Praise for Holly Chamberlin and *The Family Beach House*

"Explores questions about the meaning of home, family
dynamics and tolerance."
—*The Bangor Daily News*

"A dramatic and moving portrait of several generations of a
family and each person's place within it."
—*Booklist*

"An enjoyable summer read, but it's more. It is a novel for all
seasons that adds to the enduring excitement of Ogunquit."
—*The Maine Sunday Telegram*

"*The Family Beach House* is an exploration of life in its middle
stages and the wisdom that comes from truly understanding
yourself. It builds to a quietly satisfying end that neatly ties up
the characters' futures. Southern Maine readers will delight in
the references to local restaurants, museums and destinations
woven throughout the book. Fans of Ogunquit will be
particularly thrilled as the town itself provides a rich and
vibrant backdrop for the McQueens' story."
—*Seacoastonline.com*

Books by Holly Chamberlin

LIVING SINGLE

THE SUMMER OF US

BABYLAND

BACK IN THE GAME

THE FRIENDS WE KEEP

TUSCAN HOLIDAY

ONE WEEK IN DECEMBER

THE FAMILY BEACH HOUSE

SUMMER FRIENDS

Published by Kensington Publishing Corporation

The
Summer
of Us

Holly Chamberlin

KENSINGTON BOOKS
www.kensingtonbooks.com

KENSINGTON BOOKS are published by

Kensington Publishing Corp.
119 West 40th Street
New York, NY 10018

ISBN-13: 978-0-7582-6573-9
ISBN-10: 0-7582-6573-5

First Kensington Trade Paperback Printing: May 2004
10 9 8 7 6 5

Printed in the United States of America

As always, for Stephen.
And this time, also for Joey.

Acknowledgments

The author would like to thank Jack and Betty for their indispensable companionship and love, and the Animal Rescue League of Boston for introducing them to her.

She would also like to thank her editor, John Scognamiglio, for his enduring faith and support.

Finally, with a full heart, she would like to welcome Ella Carol Nelson to this world!

May

Gincy

The Go-to Girl

The crisis was discovered at four forty-five in the afternoon. Fifteen minutes before ninety-nine percent of the staff hurried out of the building to enjoy their sixteen-hour vacation.

My boss, Mr. Bill Kelly, Kell for short, was frazzled. He didn't handle crises well. What he did do well was delegate responsibility.

He came tearing into the center of our office area, what little hair he had on end, plaid shirttails untucked.

"Listen up, people. We have a problem. The idiots at the copy shop lost our proposal and we've got to recreate it. Now. It's got to be at the printer's tonight."

I watched the predictable reactions of my colleagues.

Curran, the senior designer, slipped out of the room backwards.

Norton, the copy editor, suddenly found the piece of blank paper he was holding extremely interesting.

Vera, the administrative assistant for our division, feigned a sudden hacking cough.

"Kell," she gasped, "I wish I could help, but I think I'm really sick. If I don't get home and into bed soon . . ."

Kell turned to me. "Gincy, you'll stay, right?"

"It's gotta get done," I said, shooting my coworkers a look of disgust. "I'm here."

That's me. The go-to girl. Virginia Marie Gannon.

I guess I got my work ethic from my father, though our choices of work couldn't be more different.

Dad manages a hardware store, the small, privately owned kind that monsters like Home Depot have mostly put out of business.

I'm the senior editor of the monthly publication sent to subscribers of a public television station here in Boston.

Come to think of it, I'm not sure how much of a choice my father had when it came to a career. He didn't go to college. When I was about twelve I heard a rumor from a cousin that he'd never even finished high school.

To this day I don't know the truth about that. I'd never ask Dad straight out. It would embarrass him, and though my parents aren't my favorite people in the world, I treat them with respect.

It's what you do. Work hard and respect your parents. In that way, I'm a typical Gannon. In other ways? Not so much.

Anyway, the job got done and at six thirty-five I left our office on Bowdoin Street.

By the time I raced through the door of George, An American Cafe, it was almost seven o'clock. The place was a cemetery.

"Where is everybody?" I barked to the dimly lit room. "There's nobody here!"

A dark-haired girl about my age stepped away from the bar. I noticed she had breasts the size of Pamela Anderson's. Almost.

How can you not notice something like that?

"Uh, hello?" she said. "We're here. Me and—Clare, right?"

Another girl, a blond one, all clean and healthy-looking, like she could star in a soap ad shot at a mountain spring or something, slipped off a barstool and joined the first girl. She nodded and looked at me warily.

Okay, maybe she had a reason to. I'd caught a glimpse of my hair in the window before charging through the door. It was pretty wild. I think I'd forgotten to comb it that morning.

I had, however, remembered to wash it. Which was more than I'd done the day before when I'd been up since four A.M. working on a report for Kell the Inefficient. Next thing I knew it was

eight-thirty and if I'd stopped to shower I would have been late
for a nine o'clock meeting.

You know how it is.

"So," I said. "I thought there was supposed to be a meeting
here tonight. You know, to hook up with roommates. For a summer place. In Oak Bluffs."

"There was a meeting," the dark-haired one drawled, "but it
seems it was over at, like, six-oh-five. By the time I got here at six-
thirty, everyone had already hooked up."

She nodded toward the girl next to her. "Except for Clare.
And me. I'm Danielle, by the way."

"Hey. Gincy."

"That's an unusual name," Danielle said flatly.

"Yeah," I answered flatly. "It is."

The one named Clare stuck out her hand and I stared at it.
She let it drop.

"One girl told me all the good houses are taken," she said. She
sounded apologetic. "I think you're supposed to rent them by
February or March and then look for housemates. Not the other
way around. I didn't know."

I propped my fists on my hips. What there was of them.

I tend toward the skinny.

"Crap," I said. "Well I didn't know, either!"

Danielle heaved this big dramatic sigh. "None of us did," she
said. "I guess."

I was seriously disappointed. I really wanted the summer to be
something special.

And then, inspiration struck.

"Wait," I said. "All of the good houses might be taken but that
doesn't mean there aren't still bad houses to rent. Right?"

"I suppose," Clare said doubtfully.

"A bad house?" Danielle rolled her eyes. I noted she was wearing a lot of eye makeup. Personally, I'd owned the same tube of
mascara for three years. "See, I don't like the sound of that," she
went on. "That means, like, a bathtub but no shower, right?
Ceiling fans but no central air?"

I guffawed.

Ms. Fresh Mountain Air tried to hide a smile. "It might be worth taking a look," she said. "I . . . I kind of had my heart set on this."

There was a beat of silence and then I said, "Well, what's it gonna be? Are we going to do this or what?"

"Well, I'm not spending the entire summer in the city," Danielle declared fiercely. "The grime is murder on my skin. And speaking of murder, I just read in the *Globe* that street crime has like, tripled from last year. And you know how they get in the hot weather."

I narrowed my eyes. "How who gets?"

Danielle looked at me incredulously. "Duh. Criminals?"

Okay, I thought. *But I'm watching closely for any signs of bigotry.*

"I'm allergic to cigarette smoke," Clare said suddenly.

I eyed her keenly.

"Well," she admitted, "not allergic, exactly. It's just that I don't like it. It gives me headaches."

Danielle nodded. "And cigarette smoke stinks up my hair, not to mention my clothes. No smoking in the house. Agreed?"

I considered this.

Truth was, I wasn't a big smoker. I was kind of a social smoker. A wimpy smoker. It was the only thing about me that was wimpy. I could live with a no-smoking rule.

Still, I kind of hated to let things go.

I kind of liked to win. It was one of my more obnoxious traits.

"What about on the porch?" I countered. "If there is one. Or in the yard?"

Danielle and Clare discussed this with eye language and then Danielle nodded. "All right. But if the smell starts getting in the house . . ."

"Yeah, yeah, fine. Anyway, we're jumping ahead making house rules before we even have a house."

Clare didn't answer but checked her watch for about the tenth time.

"Hot date?" I asked.

She blushed and hefted off a barstool what I realized was a

suit in a plastic dry-cleaners' bag. "Oh, no! I have a boyfriend. He's working late tonight. We live together. I just want to get home before he does. You know."

I didn't at all know, but shrugged. "Fine. We'll hammer out the rules later."

"Good, because I want to watch something on Lifetime at eight," Danielle said.

She suggested a time, date, and place for us to meet for an excursion to the Vineyard; we each promised to bring any rental listings we found and Clare said she'd make an appointment with an Oak Bluffs real estate broker.

After we'd exchanged phone numbers and e-mail, the odd couple left and I gratefully settled at the bar and ordered a beer and a plate of nachos. I hadn't eaten all day. The six cups of coffee I'd drunk were eating away at the lining of my stomach. I could hear them munching.

So could the bartender, who after a particularly loud growl gave me a funny look.

I smiled sweetly. "If you could hurry with those nachos?"

I'd always hated snobs.

Maybe because I grew up among people whose idea of culture was a monster-truck rally followed by super-sized sugar drinks at the local DQ.

I was pretty sure half of the residents of my hometown—which I not so fondly called DeadlySpore, New Hampshire—were related. I guessed for some people, inbreeding was a goal; incest, something to kill the slow passing of rural time.

The evidence was clear, at least to me. Every single class in our local grammar school and high school had at least one member of the extensive Brown family.

Maggie Sullivan was a Brown.

Bobby Manigan was a Brown.

Petey Ming, who looked as Asian as his last name, was a Brown; I don't know how, exactly, but he was.

Basically, you threw a rock, you hit a Brown.

Note to the uninformed: Rock-throwing was a sport of choice

in Pondscum, New Hampshire, as was name-calling, merciless teasing of anyone who ate whole wheat bread instead of Wonder white, and expert wedgie-giving.

Not that I, of course, ever participated in any of these sports except as a horrified spectator.

I swear.

See, for as far back as I can remember, say from about the age of four, I felt different from the infuriatingly dim-witted morons—okay, do morons come in any other kind?—who populated the neighborhood where I lived from the time of my birth to the day I left MooseDroppings, New Hampshire for school in Boston, Massachusetts.

Addison University. Ah, the haven for wanna-be artistes. (Yeah, use the French pronunciation here.)

Also known as losers.

That's not fair. Not everyone who went to Addison was a loser.

Sure, some started out that way and just perfected the role over time. Everybody knew these kids. Every high school had them. Kids who blustered and swaggered about their Hollywood-style future and somehow, in the end, came running home, proverbial tail between proverbial legs, to take a job tending bar at the local dive. For the rest of their lives.

Other kids started their freshman year at Addison bright-eyed and truly, touchingly optimistic about preparing for a life in The Arts. Then they became losers, usually by the middle of their sophomore year, when they realized they had absolutely no artistic talent whatsoever.

Losers or posers, or a fascinating combination of both.

Me? I started at Addison an eighteen-year-old combination of loser and poser. Pretty impressive, I'd say. Not everyone can pull off such a loathsome personality at so young an age.

Even more impressive—and rare—is that by the end of my four years of higher learning (you know, higher as in "wanna toke, man?"), I was neither a loser nor a poser.

(See? I know how to use neither/nor, either/or. Losers don't know anything about good grammar. They spell grammar "grammer." Posers don't give a crap about good grammar. They have sycophants write their stories for them.)

So, if neither poser nor loser after four years of dopey seminars on the latest fad in acting methods (taught by people whose one and only claim to fame was a television commercial for deodorant) and ridiculously unhelpful internships at the tiny offices of sadly illiterate neighborhood newspapers (whose staff always included a totally bored party boy at the switchboard) and far too many theme parties (such as, Come as Your Favorite Living South American Philosopher!), what, then, was I?

One: Highly unemployable and not proud of it. That made me not a poser.

Two: Possessed of a substandard college education and embarrassed by it. That made me not a loser. And explained my desire to teach myself the rules of grammar.

Still, I knew that if I had to do it all over again—what a joke!—I'd probably be the same jerk I was the first time around. I doubted I'd be enrolled in Harvard or Brown or Northeastern, even knowing at eighteen what I now knew at the ripe old age of twenty-nine.

And counting. Thirty loomed.

Not that calendar year, but on the first day of the next. I missed being the first baby born in WormSlime by three minutes. Nancy Harrison, married to a Brown, delivered a bouncing baby boy at 12:02 A.M., to the eternal frustration of my mother.

I wasn't sure she'd ever forgiven me for being late, let alone for being born.

Anyway, turning twenty-nine had made me think. About age and accomplishment and roads not taken. Yet. The reality was that I'd been working since I was nine, baby-sitting, mowing lawns, running errands for the elderly neighbors.

And then I'd put myself through college.

And then I'd gone on to develop a not-so-terrible career in public television.

Don't get me wrong. I loved to work, even if I didn't have any major assets, liquid or otherwise, to show for my dedication. Student loans ate most of my salary; rent ate another large portion.

The fact was that I was tired. Really tired.

And so I determined that in those last months of relative, if not starry-eyed, youth, I was going to have some fun. Meet a bunch of cute guys. Stay out all night. Sleep all day, at least on the weekends.

Before getting back down to work.

Sitting there all alone at the bar, sipping a beer, I determined to rent a house on Oak Bluffs even if it was the rattiest dump imaginable.

And even if I had to share it with the odd couple.

The blond one, Clare. She looked as if she'd stepped out of the pages of an Eddie Bauer catalog, all scrubbed and healthy. I doubted we had anything at all in common.

And worse, the Pampered Princess, Danielle. With her red nails and her gold necklaces. Seriously not the kind of person who could be my friend.

But then again, who was? I could count my female friends on a fingerless hand.

The nachos finally arrived. I dug right in, slopping guacamole on my shirt. My tummy quieted immediately.

Gincy, I told myself, *this is going to be one hell of a summer.*

Clare
She Can't Say No

I never said no to Win. I wasn't sure I knew how.

"So, get the low-fat milk," he went on, his voice slightly distorted by his speakerphone. "And Clare, sweetie? If you could also pick up my black suit, that'd be great. It won't be ready until five-thirty, but that shouldn't be a problem for you, right?"

Plus, I hadn't told him about the summer house. I didn't want to pick a fight over something as silly as dry cleaning when I knew a truly big fight was to come.

"Sure," I said, folding clean laundry while I held the portable phone between my shoulder and chin. "No problem."

"Thanks, sweetie. You know, with your afternoons free—"

"They're not free, Win," I replied, automatically. We'd been through this so many times. "I have to grade papers and review lesson plans and then there's housework and—"

Win chuckled his indulgent chuckle. "Okay, okay, I get it. Sorry, sweetie. Look, I've got to run. See you later. Oh," he added, as if just remembering. "I probably won't be home until at least nine so grab some dinner for yourself, okay?"

Win lowered his voice; now it held a note of long-suffering. "I have to take this client out for drinks after work. You know how it is."

No. I didn't know how anything was.

But I was beginning to figure things out.

"Sure," I said. "Bye."

We hung up and I finished folding and putting away the laundry. The simple task always gave me a feeling of accomplishment. At least something in this world was clean, neatly folded, and put away just where it had always belonged.

Like my so-called life?

I never could say no to Win, not even at the beginning of our relationship.

To be honest, Win had never asked me to do anything dreadful or dishonest or criminal.

He wasn't abusive. Not in any common sense of the term.

It was just—it was just that he was powerful and I was . . .

Not powerful.

But not stupid, either.

See, I'd finally come to understand that Win had power over me because I allowed him to have power over me.

I'd given it to him from the moment we'd met just over ten years earlier. I hadn't known what I was doing, not really.

And if I had?

At eighteen years of age I welcomed Win—a strong-willed, decisive, career-focused man—into my life with a sigh of relief. Not a literal sigh, you understand.

But having Win around made things easier for me. For example, in spite of my parents and professors pressuring me to think seriously about my future, I had no idea what I wanted to do or be until Win helped me decide on a career in teaching.

I liked being a teacher, very much. What was more, I was a good teacher. I was dedicated and sometimes even inspired. At least, my fifth graders at York, Braddock and Roget seemed to like me.

Win, it seemed, knew me when I didn't even know myself.

There were other reasons for my falling in love with Win Carrington.

I knew he wanted someday to be married and have a family, and I wanted those things, too.

My mother, who'd never worked outside the home, having married just out of college, urged on our budding relationship. Maybe she recognized in Win something of my father, a man who was a stellar family man if you looked at it in terms of financial support.

My father.

Daddy had always loved me, in a formal, distant sort of way. But he never paid much attention to me for the simple reason that I wasn't a boy. James, five years my senior, and Philip, two years older, were his major concerns.

His heirs.

Daddy was so old-fashioned he almost seemed like a character straight out of a Victorian novel. But he was all too real. And quite early on he assigned me to my mother.

His two girls.

Mother chose my clothes and took me to Girl Scout meetings while Daddy brought my two brothers to his beautiful office at the University of Michigan Medical Center where he was chief of urology.

Mother attended my ballet recitals while Daddy took my brothers on fishing trips up north.

Mother taught me how to sew and knit while Daddy encouraged the boys to excel in school and sports.

Nothing changed this dynamic until I started to date Win. Suddenly, I became visible to my father. Suddenly, I was worth his personal attention.

And the more Win achieved, the higher in Daddy's esteem I rose. At least it seemed that way to me.

When Win was accepted at Harvard Law, Daddy took us all to Chicago for the weekend.

When Win made Law Review, Daddy gave me a big fat check, as if I'd been the winner of the prize.

And when Win was offered a partner-track position at the law firm of Datz, Parrish and Kelleher, Daddy treated us both to a weekend at Canyon Ranch in the Berkshires.

Everything was just fine.

Still, not long before that May evening when I committed myself to spending a good part of the summer with two strangers, and in spite of my father's gifts and approbation, something inside me began to change.

I felt as if I was waking up. I felt as if I was falling asleep.

And for someone who was known for her even keel, this was frightening.

I'd feel terribly restless, then lethargic; full of nervous energy, then barely able to get out of bed.

My favorite pastimes, like knitting and power-walking along the river, suddenly held no interest.

I started to screen all calls so that I wouldn't have to fake a good humor.

I lost what little sex drive I'd had.

Clare Jean Wellman. I'd always been the girl who was so pleasant and easy to please.

But suddenly, I felt all discontent.

And angry. But I wasn't sure why.

Sad, too, but I couldn't identify the source of the sadness.

Win didn't seem to notice my altered mood and behavior. At least, he didn't say anything to me about it. I guess I was grateful for that. Strange, but true.

I was grateful for his oblivion, or what passed for it.

I started searching out articles in popular women's magazines on mood swings and hormonal shifts, on something astrologers call the Saturn Return, and finally, on depression.

But members of the Wellman family didn't go to therapy.

Besides, I asked myself time and again, why did I need therapy? I had a steady job, a good family, a nice home.

I had Win.

Maybe, I came to think, there's nothing wrong with me.

Maybe . . .

And then, one day while flipping through a magazine called *New England Homes,* I saw a promotional article about Martha's Vineyard and it occurred to me, just like that, that I could go away for a while.

By myself. At least, without Win.

Classes ended in mid-June and the fall semester didn't start until after Labor Day.

Why did I have to stay in Boston when I could be somewhere closer to nature?

I missed spending time in the country and being by the water. It wasn't my choice to live in a big city. But Win had made his decision, New York or Boston, and I'd chosen Boston as the lesser of two urban evils.

A summer in the heat of the city? Or a summer by the seashore?

Besides, Win worked such dreadfully long hours and I knew he'd be starting a major case sometime in August, which meant we wouldn't be able to take a vacation together anytime soon.

The idea was tantalizing. Going away without Win.

I felt as if I had a dirty, thrilling secret.

For two days I did nothing more but fantasize about spending part of the summer without Win.

And then I saw a sign taped to a streetlight, a sign advertising the housemate event at George.

And there it was. Just like that I made a verbal commitment to share a summer house in Oak Bluffs with two strangers.

What had I done?

I asked myself this question over and over again on the way home to our spacious loft on Harrison Avenue in the South End. It became a chant in my head, matching my footfalls: *What have I done, oh, what have I done.*

I passed a tiny, bustling restaurant called The Dish on the corner of Shawmut. It was a balmy evening and several diners were seated at the small tables on the sidewalk.

At one table sat a woman alone, her pug resting at her feet. She was about forty-five and simply dressed; she looked content and relaxed.

I could never do that, I thought. *Eat alone at a restaurant.*

Or could I?

I spent an awful lot of time alone for someone with a live-in boyfriend.

It would be nice, I thought, *to work up the nerve to actually do more on my own, like enjoy a warm spring evening at a friendly local restaurant.*

The woman caught my eye as I passed, and smiled. I returned her smile, awkwardly, and walked on.

Courage, Clare, I told myself. *Taking this house for the summer is a step in the right direction. It's a step toward independence.*

That's what you want, right?

Independence?

But what does Win want for you? a teeny voice questioned.

He wouldn't be pleased with my plan, that much I knew for sure. The real question was: Would I have the nerve to stand up to his desires?

In other words, would I have the nerve to say no to him and yes to me?

I stopped at Foodie's, a midsized market across from the big cathedral, for Win's milk and for something prepared for my dinner.

And as I waited for the plastic container of macaroni and cheese, I thought about the two women who'd likely be my housemates.

Danielle seemed okay. She was a bit flashier than most of the people I knew but she seemed like a nice person.

I liked nice people.

Niceness, I'd always thought, was an underrated quality.

Gincy?

Well, I was a bit worried about her. About how we'd get along. Already I could sense that she was a bit pugilistic. Kind of a troublemaker. Kind of wild.

Maybe, I thought, *I should reserve any further judgment until we all meet again.*

I paid for the groceries and, juggling a white plastic bag and Win's dry-cleaned suit, headed over to Harrison Avenue.

All anxiety aside, I was excited. On some level I really didn't care what Win thought about my plan. And that brought a sense of freedom, something I don't think I'd ever felt before.

I took a deep breath and for a moment imagined I was on the beach, alone with the stars and moon and pounding black surf.

My life suddenly seemed very scary.

And quite possibly, very wonderful.

Danielle

She Likes Herself

It wasn't my fault that I was late for the meeting.

I mean, in the business world, what meeting ever starts exactly on time?

I'll tell you. None. Not many.

I'd been the senior administrative assistant at the Boston offices of a large construction firm for seven years and I'd seen my share of meetings.

Not even engineers, known for being all precise and focused, are on time for meetings. Not always.

So who would expect a meeting of random twenty- and thirty-somethings with some money to spend on a nice summer vacation—a meeting held at a totally casual bar like George—to begin exactly at six o'clock?

Please.

Most people in my office, located near Northeastern's attentuated urban campus, didn't even leave the building until at least six-thirty. So they told me because I made sure to be out of there no later than five. I didn't make enough money to work until seven.

That was my husband's job.

At least, it would be when I found him.

Anyway, I left the office that day at five on the dot, per usual, giving myself plenty of time to take a leisurely stroll through the mall on my way from Huntington Avenue over to Boylston Street, almost up by the Gardens. It was a very nice day in late May and for a moment I considered avoiding a shortcut through the mall in favor of a bit of fresh air.

And then a disgusting bus roared by, belching thick black smoke, while I waited for a traffic light, and I thought: *What? I should destroy my lungs more than they're already destroyed by this foul city air?*

No thank you.

I suppose I didn't have to walk through the entire mall. It did take me out of my way.

And I suppose I didn't actually have to detour upstairs. But I did and that's when it happened. I saw the cutest pair of slides in the window of Nine West and they just called out to me.

"Danielle Leers!" they cried. "Look at us! Just imagine yourself wearing us to dinner at Davio's."

Well, as any self-respecting woman will tell you, when a pair of fabulous shoes cries out to you, you march right inside the shop and you try them on.

Of course, the slides looked spectacular on my feet, especially with the Raspberry Royale I was wearing on my toenails.

Sure, once summer came I'd be wearing Sassy Strawberry, but I was expert enough to know my color matches—without the help of *InStyle* magazine.

I bought the slides. And when I left the store, feeling that special after-purchase glow, I suddenly remembered that I'd forgotten all about the summer-house rental meeting.

I checked my watch to see it was already six and, with a shrug, headed off toward the closest exit. I figured it was better for me to stick to the streets if I were to make the meeting at all.

Which I didn't. Because by the time I got to George the meeting was over and everyone was hooked up with housemates but for me and two other girls who'd come in late.

Well, long story short the three of us decided to just go to the Vineyard and hope to find something decent to rent.

So there I was, committed to sharing a house—well, at least to trying to find a house—with two total strangers.

Neither of whom seemed anything like me at all.

Maybe, I thought, that was a good thing.

Maybe it would be fun to hang out with the one named Clare. She was okay. Her clothes were a bit bland but at least her hair was nicely, though simply, done. And she had a boyfriend, so she'd be no competition.

Though I did wonder why she was renting a house without said boyfriend.

The other one, Gincy? I wasn't so sure about her. The girl's hair was a disaster. And she hadn't been wearing any jewelry. Unless you counted ratty little silver studs in her ears as jewelry. Which I did not.

Still, she'd be no competition, either. No man I'd want to date would ever in his right mind want to date that mess of a girl.

In the end, it didn't really matter how well I got along with my two housemates. I wasn't renting a summer house to make new girlfriends.

Actually, I'd never been much for girlfriends.

True, I kept in touch with a few girls I grew up with in Oyster Bay. That's on Long Island, part of New York. We e-mailed on occasion and I saw them whenever I went home to visit my family.

But I didn't have a lot in common with Amy and Michelle and Rachel. Not only because they were all married and I wasn't.

I'd kind of been different from the start.

Like, I was the only one of the group to leave home for college.

While Amy and Rachel attended a local community college and Michelle made the commute to and from New York University every day (her parents didn't want her to live in the dorms), I went off to Boston University and majored in communications with a minor in art history.

For four years I flew home to Long Island for holidays and for summers and, though I always had a nice time, I was always happy to get back to Boston and my own life.

Then, as graduation drew closer, it became clear that my parents assumed I'd be returning home to find a job in New York.

I rebelled against the notion.

I loved my family. But I didn't want to start my so-called adult life under their gaze. They'd given me enough grief about going to Boston for college, but I'd stuck to my guns. I'd needed to be alone, to grow.

And there was just no way I could go home after those four years.

My privacy had become too important.

Amy, Michelle, and Rachel were each married by the age of twenty-three.

My father hinted that maybe I might want to marry, too.

My mother wondered what was wrong with those stiff New Englanders that they couldn't tell a lovely young woman when they saw one.

Honestly, I was in no hurry to marry. At first.

Which brings me back to the summer house. I had chosen to rent a place in Oak Bluffs because I couldn't afford to take a house on Nantucket or one of the super-expensive areas of the Vineyard, like Edgartown.

I knew I could ask my parents for money. They'd give it to me, but first they'd try to get me to drop the idea of a house and come home for a few weeks that summer.

And I didn't want to do that. Their love could be so overwhelming. I'd never stopped being afraid that I would get lost in their emphatic embrace.

And it was someone else's embrace that interested me.

I was taking a summer house in the first place because it was time to find a husband.

A husband worthy of Danielle Sarah Leers.

Who was Danielle Sarah Leers that fateful summer? Let me tell you a bit about her.

Height: five feet, four inches tall. Just right.

Coloring: medium olive complexion, brown eyes, and perfectly arched eyebrows, thanks to Studio Salon.

Hair: thick and dark brown; I liked to wear it to my shoulders and it was always perfectly groomed.

Figure: some had called me voluptuous. Others said that I resembled a young Sophia Loren.

Or a Catherine Zeta-Jones.

Or, on one of my best days, a Jennifer Lopez.

Really. People told me this. You can ask my mother.

Once, a very long time ago, a guy had the nerve to tell me I was a smidgen too fat. I told him to take a leap. What I looked like was my business and my business only. He tried to backpedal and claim he meant the fat remark as a compliment, but it was too late. He was history in my book.

See, I'd always believed that self-esteem was a very good quality to have. I owed mine to my parents. They taught me early on that I was beautiful and intelligent and entirely worthy of happiness and love and social success.

They taught, and I listened. I might not have listened so well all the time at school, especially during geography and social studies—like I've ever had my day ruined by not being able to find, I don't know, Uruguay, on a map! But at home I listened very carefully.

It wasn't that I was full of myself. I'd known girls who were full of themselves and they were just insufferable. Insufferable was, is, and always will be unacceptable. But I did advocate feeling good about myself. Feeling worthy of good things.

Why not?

As my grandmother was fond of saying, "You're dead a long time."

Think about it.

Anyway, I didn't worry obsessively about an extra pound or two. I knew I was beautiful with or without the pound.

And I didn't tolerate anything less than total gentlemanly behavior from men.

I went for regular massages and facials and had a manicure and pedicure every two weeks. Once, someone at the office asked me why I bothered to have my toenails done during the winter.

"It's not sandal weather," she pointed out. "No one sees your toes."

"Correction," I replied. "I see my toes. And I'm the one that matters."

Since high school I'd worn only yellow gold, never silver. Not that I hated silver; it's just that I'd decided to have a trademark, a signature style. And I'd learned early on that every woman should have a personal jeweler, someone she trusted.

Every woman, I believed, should have a lot of things all for herself. It all came back to self-esteem.

It all came back to self-respect.

It made me want to scream when I saw women allowing themselves to be trampled by men who wanted them to pay for their own dinner, men who didn't call when they said they were going to call, men who wore sweatpants in public.

I thought: *What is the world coming to when this bad behavior is allowed?*

Here was the thing: You gave men an inch, they took a mile. You had to set boundaries. You had to make them play by the rules. And if they didn't want to play by the rules, they were out of the game. Period.

I considered myself a good person.

I donated the previous season's clothes to a homeless shelter. You know, the mistakes, the pieces you just shouldn't have bought.

Not that I made many mistakes.

At the end of each year I wrote a check to the Women's Lunch Place.

"When you have as much as we do," my father often said, "you should give a little back."

Someday, I'd think, *when I have children, I'll teach them what my parents taught me. I'll make sure they're proud and strong and generous, and then happiness and success will follow.*

At least, that's what I was told should happen. Sometimes I had my doubts about the happiness part. Not that I talked about those doubts or anything.

Though I had doubts, I did have faith, of a sort. My family didn't keep kosher or go to synagogue, but on the high holy days we did gather for the special meals. The women cooked and the men sang and read some prayers.

Most of which I didn't understand because I'd never taken Hebrew in school.

Please. There was enough in life to keep track of, what with a job and a social life.

Still, I'd always felt that tradition was important and vowed that when I married, my husband and I would instill the importance of tradition in our children.

Back again to the topic of a husband.

I had a plan once, a long time ago, to meet Mr. Right by the age of twenty-five or so.

Maybe it wasn't so much of a plan as a felt certainty. I just never thought I wouldn't meet Mr. Right by my midtwenties.

But there I was, twenty-nine and single. And turning thirty that summer, August tenth.

Thirty.

I could hardly believe it.

Suddenly, I was very, very aware that many of the other women on the streets of Boston were younger than me. I took to scrutinizing them, the clarity of their skin, the thickness of their hair, the brightness of their teeth, the firmness of their flesh.

Rivals. Dangerous rivals.

Not that I'd lost confidence in myself, but . . .

Face it. Thirty is old for a woman.

Danielle, I told myself, *it's high time you got down to business. It's high time you tied the knot.*

Marriage was a sign of maturity, right? It said to the world, "Look, I'm an adult. I can talk about mortgages and gutters and snowblowers and property taxes and in-laws and school systems and life insurance with the best of them. With my parents."

Marriage was an end to childhood or a prolonged adolescence or something.

It was an end to something.

Well, I was ready to put an end to something.

I was ready to be an adult.
I was ready to join the club.
Now, all I had to do was find Mr. Right.
No big deal, I told myself. He was out there somewhere.
And he was going to love me in my new slides.

Clare
Nothing Can Stop Her

Win wasn't happy about the summer house.

I hadn't expected him to be. Still, his disapproval scared me a little.

Win would never hit me. It wasn't that. It was the look in his eye, the steely look, the look that seemed to cut me off from his consideration.

We were in the expensive, state-of-the-art kitchen Win had chosen for our expensive, state-of-the-art new home.

"If you're worried about the money," I said, "I'll pay for the house out of my parents' allowance."

The look intensified. "Don't ever doubt my capacity to support the both of us," he said, in a low, cold voice. "I'm the man in this relationship. Don't ever forget that."

What could I say? I turned away from him, picked up a dish towel, and began to dry the silverware.

"Clare, why do you insist on doing the dishes by hand?" Win sounded exasperated. "We have a Bosch to do that."

I whirled around. "You're always too busy to spend time with me anyway. What does it matter if I go away for a while?"

Or if I like to wash the dishes myself?

"It matters because—" Win stopped. Changed tactics.

Now his voice would be cajoling. Calculated to calm.

He came close and put his hand on my shoulder. "Sweetie, why don't you go home, spend the summer with your mother."

Why? So she can keep an eye on me?

"I'm taking the house." I moved out from under his touch. "You can't stop me from doing this, Win."

Win took a deep breath before delivering his prediction. "Mark my words, Clare, you'll regret this. But you know what? If you don't want to take my advice, fine. I'm just trying to stop you from making a big mistake."

You're just trying to stop me from living my life.

Win went back to his laptop, to some document he had to review for work. I went into the bedroom and sat on the edge of the bed.

It occurred to me again that I was so alone. I had no friends other than the wives of some of Win's colleagues.

And they weren't really friends. Not the kind I remembered from grammar school, the close friends, the kind you giggled with, the kind who knew your family almost as well as you did, the kind who knew how you liked to eat ice cream straight from the container.

An hour later, Win came to bed. I was under the covers, still in my clothes. We didn't speak.

Don't ever go to bed angry. That was one of my mother's favorite pieces of relationship advice. She swore she and Daddy had never gone to bed without first making up.

I thought she was lying.

Gincy
You Can Never Go Home

I don't know why I called home.
It's not like my parents ever called me.

Hardly ever.

It's not like I really had anything to say to them.

Stuff about my job, they didn't understand. Stuff about my personal life, I didn't want them to know. Not that anything so steamy was going on at the moment.

Still.

I called from the office the next afternoon, using my calling card. I wasn't in the habit of abusing the office phone or e-mail or copy machines, unlike some people whose names I will not mention.

For instance, my office buddy Sally. She was kind of an after-work friend, too, though at that point we hadn't hung out often. Only three times. And she'd instigated each of those drunken evenings.

Good kid, in spite of her carefully calculated tough-as-nails appearance.

"Mom? It's Gincy. Calling from Boston."

Had to rub that in, didn't you? My better self shook its head, ashamed.

"Hello, Virginia," replied my grim mother. "Is anything wrong? I hope you don't need money because we just don't have any to send you, what with—"

I rolled my eyes for the benefit of nobody. "Mom! No, I don't want money. God. Can we please just have a normal conversation? Jeez."

"I wish you wouldn't use that language, Virginia. You know how I feel about bad language."

Yeah, I thought. *Which is why it pours out of my mouth when we talk. Can't help it, Mom. That's what you do to me.*

"How are you, Mom," I said, shoving aside the urge to staple my hand to the desk. It would take my mind off the pain of this conversation. "How's Dad?"

"Oh, we're fine, what would be wrong, except for the money—"

"How's Tommy?"

My brother, just twenty-five, had forgone college for an exciting life as a check-out boy at the local Harriman's, a giant food store. We'd never gotten along, even when we were kids. Tommy had a mean streak. And, worse, though he acted plenty dumb, I suspected he was actually fairly bright. Just lazy. And I abhorred laziness.

Mom sighed. "Seeing some piece of trash he picked up in TreeStump. That town produces more garbage—"

Of course, nothing was ever Tommy's fault. His slutty girlfriend, the bad-influence best friend, the cops who had nothing better to do than arrest a young boy just sowing his wild oats. They were all to blame for Tommy's miserable life.

"Oh!" my mother was saying. "I do have some news."

The basement flooded again because you're too cheap to install a French drain or whatever it's called that prevents the flooding of basements?

"You remember your cousin Jody?"

How could I not? The kid had been a poop-throwing terror.

"Uh, yeah, Mom. I used to baby-sit her."

"Oh, yes. Well, she's dropping out of high school to have a baby!"

Now there's an interesting career choice, I noted.

"Who's the father?" I asked, as if I would know the little shit. "Is she getting married?"

"Well, of course, Virginia! Uncle Mike wouldn't dream of letting his daughter live in sin or his grandchild be a bastard. What can you be thinking? FrogPiddle is not the big city, you know."

There was absolutely nothing I could say to all that, so I radically changed the subject. "Guess what, Mom? I'm renting a house on Martha's Vineyard for the summer. With two other women. Right by the beach. A house."

There was silence for a moment.

Then: "Does that mean you won't come home for Jody's wedding?"

And there it was.

What had I expected? My mother to be happy for me?

"Put Dad on, Mom."

The conversation with my father was brief. I told him about my plans.

"Guess we won't see you this summer, then," he commented. "You be careful all on your own out there on some island."

Yeah, Dad, I'll watch for sea monsters. I hear they rise from the deep with every full moon . . .

"I'll be fine, Dad."

I always am.

I hung up and rubbed my eyes. Damn flourescent lights. And in the middle of the buzzing office, phones ringing, computers dinging, voices calling, I suddenly felt very, very alone.

And then, there was Sally. In all her chopped, purple-haired splendor.

"Hey," she said, staring at the bulletin board above and behind my head. "You want to grab a beer after work?"

I noted a new nose piercing.

"Sure," I said. "Thanks."

Danielle
The Single Daughter

The call wasn't as bad as I'd expected.

My mother lamented and wailed a little, but after I assured her that Martha's Vineyard was popular with eligible bachelors—not only gay men—she accepted my summer plans with a sigh.

"At least," she said, "you won't be wasting your time, having fun to no purpose. Danielle, I'm so glad you've decided to settle down and get married."

"Well," I said, nerves tightening, "I do have to find the man first, Mom."

"Ppff!" my mother sounded. I could picture the flip of her plump hand in the air, dismissing the silly little obstacle. "Like that will be a problem? Look at you! You're gorgeous. Any man in his right mind would die to marry you."

In his right mind.

Note to self: Watch out for lunatics.

"Thanks, Mom. Is Dad there?"

The very first thing he said was: "You know, your mother would love if you came home for a couple of weeks this summer. You can't do that?"

There it was. The guilt.

"I signed a lease, Dad," I lied. "Besides—"

"You know, David will want to see you. Him and that fiancée, what's her name?"

"Roberta."

Why had Dad always pretended to forget the names of every one of David's girlfriends?

"Maybe David will come and visit me on the Vineyard," I added, knowing Dad had at least one more guilt card up his sleeve.

"What about your poor old dad, did you think of him?" my father said, his tone now half-teasing. "You don't love him anymore? You found someone else you love more than your father?"

This was always the killer. I was my Daddy's little girl, though unlike lots of other females I'd tried hard never to take advantage of that.

"Oh, Dad, of course not. You know you'll always be number one with me. It's just that—"

"Danielle, go, have a good time. I'm only being silly, just joking around. You're a young woman, a beautiful girl, you should be out having fun."

"I'll be home for my birthday," I said, tears prickling my eyes. "In August. For a weekend."

"My little girl, thirty years old." Dad sighed. "You're making me an old man!"

"You're not old, Dad," I said, thinking: *My dad isn't old, is he?* Sixty-five. That wasn't old by modern standards, was it?

"Well, I'm getting old, and thank God. You know why?"

The comfort of the familiar. Also, the dread.

"Because if you weren't getting old you'd be dead," I recited.

Dad chuckled. "Exactly right! Now, go, have fun at the beach."

I promised I would try.

Gincy
Inauspicious Start

I suppose we could have taken the plunge and rented a house sight unseen.

Trusted the broker. Believed her tall tales.

In the end it wouldn't have mattered much. By the time we were ready to rent, all that remained on the market for summer was crap. At least in Oak Bluffs.

Our broker mentioned a few little compounds on the Tisbury Great Pond. No electricity. Dubious plumbing. Spectacular views. Lots of peace and quiet.

"We're not interested in peace and quiet," Danielle announced. Turning to me and Clare, she whispered, "And the only view that interests me is the view of a well-muscled, masculine chest!"

It hadn't taken me long to notice that on occasion Danielle lapsed into romance-novel language.

The weather didn't help sell us on the place, either. The day was chilly, wet, and gray. I'd neglected to wear a jacket over my short-sleeved T-shirt. My arms were prickled with goosebumps.

I wondered: Was the Vineyard worth the grief? It wasn't like it was easy to get to, compared to say, the Cape. First we had to take a bus to Falmouth and from there, the ferry to Oak Bluffs.

Maybe, I thought, I should just bag the whole idea of a summer place and spend weekends and days off taking day trips in a rental car to places like Sturbridge Village and the Louisa May Alcott house in Concord. Or was it Lexington?

Oh, yeah. Like I was gonna have some dirty fun in any of those places.

"Girls, not for nothin'," Terri was saying, "but listen to me. I'm not just tawkin for tawkin over heah. You don't have a choice, this late. You take this or, believe me, you'll be sayin', my gawd, we should'uv listened to Terri."

"Are you from Brooklyn?" I asked.

"Yeah, so?" Terri looked at me warily, like I was going to rat her out on some old neighborhood crime.

I shrugged. "Just wondering. I like to see if I can place accents."

"What accent? Anyways, do we have a deal? Huh?"

It could have gone either way. I mean, the house was pretty lousy even by my low standards. A lacy Victorian folly? No way. More like a shack gone to seed.

Two minuscule bedrooms, more glorified closets than actual rooms. Which was interesting, as there were no closets. A refrigerator circa 1965 or so. A smell of must so heavy we'd be airing out the place for months to come. A couch that even I wouldn't sit on without first spreading a clean sheet. And spraying several cans of Febreze.

The good thing about the house? It was in Oak Bluffs.

And Oak Bluffs was a pretty funky place. It had a history of Revivalism, which had something to do with the Methodists, a group that scared the bejesus out of Catholics and the more mainstream Protestant types.

Revivalism and all it meant somehow led to a profusion of late-nineteenth-century wooden houses built in the Carpenter Gothic style, and to the growing popularity of Oak Bluffs as a vacation spot for the average, middle-class American.

I didn't know how the history all worked but I did know that Oak Bluffs still featured a vibrant and affluent African-American community.

And that it had a lot of bars.

Danielle wrinkled her nose. "The kitchen is kind of dirty."

"I can clean it," Clare said promptly. "I mean, it has to be done."

"How much cooking are we going to do, anyway?" I said. "I'm thinking we'll be hanging out most of the time."

Where are you getting the money for all that hanging out? an annoying little voice in my head asked.

Shut up, I told it.

Danielle had another problem. "The paint's all peely."

"On the outside. Who cares?"

"Uh, maybe it's got lead in it?"

"And you're going to sit around eating paint chips?" I shot back.

"I'm just pointing out."

Terri shrugged.

"The bathroom is awfully small," Clare noted, tapping her chin with a finger.

"We'll use it one at a time," I replied.

Terri sighed. "Lookit, whaddaya gonna do? It ain't a palace. You can afford a palace, you don't come to Oak Bluffs. This is all I'm sayin'."

"That's all she saying, Clare. Danielle. Come on," I urged, even though I was still a bit unsure how I felt about taking the plunge.

Let's consider this again, Gincy. Summer weekends on the beach? Or a week in FernSpore to attend the wedding of a pregnant teen and other similarly high-class family functions?

What, was I crazy?

"Are we going to do this or not?" I said.

We stood on the tiny, rickety porch, looking at each other with tentative expressions, when suddenly, Danielle's eyes darted over my shoulder, and before I could move out of the way, she gripped my arm. Her long, painted nails were like razors.

"Ow!" I cried, yanking away. "God, you're like Vampira! Watch it with those talons."

"Sorry," she mumbled, eyes still fixed at a point down the street. "Girls, you just have to see this. Oh. Oh. Oh."

"What?" I asked irritably, turning to see what had caught her eye.

And there It was. God's gift to women. And men. Freakin' everything with eyes.

At least, the physical ideal. And in bike shorts, too. Damn.

"Oh, that just can't be real," I said. "Can it?"

The guy was coming our way and had seen us gaping at him. He didn't seem to mind the attention, if his grin and attitudinal strut were any indication.

Broad shoulders, trim waist, flat stomach, muscled legs, and, you just knew, a great butt.

"He is pretty handsome," Miss Perfect-with-a-Boyfriend said.

"Pretty handsome?" I shrieked. "Are we looking at the same guy? He's the sexiest thing I've ever seen!"

"Not a thing," Clare corrected. "A person. And yes. He is sexy."

Danielle winked and the Adonis winked back. "Hetero. Definitely."

"So?" Terri prodded with a loud clack of her gum.

What was she doing on the Vineyard anyway? Shouldn't she be filming *My Cousin Vinny Part II*?

"You want the house or not? You don't want, I've got a nice young couple who might just be interested. I—"

"We'll take it," Clare blurted. Then she looked at me and Danielle with her big baby blues. "Right?"

Danielle looked at me and nodded. "Right."

Take the plunge, Gincy.

Finalize a major decision based on a hot guy's butt.

Now there's maturity.

"Well, kids," I said, "let the fun begin."

Gincy
Three Girls in a Tub

Needless to say, phone service wasn't included in the deal. Neither were towels and bed linens.

The result was that on the first weekend of our venture, the three of us were loaded down like pack mules: Danielle with matching everything Louis Vuitton (I had to ask); Clare with assorted Vera Bradley, from ditty bag to duffel (I had to ask about that, too); and me with a monstrous blue canvas backpack a cousin had used on various hiking trips (until he fell off a mountain, conveniently leaving his pack behind) and a big black garbage bag tied in a double knot.

The bus was crowded and hot. When it came time to board the ferry, I raced to grab us three seats on deck. Danielle balked at being exposed to the "weather." I reminded her of the smelly first leg of our journey and pointed out that the day was sunny and dry.

She caved and put on a wide-brimmed straw hat she pulled—miraculously uncrumpled—from one of her many bags.

"Well," she said brightly. "So."

"Here we are." Clare smiled tentatively.

I looked from one to the other of my roommates. Disaster from right to left.

What were we thinking, three strangers hooking up for an entire summer?

"Is this going to be the level of conversation this summer?" I asked. "Because if it is, I'm thinking we should make a deal right now. No talking. Ever. Except for essential commands, like 'toss me a beer.' "

Danielle sighed magnificently. "Oh, Gincy. Please. It's just first-date jitters. Except that we're not on an actual date."

"Right," Clare said, looking suddenly all sincere. "We just have to rely on the art of conversation. You know, make appropriate small talk. That will lead to a deeper intimacy."

"We're not in therapy here, you know," I snapped. "And I'm not happy about the 'intimacy' word. Ever. Don't expect me to get all weepy and reveal a dark inner secret about my childhood. Even if I had any dark inner secrets, which I don't. Just so you know."

Clare blushed very pink and stood up from the whitewashed slatted bench on which we sat. "I think I'll go inside—"

Danielle reached for Clare's arm. "Oh, honey, sit down. Gincy's just teasing."

Reluctantly, Clare sat and I shot her a half smile of apology.

"What Clare means, Gincy," Danielle said pointedly, "is that to get a good conversation going among strangers you start with the basics. You know. What's your favorite TV show. Or movie. How do you like your martinis. Who's your favorite designer. How many brothers and sisters do you have. Stuff like that."

"*The Honeymooners. Cool Hand Luke.* Gin, onions, shaken not stirred. What designer? One brother."

"Name?"

"Tommy."

"Older or younger?"

"Younger."

"Are you close?"

"No. He asks too many questions."

Danielle beamed. "See how easy that was? Now we know something about you. Okay, my turn. I love, love, love *Legally Blond,* the first and second movies."

Figures, I thought. *Did this chick even go to college?*

"TV, that's easy. *Will & Grace* because of Grace's clothes, though she's far too skinny—I mean, you can count her ribs!"

And that was a problem Danielle did not have to worry about.

"Martini," she went on. "Lemon or raspberry vodka with olives." Ugh. Adulterated martinis disgusted me.

Danielle cocked her head and pouted. "The designer question is a tough one," she said. "Where do I begin? I'll just say it depends on my mood. And the season. And how much money I can spend, of course."

Of course. My own clothing budget was—well, it was pretty much nonexistent.

"Siblings: one brother. His name is David and he's thirty-six. He's very handsome and he's a doctor and he's engaged. It'll be a late spring wedding. And I'd better be one of the bridesmaids. And that's me!"

I shrugged. No big surprises from Danielle.

"Clare?" I said, without a trace of challenge in my voice. I still felt kind of bad about scaring her.

"Oh," she said, as if surprised she had been included in the silly game. "Okay. Well, I don't watch TV much. But I guess if I had to say . . . I guess I'd say *Murder, She Wrote*. Remember, with Angela Lansbury as Jessica Fletcher? It's on a cable channel. Repeats, of course."

Clare's favorite TV show featured a widowed senior citizen? Okay. Maybe Danielle did have a point about simple questions revealing complex clues to the self.

"How nice," Danielle said blandly, crossing her already tanned legs. Maybe they just looked so tan because of the white shorts she was wearing. I made a mental note to check her bathroom supplies for spray-on tan.

"That's very . . . nice."

Clare seemed oblivious to our dismay. "I have several favorite movies," she went on. "I'm not sure I could pick just one. Each one has its own merits, of course."

"I'm sure they do, honey. Just pick one from, say, the top ten. Off the top of your head. Just, you know, without thinking."

Did Clare ever speak without, you know, thinking? I wondered.

"Well, all right. Then, *It's a Wonderful Life*. And *On Golden Pond*."

"Fine. Martini preference?" *And don't say chocolate*, I warned silently.

"I don't drink martinis. And I don't really pay attention to designers."

Here, Clare pulled lightly on the fabric of her short-sleeved, pink polo shirt. "I mean, I buy quality clothes that never go out of fashion. Classics, I guess. Usually from Talbots. L.L. Bean. Sometimes Ann Taylor. But I only go shopping twice a year. There are always so many other things to do, you know?"

Danielle lowered her massive white sunglasses and peered warily at Clare. "Like what?" she said.

"Well, like read. Or knit. I love to knit. Or grade papers. Or power-walk along the river. Or do the chores, like pick up Win's suits and shirts from the dry cleaners and buy the groceries. And handwrite letters to my family back in Michigan, which is so much more personal than typing. And—"

"We get it," I said. Danielle looked too horror-stricken to stop the madness. "What about siblings?"

"I have two older brothers, James and Philip. James is an orthopedic surgeon. He's married and has a two-year-old named James, Jr."

How original, I thought nastily. *And how self-congratulatory.*

Not that I ever had strong opinions or anything.

"And Philip?" Danielle inquired.

"Philip is a communications director for a big pharmaceutical company."

"Is there a Mrs. Philip?"

Clare's eyes shifted to the horizon. "Well, yes, but . . ."

"But what?" Danielle asked eagerly.

Ah, I thought. Watch what you say around this one. She craves juicy gossip.

"Well, she asked for a separation, but Philip hasn't agreed to it yet. She said Philip spends too much time at the office and not enough at home, with her. But he's the one who makes the money." Clare turned back to us, pleading in her voice. "Doesn't she understand that he's only doing what he has to do?"

"Maybe," I said, "he doesn't have to do it so excessively. Maybe she'd like it better if they had less money but more intimacy."

What the hell was I saying?

Clare shook her head. "But they're trying to have a baby. And babies cost lots of money these days."

"Yeah," I snapped, "if you treat them like freakin' royalty. When I was a kid—"

"Does Mrs. Philip have a career?" Danielle asked, cutting off what was sure to have been a tirade on one of my pet subjects.

"No. She married Philip right after she graduated from college. She's only twenty-five. She's been home trying to get pregnant."

I swear Clare delivered that bit of information without a trace of sarcasm.

Danielle cleared her throat and adjusted her hat, which, as far as I could see, didn't need adjusting.

"Unless I'm seriously out of touch with contemporary culture," I said, "Mrs. Philip needs Mr. Philip at home with her for that particular task. What does she do while she's waiting for him to show up?"

"She runs errands, I suppose. They have a housekeeper. I don't know. Maybe she volunteers." Clare lowered her voice, as if anyone cared about this silly exchange. "Honestly? I think I'd go out of my mind if I didn't have a job to go to. If I weren't being productive somehow."

Danielle sighed. "No wonder your brother spends so much time at the office. Honey, don't take offense, but I think what Mrs. Philip needs isn't Mr. Philip, it's a life. Of her own. Now, before it's too late. That's just my opinion."

"There's never been a divorce in the Wellman family," Clare retorted, as if that put an end to that discussion.

Which it did, because then there was a lull in the chatter. Lulls drive me nuts. They make me feel like I'm failing to hold up my part of the social bargain. They make me feel responsible for everyone's entertainment.

Okay, I thought, standing and stretching. Now what?

"I'm going to get a soda," I said, suddenly eager to be alone. "Does anyone—"

But I wasn't about to get away so easily.

"Here," Danielle said. "I've got bottled water for everyone. Sit down, Gincy. I have another fun question."

Grudgingly, I sat. And accepted the free water. Free stuff was good.

"What's the question?" Clare looked as dubious as I felt.

"Okay. Here goes. Who's the most recent person you've had a sex dream about?" Danielle looked as if she was dying to share her own juicy nocturnal adventures.

I was not. But she wanted conversation? She was going to get conversation.

"That's easy," I said, wiping water from my chin with the back of my hand. "Hank Hill."

"Excuse me, what?" she said. "Hank Hill? As in the 'star' of *King of the Hill*? Hank Hill the cartoon character with the saggy gut and bad glasses?"

"Look, it was a dream, okay?" I shrugged elaborately. "You can't help what you dream. Your head gets all weird when you sleep."

"His character is very upstanding," Clare offered. "Except for always wanting to kick people's asses, he's very socially acceptable."

"I thought you didn't watch TV?"

"Well, not a lot of TV. See, Win stays late at work several times a week so, well, I guess lately I've gotten into the habit of watching TV while I eat dinner. It's—It's not so lonely that way."

You don't have to apologize for watching TV, I almost said. But didn't.

"Was he good?" Danielle asked.

"What?"

"Was he good in bed?" Danielle repeated. "Was the dream worth it?"

"Oh. Well," I admitted, "nothing actually happened. You know, sexually. It was more like I was attracted to this guy and then I realized he was Hank Hill, but a real guy, not a cartoon. He was a teacher in a boarding school. So was I, come to think of it. And then he had a nervous breakdown."

"Before anything sexual could happen?" Clare asked.

She looked truly interested in my answer. Maybe she had a secret crush on Hank Hill.

Hmmm.

Jessica Fletcher, New England-based mystery writer and amateur sleuth, and Hank Hill, a tall Texan specializing in propane and propane accessories.

Interesting.

"Right," I confirmed.

Danielle sighed. "Gincy, honey, you are one weird chick. Clare, your turn."

Clare squirmed in her seat. "Oh, this is silly," she said, "but I had a dream once about Niles, from *Frasier*. It was very romantic. He was a total gentleman. He never even took off his suit jacket. We didn't, you know. We just had dinner."

"Niles Crane is no Hank Hill," I pointed out. "I'll take a T-shirt over a suit jacket any day."

"Am I the only one on this bench who actually has sex dreams that involve actual sex?" Danielle demanded.

"Okay, kiddo," I said, "let's have it. Who have you been boinking in REM sleep? You've been dying to tell us since this conversation started. Spill."

Danielle preened. "Well," she said, "I had a totally hot dream about Dr. Phil. He was a-ma-zing. First—"

"The bald TV psychiatrist?" I blurted.

"Now you're making fun of bald? You fantasize about a cartoon character."

"He's also kind of fat," Clare said.

"And this from the girl who fantasizes about a nonexistent

person," Danielle said. "A TV character. Niles Crane isn't real. Dr. Phil is."

And so the journey passed. It took only about forty-five minutes but it felt much, much longer.

If this is what friendship is about, I thought, maybe I should throw myself overboard now.

Gincy

She Is What She Is

That evening, after having unpacked and picked up a few basic groceries, the three of us decided to go to a popular restaurant called Truce and to split up after dinner. In case any one of us wanted to do something the others didn't.

Danielle came out of the bathroom with hair bigger than any I'd ever seen on Jennifer Lopez.

"Whoa!" I said, feeling my own measly mop.

Someone had told me that if I bothered to style it I could look very gamine. I knew what that meant but I pretended not to know. Sometimes I can be quite perverse.

"I didn't know you had that much hair!"

"It looks real, doesn't it?" Danielle beamed. "It's a hairpiece! Isn't it fantastic?"

Clare didn't look so sure. "Why are you wearing a hairpiece?" she asked.

"Why aren't you wearing a hairpiece?" Danielle shot back.

Clare? In a hairpiece? Miss straight-and-shiny pageboy, Miss Eddie Bauer catalogue model? I was curious to hear what she had to say.

"Because it's kind of much. That's just my opinion," she added quickly.

Always the peacemaker. The girl needs to cause some trouble, I thought. It would do her a world of good.

Danielle took a sip of the pinkish martini I handed her before retorting. "It's a legitimate accessory. And it wasn't inexpensive."

"I'm sure. It's just that, well, I'd be embarrassed to wear a hairpiece."

"Why?" Danielle demanded. "Why would you be embarrassed if it made you look gorgeous and glamorous?"

"Well, still." Clare kind of squeaked. "I don't think I could be seen in public that way."

"What way? Gorgeous and glamorous? Well, honey, that's your problem."

"I'm naturally suspicious of artifice," Clare admitted.

I grinned. The poor kid. "I wonder. Can you be artificially suspicious of artifice?"

"What's natural, anyway?" Danielle said. "Besides, I don't know, nature. Trees and flowers and rocks. You can't tell me that every decision a person makes isn't about artifice. About selling something, getting a message across."

Clare took a sip of orange juice before speaking. "A starving woman in Ethiopia who has to decide whether to share her family's tiny bit of food with another woman's dying baby isn't thinking about getting a message across. She's thinking about how she'll survive another day in such a dreadful life."

"Well, okay," Danielle admitted, "so let's just talk about people like us, privileged people, people who aren't starving, people who aren't living in refugee tents."

"People choose to wear L.L. Bean instead of Prada," I said, enjoying myself mid-Martini, "because they want everyone to know they're about comfort. Or, I don't know, family values. Vacations on Nantucket with the sailboat and the perfect blond children. Tomatoes and corn on the cob. Weekends in Maine at the family camp. Blueberry pie. Maple syrup."

"I don't dress to send a message to anyone," Clare protested. "I dress for me. I like to be comfortable."

"But your L.L. Bean ensemble is a costume anyway," Danielle said. "A uniform."

"It is not! I've never worn a uniform in my life! Except for my Girl Scout uniform."

Danielle sighed magnificently. "Don't get me started on those uniforms. Anyway, I am so tired of this conversation. Look, all I'm saying is that men appreciate a little artifice. It makes them feel the woman went out of her way to impress them."

"Some men, maybe," Clare said. Self-righteously? "Not the kind of man I want to be with."

Now it was my turn to sigh dramatically. "God, you are boring, Clare."

BANG!

I jumped at the sudden loud noise. Clare had slammed the glass bottle of orange juice on the counter; juice was running down the outside of the bottle and pooling.

"How dare you say that about me!" she cried. "You know nothing about me, nothing! Until a few weeks ago you didn't even know I existed. How can you possibly have the right to judge me?"

It was not the reaction I had expected.

"Hey, look, I'm sorry. I was just goofing around. I thought, you know, you'd just tell me to go stuff myself."

Clare hung her head and I saw her taking a deliberate deep breath. Danielle raised her perfectly arched eyebrows at me.

"Fine," Clare said then. "But I don't think calling people 'boring' is funny. I am the way I am for a reason. For a lot of reasons. I—"

"Okay," I said. "I got it. Really."

A cell phone rang just then.

"It's me," Clare declared, reaching into the pocket of her chino shorts. "It's Win. Hello?"

Danielle and I watched her hurry out onto the raggedy porch.

"Well," Danielle drawled, "there's more to that girl than meets the eye."

Gincy

All by Her Lonesome Lone

"Morning, sleepyhead," Danielle singsonged. "I was just about to show Clare my dating system. Grab a cup of coffee and I'll show you, too."

I dragged myself into the kitchen and poured a cup of coffee from the old perk pot we'd found under the sink.

"Who made this?" I grumbled.

I didn't know about my roomies, but I'd been out very late the night before, flirting heavily with a guy at a bar with a crappy pool table. Things were going great until I beat him, in itself a minor miracle as I suck at pool.

Some men just can't handle a strong woman.

"It's too watery," I went on. "And what do you mean you have a system? Why do you need a system to meet men?"

"Duh! It's not a system to meet men. Men are all over the place. The world is lousy with men. It's a system to weed out the losers. To separate the wheat from the chaff. To evaluate potential husbands."

I grunted. Pre-coffee was also pre–witty reply.

"Okay," Clare said musingly. "But it sounds like an awful lot of work."

"Do the work up front and you won't have to do it on the back end."

"The back end?" Clare asked.

"Yes. After the wedding. Make sure they're properly trained right from the start and you avoid problems down the line."

"Men aren't dogs, Danielle," I said, sitting next to Clare at the kitchen table. "Well. You know what I mean."

Clare shrugged. "I'm kind of curious about this system. Can we see it?"

Danielle looked oh-so-smug. "Of course. You can adopt my basic structure and tailor it to your own particular needs."

And she proceeded to walk us through a binder full of lists and charts. By page five, my eyes had glazed over but Clare, oddly, seemed still interested.

"Under 'Style,' see," Danielle was pointing out, "I've included 'Hair' (natural color & texture, cut, maintenance); 'Clothing' (casual, office wear, formal)—absolutely no white socks except on the tennis court!"

"What about at the gym?" I said.

"Oh. Well, that's okay. As long as I don't have to see them. Or wash them. Anyway, here's 'Personal Grooming' (cologne, nails—length & cleanliness, breath, etc.), and—"

"You're unbelievable!" I burst out, caffeine all kicked in. "You know that?"

Danielle beamed. "I know. Let me tell you, my method is fool-proof. Also, look, I rate his 'Relationship Quotient.' For example: Has he been in a long-term relationship? If so, how long-term was it and why did it end? Has he ever been married? Etcetera."

"What if he doesn't tell you right up front about his past?" Clare asked.

"Well, then I ask him. Of course. I have a right to know."

"And he has a right not to tell," I countered.

"Fine. Then he's not the right man for me. Full disclosure is very important."

A date is not a court of law, I thought, but all I said was: "But—"

"But nothing, Gincy. End of story. He's history. Now, would you like to hear the rest of my categories? I'm always refining the system."

"Uh, no thanks. That's okay." I got up and left my roommates poring over the binder.

I wondered as I walked down the porch steps and headed toward the beach. What had I gotten myself into with these two? They were so totally unlike me. I couldn't imagine we'd get through the summer without a major meltdown.

Truth is, I'd never been very good at making or keeping friends, male or female. I'm not really sure why.

My best friend in grammar school was a doofus named Mark. We were an odd pair, to be sure; Mark chubby and klutzy, me skinny and speedy. But it worked, our friendship, especially since we shared a general cynicism none of the other kids in DeerPlop seemed to have.

When Mark's family moved away just before seventh grade, I was down for about a week until one day I realized I didn't even remember Mark's last name.

Maybe I was just unfit for true friendship. I didn't know.

In sophomore year of high school I struck up a sort of buddy-ship with the new girl in town, Kathy O'Connell. I never found out why her divorced mother had dragged them both to WormSlime, New Hampshire, where there was virtually no career opportunity of any kind.

But there was Kathy and she was wild. I mean, really bad. I liked her immediately and she liked me. Maybe because I sort of worshipped her. Kathy was who I wanted to be but didn't have the nerve to be. Anyway, I was like her acolyte or something, the driver of the getaway car, her personal assistant in mischief and crime.

Our brief and totally unequal friendship came to a crashing halt when Kathy schemed to break into the Kmart out on the highway one night and see what she could make off with. She was especially interested in the electronics, which she then planned to sell.

I just couldn't go along with her plan. I was ashamed of my cowardice but also kind of proud of my ability to distinguish right from wrong. Kathy was disgusted with me, called me every foul name in the book, and told me never to even look at her again. I kept my promise, which wasn't hard because she was arrested while stuffing a Nikon camera down her pants, and sent off to a juvenile detention center in BarfVille.

Soon after, her mother moved on, ostensibly to be closer to her wayward daughter.

For the rest of high school, I remained pretty much a loner. It didn't bother me. Occasionally I'd go to a movie with some kids, but most of the time I hung at the crummy little library where I could go online on its crummy little computer and pore over its crummy little collection of books on art and film.

Once, I went on a date with a guy home from college for spring break. I don't know why. I wasn't really attracted to him but it seemed an interesting thing to do. It wasn't.

Ah, the ocean. And sand. And a few teeny, white puffy clouds. A view. A vista.

I took a deep, cleansing breath of the fresh morning air. I loved living in the city but the great outdoors definitely had its benefits. Still, I'd stick to the beach, I vowed, plopping down on the sand, still slightly damp with dew. There was plenty of nature back in HorsePoop, New Hampshire, but I was never going back there.

And I wasn't the only one who'd made that vow.

I closed my eyes, let the sun warm my upturned face, and remembered.

When I was a senior in high school I got a letter from a guy named Mark Tremaine. It took me a moment to realize the letter was from my old friend, and not just some prank or misdirected mail. Mark wanted me to know that he'd come out of the closet. I was happy for him for about a minute and then tossed the letter on my mess of a desk. I never saw it again. And it was the last I ever heard from Mark.

When I got to college, I finally experienced the artificial

frenzy of oh-my-god-best-friend-dom. For the first two years of college I had a new best friend approximately every three weeks. Nothing stuck. Probably a good thing.

By junior year I was back to spending a lot of my time alone and enjoying it. After four years at Addison I graduated with nothing more than a handful of passing acquaintances.

Throughout my twenties I continued this habit of not forming or keeping close relationships.

I dated my share of guys but bailed on the few who seemed interested in sticking around.

The office provided a pool of people from whom I could chose companions for the sole purpose of a drink after work. Sally was a fairly recent addition to that list of drinking buddies, and while I liked hanging out with her a couple of hours a week—she was good for a laugh and a verbal wrangle—I never saw us becoming real friends.

Whatever real friends were.

Maybe, I thought, gazing out at the glittering ocean, *I'm a social freak.* Or maybe I was meant to be close—really close—to just one or two people during the course of my lifetime.

If so, I hadn't met that person or those people yet. Clare and Danielle were just not going to fit the bill.

The sun was getting hotter by the minute. It was going to be a scorcher and I'd forgotten to pack sunblock. That was one thing Danielle and Clare were good for. Borrowing things from.

Not that my roomies were horrible or anything. They were okay. A bit odd, but who wasn't? We just had the usual living-with-strangers stuff to work out. Each of us came with a bundle of habits acquired over almost thirty years. That meant approximately ninety years of habits all told, a lot of crap crammed into one leaky old house.

Clare, for example, was very, very neat. Maybe it had something to do with her Midwestern values. I didn't know. I'd never been further west than Chicago. I suspected Danielle and I might be witnessing a borderline obsession with cleanliness.

Danielle, on the other hand, was completely averse to the most basic cleaning chores. The girl had had a housekeeper all her childhood, still had one for her small one-bedroom apartment in Boston.

Wash a dish? Damp mop a floor? Ew. You paid people to do that. Like, maids.

Me? Well, I'd been told by former college suitemates that living with me was like living with a frat guy. I could see why some people would make the comparison.

I did on occasion leave the lights on all night. I did sometimes blare music at odd hours. I did tend to sing loudly and badly in the shower. And once I did forget to put the top back on a container of sour cream.

I still didn't think that one isolated incident should have earned me the nickname Moldy.

Maybe that was the deciding factor. Because come graduation I vowed that I would never, ever have another roommate again. Since then, most of my income had gone toward rent—in other words, down a black hole—but at least I had my privacy and independence.

Except for this summer.

I started back for the house, thinking now of breakfast and a shower. And hoping Danielle wasn't hogging the bathroom. And that Clare hadn't finished the Cheerios.

Well, I thought, as I walked under the strengthening sun, *it doesn't much matter what I think of my roomies or how well we get along. I've signed a lease and now I'm stuck with them.*

Suddenly, I remembered one of my father's many favorite clichés. "When life gives you lemons," he'd tell me, like when I'd get assigned a lousy science lab partner, "make lemonade."

I grinned. With Danielle and Clare as my roommates, I'd need lots and lots of sugar.

Gincy

Musical Sheets

Though I loved the sun and sand, I'd never been much for lazing around on the beach. I'm too full of nervous energy for laying flat in public.

Unless, of course, I'm hung over.

But I agreed to hang with my roomies for a while later that morning while they sunbathed on the Oak Bluffs Town Beach. What else did I have to do?

Face it, Gincy, I told myself, throwing a threadbare towel in a backpack, you're a workaholic. If you're not working, you want to be working.

My father, I thought, *would be so proud. If he really knew anything about me.*

We found a relatively empty section of beach and settled in, Danielle on her plush beach towel and matching chair; Clare on a bright blue mat; and me on half an old sheet.

I watched as Danielle shrugged out of her belted terry cover-up.

"What the hell are you wearing!" I cried. "You look like a World War Two poster girl, you know that? What's-her-name, Lana Turner. You're poured into that bathing suit. And what's up with the torpedo bra?"

Danielle rolled her eyes. "It's a retro look. It's very popular this year. I'm supposed to look like Ava Gardner. Mimi Van Doren. Marilyn Monroe. And it's more a late-forties, early-fifties look, post–World War Two. Have you ever read a fashion magazine in your life?"

"No," I lied. "Never."

They didn't need to know I bought and read, cover to cover, every September issue of *Vogue, Bazaar, Elle,* and *Marie Claire.* It was cultural research, that's all.

"I think you look nice," Clare told Danielle. "I could never wear a white bathing suit, though. I'm too pale. And since I don't allow myself to tan . . ."

"Let me guess," I said, eyeing Clare's navy, one-piece, conservative tank suit. "L.L. Bean?"

"At least I didn't raid my brother's underwear drawer this morning!" Clare retorted.

Danielle whooped with delight.

I was wearing my standard beach fare. A thin tank top and a pair of boys' boxer shorts. With a thong underneath. You know. For modesty.

I grinned. "Touché."

"Why don't you try one of the super-advanced self-tanning lotions?" Danielle said to Clare.

For the next few minutes my roomies discussed the merits and pitfalls of various expensive beauty products. I slathered on more drugstore-brand sunblock and watched a chunky, middle-aged, fish-belly white guy in a teeny Speedo-type bathing suit play Frisbee with a girl I seriously hoped was his daughter and not his girlfriend.

Men. You can't live with them, you can't . . .

"I was thinking," I said, interrupting my roomies' deep discussion. "We should talk about what happens when someone wants to bring a guy home for the night."

Danielle nodded. "Good point. We have only two bedrooms. As it is, we rotate getting the couch. Okay. So if someone brings home a guy, I say she should get the second bedroom for the night. And the girl she's displacing takes the couch or shares the first bedroom with the girl who's got the first bedroom for the night. According to the schedule."

"That could get messy," Clare said. "The way I see it, the girl who's been displaced should get a substitute night alone in the second bedroom since she lost her turn to the girl with the unexpected guy."

Danielle scrunched up her nose. "What?"

"Or," Clare went on, "this is a better idea. Each girl is assigned a particular night when she can bring home a guy and use the second bedroom. That way there are no surprises!"

"But what if I don't meet a guy on my appointed night?" Danielle argued.

"Then you forfeit," Clare said matter-of-factly. "It's only fair."

"It's only a freakin' fascist state is what it is," I commented, reasonably.

"Why does it even matter to you, Clare? You've got a live-in boyfriend back home!"

"Yeah, are you planning on fooling around behind his back?" I said. "You don't seem the type."

"No, of course not! And I'm not the type. But—"

"So, stay out of it. Let me and Dani handle the sexual logistics."

"Danielle. It's Danielle, not Dani."

"Whatever." I stood and stretched. The sun on my shoulders felt electrifying. "I'm going for a swim," I announced. "Nobody touch my Snowballs."

Clare

The Root of All Evil

I couldn't sleep.

Danielle was snoring lightly in the other bedroom; Gincy was passed out on the couch in the minuscule living room. Usually, a few hours at the beach tires me enormously, but for some reason I found myself staring wide-eyed at the dingy white ceiling.

And worrying. About everything.

Maybe Win was right, I thought. *Maybe my renting this house is a big waste of hard-earned money.*

What would I know about real value?

Money had never been an issue in my life until then. Meaning that until renting the house with Gincy and Danielle, I'd never had to think about things like paying bills and sharing expenses. First my parents, and then Win, had taken care of those matters.

And there was something I hadn't told my roommates. My parents supplemented my fairly small income with a monthly check. Though I religiously deposited each check, the fact was that the money was there if I needed it.

My father had made sure I knew that the monthly supplement was part of my inheritance; that when he died, my portion of his estate would be that much smaller. Still, I didn't feel comfortable letting anyone but Win know about my financial arrangements.

Anyway, that summer I was writing checks of my own for pretty much the first time. A fairly hefty sum each month to the owners of the little house in Oak Bluffs, sent off via Terri at People's Properties. It was both satisfying and slightly scary, sealing the envelope and knowing that my portion of the house was secured.

What I hadn't considered before signing the lease was that unless the entire amount of rent was paid on time, our right to the entire house was jeopardized. All three names were on the lease. Clare Jean Wellman. Danielle Sarah Leers. And Virginia Marie Gannon.

And Gincy had been late with the first installment of rent. She apologized and explained she'd had to get an advance on her salary, but still. It annoyed me. I wondered if she realized what was at stake. Her carelessness could have ruined the summer for us all.

But I'd kept my feelings to myself, something I was very good at. Mostly. I just couldn't keep quiet whenever Danielle insisted we chip in for a housekeeper, a luxury Gincy clearly couldn't afford and one I didn't think necessary.

It was about time Gincy learned how to clean up after herself.

And Danielle, who knew all about cleaning by watching her housekeeper, simply had to pull on a pair of rubber gloves and get busy.

Clare, I told myself, *you're becoming a grumpy old lady.* I shook out the crumpled sheet and turned on my side, still hoping to catch an hour of real rest. I'd worked myself into a bit of a state.

And another thing, I told the ugly papered wall. *I simply refuse to split the grocery bill in three equal parts when Gincy routinely brings home those disgusting pink-and-white Snowballs which I wouldn't eat if I were starving to death.*

Danielle agreed with me on that issue, though she was the one who suggested the three-way split in the beginning. I don't think she had any better idea than I did about what constituted Gincy's diet. The girl ate junk food by the pound and yet was skinny as a rail.

I sighed, tossed off the sheet, and got out of bed. A nap just wasn't going to happen. I tiptoed past Danielle's room; she was still out cold. Downstairs I crept into the kitchen, hoping not to wake Gincy, who was collapsed on the couch, mouth open, legs dangling.

She looked silly.

I smiled.

Okay. So far, things hadn't been as bad as they could have been with my roommates.

But I wondered when I would start to have fun.

Danielle

Bad Things and Good People

My paternal grandmother was a very wise woman.

"Sometimes," she would say, "God tests us.

"He challenges our faith in Him by putting terrible obstacles to happiness in our way.

"He tests our inner strength by forcing us to face trials of spirit and patience and perseverance.

"He urges us to meet those trials and overcome those obstacles and be the best people we can be.

"And when we do," Grandma Leers would say, "we are rewarded. Not necessarily in this lifetime but definitely in the next."

This was what I added to her words of wisdom: "If I'm going to be rewarded for tolerating slobs and enduring cretins, I want to be rewarded now. In this life. In a big way."

This was another addendum: "Sometimes, there is no reward. Sometimes bad things happen to good people. And no matter how much faith and patience and other superhuman qualities you display, you still get screwed in the end."

That fateful summer, God decided to test me by putting Gincy Gannon in my path. What I ever did to annoy Him, I didn't know.

Gincy Gannon was beginning to convince me that God had a sick sense of humor.

My midafternoon beauty rest was very refreshing. I felt really wonderful. Until I joined my roommates in the kitchen.

"What are you wearing?" I demanded, stopping short at the entrance.

Clare looked at me quizzically.

"Not you," I said. "You! Gincy. What's that you're wearing?"

Gincy looked up from the Sno Ball she was eating with a fierce concentration. "What? I didn't hear—"

I pointed with a trembling finger.

"That's my T-shirt. And it's got—Sno Ball!—all over it!"

Gincy wiped her hands on her shorts and peered down at her flat chest. "Oh. Sorry. I didn't bring enough clothes for the weekend. I found this—"

"In my dresser drawer!"

"Jeez, don't shout. Yeah. Look, I'm sorry, I'll wash it—"

"You'll buy me a new one is what you'll do, missy!"

"What? It's a lousy T-shirt!" Gincy protested.

"It's a hundred-and-fifty-dollar Ralph Lauren T-shirt, you moron!" I screamed. "And you got that disgusting Sno Ball all over it."

Gincy pulled the shirt away from her chest. "It's not Sno Ball," she pointed out. "It's hot sauce. I had chili for lunch. And it's not all over. It kind of makes a pattern. An abstract pattern. You could say it's art. Hey, I could borrow more of your shirts and spill stuff and we could market a whole line of T-shirts and make some real money!"

Clare looked downright afraid. But I was too drained to continue the argument. Instead, I sank into a chair.

An herbal wrap, I thought. *I need an herbal wrap because of this girl.*

Clare
Other People's Children

I don't understand why people can't treat other people with respect.

That's what I was taught to do. It's not all that hard, either. Respect for other people and their feelings and their property quickly becomes second nature.

Danielle didn't even claim it was an accident that she had eaten one of my nonfat yogurts for breakfast that Sunday morning. I came shuffling into the teeny kitchen and opened the old refrigerator—the one I'd thoroughly scrubbed—only to find the last of my yogurts gone.

Confused, I turned around to ask my roommates if they'd seen it.

Gincy was sucking down black coffee from a chipped ceramic mug, her feet up on the Formica kitchen table.

Danielle, dressed in a black silk robe, was sitting next to her, licking a spoon covered with raspberry yogurt. In one hand was a container that clearly read "nonfat."

"That's my yogurt!" I cried.

Danielle shrugged. "I just thought I'd give it a try. You can have one of my low-fats."

"But I don't want one of your low-fats," I protested. "I want *my* yogurt."

"You don't have to be so fussy," she snapped. "Just eat the stupid low-fat. There are, like, three flavors in there."

"Low-fat is not the same as nonfat," I said.

Gincy muttered, "Somebody needs to get laid."

I slammed the refrigerator and turned on her, furious. "Shut up!" I shouted. "Every word out of your mouth is foul! Don't you ever just—just—"

"Just shut up? Rarely. Sorry."

I clapped my hands to the sides of my head. Since when had I become so dramatic? "Oh, this fighting is killing me! Aren't we supposed to act like a family?"

"What do you think we've been doing?" Danielle laughed, got up, and tossed the spoon in the sink. "Doesn't your family argue? Don't they act like freaked-out lunatics every time someone won't get off the phone or out of the bathroom fast enough?"

"No. No they don't."

"What, is everyone all polite and stuff?" Gincy asked with a snort.

"Yes," I told her. *Unlike you.*

Danielle came over to where I stood and took my hand. I tried to pull it away but Danielle hung on.

"Clare, honey," she said. "Maybe things are different where you come from. You know. Out there. But where I grew up, it's normal for a family to scream and yell and slam doors."

"And hate each other and call each other toilet scum and douche bags," Gincy added enthusiastically, reaching for the half-empty coffeepot.

"That's what family is all about, honey. Love. Unconditional love. It's where you can hang your hat and throw silverware and where you and your cousins can pee in the pool—"

"And projectile vomit after drinking your uncle's secret beer supply." Gincy laughed. "Once, my cousin Mikey hit the side of the garage from the back steps. It was like fifteen or twenty feet!"

For a moment I just stared at them. My roommates. I was stuck with them for an entire summer.

And then I burst out crying.

"I guess she's not a morning person," Gincy whispered loudly as Danielle finally let go of my hand.

June

Gincy
Guys and Dolls

K ell had asked us to come to a quick meet-and-greet session at which the new director of daytime programming would be introduced.

Everyone from our department showed up but Sally.

I snatched a bagel from the tray of goodies provided for the occasion and poured a third cup of coffee. Then some bigwig named Weinstein introduced Rick Luongo.

Mr. Luongo seemed a bit embarrassed by the fuss, and after mumbling something about "looking forward" and "teamwork," he melted into the crowd of about twenty.

I spotted him again just before leaving the conference room. He was shoving a jelly donut into his mouth. Powdered sugar covered his chin and a big blob of raspberry jelly was about to plop onto his tie.

Hiding a smile, I returned to my office. Anyone who was brave enough to eat a jelly donut in public, on the first day at a new job, couldn't be all bad.

Later that morning, Sally stopped by.

"Have you met the new guy?" I asked. "I didn't see you at the meeting this morning."

"I was late." Sally made an ugly face. "And I met him later. He's just like all the rest of the corporate scum."

"How do you know?" I asked, not really expecting a sensible answer.

Sally was so predictable.

"Uh, he's wearing a tie? And a blazer. A navy blazer."

I decided to give her a hard time. "His tie was sort of funky. Those abstract patterns? Well, if you look real close, they're not abstract at all. They're puppies."

I wasn't kidding about that. Rick Luongo wasn't exactly Mr. GQ, at least in terms of his clothing.

Sally snorted. "A typical man. Using his tie as a conversation piece. Tie as penis is what it really is. He lures you in with his pathetic wit and the next thing you know—"

"His mother gave it to him," I said. "I asked."

I was lying, of course, but . . .

Sally glowered and folded her arms across her chest.

No matter how hard Sally argued, I wasn't going over to her side.

Something about this Rick guy struck me as okay. In spite of the nerdy outfit, which now boasted a jelly stain.

I think it was his face. His entire manner, actually. There was something open about him. And, okay, he was pretty damn good-looking in a slightly swarthy male sort of way.

The kind of way that makes you think of Mediterranean beaches, salty skin, and fresh-caught calamari for lunch.

"Whatever," I said to Sally.

She huffed and walked out of my office.

Sally hated men and it wasn't because she was a lesbian. I've known plenty of straight chicks who loathed and despised men and enough gay women who thought that, on the whole, men were no better or worse than women. But Sally did happen to be gay, openly and proudly so.

It didn't bother me that she was gay. So what?

What bothered me was when she got in a mood that dictated the only topic worthy of discussion was Being Gay. For obvious reasons, I had little to contribute to those so-called discussions.

After a half hour of her ranting about rights and privileges and identity crises, I was bored and angry.

Sometimes just angry.

Like a few nights before Rick Luongo's debut. We were at Jillian's, shooting pool. Sally sucked, by the way, even worse than I did. And she was rattling on about gay this and gay that. Like the right to get married and job discrimination and blah, blah, blah.

Now, I was all for legalizing gay marriages, and job discrimination of any kind made me sick, but all I was trying to do was have a good time. Not change the world.

"Can we please, please talk about something else?" I begged, after missing yet another shot. "There's more to life than being gay, you know."

"We are our sexuality," Sally responded. "Our sexuality defines us."

"If it defines us, why don't I talk only about how great it is being hetero?" I asked cleverly.

Forgetting that Sally had an answer for everything.

"Because you're the majority," she replied with an utterly annoying air of superiority. "Or so you say. The world is the way you made it, not the way we would make it if we could. You don't need to talk about your sexuality. The world as it exists *is* your sexuality."

You know what, I thought, not for the first time, resting my forehead against the pool cue, *I just don't have enough schooling, formal or informal, to argue this sort of thing.*

And I definitely don't have the patience.

"Fine, whatever," I said, giving up. "I'm the enemy. Now, just shoot. I want to wrap up this game before midnight."

Since I'd been hanging out with Sally, I'd been thinking a lot about the whole gay thing. I mean, things had really changed in the past ten years. All the good stuff—the relative tolerance on the streets of major cities, programs for gay teens dealing with the horrors of coming out—all that was great.

But some stuff struck me as odd. For example, one day while watching MTV it hit me that contemporary pop culture was insinuating that women having sex with women was totally common.

And I don't mean hot Bunny-on-Bunny action for the voyeuristic pleasure of balding straight men in paisley silk bathrobes.

I mean, one average straight girl and another average straight girl deciding to date each other rather than the two cute guys in Accounting, even though they'd never dated women before and weren't considering coming out of any closet because they'd never been in any closet.

Music, magazines, TV, and books—the voices of every medium said it was no big deal to suddenly decide, hey, I really like her, I think I'll have sex with her.

Even if you'd never had a homosexual thought in your life.

But I thought it was a big deal. I found it a huge deal to suddenly develop a passion for a body part you'd otherwise never had a passion for.

I mean—a vagina? Suddenly, that often leaky, smelly . . . thing was something you wanted to touch on someone else? I didn't think so. Not for me, anyway. You could count me out of the lesbian sex thing.

Sure, I admitted, I might really like another woman, as in maybe sort of have a crush on her, in the way you look up to someone who is totally more talented than you are.

Like, if I ever met Hillary Rodham Clinton I might gush and make a fool of myself in the presence of so much talent and intellect and incredible loving patience.

Bill was one lucky man and Chelsea one lucky daughter.

And don't get me started on Mother Theresa.

But were those feelings romantic? No. Well, maybe in the capital R sense of the word.

But were those feelings sexual? No they were not. Not in any sense of the word. Ever.

At least, not for me. God knows I didn't want to offend anybody by speaking for them.

Just like I didn't want anybody else speaking for me. Like

telling me that if all factors were in place—like luck and timing—I might someday have sex with another woman. No big deal.

No, thank you. Not happening.

And neither was work. I'd been sitting at my desk for almost ten minutes by then, staring blankly at the computer screen, on which neon spirals danced.

Damn, I thought. *Focus, Gincy.*

But it was no use. Sally had pissed me off with her automatic dismissal of Rick Luongo. And now all I could think about was how, when she wasn't hating men, Sally was assuming that a lot of the heterosexual women around her were lying to themselves about their sexuality.

How would Sally feel, I wondered, if I assumed that she was lying to herself about being a lesbian? Huh? How would she feel?

She would feel royally pissed off, and she'd have a right to be.

Royally pissed off is how I felt when she gave me the lifted eyebrow, that same smug expression I used to see on my mother when she wanted to imply that she knew better than I did about myself. That I was too blind and stupid or young and naive to know anything better than she did. That no matter what I said or avowed or claimed, it was worthless, it was wrong, it was stupid.

I groaned and clutched my head. Nice. Now I was obsessing about my mother. At work. On sacred turf. And it was all Sally's fault!

My mother. Ellen Marie Gannon.

The way I saw it, my mother assumed I was a failure because she wanted me to be a failure, for a whole bundle of sick, self-serving reasons, only one of which was that she was a failure and misery loves company. Mom wanted me to be what she needed me to be.

Of course, I knew that if I ever confronted her with my knowledge, she'd deny everything.

My mother, I'd realized, was similar to Sally in a way neither would ever have imagined. See, though she'd never come right out and said it, I knew that Sally assumed I was gay.

Why? Because she wanted me to be gay. She wanted to be right about me. She wanted me to be what she needed me to be. Her lesbian buddy.

Why does she need me to be lesbian? I thought, truly puzzled. *I'm already her buddy. Jeez. Talk about selfish.*

Back to work. Determinedly, I opened a file that needed attention that morning. A draft of a presentation. And I stared at it, seeing only a collection of letters.

Damn that Sally! And my mother. And their assuming things about me.

Fine. If they could assume, so could I. I could assume—in my less generous, darker moods—that they were both smug, self-centered, pathetic losers.

I'm not, I'd tell Mom, *slinking home to YellowBelly, New Hampshire, shamed and beaten, to wither away the rest of my days in trailer-park misery.*

And I'd tell Sally, *Look, kiddo, I am so not going to have a eureka! moment and discover that lo!, I am gay. At least not until you have a eureka! moment and discover that lo!, you are straight.*

I squinted hard at the document open on the screen before me.

Fine. Back to work.

Sally and Mom would just have to deal with my reality. In spite of their best efforts to convert me, I was not going to succumb to either of them.

Ever.

Clare

The End of an Era

I knew something was wrong the moment I walked through the front door.

Win was home and it was only six-thirty. Usually he didn't appear until almost eight.

"Hi," I said warily. "What's wrong?"

Win grinned. "Nothing's wrong. Why?"

"Because you're never home this early."

"Aren't you happy to see your boyfriend?"

"Of course. I didn't mean that."

Win opened his arms and, dutifully, I went into his embrace. *Sex,* I thought. *He wants sex.*

But he didn't. Win stepped away and said, "Come sit down, Clare. Over here, on the couch."

I sat and Win perched next to me. Without preamble, he took a small black ring box from the front pocket of his suit pants.

"I want you to marry me, Clare," he said. "I want you to be my wife."

What Win wants, all about Win . . .

Not, "Clare, will you please marry me? I would like to be your husband. Would you like to be my wife?"

"You haven't asked me," I said.

I eyed the ring box in Win's hand as if it were a can of coiled snakes.

"Yes, I did," he cried. "I just did! What do you mean?"

I sighed. I'd spent so many years explaining . . .

"You told me what you wanted. You didn't ask what I wanted. I get to say yes or no. That's the way it goes."

Let him indulge me, his silly little fiancée.

"Of course, sweetie," Win said soothingly. "I'm sorry. So: Clare Wellman, will you marry me?"

"It's so—so sudden," I mumbled.

"Sweetie, we've been together for ten years, this is not sudden!"

"But we haven't even talked about getting married. I—"

Win eyed me oddly. "Hey, I thought you girls liked to be surprised. I thought you girls wanted the romance."

You girls . . .

A question kept nagging at me: *Why is he doing this now? Why now?*

And an answer kept flashing.

He thinks you're slipping away.

He thinks he's losing his control.

He's trying to reel you back in.

He knows you can't say no.

"Besides," Win was saying then, "let's face it, Clare, we're not getting any younger. You're almost thirty and if we want to have kids, which of course we do, then we'd better get moving. Am I right? You know I'm right."

"You're right," I said.

You're always right.

"Of course I'm right. Now . . ."

Win handed me the ring box with a look of such anticipation I almost burst out laughing. Almost.

Like he didn't know what I would say.

I opened the box.

"It's beautiful," I said.

It was. But the ring wasn't my style. It wasn't me.

Win should have known that.

"I knew you'd love it," he said, jumping to his feet, a man with a mission. "So, I'm thinking sometime soon. Say, September."

"September!" I felt sick to my stomach. "No, Win, that's too soon, there's no time to—"

"Oh, come on, sweetie. You're a whiz at getting things organized. Plus, your mom can help, and your friends . . ."

"But the fall semester starts September tenth," I argued. "How can we take a honeymoon? I'll need to go back to work."

"I'm sure the school will give you a leave of absence," Win said smoothly. "Or a sabbatical. Isn't that what you teachers call it? After all, it's not every day a girl gets married!"

More weakly, I said, "But you start that big case in August. It'll never be over by September. How can you get away . . ."

Win reached out to stroke my hair. I winced at his barely perceptible touch.

"Sweetie, I'll work it all out, don't worry about a thing. All you need to do is have fun planning the wedding. Okay?"

I nodded, hardly aware of the motion. Win talked on and I tuned out.

What friends? What friends will help out? Maybe I don't want help. Maybe I don't want—

"So, are we set?" Win's voice, intruding. "September? Late September. Hey, you'd better start calling around now, book the church and a place for the reception, and, you know, whatever else needs to be done. You girls know these things."

I stared at the huge diamond ring on my finger and felt only disbelief. What was happening to me?

And then Win was on the phone.

"Mrs. Wellman? Hey, it's Win. No, nothing's wrong. In fact, we have some big news. Hang on. Clare, sweetie, pick up the other receiver, okay?"

Numbly, I did. And we announced our engagement to my family.

Danielle

When You Least Expect It

Things were going swimmingly.

I'd lined up a date for Friday night. Saturday was open but I was planning on dinner at Lucca's and then drinks at the club next door. With any luck I'd meet someone before the end of the night and line up a date for the following weekend.

And then I met him. Coincidentally, unplanned, a surprise.

Here's how it happened.

The sun was high and bright and I had a sudden, intense craving for an ice cream cone.

Intense cravings should always be satisfied.

So, carrying my beach bag equipped for a lazy afternoon of sunning, and wearing my broad-brimmed straw hat, I first headed to this tiny little place called SusieQ's for a cone.

The line was long, which gave me plenty of time to decide what flavor I wanted. Peach? Mocha Java? Or maybe decadent Chocolate Supreme!

Suddenly, my hat was knocked forward over my eyes. I let out a little scream. I mean, who knew what deviant was trying to blind me before he grabbed me and my overflowing bag!

"I'm so sorry!" a male voice said. "Can I—"

"No, I can—" I righted my hat and with a deep breath looked at the person now standing before me, a look of sincere apology on his face.

"I'm sorry," he repeated. "I was standing behind you and I— Well, I'm not used to judging the circumference of, uh, that kind of hat. Not that there's anything wrong with it," he added hastily.

I considered him keenly before replying. Physically, he wasn't my usual type—dark hair and eyes, clean-shaven, not too tall— but I was woman enough to appreciate masculine beauty in any form.

His wild hair was light brown, randomly streaked by the sun. His eyes were an amazing light blue-green, like Richard Burton's eyes, intense, penetrating, framed by dark lashes. He hadn't shaved in a few days; his stubbly beard was blond and brown and red. And he was tall, at least six-two.

Very nice.

"That's all right," I said graciously. "I forgive you."

Mr. Sunkissed smiled back. "At least let me buy you an ice cream for any trouble I caused."

Ah, a gentleman!

I graciously accepted.

By that time we were near the head of the line and I'd had plenty of time to note his clothing. Nothing spectacular. A dark T-shirt, jeans, and, oddly for the weather, work boots. He was clean and the jeans fit very nicely, but overall, he was too casually put together for my taste.

"What'll it be?" he said when we reached the window.

"A peach cone, please," I said.

Mr. Sunkissed also asked the server for a gallon of cherry-vanilla.

"For my dad," he explained. "It's his favorite. He doesn't get around too well anymore so I stop here when I can and get a supply."

"Oh, how nice," I said. A respectful son. Good sign. "So, your father is vacationing with you?"

Mr. Sunkissed handed me the cone and I noticed large, well-sculpted hands. Then he took his package from the server and we stepped out of the line.

"No," he said, "we live here year-round. In Chilmark. But you're here on vacation?"

I told him I lived in Boston and had rented a house with two other girls. Before he could reply, his beeper went off. He checked it and, with a frown, told me he had to get going.

"I'm sorry, again," he said, grinning. "About the hat."

"That's quite all right. It was nice talking to you."

There was a moment of awkward silence, Mr. Sunkissed poised to run off, my cone beginning to melt over my fingers.

"Well," he said, "maybe I'll see you around town again."

I nodded and he dashed off. I watched as he got into a black pickup truck and drove away.

I didn't even ask his name, I realized. Not that it mattered. I could never get serious about a guy who drove a pickup truck.

With a shrug, I headed toward the beach.

Gincy

The Ship and the Ocean

Danielle was curled up on the couch, busily at work updating her husband-hunting schedule.

"So far, so good," she murmured. "Three dates down; a second date with bachelor #2; two new prospects on board, not counting Mr. Pickup Truck . . ."

"You're rapacious," I blurted, tossing aside the week-old copy of the *Globe* I'd never had time to read. "You're like a starving cat working its way through a bowl of tuna fish covered in heavy cream."

"That reminds me," Danielle said, closing her account book. "I'm hungry! Who wants to go to lunch?"

Clare came into the living room from the kitchen. "I do. There's nothing in the fridge."

"And, we can't meet men in our own kitchen," Danielle pointed out, grabbing her purse. "Not that it matters for our bride-to-be!"

Clare gave a half smile. "I've got the keys," she said. "Are you coming, Gincy?"

I was. We wound up at the Beachcomber. Someone had left a copy of *Esquire* on the next table. Danielle began to leaf through it.

"Ha!" she cried. "You've got to see this ad!"

She passed it around. It was a full-page ad for penis enhancement. A larger penis, it seems, was guaranteed to "get the job done."

"Do you think that's how men really think about sex?" Clare seemed disturbed. "That it's all about 'getting the job done'?"

Danielle shrugged. "I don't know. Maybe the ad is saying that men don't really care about women, just getting done what they have to get done to make the women continue to have sex with them. I guess."

"All men care about is getting off," I declared. From experience. "If they can get off without getting the job done, that's even better."

"Oh, Gincy," Clare protested. "That's not true!"

Danielle returned to studying the full-page ad. "So," she said, musingly, "you think 'getting the job done' means giving a woman an orgasm?"

"Yeah. I think."

"But you don't need a big penis to do that!" she cried. "You don't need a penis at all!"

"True. So maybe they mean getting the job done is the whole sex act. The whole shebang, start to finish. God, who writes these ads, anyway?"

Clare seemed very interested in her crab salad.

"Why should any of this be surprising?" Danielle said, tossing the magazine to the floor. "Isn't that what men are really all about? Fixing broken car parts. Solving messy plumbing problems. Seeking leverage. Building decks. Grilling hamburgers. Punching out bad guys. Getting the job done. Don't talk and muse and ponder. Just do something. Just get it done."

Clare put down her fork suddenly. "That makes men sound so simple," she said. Was she upset by this? "So easy to understand."

"They are simple," I said. "They're right out there, getting the job done. End of story. Nothing complicated about it."

"But every man is different," Clare protested. "Every man's an individual!"

"Okay, to some extent," Danielle admitted. "But ask a cross

section of men what they want in life and they'll all say, 'to get the job done.' I guarantee it."

"I don't know . . ." Clare said.

"Women, on the other hand—"

I clapped my hands to my head. "Oh, boy, here we go."

Danielle smirked. "We are unclassifiable. We fit no one mold. We are complex and ever-changing."

"We sound highly annoying," I said.

"Chameleon-like. Seasonal. Cycling with the moon. Rising and falling with the tides."

I pretended to gag. Clare winced.

Poor Clare. Half the time she didn't know what to make of us.

"I think I'm going to be sick," I said. "Like, seasick. I want stability. I want my feet planted firmly on the ground. Maybe that's why I don't have any women friends. I'm enough of a woman for me to handle."

Danielle rolled her eyes. "Okay, we'll change the subject."

Then she leaned toward Clare, eyes gleaming. "So, Clare, are you totally psyched about the wedding?"

Clare twisted her massive engagement ring, right to left, left to right. It almost freakin' blinded me.

"Well, you know. I guess. I mean—"

"Having doubts?"

Clare looked at me, horrified. "Of course not! Why would you say that?"

"Did you hear how you answered Dani's question? Talk about equivocation."

"It's Danielle. Clare, honey, don't worry. Every bride feels overwhelmed. But I'll tell you what. This is your lucky day. I'll be your wedding planner! No charge, of course, except an invitation to the big event. How's that? Feel better?"

Clare managed a small smile. I thought she looked sick, but Danielle was elated.

"Excellent! Let's get started right away. There's so much to do! Okay, we know it's an early fall wedding. Hmm. Tricky. The weather could go any which way. I'd go with an indoor reception and as for the dress, well, let me do some research. No short sleeves, but maybe sleeveless, with some sort of bolero jacket or wrap for modesty in the church—do you want a church cere- mony?—and—"

I dug into my burger.

Clare picked listlessly at her meal.

Danielle chatted on.

Danielle
Love American Style

Oak Bluffs may be chock-full of vacationers, foreigners, outsiders, but still, it's a small town.

I was pondering the selection of bath oils in the window of a charmingly old-fashioned pharmacy when the door to the shop opened and who should walk out but Mr. Pickup Truck.

"Well, hello," I said brightly, as he caught my eye. "Remember me? We met in line at SusieQ's."

"Of course I remember you." He laughed. "I almost knocked your hat to the ground."

I favored him with a dazzling smile. "As you can see, I'm wearing a much smaller brim today."

"It's pretty," he said. "Your hat."

This guy was too cute.

"Thank you."

"So," he asked, shoving a small white bag into the back pocket of his jeans. "What's your name?"

I extended my hand, and he took it promptly. His skin was rough but not in an icky way. His hand, as I'd noticed the first time we met, was wide; his fingers were thick but not at all fat.

A very manly hand, I thought. *Strong and manly.*

"Danielle Leers," I told him.

"Hi, Danielle. I'm Chris Childs."

We released hands.

"What kind of name is Childs?" I asked.

Chris looked puzzled. "It's my name," he said, finally, laughing.

"Oh, I mean, is it Irish or—"

Chris shrugged. "My family is Protestant. My dad says our ancestors came over from England. I don't know how the name came about. You could ask the town librarian, though. She's into genealogy."

My heart sank. Rats. Christian and a pickup truck. Totally all-American.

Oh, well, no one was perfect.

"Oh, no, that's all right," I said, with a less-dazzling smile. "I was just wondering."

Where did we go from there?

"My family's lived on the Vineyard forever," Chris said, though I hadn't asked. "Well, for a long time. Generations."

"Oh. My family lives on Long Island," I told him. "My great grandparents came from Europe. Poland, mostly. They lived in Brooklyn and then their kids moved out to the Island. Some went to New Jersey, but we don't talk to them anymore."

Chris looked puzzled. "Because they live in New Jersey?"

"Oh, no," I assured him. "Because they didn't invite any of us on Long Island to their son's Bar Mitzvah."

"I've never been to Long Island," Chris said, skipping right over the reference to my family feud. "I hear the beaches are great."

"They are. Just beautiful. Next time you're in New York you should try to get out to the Island."

Chris kind of shuffled from foot to foot.

"Well," he said, with an endearingly tentative smile, "I've only been to New York once. Most of the time I was in Manhattan. But I did get to the Bronx Zoo one day. The Big Apple. It was interesting. Boy. But it wasn't my thing. I could never live there, you know?"

Not really, I admitted silently.

Who wouldn't want to live in Manhattan? Or at least visit every month or so? The shops, the restaurants, the museums, the galleries . . .

I felt city-lust rear up through me right then and there. *Carrie Bradshaw,* I called silently, *wait for me!*

"So," Chris said abruptly, as if he'd sensed my silence was maybe not a good thing. "I have to be going. My dad is waiting for his medicine. So, bye."

"Okay," I said, sorry to see him go but not knowing how our conversation could recover from the Manhattan crisis. "Bye."

"Bye." He walked off a few feet and then turned. I was still looking after him. I wonder if that surprised him. "There's a storm watch tonight," he called. "If you're out on the water this evening, well, be careful."

"Oh," I said, with a little wave. "Okay. Thanks."

He didn't have to know that boats other than ferries and I were not close friends.

Chris waved back and off he went. I continued to watch.

What. A. Hottie. I'd never seen a guy look so excellent in jeans. Never.

Now, I thought, turning back to the body-oil display, *if only I could meet an eligible man, real husband material, an urban guy, a professional, who looks like Chris.*

Wow.

I'd be in heaven.

Gincy

Mr. Romance

He cornered me in the break room.

Well, not cornered.

It was more like he was pouring a cup of coffee for himself when I walked in and got a can of soda from the fridge.

"Hey."

"Hey," I replied. "Jeez, watch—!"

"Oops." Rick grabbed a handful of paper towels and mopped up the coffee that had sloshed on the counter when he'd replaced the pot on the burner. Then he tossed the wad of wet towels at the garbage can.

They landed on the floor with a plop.

"I'll get it," I said. "You're a menace, Rick."

He laughed and blew on his coffee. "Yeah, I know. But, see? I'm trying not to burn myself."

"Good boy."

I was on my way out of the room when he said, "Hey, Gincy, can I ask you a question?"

I turned back and shrugged. "Sure. Ask away."

"I was wondering. Would you like to go out sometime?"

Now that was the last thing I'd expected to hear from Rick Luongo.

"With you?" I blurted.

"Yes."

"To do what?"

Rick shrugged; I noted a wet spot on his tie where coffee had splashed. *Why*, I wondered, *does he even bother with ties?*

"I don't know. Whatever you like to do on a date."

I glanced into the hall. No one coming. Good. This was weird.

"You want me to go out on a date with you," I repeated. Just to be sure.

"Yes," Rick said, with a big smile. "That's the idea."

"But we work together."

"True. But I'm not your boss. We're in different departments."

"It could be awkward. No matter what happens."

"Life is awkward."

He had a point there. And he had great hair, all dark and wavy, and a sexy, slightly rapacious smile.

Hmm. Kind of like a pirate . . .

"You don't know how to fix a paper jam," I said.

"But I do know how to ask for help."

"You're clumsy. Since you've started working here you've dropped five cups of coffee, knocked over three soda cans, tripped over the doorsill to the conference room at least once a day, and stapled your tie to your notepad. Twice."

"But I am endearing," he countered.

Again, that smile.

"Yeah," I admitted, smiling now myself. "In an oafish sort of way."

"So, will you go out with me?"

I scrunched up my face as if seriously considering a life-altering decision. "Okay," I said. "What the hell. But I'm not getting into a car with you unless I do the driving."

"Deal."

"And don't make a big to-do out of it at work, okay?"

"Why does anyone have to know?"

"Saturday. Daytime."

"Fine. I'll meet you—?"

"On the corner of Tremont and Boylston. Ten o'clock. Don't be late."

"I won't," he said.

And so it began.

Clare
Wed Lock

It happened at the dry cleaner's, and at the corner bodega, and the next day, at the greenmarket in Copley Square.

Three women, all about my age, stopped to comment breathlessly on my engagement ring.

"It's so big!" the first woman exclaimed, eyes sparkling with envy. "Oh, my God, I'd kill for a ring that big! You are so lucky."

"Thanks," I murmured, grabbing the box of Win's shirts off the counter. Before she could kill me for the prize, I was gone, cheeks flaming.

Later that day, while preparing a casserole for dinner, I realized we were out of milk so I dashed to the nearest independent market. Just as I was reaching into one of the cold cases for a half gallon of 2%, someone screamed.

I jumped, the door to the cold case slammed shut, and I whirled around, ready to find myself at gunpoint.

But there was only a woman in workout gear, a yoga mat on her shoulder, her mouth hanging open and her finger pointing to my hand as if I were holding a snake.

"That is the most gorgeous ring I have ever seen, ever," she whispered.

I wanted to slap her for scaring me so, but all I said was, "Thanks," and hurried past her, milk forgotten.

I knew that newly engaged women were supposed to be just dying to show off their ring.

They got weekly manicures with O.P.I. or Essie sheer colors to assure their hands were in perfect shape.

Kiss the Bride, Ballet Slipper, Rosy Future.

They frequently touched their hair and adjusted their necklaces with their left hand.

Occasionally they stopped dead in the lingerie section of Express or the handbag section of Lord & Taylor to admire their new possession.

I didn't do any of those things. I didn't want to show off the fact that I was now, more than ever, committed to Win.

I didn't own that ring. That ring—that monstrous ring!—owned me.

So why didn't I put it in a drawer and wear it only when Win was around? Why didn't I tell him it was too big and fancy for me, even though that wasn't really the main issue?

Because I was possessed of absolutely no courage.

I was selecting tomatoes from my favorite farm stand the following afternoon when suddenly I became aware of a sleek, ultra-sophisticated, super-tan, professional blonde staring at me.

I looked back at her, wondering if I knew her from someplace.

"You have it insured, don't you?" she said, by way of a greeting. "Because that ring's got to be worth fifteen, twenty thousand, easy. You should probably have a copy made up in cubic zirconia to wear just around, you know? Like to this market. Or on vacation to the Islands. You know how the locals can be. You don't want to take any chances on losing it or having it stolen. On the T? Turn it around so no one can see the center stones. Do yourself a favor."

I opened my mouth to mumble something incoherent but the woman went on.

"And don't wear it to the beach," she said, "because your finger will shrink in the water and the ring will fly right off. I've seen it happen, trust me. Well, I haven't actually seen it but a friend of a friend lost her engagement ring that way. Or was it at a pool? Either way, avoid water."

Dumbly, I nodded. The oh-so-helpful woman sauntered off, and as she went, I caught a massive flash from her left hand.

I was petrified.

There was a time bomb on my finger. Something too big, too outrageously noticeable, too expensive for comfort.

I considered taking the ring off right there and putting it in the front pocket of my chinos. But it would be too easy for it to fall out. And Win would have spent twenty thousand dollars for nothing.

Twenty thousand dollars? For a ring?

I felt sick and stunned.

Then I considered slipping the ring into my purse, but what if my purse were snatched?

What if I just left the ring on and I was snatched? What if the thief cut off my finger to get the ring?

Twenty thousand dollars could feed a lot of poor kids for years. Or one very devoted drug addict for a week or two.

"You ready?" the farm-stand guy asked.

I nodded and handed him the plastic bag filled with tomatoes. He weighed them and I gave him a five-dollar bill. As he took it, he put his other hand over his eyes as if to shield them.

"Whoa," he said, laughing. "You almost blinded me!"

I just wanted to cry.

Gincy

Just Full of Surprises

*C*ancel the date.

That was my first thought upon waking at six-thirty that Saturday morning.

If I called Rick right then, sure, I might wake him up, but on the other hand, I'd be giving him plenty of notice to replan his day.

Right?

And then I had to ask myself: *Why do you want to cancel?*

You like Rick. You've got nothing else to do now that you bagged out of the Vineyard for the weekend. Except go to the office and get a jump-start on next month's issue.

So what's the problem?

With a loud, old man groan I got out of bed and flipped on the drip coffeemaker.

And while I waited for the mud to brew, I tried to figure it all out.

The problem was this:

My track record with guys sucked. I mean, in spite of my lack of fashion sense—reading the September issue of *Vogue* didn't mean you had the skills to tranlsate what you'd learned to your own life—or maybe *because* of my lack of fashion sense, who knew, I'd never had a problem getting guys.

All guys always want to have sex. Always. So if a girl's got a good sense of fun and is willing to play the game, hey, guys are gonna like her.

Which is not to say I was a sleep-around or that I let guys walk all over me.

No way. I called the shots. I was tough.

I dumped them way before they could get around to dumping me for the girl they'd marry, someone all cute and cuddly. Blah.

Gincy Gannon was not a stupid person.

The mud was ready. I poured a cup and took a first trembling sip. Ah, scalding! Just the way I liked it. A few more sips and maybe I'd feel all better.

All calm.

No more butterflies in my stomach.

No such luck. I drank two cups and still I felt no more courageous than I had upon waking.

There was something about Rick . . .

I don't know. Maybe, I thought, *it's my age. Maybe I'm hitting some major hormonal peak or valley that's making me . . .*

Afraid. I felt afraid. Almost afraid.

Not of Rick, exactly. Jeez, it was pretty clear I could totally take him in anything from arm wrestling to kick-boxing. If I kick-boxed. Which I didn't, but with Rick's native clumsiness, I was pretty damn sure he'd be no challenge at all.

Was it because he was older than me by about six years? (The receptionist had told me his age.) Was it because he wore adult, dress-up clothes to work? Even if they weren't the height of fashion—like I would really know that—they were clearly adult clothes.

Or was it simply because, unlike virtually every other datable guy I'd ever met, Rick was just—himself. No posturing, no blustering.

He was unself-conscious in a way that made me take notice and approve.

And that made me wonder if by being with him I'd have to learn how to be self-truthful, too.

I dropped the empty coffee cup into the sink. It made, of course, an annoying clatter and I asked myself why I never learned from my annoying habits.

You're getting ahead of yourself, Gincy, I scolded. *Sure, Rick seems nice and genuine and all down-to-earth. But is he, really?*

For all you really know he's a self-serving slime just like every other guy you've met and had to toss aside.

So, relax. Calm down. Just go on the freakin' date and see what happens.

But keep your wits about you, your eyes open, your senses tuned.

At exactly ten o'clock, Rick and I met at the assigned corner.

"You're on time," I noted.

Rick shrugged. "I'm always on time. It just happens."

Rick looked different. In a good way.

I'd never seen him out of the office, in daylight, not in a tie—even if the tie was stained with jelly. He wore slouchy chinos and a navy T-shirt that revealed he had muscles. Big ones. And a pretty flat stomach. Hard to tell the truth in his work attire.

Note to self: Reconsider the ease of the arm-wrestling victory.

I was scrappy but no one had ever called me muscular.

"Hey," he said, then. "I thought you had a house on the Vineyard?"

"Who told you that?"

"Kell mentioned it. So why are you in town on a Saturday?"

The question was delivered in an innocent way, but I sure as hell wasn't going to tell him I'd rearranged my schedule to go on this date.

"I've got a prior commitment tomorrow," I lied. "A distant family thing. So my being in town has nothing to do with you. Just so you know that."

"I wouldn't think anything of the kind," he said without a trace of sarcasm.

And I believed him.

"So, I had a couple of ideas," he said, sticking his hands in the front pockets of his pants. The gesture struck me as very youthful. And it made a tendon or something in his forearm flex. "About what we could do."

"What?" I said, momentarily distracted by lust. "Oh. Right. Shoot."

"We could go to the Science Museum."

"The Science Museum? Isn't that really for kids?"

Rick smiled. Again, I noted big strong sexy teeth. "Yeah. Or we could go to the Aquarium. Afterwards, I thought we could walk to the North End, get some pizza. What do you think?"

I grinned. "Sounds great. Let's do the Aquarium. I love the seahorses."

We headed through downtown towards the waterfront.

I watched him walk from the corner of my eye.

Nice gait.

Tendons. Teeth. Gait.

I gave myself a mental boot to the head.

What is he a horse, Gincy? Snap out of it!

"Hey," I said, utterly casually. "What do you like on your pizza?"

Rick shrugged. "Everything. Except anchovies. They make me burp. I don't know why."

Excellent.

"They give me the skeeves," I told him. "No anchovies."

Rick and I had the best day. Totally easy and fun. I paid for the Aquarium and he paid for the pepperoni pizza. And the cannolis afterwards.

We discovered we both liked walking and hardly ever took the T unless it was absolutely necessary.

He admitted to being a reality TV addict.

I mocked him, then admitted to sucking at all sports.

We both admitted to being Hunter S. Thompson fans.

We were sitting on the steps of City Hall when Rick looked at his watch and sighed. "I wish we could hang out more. But I've got to get home."

"Why?" I asked. "What's the rush? It's only—" I looked at his watch as the battery in mine had been dead for weeks, though I continued to wear it. "It's only five-fifteen."

"Yeah, I know, but Justin's sitter is only available until six, so—"

"The what now?" I interrupted. "Who's Justin?"

Rick looked thoroughly perplexed. "Justin. My son. You know about him."

I'd known it was too good to be true! I scooted away from Rick a bit so I could look straight at him.

"Uh, no," I said. "I don't. When were you planning on telling me you have a kid? When you got around to telling me you have a wife, too?"

Rick looked truly stricken. "Gincy, I'm sorry. I thought you knew. It's common knowledge around the office. At least, I thought it was. The receptionist knows. Don knows. Sally knows. Even Kell knows, and he's kind of oblivious to . . . Sorry. I didn't mean to say that you're oblivious . . ."

"Sally? Sally knows?"

And she'd never mentioned it to me? Okay, I hadn't told her I was going out with Rick. But still.

"Yeah. I've even got a picture of Justin on my desk."

"I've never actually been in your office."

"Oh."

I took a deep breath. "So—about the wife?"

Divorced creep. Probably dumped her for a newer model.

Cheated on her. With her best friend. Or her younger sister!

Stiffed her in the settlement so now she was raising a kid on her own—except for Saturdays when her slime of an ex-husband had him but tossed him off on a baby-sitter—and working two jobs and—

"I'm a widower, Gincy. My wife died about four years ago, a few months after Justin was born. Breast cancer."

Oh crap, crap, crap.

I put my head in my hands. "Jeez. I'm sorry, Rick. Jeez. So, uh, that makes Justin how old?"

"He's five. His birthday was in February."

The poor kid probably didn't even remember his mother.

"Oh," I said lamely. "Happy birthday. Belated."

"Thanks. From Justin."

What now?

"So, he's in kindergarten?" I asked. "Do they have kinder-garten anymore? I don't really know anyone with kids. Little kids. My sixteen-year-old cousin is pregnant, though."

Now that would impress my date . . .

"Oh. Congratulations. I guess."

"Well, she is marrying the father," I said inanely.

We ended our date awkwardly, both visibly upset.

Rick didn't try to kiss me. I still kind of wished he had, even though I knew our relationship was over before it had ever really begun.

I sat on the cooling steps and watched Rick walk off, on his long way back to Charlestown. I felt queasy. Suddenly, the pep-peroni pizza we'd shared didn't seem like such a good idea.

I liked Rick. A lot. Man, I'd had a great time with him, just hanging out.

But a kid?

No. It wasn't in my plan.

It just wasn't.

Clare
Personal Space

Having summers off is a mixed blessing.

On the one hand, the free months stretch out like a wonderful promise. Plenty of time to catch up on all the things you just didn't have time to do during the school year.

Like sleep.

One the other hand, the free months come as a shock to the system. From September through June you had virtually no downtime and suddenly, there you were, cut loose and swinging in the wind.

Lost and alone, while most other people you knew were still heading to the office every Monday through Friday morning.

I often felt out of sync with the average adult world.

That summer, as always, I vowed to fill my "time off" constructively.

Back in high school and the early days of college I'd kept a journal. Journaling gave my daily life a structure and a sense of importance.

It gave me time to be alone with my thoughts, and it allowed me to create a sense of relative peace.

Shortly after I met Win I stopped keeping a journal. I don't

know why, exactly. It was like Win took up so much space there
was no longer room for my private self.

Back then, it felt like a relief.

But now, eleven years later? It was time, I felt, to start looking
for my private self, wherever I'd misplaced her.

I would start another journal. But where could I keep a journal that would be truly private?

And then I began to wonder if I had a right to total privacy.
Weren't couples supposed to share everything—every thought
and dream, every success and failure?

Maybe in romance novels and chick flicks couples shared
such intimacy. But my reality was different.

Win and I hadn't had a truly meaningful conversation in
years. We never talked about spirituality or ethics or philosophy.
We never really had, not even in the beginning.

The myth of the Start of the Romance: During those heady
times the two lovers sit up all night talking; they ask penetrating
questions and share intimate longings, they laugh and they cry,
they voice deep desires and exchange fanciful hopes.

To be fair, in those early days of our relationship Win and I
had shared a few amusing family stories, a few childhood memories, our tastes in music and film. Shorthand for our personalities.

But as for our souls?

I couldn't speak for Win but my soul had never been touched.
A virgin soul.

Maybe, I thought, *it's asking too much to have your spouse touch
your soul.*

*Maybe it's enough that he be generally pleasant and hardworking
and tolerant of your parents as they age.*

*Maybe it's just fine if your heart doesn't swell with affection when you
run into him on the street, all unexpected.*

Maybe.

And maybe it wasn't.

I'd done nothing more than consider keeping a journal, and
yet I felt guilty.

Was it cheating somehow to pursue a completely private, separate venture without telling Win that I was embarking on such a course?

But if I told him, the venture would no longer be truly private and separate, would it?

Oh, Clare, I thought. *Why is everything so complicated with you?*

With some effort, I put aside my reservations and bought a five-by-seven spiral bound notebook with a floral cover. Lined, cream-colored pages.

My journal.

One afternoon while Win was at work, I determined to begin. For a long moment I stared at the blank page. And then, the words flowed.

I think it's all over for me, sexually. In spite of Win, sometimes I feel sure I'll never have sex again. I know I'll never be kissed—really kissed—again. It's horrible to contemplate. I want to be wanted. I want that very badly.

I dream all the time about being kissed. Not by Win. I dream about being with a man who's so, so beautiful. His body is beautiful. I crave him in a way I've never craved anyone in real life. When I'm awake. I— it's like I'm in love but also—the feeling in the dream is like—adoration. The man almost isn't a person. An individual, you know, with a particular past and particular flaws and . . . He's not real. I think he's supposed to mean something or represent something beyond any one man. I never see his face clearly, but he kisses me and I rub my cheek against his. He's tan but not like from the sun. His skin is a color I don't think I've ever seen in real life. His shirt is often off. I cling to him, mostly.

Sometimes, he's someone I know from the past, from early years, oddly enough, from grammar school. He's someone who's mysterious, has a life I know nothing about. He just seems to appear. He comes back into town unannounced. He leaves again without warning. He's not unkind. We're friends. He's never shown any interest in me, romantically. Or, sometimes, we've kissed but it's never gone far. He's drawn to me but—but he's always chosen someone far more glamorous to be with. Often I don't know where he lives or what he does for a living or if he's married. Sometimes I wonder if he's gay. Sometimes I wonder if he's dying.

He's somehow—popular. Other people wait for him to come back home, not only me. He's part of a group but he can't be expected to act like it. He's a member of a graduating class but no one expects him to come to graduation exercises. And he doesn't. And I'm waiting for him, desperately waiting. Wanting some small bit of affection. When he does appear later, unexpected, he's always glad to see me but loses interest before long. And he's never come back for me. He's got his own reasons for showing up. And I never know those reasons. I'm too afraid to ask and he doesn't volunteer.

I care for him like no one else does, I just know that. I feel almost like his mother, or a big sister. I want to be his lover. I want to be an integral part of his mysterious world. I want to be indispensable. But I'm not. I'm highly dispensable.

He goes away, and by the time he does, I'm almost forgotten. And I wait, desperate for his next return.

These dreams are plaguing me. I yearn for them—for the intensity of emotion I feel in them, for his beauty. The days after the dreams, I try to hold on to them. I look forward to the next dream. And I want to find this man in the real world.

Even for a moment.

Does this mean I shouldn't marry Win? Of course not. This man of my dreams is no rival to Win. Of course not. Win has nothing to worry about. I'm not cheating on him by dreaming. I'm not.

Gincy

Fashion Victimista

Our weekend on the Vineyard was off to a lousy start.

See, I was learning that you couldn't always ignore your roommates, much as you might want to. When someone was in trouble and you were looking right at them, you pretty much had to help out.

Unless you were okay with being a horrible person.

It sucked, but what were you going to do?

Saturday morning, Danielle came hobbling out of the bathroom and sat at the kitchen table with a grunt.

"What's wrong with you?" I asked, not so graciously.

She pointed at her left foot.

The entire side of her foot was swollen and red. Where it wasn't full of pus under the stretched skin.

"That is hideous."

"Thanks," Danielle said, gingerly poking at her foot. "Your remarks are so helpful."

Clare squinted at the abomination that was Danielle's foot. "I think you should see a doctor," she said. "But I'm not sure you should wait until you get back to Boston. See those red streaks forming? That's bad. You could go septic and die."

Danielle put her hand to her head. "Oh, my God. I think I'm going to faint."

"Don't faint," I ordered. "We'll take you to the emergency room. You can faint there if you want."

"Do I have to go?" she wailed.

"I'm no doctor," I told her, "but I'd say, yeah. You need to get that drained or something. Get some antibiotics."

"Why do you wear shoes that like, anyway?" Clare asked, pointing to the skinny purple sandals that had cut Danielle's foot so badly.

The night before she'd been bragging about finding them on sale, but I'd noticed that the moment we got home from the bar she'd wrenched them off and left them by the back door.

"They're sexy. They make my legs look fabulous."

"They're sending you to the emergency room, Danielle."

Danielle glared.

"You know," Clare went on, "wearing high heels can cause back problems later in life. You might want to try more practical shoes. There are plenty of fashionable flats these days, and sneakers—"

"My legs," Danielle said, between gritted teeth, "look stumpy in flats. Now, get me my makeup bag!"

Clare jumped and I grabbed a shiny zippered bag from beside the sink.

"No, no, no!" Danielle cried. "Not the black one. That's my resource bag. Get me the red makeup bag!"

"Well, why didn't you say so in the first place? Jeez. I'm not a mind reader. Who has two makeup bags anyway?" I mumbled, searching the room for the red bag. "What's so special about the red one?"

"The red one contains the palate I'm currently using on a daily basis. The black resource bag contains the colors I'm not currently using on a daily basis."

"The special colors?" Clare asked.

"Not necessarily. It's just that . . ."

I spotted the red bag on the small coffee table in the living room and grabbed it. "Uh, kids? Could we get moving here? We're not going out to a club. We're going to the hospital, remember?"

"I still want to look my best," Danielle said with a pout.

"You're already wearing makeup," I shot back.

"I might need to touch up."

"You're not going to meet anyone in the ER."

"Uh, hello? Doctors work in the ER. Jewish doctors."

"My father thinks the doctors who work in the ER are failures," Clare said.

"What?" I said, checking my wallet for cab money. Three lousy singles. "What are you talking about?"

Clare shrugged. "That's what he says. He says the successful doctors work in specialties and private practice."

"What about at a teaching hospital?" I shot back. "Every young doctor has to rotate through every department, right? You know, as in rotations."

Danielle nodded. I noticed her color was bad, and grabbed a plastic shopping bag in case she needed to hurl in the cab.

"Gincy's right," she said, a bit weakly. "I could very easily meet a gorgeous, brilliant, and potentially highly successful—i.e., rich—doctor today. Besides, it never hurts to look your best."

I laughed. The girl was amazing. "Yeah, in case the druggies and poor folk who hang at the ER give a shit about the little rich girl in for an infected blister."

"I'm not rich," she protested, wiping sweat from her brow with the back of her hand. "Exactly. Though I'd like to be. I aspire to be. In fact, I think I was born to be."

"That's nice for you," I said, squatting and wrapping her right arm around my shoulders. "Now, heave ho! We're out of here before you're sprawled on the floor."

Danielle
Cruel and Unusual

Gincy and Clare got me to the emergency room—though Gincy stepped on my good foot twice on the way to the cab— and after a lengthy process called triage, I found myself alone in a curtained-off section of the room, sitting on a hospital bed without even a pillow for comfort, wearing nothing but a flimsy wraparound gown called a johnny.

The johnny was a pallid pale blue. It did absolutely nothing for me.

I felt cold and scared and lonely. Some evil nurse told Gincy and Clare they couldn't stay with me. Something about their not being family.

Stupid.

"BLLLAAAAAGGGHHH!"

And behind curtain number two, Mr. Retchie McRetcher.

I put my hands over my ears and hummed loudly. Couldn't they have put the guy in, like, a soundproof room or something?

After almost an hour a doctor came in through the ugly pale blue curtains. She was barely five feet tall and had a massive amount of shiny black hair gathered in a bun at the nape of her neck. She introduced herself as Dr. Alotofsyllablesinverystrange-order.

And then she said a lot of words I couldn't understand at all.

"Excuse me?" I said, trying to look all apologetic. I'd never been very good at catching foreign accents.

Without changing her no-nonsense expression, Dr. Alotofsyllablesinverystrangeorder said more words. Maybe she repeated what she'd said earlier. I don't know.

"I'm sorry," I said. "I don't know what you're saying. Maybe you could get a translator?"

Dr. Alotofsyllablesinverystrangeorder ignored my suggestion and babbled on while poking vigorously at my injured foot with a gloved finger.

Maybe, I thought, *if I just blank my mind and then start listening all over again, I'll catch the cadence and the meaning will follow.*

"Verystupidyouareagirlsotobesostupidthatyoudothistoyouastowearthestupidshoes.Very."

Darn. I got nothing.

"I'm sorry." I shook my head, grimaced, raised my palms in questioning defeat. *Please, could a nice Jewish doctor—without any accent—please, please just come through that flimsy curtain right . . .*

"Blaahhhhrrrrggghhhhh!"

I clapped my hands to my ears and hunched my shoulders while Mr. Hurly McVomit in the next "room" retched his brains out for the tenth time and Dr. Alotofsyllablesinverystrangeorder babbled on incomprehensibly, obviously to further torture me.

And then the real torture began. Dr. Incomprehensible—as I'd come to call her in my head—tore open a cellophane packet and pulled out a needle.

The needle was long. And fat.

Dr. Incomprehensible smiled. I swear, she smiled.

And then she stabbed me.

"Ow! Ow, ow, ow!" I wailed.

Nothing, I thought, *could ever be more painful than what Dr. Incomprehensible has just done to me. Nothing! Bring on childbirth! It will be a breeze after this!*

My shrieks brought a nurse running. Tears streaming down my face, I pointed to my poor foot.

Nurse Mary spoke English with a Southie accent. Fine. That, I could understand. She peeked at Dr. Incomprehensible's notes and explained that I'd just been given a shot of something to numb the infected area. And what would happen next would be an "unroofing" of the blister. To allow it to drain.

Nurse Mary winked, patted my knee, and promised she'd be back with antibiotics; I'd need to take them for the next five days.

"Thank you, Nurse Mary," I gulped.

Dr. Incomprehensible glared at me and, with a fierce move, stabbed my poor foot again, this time with a knife.

I think I passed out. When my head cleared I was flat on my back. Dr. Incomprehensible was gone. I took a few deep breaths and sat up.

My foot was loosely bandaged. Okay. Now all I had to do was wait patiently for good, sweet Nurse Mary to bring me my drugs.

I reached for my makeup bag. A fresh coat of lip gloss would definitely help my spirits. Plus, I reasoned, the super-sweet raspberry smell might help distract my nose from the icky smell of throw-up.

But the bag was gone. At least, it wasn't on the little table where I'd put it. I leaned over the side of the bed and checked the floor.

Nothing.

I checked the other side of the bed.

Still nothing.

And then the ugly truth dawned. While I was unconscious, someone had stolen my makeup bag!

What was the world coming to when you couldn't go to the emergency room without being robbed! Quickly, I checked my jewelry and was relieved to find it all still intact.

Still, I started to cry. I'd never felt more miserable. Right then I made a bold-typed mental note to cross hospitals off the list of potential husband-meeting places.

Forever.

Gincy
The Marriage Game

Danielle lay propped up on the couch, surrounded by magazines, the TV remote, a pitcher of some fluorescent low-calorie drink, and a box of low-fat cookies. She was making a list of makeup she needed to replace.

"Did you take your antibiotic?" Clare asked her.

Danielle nodded. "They're so disgusting. Did you see the size of them?"

"Just take them," Clare said, dropping into an armchair. "Infections are no laughing matter."

"Is there any beer or do I need to go out for more?" I said.

"There's a six-pack in the fridge. Bring me one, please?" she asked. "Only if you're going to the kitchen."

Yeah, I thought. *The extra ten feet will kill me.*

I brought us each a beer and a big bag of pork rinds.

Clare refused the pork rinds with a grimace. I offered some to Danielle, but she gave me the "oh, please" look.

I shrugged. "More for me. Hey, Danielle," I said, plopping into a rickety wooden chair that was going to fall completely apart before long if I kept plopping into it. "I don't get it. If you want so badly to marry a doctor, why don't you just ask your brother to introduce you to one of his colleagues?"

Danielle sighed. "It's not that I want to marry a doctor, as opposed, say, to a lawyer. He doesn't have to be doctor. Besides, I've already dated David's eligible colleagues. Let's just say that none of them were in my league."

"Doctors are under so much stress," Clare added. "It can be hard to be married to one."

"Your mother's married to a doctor," I pointed out. "Are you saying she's had a rough time of it?"

Clare looked uncomfortable. "No. I'm not saying anything about my parents. Their marriage is just fine."

Clare was a lousy liar but I let the subject go.

"Hey," Danielle said from her throne. "Here's an article about friendships among couples. It says it's hard for a couple to find another couple to hang out with. Where all four people get along. I can see that."

"I have no opinion," I said. "I've never been in a couple long enough to have to deal with that situation."

Danielle tossed the magazine to the floor. "I'd settle for my husband liking my girlfriends. I don't care if he likes their boyfriends or husbands."

"But then you might not see your girlfriends so much," Clare said.

"Why?" I asked through a mouthful of grease.

"You aren't supposed to see your girlfriends a lot once you're married," Clare said.

I swear it sounded as if she were reciting from a manual.

"At least, not as much as before you were married. You're supposed to spend most of your time with your husband. And if he doesn't like your girlfriends' husbands, well then—"

"That's just fucked up!" I said. "I am so never getting married."

Danielle grimaced. "With a mouth like that, I doubt you'll ever have to deal with the issue."

"And if you keep making those ugly faces, neither will you."

"I am in pain. I just endured a terrible medical trial. I think I'm allowed to make faces if I want to."

I shrugged.

After a moment Danielle announced: "I was thinking."

"Call the papers!"

"I was thinking," Danielle went on, "that it wouldn't be wise to marry a guy with more than two siblings. Too many gifts. Birthdays, anniversaries, nieces and nephews graduating from high school. And too much travel at the holidays. And it totally wouldn't be wise to marry a guy whose mother lives within a fifty-mile radius. You'd be pressured to spend every Sunday afternoon eating dried-out pot roast and listening to stories about how perfect your husband was."

"Oh, come on," Clare said, with a small, worried little laugh. "You're overreacting, Danielle. You don't marry a family. You marry a man. One person."

"Are you high?" I asked. Rhetorically, because I so knew she'd never done drugs. Not that I had, either, but I seemed the one more likely to have dabbled.

"Marriage is a social institution," I announced, with all my years of wisdom. "Forget about what goes on in the privacy of your own home. When you marry a guy you marry his family, believe it. You marry his past and his present and his future.

"You marry the detergent his mother used to wash his diapers and the teacher who crushed his youthful spirit and the first time he got laid.

"You marry his health insurance and his retirement account.

"You marry his midlife crisis. You marry his parents' aging and getting Alzheimer's and you marry the nieces and nephews you'll be buying birthday presents for.

"Because we know men don't buy the presents and send the cards. That's women's work."

Danielle sighed. "It all sounds so exhausting, doesn't it? When I'm married I'm hiring a personal assistant to handle my correspondence and gift shopping. Like I'll have the time? Supervising the nanny and organizing dinner parties and hosting fund-raising events? Please."

Clare got up and headed for the kitchen. "Another beer?" she asked as she passed me.

Poor thing. She looked sad.

Could it be that Clare wasn't entirely thrilled with her impending fate?

Danielle

The Right Moves

I'm still not sure why I accepted a date with Chris Childs in the first place. He so clearly didn't meet several of my criteria for a husband.

He wasn't Jewish.

He didn't wear a suit to work, which meant he probably didn't have things like investments and stocks and a four-week paid vacation during which he could take me to Europe while our kids spent the month in sleepaway tennis camp.

And something told me he wouldn't necessarily appreciate the new Missoni skirt I'd picked up at Filene's Basement for only three hundred dollars.

Also, at that moment in my life, I wasn't particularly interested in casual sex, a fling, an affair. I viewed a quickie as a waste of precious time. Why be rolling around in some hottie's rumpled bed when I could be out scouting for a lifelong relationship?

A woman on the verge of thirty had to carefully budget her time.

Still, when Chris called the house and suggested a sunset picnic, I readily accepted. I mean, I didn't have a date scheduled for that evening, so why sit at home?

He came for me in the black pickup. Thankfully, neither

Gincy nor Clare was home. I could all too easily imagine Gincy's smirk and Clare's frown of concern.

God, I thought, as Chris smiled and opened the passenger-side door, *I hope the seats are clean because I'm not sure even a dry cleaner can get grease out of taupe linen pants!*

Frankly, I knew nothing about truck attire.

Chris wore a gray, long-sleeved T-shirt and his standard jeans. Everything was clean. Honestly, I'd never seen him look anything but spick-and-span. *Maybe,* I thought, *he pays a mechanic to do all the work on the truck.*

"By the way," I said as we drove off, "how did you get my number?"

Chris blushed. Through his tan I actually saw a blush!

"Don't freak, okay?" he said. "I was driving through town the other day and I saw you come out of a house. I took a chance that you were staying there and not just visiting. So I looked up the number in the phone book. Everyone here knows the people who own the house are the Simpsons, so . . ."

Huh. Determination. That was good.

And honesty. Also good.

And the blushing was unexpectedly sexy.

I watched him drive—his hands firm on the wheel and shift knob, his thigh muscles bulging when he put in the clutch.

Watch yourself, Danielle, a voice in my head warned. *This guy could be big trouble. He could divert you from your chosen path. He could delay your process.*

Stick to the program, Danielle, the voice said before I closed my ears to it.

For our picnic Chris had chosen a totally unoccupied stretch of Lucy Vincent Beach. Unoccupied by humans, that is.

"Do we have to sit here?" I asked nervously, as Chris spread a large plaid blanket on a flat, dry area of sand.

"What's wrong with here?" he asked, oblivious to the threat.

I pointed to the herd or flock or gang or whatever it was of seagulls a few yards away.

"The gulls?" Chris looked confused. "They won't hurt us. Come on, have a seat."

I did, but I never took my eyes off the gang of feathered hood-lums.

"That one's looking at me!" I cried, clutching Chris's arm.

Let him sit with his back to the enemy! Not me.

"Which one? The little brown one? I don't think he's looking at you, Danielle. I think he's got a lazy eye or something."

"No, no, no! Not the little brown one. That one! The big one! Oh, my God, it's as big as a car!"

Chris laughed. "They're kind of cool, don't you think? Their breast feathers are so amazingly white."

I shuddered. What was wrong with him? "They're disgusting. They're scavengers. They eat garbage. I think they know I don't like them. Chris, I'm scared. Let's get out of here."

"You sure you don't want to have our picnic first?"

I considered. I was awfully hungry. "Okay. As long as you promise to keep those—things—away from our food. If even one comes within twenty feet of us I know I'll have an attack."

"Are you subject to, er, attacks?" he asked.

I thought I saw a smile playing around his lips.

"No," I admitted. "But a seagull snatching my dinner could definitely start a bad habit. They're just rats with wings, you know."

"Pigeons. Pigeons are rats with wings."

"You have your rat and I'll have mine."

Leather and lace, I thought. *Town and country. Jew and Christian.*
It would never work. In the long run.

But tonight?

I was sure it would work just fine. Especially after I saw the contents of the big picnic basket Chris had brought.

He'd brought wine—it wasn't very expensive, but it was tasty—and a baguette and a piece of brie and grapes. Standard picnic-date fare. It was very nice. He'd even thought to bring napkins! Not a lot of guys remember napkins. And a corkscrew. And plastic cups.

Chris had thought through the details.

That was a good thing. In my experience, most guys were not detail-oriented about anything other than cars and computers.

We ate and talked, and though the conversation wasn't about politics or art, it flowed easily.

And the sunset was spectacular. I mean, I'd seen my share of sunsets, but this one was really something.

"I'd love a wraparound dress in those shades of orange," I said, pointing to a band of fire along the horizon. "See?"

"You'd look beautiful in those colors."

I sighed. "I know. I wish I'd brought my camera tonight. I could take a photo with me when I go shopping . . ."

Chris touched my chin with a finger and turned my face to his. His eyes were brilliant in the light of the setting sun.

"Danielle, I've never met anyone like you. You're so . . . I don't know, just so alive. And fun. And you just seem so yourself."

Well, of course, I thought. *Myself is an excellent person to be.*

"Thank you," I said.

I didn't compliment him in return. It wasn't smart to be too free with compliments. A man might think he could stop trying.

And even though I had no intention of seeing Chris after that night, I did still want him to try for the duration of the evening.

Just as the sun was touching the horizon, Chris kissed me. It was a long, deep kiss, not all slobbery though. The man was an artist, a master of the kiss.

But I didn't tell him I thought so.

Forehead to forehead, Chris's sweater draped around my shoulders, fingers entwined, we sat there in the growing dark.

I wish a professional photographer would stroll by right now, I thought. *We'd make a wonderful cover shot.*

Gincy

You Scratch My Back

The things we do for friends.

Or acquaintances.

Or roommates.

Basically, for people we hardly freakin' know.

Clare called me at home one night—a first—and asked if I'd go with her to a baby shower the following afternoon for one of her colleagues.

"Since when do you take a date to a baby shower?" I asked, stomping a roach with my bare toe. "I don't even know this chick. And do I have to bring a present?"

Clare was silent, as if trying to come up with a reasonable explanation for her request.

She should have thought of one before picking up the phone and wasting my time.

"Well?" I prompted.

"Can you please just come with me? You don't need to bring a present. And I'll say you're a friend visiting from out of town. We won't have to stay long. Please, Gincy?"

How lonely is this girl, I thought, *when she has to ask me, a virtual stranger and someone who's always poking fun at her, for such a big favor?*

"Yeah, all right, I'll go," I said. What a softie I was becoming. "I have lots of sick days built up. Just tell me where to be and when. And what to wear."

Clare sighed. "Thanks, Gincy. I mean it. I owe you one."

The shower, it turned out, was afternoon tea at the Four Seasons. The freakin' Four Seasons!

I pictured the baby showers my mother and aunt had given— Jell-O mold, ambrosia, cake from a Duncan Hines mix. Soda. Not a vegetable in sight. Certainly not finger sandwiches. Unless you counted squeeze cheese between two Ritz crackers as finger sandwiches.

Sitting there next to Clare, all dressed up in my one good black suit, a snowy white napkin on my lap, I had a sudden, serious craving for sliced bananas suspended in red goo.

But alcohol would do.

Clare
Baby-o-Rama

"Isn't there booze? Can't I get a drink?" Gincy asked.

I sighed. Maybe it hadn't been such a good idea to ask Gincy along. She was the only one at the table wearing black. She was a beetle among pastel butterflies.

"It's tea, Gincy," I whispered. "Not cocktail hour."

"I know but I'm having a few problems with this," she hissed. "First: I don't like tea."

"You could order coffee," I suggested reasonably.

"Second: I hate hotel coffee. It's just flavored water."

"Seltzer? Iced tea? Everyone likes iced tea."

"Third: No iced tea. Fourth: I am bored out of my mind. I don't know Ms. BabyMaker. Why am I here, Clare? Do I care about receiving blankets? No, I don't care about receiving blankets. What the hell is a receiving blanket anyway? The least they could do is provide alcohol for the single women."

Why, oh, why hadn't I asked Danielle to come with me?

I shot a look around the table of twelve smiling women. My colleagues: Tara, the mom-to-be; Rita, a third-grade teacher; and Alana, an art teacher, only fifty-eight and grandmother of three. The other women were Tara's family and friends.

Thankfully, no one seemed to be paying any attention to my grumpy, out-of-town visitor.

"Well," I whispered, "I suppose you could ask the waiter . . ."

Gincy rolled her eyes. "For a Manhattan? And have everyone look at me like I'm an alcoholic? No thanks. I'll just grin and bear it and nibble this—what is this, anyway?"

"It's a tea biscuit," I pointed out. Really, sometimes I wondered if Gincy had been raised in a cave.

"Figures. Not even a bagel on the table. And no cream cheese. Do you see any cream cheese?"

"It isn't breakfast. It's tea."

"More petits fours?" Tara's mother asked, offering me the doily-covered plate of pastel sweets.

I smiled politely, put one on my plate, and passed it to Gincy. She frowned and practically tossed the plate to the woman on her right.

"All I'm saying," she hissed in my ear, "is that this is America, not bloody old England. I should be able to have bagels and cream cheese when I want them. And Sno Balls. Not these little square things."

It was time to put an end to our mutual agony. *Besides,* I thought, *the semester has just ended. I won't have to face my colleagues again until September. Maybe by then they will have forgotten about my odd little friend.*

"Look," I said, pretending to dab my lips with a napkin, really trying to hide from any lip-readers at the table. "How about we cut out now? We'll tell everyone one of us suddenly feels sick, and go, I don't know, go someplace with other single people. And have a drink. Okay?"

Gincy looked at me with dawning amusement. "You're bored, too, aren't you?" She chuckled. "Oh, my God, you had me totally fooled but you're bored, too!"

"Gincy," I admitted, "I am about to stick a fork in my own eye. And twist it sharply."

"Then why did you want to come in the first place? Why did you drag me along with you?"

Why, indeed.

I stood and excused the two of us, indicating that we were paying a visit to the ladies' room. And once outside the dining room we made a dash for the lobby.

Clare

Let Me Get What I Want

Gincy called Danielle on her cell phone as we walked toward Joe's American.

"She'll be there." Gincy snapped shut her phone and laughed. "She says she's been dying for an excuse to wear her new sandals. She's such an airhead."

"She's more than an airhead," I countered.

"Whatever. I just don't want to have to pay another visit to the emergency room. It took three showers before I got the smell of wet gauze off my hands. And I hadn't even touched any gauze."

When we were settled at the upstairs bar and Danielle had come rushing in, cheeks red with heat, Gincy said: "Okay. I know why that little society event freaked me out. But why did it make you so wiggly, Clare?"

Good question.

It couldn't be jealousy. I was engaged. My ring was massive, a good thing in a world in which size seemed to matter. I'd soon be on the mommy track and living in a sprawling suburban house, complete with deck and in-ground pool.

So, what then?

Fear.

Of motherhood? Delivery? Pregnancy?

Or of that first step.

Marriage.

And if not fear, then—reluctance?

Maybe I just wasn't ready for marriage.

Maybe I wasn't ready for marriage with Win.

But I'd accepted his proposal. Reluctantly, but I'd accepted.

How could I explain how I felt to Gincy and Danielle when I couldn't really explain my feelings to myself?

And then words were pouring out of my mouth. "I don't know," I said, twisting a napkin to shreds. "Today I'm single and dancing till dawn at a club in downtown Boston . . . Not that I'm into the club scene—all right, I've never even been to a Boston club—but you know what I mean. And tomorrow I'm nine months pregnant and soaking my grotesquely swollen feet. It just—"

"I thought you wanted children," Gincy said, eyeing me keenly.

"I do! Just not . . ."

"Now?" Danielle, too, speared me with her eyes.

Their intensity pinned me. "I don't know," I admitted, unable to lie or prevaricate. "I don't know if I was going to say not now or not with Win. Maybe that's the same thing."

Gincy and Danielle continued to stare at me, waiting.

I took a deep breath and prepared to admit something I'd never told anyone. "Look," I said, lowering my eyes, "Win's my first real boyfriend. I mean, I've never slept with anyone else. Okay? I know, it sounds so old-fashioned . . ."

"It sounds pathetic," Gincy snapped. "Sorry."

What was she sorry for? It was pathetic. At least, I'd come to think so.

"I know," I said, looking back up. "And now I can't help but wonder what I'm missing. And if it matters that I'm missing it."

Danielle shook her head. "Honey, only you can answer that. Personally, I can't imagine never having had sex with other men before marrying a guy. But then again, I've never been in a long-term relationship like you. I mean, my record is three, no, four months. Once, with a much older man. We've had totally different romantic lives, you and me."

"I just don't know what to do," I admitted again, continuing to surprise myself with every word. I'd never, ever given voice to my doubts and fears.

"Is Win the right one? Or am I marrying him because I'm turning thirty and it's the thing to do? I didn't ask him to propose," I said, almost pleadingly. "I never even mentioned a wedding. But now that I'm engaged . . . I mean, there are so many horrible guys out there and I've been with Win for so long. We really know each other. In some ways. Would I be stupid to walk away from this? It's a sure thing with Win. Right?"

Please, I prayed. *Someone say I'm right.*

Gincy excused herself to go to the ladies' room.

Danielle cleared her throat and took a compact from her purse.

"Another round?" the bartender asked.

That question I could answer all on my own.

Gincy

Missing Socks and Shining Armor

It had been one of those typically crappy evenings.

The Chinese food delivery guy brought the wrong order, which I didn't discover until he'd gone off with my money.

The water from the kitchen faucet was running rusty so I had to settle for flat Dr Pepper.

The water in my tiny Allston apartment often ran rusty. When it ran at all.

And then there was the phone call that came while I was in the bathroom.

The phone rang. And rang. And rang. Clearly, the answering machine was on the fritz. Again.

When I was free, I dashed into the mini-kitchen, grabbed the receiver from its cradle, and barked, "Hello?"

A highly chipper female voice said, "Hi! May I please speak to the lady of the house?"

"The what?" I hadn't meant to be rude. The words just shot out of my mouth.

The owner of the highly chipper voice wasn't in the least fazed. "Is the lady of the house at home?" she repeated.

"Excuse me," I shot back. "Are you calling from the nineteenth century?"

Now there was silence. Clearly the telemarketer's script had not anticipated this particular remark. I took advantage of the silence.

"What are you selling, anyway?" I asked. "Corsets? Smelling salts? Chastity belts?"

The telemarketer disconnected the call without further remark. I suspect she thought she'd dialed the home of a lunatic lady, someone better suited to a life in a musty attic than to domestic bliss in a well-appointed kitchen.

I shrugged and replaced the receiver. No one had ever called me a lady and gotten away with it.

I ate what I could stomach of the cashew-and-bean-sprout mush and flopped into bed. But sleep didn't come easily. I tossed and turned for almost an hour before I fell into a deep sleep and dreamed of a parade with a big balloon of a naked, hairless man. I was one of the handlers, or whatever you call the people who hold the strings beneath those balloons, and I kept looking up to check on the balloon's genitals.

Yup. They were there and they were dangling.

I was wakened from this odd but oddly enjoyable dream by a sound I couldn't at first identify.

A wrong sound.

A sound that should not have been.

I sat up as if that might allow my ears to better detect the origin of the sound.

No doubt. Someone was at the door. And there was no way out except down the rusty old fire escape which, if I was any judge of anything, would crumble to dust the moment I put a foot on the first rung.

"Oh, shit, oh, shit!" I muttered.

As quietly as I could, I slipped from bed and scurried over to the phone.

Don't turn on the lights, Gince! The burglar—rapist!—would know I'd heard him and that would infuriate him and he'd hack down the door with the axe he was sure to have in his utility belt and I'd be in bloody shreds before I could dial 911.

An easy number to dial, Gince. You don't need a light to dial 911. Carefully, I lifted the receiver of the portable phone and dialed.

And prayed. *Oh, please, please pick up!*

After three rings, an emergency operator!

"Someone's trying to break into my apartment," I whispered.

"Are you sure, ma'am?" she asked. I swear she sounded bored.

"What! Yes, I'm sure. Someone's at my door!"

"Ma'am, what is your address?"

I told her. "Hurry, please! I'm too young to die!"

"Ma'am," the voice droned, "we have no cars in the vicinity at this time. We'll send one as soon as possible. In the meantime, don't let the person in."

Don't let the person in?

"Ma'am?"

"What does that mean?" I hissed, shooting a look at the now rattling door. "Do you really think I'm going to invite a murderer in for coffee? Are you crazy!"

"Ma'am, there's no need for—"

I hung up on the bitch. *Who to call? Who to call!*

Rick. I'd call Rick!

I grabbed my backpack and dumped the contents on the table. Who cared if the killer heard me!

There, my address book! I hit the table lamp and made the call. "Rick!"

"Gincy?" he mumbled. "What's wrong. It's—it's two o'clock in the morning."

"Someone's trying to break in to my apartment!" I wailed.

God, I was getting hysterical.

I thought: *How will I ever live this down?*

And then I thought: *You won't have to if you're dead.*

"Did you call 911?" he snapped.

"Yes, yes, and they said they had no one to send and—"

"I'll be right there. Barricade the door. No, stay away from the door in case—in case he has a gun. Lock yourself in a back room or a closet or something. I'll call the police again on the way. Gincy?"

"Yes?" I sobbed.

"It'll be okay. Now, go!"

I did. Directly under the bed. There are benefits to being

scrawny. I scooted back against the wall and covered my mouth with my trembling hand. The dust under there was awful.

And I waited. The rattling and fumbling continued, and slowly I began to wonder what kind of thief this guy was.

New to the game? Drunk? Oh, God, or high on crack!

People got very violent when they were high on crack. I'd seen it on HBO.

I don't know how much time had passed when I finally heard the siren. And then, the heavy tramping of feet up the hall stairs, male voices shouting, and then, a brief confused silence.

"Gincy!"

Rick! I scrambled from under the bed and cried out. "Rick!"

"It's okay," he called back. "The police are here. You can open the door."

All dressed up in sweats and a ratty old T-shirt I tore open the door and flung myself into Rick's arms. He held me and stroked my back and I cried and kissed his neck.

It was a moment before I was aware that we had an audience. I pulled away, wiping my tears with the back of my hand.

"Did you get him?" I asked the policeman watching us too closely. Pervert.

Officer Beefy McBeefster grinned. "There was no burglar, ma'am."

Why did everyone keep calling me ma'am?

I turned back to Rick. "Yes, there was! Someone was trying to break in!"

"Uh, Gincy." Rick pointed to the far end of the dim hallway. Another policeman was talking quietly to a frail, stooped old lady in a housecoat.

"What's Mrs. Norton doing out here?" I said. "Oh, my God, did the burglar try to get into her apartment, too!"

Rick cleared his throat. "Gincy, Mrs. Norton is your burglar. I mean, she left her apartment for whatever reason—you do know she has Alzheimer's? We called her son, he's coming right over—and then she thought your door was hers and—"

I looked again at Mrs. Norton. The poor thing seemed very frightened.

"Oh," I said. "I—I'm sorry—"

The big policeman continued to grin annoyingly. "Better safe than sorry, ma'am," he said.

"You did the right thing, Gincy." Rick turned to the Beefster. "Can she go inside now?"

He shrugged. "Yeah. There's been no crime."

As I walked back into my apartment I heard him add, "Except a waste of police time."

Rick heard him, too, because he shoved me ahead of him and closed the door. "You don't want to pick a fight with the police," he warned.

Now I was angry and mortified. Not a great combination.

I mean, I hadn't even thought about finding a household item I could use as a weapon! No. I'd called for help and hid under the bed.

And now, everybody was laughing at me. "You'd better not be laughing at me," I warned.

"Does it look like I'm laughing?

"Well, inside. You'd better not be laughing inside."

Rick sighed. "Gincy, let's sit down. I'm going to call my neighbor and ask her if Justin can stay with her until morning. Then we're going to have a drink and toast to your being alive. Okay?"

"You don't have to be all hero, you know."

I wrapped my arms around my chest and shivered.

Residual fear. Cold.

"Put on a sweater," he instructed. "And deal with it. Tonight, I am the hero. Next time, no doubt you'll be the hero."

I looked at Rick, at his sleep-rumpled hair, at his sockless feet shoved into mismatched sneakers, at the dark circles around his eyes.

My hero.

I burst out crying.

Clare

Communication Breakdown

The television was on but I wasn't paying much attention to the show.

Something on the History Channel. Something about the French Revolution.

Daddy was right. It should really be called the War Channel. Or the Warmongers Channel.

Or the How Bloodthirsty, Power-Hungry Men Have Made a Mess of Things Channel.

I scooped another spoonful of ice cream from the pint on my lap and let my mind drift along.

Random thoughts.

My third-grade teacher, Mrs. Healy, in her baggy orange cardigan.

My grandfather's grumbly voice, silent now for ten years.

The first day of college, the temperature almost ninety.

The night I met Win, the first chill wind of the fall.

At almost eleven P.M. I heard a key in the door. A minute later, Win came into the living room and tossed his suit jacket on the back of a chair.

I, of course, would hang it up later.

"So, who did you have dinner with?" I asked.

Win slipped off his tie and tossed that, too. "Hello. And, no one you would know."

I lowered the volume of the TV and sat up. "I guessed as much. But I want to know anyway, okay? I'm curious. About your work."

Win looked at me strangely. "I know. I just don't want to bother you. You've got enough on your mind right now."

"How do you know what I have on my mind?" I snapped. "You're always—you're always—"

Win sighed. "I'm always what?"

I sat back again. "Nothing."

Win left the living room. I heard him rattling around in the bathroom for a few minutes. When he returned he was in his pajamas and glasses.

"I'm going to bed," he announced.

I shrugged and turned the volume back up.

Win stood there. I waited for it.

"Hey, sweetie?" he said. "Why don't you put down that ice cream, okay? I think you've had enough. You don't want to be putting on weight with the wedding coming up, do you?"

I said nothing and continued to stare at the TV. At the portrait of King Louis the Something-or-Other.

Finally, Win left the room.

Deliberately, I ate my way to the bottom of the pint.

Win didn't see me anymore. Not really.

If he did, he'd have noted that I'd lost seven pounds since our engagement.

When Win looked at me he saw what he wanted to see.

I wondered: *What was that, anyway?*

Danielle
If This Is Love

I'd always prided myself on my ability to self-entertain.

And I'm not talking about anything sexual, thank you very much.

See, as far back as I can remember I was a bit of a loner. Not antisocial or anything, just perfectly fine on my own.

But loners and individuals make the average person uncomfortable. Especially when the loners and individuals are children.

For years adults tried to get me to join things. The average adult just doesn't understand kids who aren't joiners.

In grammar school, my mother took up the cause.

"But every little girl wants to join the Girl Scouts," my mother said, pleading.

"Not me," I answered simply.

"But why, Danielle? It will be so much fun."

I considered this for about thirty seconds.

"No thanks," I said, smoothing my new pink skirt, a recent gift from my grandmother. "Besides, those uniforms are ugly. The greens and browns are so muddy."

In high school, the administration took up where my mother had left off.

In my junior year the guidance counselor warned me I wouldn't get accepted into a good college unless I joined an athletic club or got involved with some other kind of after-school activity.

"Like what?" I'd asked.

"Like cheerleading," he suggested. "Or, I don't know, the school newspaper. What are your interests, Danielle?"

"Clothes and jewelry."

"Well, we don't have a sewing club, but maybe you could start one! Now that would show initiative and—"

I suppose it was the look of incredulity on my face that stopped Mr. Burns in midsentence.

"Well," he finished lamely. "Just think about it, okay?"

"Okay," I said, getting up to leave his stuffy little office. "But I wouldn't get your hopes up."

Thankfully, by the time I started college most adults had decided to let me live my own life. Maybe because I was almost one of them.

Whatever the reason, no one protested when I declared my intention to live on my own. I juggled several jobs each summer—not an easy thing when you're also trying to have a social life—in order to pay for a single dorm room.

I mean, the possibility of getting stuck with some horror show of a roommate who wanted to chat 24/7 was not one I was willing to chance.

Truly, I'd never, ever been bored by my own company. And I'd never once felt dissatisfied just spending an evening alone at home.

Until that particular night in June, six weeks or so before my thirtieth birthday.

My very adequate Back Bay apartment was newly cleaned.

The air-conditioning was gently humming.

The fridge was stocked with all the essentials: champagne, diet soda, yogurt.

I'd just been to my favorite nail salon for a manicure and pedicure.

Everything was perfect and in place.

Except for me.

I found myself standing in the center of the living room.

Just standing.

See, ordinarily, I don't just stand. Or sit.

Sure, I lounge. But that's an activity, some might say an art. This was different. This was new.

I'm restless, I realized. *This might be what people call being at your wits' end.*

I had absolutely no clue as to what to do with myself.

I didn't want to do anything in particular, yet I wanted to do something special, something meaningful, something . . .

That's it, I thought. *I'll call my mother. When all else fails, make a phone call.*

But halfway to the phone I rejected the notion. She'd ask how the husband-hunting was going, and suddenly, I wasn't in the mood to review my progress.

Especially when my progress had been interrupted by a hunky Christian guy who was occupying far too much of my time.

My mental space.

My heart?

TV, I decided. *That's what I'll do, watch TV. Then I won't have to think. About anything or anybody.*

But a quick flip through the channels I received proved that none of my favorite shows were on. *Danielle,* I scolded, *you really must get TIVO.*

I looked around the living room as if expecting a brilliant idea to be sitting on a shelf or side table, just waiting to be noticed.

But there was nothing.

Danielle, I scolded again, *you really should develop some hobbies. Maybe knitting. Or beadwork. Or sewing. You could make your own clothes . . .*

Like that was ever going to happen.

I flopped down on the couch and sighed.

I considered reading. Reading was something.

But I owned only two books. A dictionary from college days. And a Bible, a gift from many years before that.

The truth was that I hardly ever read. Except magazines, and I'd gone through each one in the house at least twice.

A third flip-through wouldn't be too bad, though. I grabbed the latest issue of *Vacation.*

About halfway through I came across a photo of a couple on the beach at sunset. They were gazing into the distance, the remains of a picnic around them. No nasty gulls fouled the scene.

Great. Now I was thinking about Chris again.

In my experience, Christians and Jews just didn't work out as couples, with the rare exception of Charlotte and Harry on *Sex and the City*. And for a while, it had looked like a total disaster. She'd even converted for him, and poof!

Instead of a marriage, a breakup. Instead of a ring, a slammed door.

Okay, so it had worked out in the end, and Charlotte had gotten a huge diamond from her future husband the lawyer, but Charlotte and Harry were a fictional couple.

Cute, but fictional.

Maybe, I thought, *I should get out of the apartment. Maybe go out for a drink.* But when I started to consider what I'd wear and where I'd go and how I'd get there, the whole thing just seemed too complicated.

I went into my bedroom, thinking maybe I'd just go to bed, try to sleep. And then I spied the computer. I could, I thought, e-mail my old Long Island friends. They just might be at their computers and ready to chat.

And then I realized how unlikely that was.

Michelle had a three-month-old baby and Amy had a manic toddler and, God knows, Rachel and her new—second—husband wouldn't want to be disturbed at nine o'clock at night.

Besides, what did I have to chat about? The weather, who had just bought a new house, whose grandmother had gone into a nursing home.

I doubted the girls would be interested in the dating exploits of their remaining single friend. About the totally ineligible guy who was worming his way into her life.

And honestly, without a family of my own, I wasn't really interested in stories of diaper rash, breast-feeding, and baby-sitters.

I sat on the edge of the crisply made bed—Ralph Lauren sheets and comforter—dejected. On the dresser were framed photographs of my parents, grandparents, and David.

THE SUMMER OF US

David alone.

David and me.

David and Roberta in their official engagement photograph, David's hair all neatly combed and glossed.

It was too late to call David. He was religious about getting to bed and rising early. Healthy, wealthy, and wise, that was my brother.

What about my new friends, I wondered. Gincy and Clare. *I could call one of them.*

Maybe.

The idea was both appealing and disconcerting.

I'd never called either of them just to chat. I wasn't sure we were close enough for that. I wasn't sure I'd ever been close enough to anybody outside my family to call just to chat.

Besides, Clare was likely to be out with Win, and Gincy was sure to be out partying at some club. Or working late on some project for work. She was a bit of a workaholic. An unlikely one, but definitely more devoted to her job than I was to mine.

Are you devoted to anything, Danielle, a strange new voice in my head asked. *Besides your family? Or your notion of who they are and what they want from you?*

Nasty, meddling voice. I tuned it out.

What to do, what to do!

Activity. Action.

I went to my desk and reached for my account book. I reasoned it would boost my spirits to note all the men who had shown interest in me recently, the men I'd dated, the ones who'd given me their numbers.

The eligible men.

The ineligible, that strange new voice whispered.

Chris. Again.

And then I was flooded by sense-memories. His touch. The salty-sweet smell of his neck. How beautiful he had looked in the light of the setting sun.

I put my face in my hands.

Oh, Danielle, I cried. *Don't let this happen.*

July

Danielle
The Ties that Bind

I loved my brother.

David was probably the person I felt closest to in the whole wide world.

Sometimes he could be bossy, but that was just a function of his being the older sibling.

Maybe it also had something to do with his being a doctor, someone in a position of authority, someone on the front line of life and death.

Whatever. It didn't matter. David was king. King David.

I loved and admired him.

And part of me wanted to introduce him to Chris. I wanted to share with David this sweet guy in my life.

Another part of me wanted to keep Chris far, far away from my brother.

The latter feeling was so strong that when David agreed to spend a weekend on the Vineyard, I skillfully arranged to keep the two men apart.

Besides, the visit would be difficult enough with Roberta in tow. My brother's twenty-five-year-old fiancée.

I didn't like the fact that I was losing my brother to Roberta, but I had to accept the reality.

When a man married, he joined the woman's family. It was just the way it went. Forever after, his parents and siblings would come second.

In the beginning years of marriage, though, there was a constant tug-of-war for the son/brother/husband. A new wife tended to be suspicious of her husband's relationship with his mother and sister; even a casual reference to his old girlfriends could wreak domestic havoc.

All of it was normal. Wives most often won the prize and that was the way it should be. Even the Bible said so. A man shall leave his mother and a woman leave her home and all.

So, when I first met Roberta I was wary, naturally. But I came to tolerate her. Even sort of like her. She seemed to want to be friends.

Maybe that was just her tactic, to befriend the sister instead of to antagonize. Whatever. Her pleasant behavior made David's moving on easier for me. And for that I was grateful.

Also, Roberta and I shared an interest in clothes and jewelry. For example, she had this gold-and-ruby pendant I would have died to own. She told me it was one of a kind, but I made a mental sketch at that very moment and, later, put it down on paper.

My future husband, I thought, would appreciate my input on his gift choices.

Anyway, I was thrilled that David had agreed to come to the Vineyard for a long weekend. I didn't see him as often as I would have liked and I knew it cost him to leave the practice.

David, unlike me, had chosen a career he was passionate about. Maybe it had chosen him. I'd heard passions often chose their people.

My brother arrived at the house that Friday in the late morning, lugging four large overnight bags. His fiancée, trotting behind, carried a small Kate Spade summer plaid tote. I showed them to the second bedroom and waited in the kitchen with Gincy and Clare for them to get settled.

"David seems sweet," Clare said earnestly.

"The poor guy looked like a pack mule," Gincy said. "A sweet pack mule," she added when she saw my glare. "But I guess he's used to carrying bags, what with having you as a sister."

"Ha. David's a gentleman," I retorted. "Maybe you're unfamiliar with the type."

About half an hour later David and Roberta reappeared in the tiny kitchen. I thought I sensed a strain between them, but David's sudden bright smile set me at ease.

"My little sister gets more beautiful by the minute," he said, throwing his arms around me.

"Thank you," I told his chest. "I know. And you get more handsome!"

David pulled away and sighed dramatically. "It's a family burden, what can I tell you."

"Oh, you silly!" Roberta squealed, pulling on David's arm so that he was forced to turn to her.

My smile changed from natural to forced but I said nothing.

Roberta announced that she and David were going off right then to see the beachfront. Before I could suggest we all go, they were gone, Roberta tugging David along behind her.

Gincy gave me a funny look.

"What?" I demanded.

"I wouldn't let my brother touch me with a ten-foot pole," she said.

"You've told us your brother is scum."

"True."

"Neither of my brothers ever hugs me," Clare said. "Not really. Not like you and David. I wish my brothers and I were closer. But I guess it's too late for that."

"I don't know," I admitted. "David and I were always close. My mother says that from the moment I was born he was totally a protective big brother. And naturally, I adored him."

"Yeah, well, lucky you," Gincy said. "Personally, I've done just fine on my own. If Tommy fell off the face of the Earth tomorrow I doubt I'd give a—"

"Don't say that!" Clare scolded. "Family is precious. Even if it's not perfect."

"She's right," I said. "Maybe Tommy deserves another chance."

Gincy grinned menacingly. "Maybe," she said, "you both should just butt out of my business."

Danielle

Girl on the High Seas

The next morning I tiptoed out of the house so as not to wake the others.

Who was I kidding? The next morning? It was the middle of the night!

Four A.M. might technically be morning, as in not P.M., but no sane person really thinks it's morning.

Except fishermen. But maybe they're not sane by nature. I don't know. All I know is that Chris was waiting for me just outside the house, pickup truck engine rumbling.

"It's still dark," I whispered, climbing into the front seat.

"You don't have to whisper," he answered with a grin. "It's only me and I'm already awake."

"Well, that makes one of us."

Chris leaned over and kissed me.

"I'm awake!" I said brightly. "That was quite a trick, Mr. Childs."

"No trick. It just comes naturally."

"You!" I swatted him playfully and we drove off to the dock or pier, or wherever he parked his boat.

But the rocking of the truck lulled me back to sleep. When

Chris cut the engine, I startled awake. I tried to stop a huge yawn, but no luck.

"This hour is ungodly," I pointed out, drawing the rain slicker I'd borrowed from Clare more closely around me. "No sane person should be awake at four in the morning, let alone heading out to sea. You know that, right?"

"Do you want to forget the fishing?" Chris said, all serious. "I could take you home—"

I touched his arm. "No. No, I want to do this. Really. Look, I brought this tote full of stuff we might need. Like tissues and Band-Aids and juice. And a camera. I'm all set. All prepared. Ready to go."

On a boat.

I stared at the thing bobbing in the water. In the big, cold expanse of water.

"Danielle," Chris said carefully, "are you afraid of the water?"

"Of course not!" I lied, as he helped me board the boat. "I did grow up on Long Island, you know. We have beaches. And backyard pools. My uncle had a pool. My cousins and I played in it all the time when we were kids."

"Oh, so you can swim."

"Well, no," I admitted. "But I can do the doggie paddle."

Chris frowned and reached into a compartment for something big, bulky, and an ugly shade of green. "Here. Wear this life vest. It's the best one I have."

As long as no one sees me, I thought, shrugging into the vest.

We set sail or whatever you do in a motor-powered boat. Chris waved to some guy in another boat. Other than him, we were all alone in the world.

The water was choppy and gray; the sky, gray and silver. Drops of water shot up onto exposed areas of skin and made me shiver.

Suddenly, I was aware that I couldn't see the shore. "Chris," I said, voice quivering, "I don't feel so good."

"Keep your eye on the horizon," he said. "Try not to blink. There you go—"

"Blllaaaaggghhhhh!"

I felt someone's hand on my back. Who ... The world was spinning, my head was pounding ...

"It's okay, Danielle." Chris. It was Chris. "It happens to everyone. Well, a lot of people. Next time you go out on the water you'll know to take a Dramamine beforehand."

Next time? Was he kidding?

I crumpled to the floor of the boat, too dizzy to be mortified. But in another minute, I was back at the rail.

The one thing I'd neglected to stuff into the tote was a barf bag. Throwing up into the sea was simply terrifying. Even through the nightmare of nausea I was beset by a horrifying vision of hurtling headfirst into the briny deep.

And I almost didn't care. Drowning was sure to solve the vomiting problem.

"Good thing I didn't eat breakfast this morning," I mumbled after some time.

"Well, if you feel better soon, I did pack some muffins," Chris offered.

When I'd emptied my poor stomach again, I gasped, "People actually eat on these things?"

"People actually drink beer," he said.

Well, you know what happened next.

Oddly, after a long half hour or so, the nausea passed and I was able to enjoy the experience of being out to sea with Chris.

Or so I let him think. It was one of my best performances, ever. I oohed over the sunrise and ahhed over the sparkling waves ...

"Danielle," Chris asked suddenly, "is this the first time you've ever been on a boat? I mean, aside from the ferry?"

"Of course not! I went on a dinner cruise once."

"Did the boat actually leave the harbor?"

"Uh, yeah. That's why it was called a cruise, silly."

"Just checking. I'm going to cut the motor here and drop a line. If we're lucky, we'll catch some fish."

Actually, he didn't say fish. He said what I think must have been the name of some type of fish. But the moment he said whatever it was he said, I forgot the word.

Chris busily tied a brightly colored lure to the line. There was a big, barbed hook hidden among some feathers at one end of the lure.

"So, the hook actually goes in the fish's mouth?" I asked, trying to imagine just what that meant, and failing.

So I'd never watched a nature show or a *National Geographic* special in my life. Big deal.

"Right. Now, stand back while I cast."

I did. And only moments later I discovered exactly what happened to the hook and the fish's mouth.

"Bingo!" Chris cried. "I think."

I watched him work to haul in whatever it was he'd caught.

Finally, Chris pulled a big, wet, flapping fish over the rail and I leapt back and stumbled into a bucket.

Chris laid the fish on the deck and started to yank the hook from its poor mouth.

"Ew, ew, ew!" I shrieked. "How can you do that to the poor thing? Doesn't the hook hurt the poor fishies? Oh, I can't watch!"

"I thought you liked fish." Chris's lips twitched.

"Cooked and seasoned, yes," I replied haughtily. "Not alive and squirming and suffering. Ew."

"So, I'm guessing you won't stop by the house later and help me wring the necks of some chickens I had my eye on for dinner."

I feigned horror and we kissed. And then we kissed some more.

I hasten to add that first I'd thoroughly rinsed my mouth with Scope. I always carry a travel-size bottle in my bag.

I was home by nine o'clock, little worse for the wear.

Truthfully, I'd surprised myself. I'd been quite the sport. Quite the trouper.

Maybe this outdoor life isn't all bad, I thought, unlocking the front door of our little house.

Not that I wanted to do anything drastic like run off to sea.

But if I was going to spend more time in nature, I was going to need an appropriate wardrobe.

I made a mental note to borrow one of Clare's L.L. Bean catalogues.

The thought of shopping made me smile.

Clare

Gabfest 2004

"So, how was your fishing date with Nature Boy?" Gincy asked, pouring a third cup of coffee.

Not that it mattered to me how much coffee she drank, though I didn't want to imagine the state of her stomach lining. It was just that she had a habit of finishing a pot and neglecting to make another.

I know Gincy wasn't inconsiderate on purpose. But still . . .

"I wouldn't call him that," Danielle protested. She was fresh from the shower and dressed in a white shorts-and-halter set. "And it was a lovely date. Chris caught a few fish. I can't remember what he called them. Anyway—sshhh, here comes David."

"Why—" I began, but Danielle cut me off with an impatient wave of her hand.

"I'll explain later," Gincy whispered. "Basically, she doesn't want her ideal brother to know she's dating a mere fisherman."

David was a friendly sort. He and Danielle shared olive coloring and dark hair and eyes. But where Danielle was voluptuous, David was lanky. He had the look of a runner, though Danielle told us he'd never been much of an athlete. He preferred to spend his time at the library or at his computer.

David, she said fondly, was kind of a nerd. It was, she claimed, what made him such a good doctor, technically speaking.

That morning he was dressed like most other casually dressed professional men, in a pair of chinos, a navy polo shirt neatly tucked in, and dress-style moccasins.

Win had a similar pair.

"Well, we're off," he announced, after greetings all around. "Seems we have to do a little shopping this morning."

Roberta smiled hugely. She seemed pleasant enough but also struck me as terribly spoiled.

But that was just my impression, based on nothing more than her appearance and the fact that the night before I'd overheard her complaining to David that our house was awful and that he should have booked them into a hotel.

They were staying in the second bedroom, which meant that I was bunking with Danielle in the first bedroom. Gincy had offered to take the couch for the duration of their visit.

As I had closed the bedroom door behind me, mostly to block out Roberta's whining, I heard David mumble something about not hurting his sister's feelings.

David, I had thought, was henpecked.

But this morning, there was no sign of trouble in paradise.

"Isn't he sweet?" Roberta asked rhetorically, petting David's arm. "He buys me a present from every place we go. Of course, I wouldn't be marrying him if he didn't! Right?"

Gincy's mouth opened, but a stern look from me kept her quiet. Amazingly.

Maybe she was trainable after all.

When David and Roberta had gone off, Danielle suggested we go out for breakfast.

We strolled into town and settled at a tiny table at Bessie's Breakfast Bests, a place dubbed "Triple Bs."

"I was thinking about that article," Danielle said, "you know, the one on couples having trouble finding other couples to hang out with. So that everyone gets along. Do you think it's, like, a duty for the wives of male friends to like each other?"

Gincy took a gulp of her fifth cup of coffee that day.

"I think most men expect that when they get married they'll never see their buddies again," she said. "Or only when their wives allow them to. Take my family. My mother was ironfisted about my dad seeing his buddies. Once she caught him sneaking out to catch a beer with this guy Bill and she freaked. At the time I was too young to know what was going on but I found out later.

"I kinda had a thing with one of Bill's sons. A minor thing; it lasted about ten minutes. Anyway, I never saw my mother hanging out with Bill's wife. Come to think of it, I never saw my mother hanging out with any women friends. She's not very likable, my mother."

I didn't share my thoughts just then for fear of insulting my housemates needlessly. But the truth was that Win would have far preferred me to have taken a summer rental with two wives or fiancées of his colleagues than with two strangers, neither of whom was seriously involved with a professional man.

He'd told me so.

And then I'd pointed out that none of the wives or fiancées ever went off without their men. And that I wasn't particularly close to any of the women, anyway.

And then Win had said, "Maybe that's your fault, Clare. Maybe you should try harder, learn to be a better hostess. Entertaining is important in my profession. I need to know I can rely on you.

"A man needs to know he can rely on his wife."

"You can rely on me," I'd answered automatically.

"I hope so," he'd responded before going back to the computer.

"I think lots of guys are like Gincy's dad," Danielle was saying, when next I tuned in. "I bet the last thing Mr. Gannon wanted was his wife and Bill's wife banding together and forcing them to stop smoking cigars or eating Cheez Doodles."

"I love Cheez Doodles," Gincy said. "Why is it that TV commercials always portray the wife as the one who knows best? Why is she the one who eats low-fat food and the hubby the one who scarfs donuts? Plenty of women scarf donuts. I scarf donuts."

"The contemporary myth of American domesticity," I replied,

poking at my own healthy fruit salad, thinking of how I routinely nagged Win to eat properly. "Why do you even pay attention to commercials?"

"Because half the time they're more interesting than the shows. You can't tell me that *Big Brother XXV* is more interesting than the latest round of Nike ads."

"I wouldn't know," I admitted. "I've never watched any reality TV show."

"Women," Danielle proclaimed, "don't want their men picking friends for them. Women have their own selection process."

Yes, I agreed silently, *we do. But tell that to Win.*

The waitress cleared our table then, though we lingered over final cups of coffee and for me, another glass of water.

"Wouldn't it be nice if our guys got along?" Danielle said. "I mean, assuming we each had a steady guy. Then we could hang out as couples."

Gincy laughed. "We three barely get along! What are the chances of us finding three compatible men to add to the mix?"

"I hate that cliquish couple thing," I blurted, surprising myself with my boldness.

Maybe it was due to the fresh, invigorating breeze coming off the water.

"It's like there's a law," I went on, "a law that dictates that once you're in a couple it's only valid to socialize with other couples. Anyway, that's what Win likes to do. Socialize only in couples. Only with people he knows from work."

"Sleazy corporate lawyers," Gincy mocked.

Boring corporate lawyers, I amended silently. *At least the people Win chooses to spend his time with.*

"You know," Gincy said, fiercely.

She often spoke fiercely and with conviction, even on topics that couldn't possibly matter in the long run. Like people who spelled Stephen with a "ph" versus those who spelled it with a "v."

"I hate those women who stop saying "I" once they're part of a couple. It's like they can only say "we." Like, 'Oh, we just hung around on Saturday afternoon' instead of telling the truth, which might be, 'Bob simonized the car and I read a book.' "

"Well, isn't the point of being a couple spending time to-gether?" Danielle countered.

"Yeah, but you're not a couple first," Gincy argued. "You're an individual who's 'in' or 'part of' a couple. See the difference?"

"I don't know about that," I admitted. "Lately, it doesn't feel like I'm me first, then part of a couple. Mostly it feels like . . . it feels like I'm just part of Win. I don't know if there's even a couple anymore. I don't know if we have a partnership."

Did we ever have a true partnership, I wondered. A blasphemous thought.

"Win and sub-Win." Gincy considered. "I think that stinks."

"Why don't you tell us what you really think?" Danielle commented dryly.

Gincy grinned. "I think I just did."

The morning breeze was suddenly gone, sucked away by a heavy, early-afternoon heat.

I decided I'd said quite enough about my personal life for the moment.

Gincy
And Another Thing

Stupid Rick Luongo.

There I was, strolling along the shore at the Edgartown-Oak Bluffs State Beach, water gently lapping at my ankles, the sun toasting my skin, and all I could think about was that stupid Rick Luongo.

Since he'd come to save me from the burglar-that-wasn't, he'd risen yet another notch in my estimation. Make that two notches. Because not once had he lorded over me his middle-of-the-night ride to the rescue.

Believe me, I watched and listened for any signs of mockery or derision from our colleagues. And when I could find none, I confronted Rick.

I walked into his office and closed the door behind me. Rick looked up from his computer and, in doing so, somehow managed to knock several fat files off his desk.

"Hi," he said, looking momentarily at the new mess on the floor. "What's up?"

"So, who did you tell?" I demanded. "Everyone's acting all oblivious. How much are you paying them to keep quiet?"

Rick eyed me carefully. "You're a bit insane, do you know that?"

"That's beside the point," I said, though of course, it was exactly the point.

Rick stood and came around the front of his desk. I moved aside as he perched on the edge, nearly impaling his butt on a pair of open scissors.

"Gincy, I didn't tell anyone about the other night. Assuming that's what you're referring to. The alleged break-in?"

"Alleged? What are you now, a cop? Mr. Law Enforcement with the lingo. And yes, that's what I'm referring to. The incident to which I am referring."

"I didn't tell anyone," Rick said, matter-of-factly. "Except Justin. I wanted to explain why I dragged him out of bed in the middle of the night and left him with Mrs. Murphy. I told him a friend needed help. Which was the case. End of story. Why?"

Rick had called me a friend. At least, he'd referred to me as a friend.

Oh, boy, Gincy, I told myself, looking stupidly at him sitting on his desk, noting how the muscles of his thighs were outlined through his pants. *You really want to be something more, don't you?*

Oh, yes.

Still, I said nothing.

Rick crossed his arms across his chest. His sleeves were rolled halfway up his forearms. Which were strong. His wrists were broad.

"Do you think there was something funny in it all?" he asked.

The question took me totally by surprise.

"No! Absolutely not! I mean, I was scared out of my mind, and poor Mrs. Norton, I don't know how long she'll be able to live on her own—"

"Then why," he interrupted, "should I find something funny in it all?"

I shrugged. *Gincy,* I thought, *you are a big fat idiot.* "I can be a bit defensive," I admitted. "Sometimes."

"We all have our things," Rick said, grinning.

"Like you're klutzy?"

"Among other things."

"What other things?" I asked, wondering if we were flirting.

"How stupid would I be to tell you all my faults?" he replied.

Oh, yeah. Flirting.

"That bad, huh?" I said.

There was a beat of silence during which we looked at each other eye to eye and, unless I was imagining it, the sexual tension was running rampant.

I'd never been prone to misreading sexual signs. At least the ones I'd been interested in following.

Finally, Rick opened his mouth to reply and just at that moment Kell was at my shoulder.

"There you are!" he cried, breathing garlic fries all over my neck. "I need you, now."

Kell grabbed my arm and half dragged me from Rick's office. I shot a look back at Rick as I went. His eyes were still smoldering.

Smoldering?

Watch it, I warned myself. *Danielle is rubbing off on you.*

I dodged a gang of delinquent ten-year-olds charging toward the water. Kids. Whose idea were they, anyway?

Rick had a kid.

Damn! In spite of the dazzling sun and sparkling water, I just couldn't get the feel of Rick out of my head. That hug when I'd flung open the door. My kisses on his neck. God, how embarrassing!

I reached the end of the two-mile stretch of shoreline and turned back for home.

A few strides later I spotted David and Roberta, up toward the road, away from the rolling water.

David was wearing what seemed to be his standard vacation garb, chinos and a polo shirt neatly tucked in. Roberta wore a hot-pink midriff-baring top and super-low-rise white pants.

It looked as if they were having an argument. Rather, it looked as if Roberta was having the argument all by herself. She was shouting and waving her arms wildly at David who stood stock-still, arms at his sides.

I looked away and walked on.

It had to be as embarrassing for the onlookers of an argument between a couple as it was for the member or members of the couple who were aware of the onlookers. No one liked their dirty laundry to be aired in public. And no one wanted to witness anyone else's dirty laundry flapping in the breeze.

At least, I didn't. I knew that some—most?—people derived a rabid, hand-rubbing pleasure from watching other people's civilized facades crumble. I mean, isn't that what *E!* was all about? *People* magazine? Katie Couric interviews?

After another minute, I snuck a peek over my shoulder. David and Roberta were gone.

I wasn't sure if David had seen me. I hoped he hadn't. He was okay. A bit spineless if his choice of fiancée was an indication of his larger personality, but okay.

Roberta must be dynamite in bed, I thought. Because it wasn't like she had a lot else going for her. The scene I'd just witnessed simply confirmed the impression I'd already formed of Danielle's future sister-in-law.

Roberta was your classic spoiled bitch. And I was sorry a good kid like Danielle was going to be stuck with her.

Not that Danielle was suddenly my best friend or anything. I wasn't ready to attest before a jury that she was of the highest moral character or that if we were stranded on an island she'd willingly sacrifice herself for me by feeding herself to a tiger. Or whatever wild beast had attacked us. A boar, I imagine.

Still, I wasn't a terrible judge of character and it was pretty clear that under Danielle's bright and sparkly airhead exterior was a good person. Someone of some depth.

Maybe she was a bit confused, maybe a bit in denial, but hey? Who wasn't confused and in denial?

Roberta. That's who. And people like her.

I swear she was as transparent as a pane of glass, as insubstantial as a sliver of styrofoam, as shallow as a wading pool. I wouldn't trust her as far as I could throw her, which wouldn't be far, what with all the hairspray and jewelry she wore.

Nice, Gincy, I scolded. *It's so easy to slam other people, isn't it? Keeps you from getting your own life in order. How can you work through this Rick infatuation if you're spending all your time mocking some bubble-head from Long Island?*

I continued home along State Road, feeling a bit too much like the rabid, hand-rubbing voyeurs I claimed to loathe.

Clare

The Calm and the Storm

The skies opened up around one o'clock that afternoon.

I'd always found rainy days so terribly depressing. They brought back memories of the summer vacations when my mother wouldn't let my brothers and me into the lake during the slightest bit of rain.

There was the big beautiful lake, only feet away, and yet it was forbidden territory. My mother's rule seemed so horribly unfair.

What could happen that would be so bad?

Lightning might strike and burn you alive. A wave might rise and drown you. A wayward boat might knock you on the head and force your body down, down into the muddy deep.

The rain itself and my mother's extreme caution seemed to cut short the vacation. They forced me to think of summer's end. Of going back to school. Of returning to the daily sameness of ordinary life.

When I was a child I felt there was real magic in difference. Change of place meant changes of thought, perceptions, feelings. Different clothes, different food, different people. Change meant excitement.

When I was a child. Children are brave.

Starting at about the age of twelve, I began to feel differently.

I began to feel that change was messy and frightening. Difference was just too challenging. Sameness meant safety and security.

For most people, I guess, adolescence is a time of rebellion, testing limits, sexual exploration. For me, it was a time of fear, a time of closing up and shutting down.

Of course, I didn't realize all that until years later when it was far too late to recapture my youth. Until I'd been with Win for close to a decade.

I could hear Gincy quoting her father: "Hindsight is twenty-twenty. Youth is wasted on the young."

I could hear Danielle chiming in with her grandmother's words of wisdom: "You're dead a long time. Seize the day."

Carpe diem.

Well, I wasn't sure I'd ever seized anything, let alone the entire day.

I mean, what kind of person was I that at the age of twenty-nine I was still haunted by those dark, depressing days at the lake?

The rain worsened and by two o'clock all thoughts of salvaging the day had disappeared. We settled in the living room with books, magazines, and the TV.

Gincy groaned. "I can't believe the only thing on is *Antique Roadshow!* This has got to be the most boring show ever produced."

"Are you crazy?" Danielle cried. "It's great! Though I will admit it bothers me when some semi-illiterate, toothless, three-hundred-pound woman in a caftan finds out she's got a bedpan worth three hundred thousand dollars or something. I mean, someone like that doesn't deserve a lot of money. She obviously has no idea what to do with it!"

"And you do," Gincy shot back. "Wait. You probably do know what to do with money."

Danielle nodded. She had a very queenly sort of nod. It seemed completely natural to her. "I was born with a dominant taste gene and I've honed my talent over the years. You know, it says in the Bible that you shouldn't hide your light under a bushel. Meaning if you have a God-given talent, you should use it."

"I thought you attributed your taste to genetics," Gincy said slyly, "not God."

Danielle gave Gincy one of her now-famous looks. The one that said, "Okay, we all know you're smart, so why don't you just shut up now?"

"Clare, don't take this the wrong way," she said, turning her attention to me, "but honey, you're looking a little dragged out these days. A little peaked. A little undernourished. I'm not seeing that glow in your cheeks. I'm seeing dark circles around your eyes and tiny lines around your mouth."

"What Danielle is trying to say is that it looks like you've lost weight," Gincy said.

"Oh, I'm okay," I said dismissively. "I guess I've just been running around a lot lately. I guess I've skipped lunch a few times."

"Honey, again, with all due respect, but you don't want to be a skinny bride. You want to be a healthy, glowing bride. Am I right? You don't want the dress to hang off you on your big day. You want it to fit."

"It will fit," I said, without any conviction at all. I hadn't even thought about a dress, though of course I'd lied about that to Danielle.

Danielle leaned forward in her chair and clasped her hands on her knees. "Clare, be honest with us. You're not having an attack of anorexia, are you?"

"What!" I cried. "No! Besides, I don't think anorexia comes in attacks, like cluster headaches. Anyway, no, I'm not anorexic. God, Danielle."

Danielle shrugged. "All I'm saying is that if you are having an attack of anorexia, there are people who can help you. There are places you can go. Just keep in mind you don't have to suffer."

I bit my tongue. Literally.

Gincy seemed to sense my outrage. "I'd offer you a Sno Ball," she said, smiling coyly, "but I know you'd just throw it up."

I laughed. "No, I'd toss it right back at you! Ugh! You know there's absolutely no nutritional value in those packaged desserts."

"Yeah, well, at least I don't smoke. Much. Everyone's got her bad habits."

"What are your bad habits, Clare?" Danielle's voice betrayed some annoyance. I suspected she didn't appreciate being teased or ignored by both housemates in the same sitting.

"I'm afraid of change," I blurted. "I don't take risks. At least, I haven't for a long time."

Danielle waved her hand dismissively. "Everybody is a bit afraid of change. It can be very exhausting. And sometimes it's not worth the effort and things don't work out to be better than before."

"I'm not talking about change that just happens, like accidents you can't control," I explained. "I'm talking about change that you choose. I never choose to change. Almost never."

"Fear of change isn't exactly a vice," Gincy pointed out.

"It's harmful enough," I shot back.

Gincy got up and went to the kitchen. Danielle raised the volume on the TV.

I stared at the screen and thought.

Oak Bluffs is a new venue.

Gincy and Danielle are new people. New friends?

Maybe. If we didn't kill each other by the rainy day's end.

And I was . . .

Well, that was still to be determined.

On TV, a tiny woman in a flowered dress was crying tears of joy. She'd just learned her grandmother's teapot, a piece she'd always thought worthless in terms of price, was, in fact, quite valuable.

"This changes everything," she sputtered.

Maybe change isn't all bad, I thought. *I'll just have to wait and see.*

Gincy

She Doth Protest

The TV show droned on.

Antiques. I just didn't get the appeal.

I mean, I enjoyed reading about historical events. I just didn't want to live with history's musty, bloodstained relics.

Hair jewelry? Can you get more disgusting?

"I don't know one man who would choose to go antiquing in Vermont," Clare said musingly. "Win certainly wouldn't. He'd suggest I go with my mother."

I laughed. "Have you ever asked him? A man who wants to get laid will do anything the woman asks."

"That's not about choice," Danielle corrected with that "Let me tell you how it really is" voice of hers. Which pissed me off, even when what she had to say was right.

When someone declared she was right, she was also declaring you were wrong.

"A man who wants to have sex has no choices," Danielle said. "He is a slave to the sexual imperative. He does what needs to be done, and if he's really smart, he keeps his mouth shut about things like going antiquing in Vermont. And if he's supersmart and wants to get lucky more than once, he buys the woman a fantastic meal and maybe even a nice piece of jewelry."

"How much jewelry do you have, anyway?" I asked, surveying the quantity of heavy gold adorning Danielle. She and Roberta could open their own jewelry mall. "How much jewelry do you need?"

My own collection of jewelry—if it even deserved the title of "collection"—consisted of a five-year-old Swatch I'd paid twelve dollars for; a 14-carat gold Claddagh ring I'd gotten for my grammar school graduation and which now didn't even fit on my pinky—where was that ring, anyway; and a pair of tiny silver studs I'd put in my pierced ears a year earlier and had never bothered to remove.

Danielle smiled smugly. "It's not about need. And, would you like to see my catalogue? Detailed written descriptions. And photos. For insurance purposes."

"A gay man might want to go antiquing in Vermont," Clare mused.

"Only if he's genuinely interested in antiques," Danielle said. "Or if he's trying to have sex with a much younger, supercute guy."

"Well, I'd never go antiquing in Vermont," I said. "Even to get laid. It sounds colossally boring."

Clare looked genuinely surprised. "Not even if you could stay in a charming B&B?"

"Huh. Especially if I had to stay in a B&B! You have to talk all hushed and smile a lot and oooh and aaah over chintz-covered couches and needlepoint pillows. And you can't even get seconds for breakfast like in a hotel with a buffet. And you can't scream during sex. And forget about the bathroom situation. Have you ever tried to take a crap and make no sound at all?"

Danielle looked at me disapprovingly so I went on. "Or leave no smell? That's a vacation, a shared bathroom? That's visiting my father's family at the trailer park."

"So," Danielle said sharply, as if she were talking to a naughty, antisocial child, "I gather you've stayed in a B&B before."

I smiled blandly. "Oh, no. I've only heard about them. Where would a lowlife New Hampshire kid like me get the bucks for a charming Vermont B&B?"

"While we're on the subject of charming," Danielle said with mock weariness, "I think I'm going to enroll you in charm school, Ms. Gannon. Your lack of it is wearing on my nerves."

Ah, mission accomplished!

Danielle
In a Mirror

Poor David had one of his migraines, a condition he'd suffered since childhood, so just we girls went out for dinner the last night of David and Roberta's long weekend.

I'd hardly spent any time alone with my brother during his visit. I wasn't happy about that. I offered to stay home with him that last night, but he urged me to go out and have a good time.

Maybe he just needs to be alone, I thought. *Totally alone.*

Sometimes I forgot how much of a loner David had been as a child. Even more of a loner than I had been.

Reluctantly, I agreed and left David to the peace of his own company.

Over our lengthy meal at Lucca's, I listened to Roberta chatter on about the cute instructors at her tennis club and the bitchy Korean girls at her nail salon and the Saks Fifth Avenue charge card her daddy had just given her, and how she planned to have her first plastic surgery by the age of thirty, and something hit me.

Just hit me smack in the face.

Roberta was boring. So awfully boring.

And she was shallow. Terribly shallow. Like a puddle.

I mean, I'd never found her to be fascinatingly interesting or a careful, deep thinker.

But this vapid?

God, I thought, *what had David been thinking when he proposed?*

I looked across the table at my future sister-in-law. She was still rattling on. Not once had she asked any of us a question about our own lives.

A vision of Roberta having an affair with one of the tanned tennis instructors she so admired flashed across my brain.

Poor David! So intelligent and caring and sensitive. This woman would eat him alive!

Why hadn't my brother seen the real Roberta yet? Why hadn't he seen past the pretty face, artful hair, and toned limbs?

Because he was only a man.

I wondered. David had an excuse for being blinded by Roberta's flash—testosterone—but what was mine? Women were supposed to be more sensitive to nuances, to reading character clues.

And then, right there over glasses of Merlot and plates of pasta, I was hit by another disturbing thought.

There was something oddly familiar about Roberta.

Roberta reminded me of—me.

At least, on the surface. Who knew what went on in Roberta's mind, in her heart of hearts. Who knew if she even had an under-surface.

I have a mind, I protested silently, noting an unfamiliar—new?—sparkly bracelet on Roberta's wrist. It had to have set David back at least five hundred dollars.

If it was from David and not from some tennis club gigolo.

I have a heart.

I don't know how spiritual things work but I think I might even have a soul.

But had I ever let anyone see those real valuables?

The answer was no. It was a startling, uncomfortable answer.

I shot a look at my housemates.

Gincy was rolling straw paper into little balls, mini-bullets I just knew she'd love to aim at Roberta's head.

Clare seemed inordinately interested in her fettucine alfredo.

Every so often she mumbled, "Oh?" or "Ah," but it didn't fool me.

Clare was bored. Gincy was disgusted.

Suddenly, I felt strangely embarrassed. It was clear what my housemates thought of Roberta.

But what did they think of me, really?

Did Gincy and Clare see a resemblance between me and my brother's fiancée?

And if so, did they even like me? Or were they simply tolerating me for the duration of our house rental?

By the fall, would I be just an unpleasant memory, the typical spoiled JAP, a figure of fun?

I stuffed a garlic bread stick in my mouth and fervently hoped not.

Gincy

You Never Know Unless You Try

Okay. So I went out with Rick again.

Maybe I thought that as long as I didn't actually see his kid, live and in person, the kid—Justin—didn't exist.

Honestly, I don't know what I thought. But after that heated moment in Rick's office, the moment interrupted by Kell, I was a goner.

In fact, I asked Rick for our second date.

"You beat me to it," he said. "And, yeah."

We went out another time after that. First to the movies, then for burgers, beer, and pool at Jillian's.

Things progressed. There was no choice about it. I was too powerfully attracted to be all cautious and wary.

Rick had the physical attributes I found most appealing: wavy dark hair, dark brown eyes, olive skin, a compact body. It was a body built for power.

Where the clumsiness came from, I had no idea.

He was also really smart and keenly interested in everything from food to music to the history of European cinema. We belonged to the same political party and our stand on the big ethical issues of the day, from war in the Middle East to the potentially explosive issue of stem-cell research, were utterly compatible.

Finally, I was drawn to Rick by his total lack of guile. The guy just didn't seem capable of telling a lie, even a social, white lie.

He was the original foot-in-mouth fellow, infuriating at times, but a huge relief after years of wasting time with cheats and guys so full of crap you could smell it a mile away.

"How do I look in this blouse?" I asked him once.

He frowned and said, "Not good."

"How do you mean?" I asked, blood simmering. I'd paid a whole ten dollars for the thing!

He shrugged. "I don't know. It just doesn't look good."

Well, I'd asked.

When I got home later that night I took a good look at myself in the mirror.

Rick was right. The blouse sucked on me. I looked like a starving nineteenth-century peasant.

Score one for the guy in my life.

So, we went out a fourth time, to a movie and then for Indian food.

And after dinner we went back to my place. It was the first time Rick had visited—not counting his rescue mission—so I gave him the tour. That took a whopping two minutes.

There we were, standing face-to-face in my minuscule living area. Rick's hair was tousled from the evening's unusually cool wind. I wanted very badly to climb all over him.

"So, uh, we're going to do this, right?" I blurted.

"Yeah," he said. "If you want to. I want to."

"I want to, too."

"You know I can't stay over. Justin. I have to drive the sitter home."

"Who said I want you to stay over, Mr. Presumptuous?"

"Sorry. It's been a while since I was last single. And then I didn't have a five-year-old. I know far more about *Nickelodeon* than I do about current dating etiquette."

"Forgiven," I said, putting my arms around his neck. "Now shut up and let's get busy."

And we did. And it was great.

Totally freakin' great.

Gincy
Venus and Mars Collide

L ife can suck, but sometimes it's just incredibly good. Like when you're blessed with yet another weekend of perfect weather.

Danielle chose to spend the gorgeous day shopping. When she returned later that afternoon she was lugging three large and overflowing shopping bags. Her purchases included a gold and enamel charm in the shape of the popular Nantucket basket (for her mother), a bright red Martha's Vineyard sweatshirt (for her father), and several pairs of sandals. They were for Danielle.

I'm not sure where Clare disappeared to exactly but she returned all glowy and energized, babbling something about five miles and running and needing new a heart-rate monitor and about how kayaking was her new favorite sport.

Me? I'd spent the day popping in and out of art galleries and paying my first visit to the Vineyard Museum in Edgartown.

At about five, Danielle, Clare, and I met for drinks and appetizers at a popular place called Keith's. It overlooked the water with a large deck and both indoor and outdoor bars. We were lucky to get a table with a good ocean view.

I suspected our luck had something to do with whatever it was Danielle had slipped the hostess.

Funny.

At the start of the summer I hadn't expected to be spending much time at all with my roommates, outside of the house, that is. But somehow, without effort, we'd begun to bond.

Sometimes, it weirded me out. Other times, it was okay.

Okay, a little more than okay.

"Hey there!" Danielle waved to someone and then turned to us. "I hope you girls don't mind. I told him we'd be here. He's only stopping by. He's got to work."

"Who?" Clare asked.

"Chris."

"Wait, David's too lofty to meet him but we're low-class enough?"

"Oh, Gincy, it's not like that at all! Now, sshhh. Hello!"

We were joined by Danielle's Man of the Sea. He was extremely cute in a very outdoorsy way. Far more Clare's type, I thought.

And he was very charming. Truly charming, not smarmy and sly.

After introductions, I asked him if he wanted to join us for a drink. I figured Danielle wouldn't mind.

"Oh, no thanks," he said. "I never touch alcohol when I'm going to work."

"That's wise," Clare commented.

Chris grinned. "Let's just say I learned wisdom the hard way. The way most of us do."

"Ain't that the truth!" I said.

Danielle got up from her chair and took Chris's arm. "Don't you have to be going, Chris?" she cooed. "You don't want to be late for work."

Chris looked at his watch. "Yeah, you're right. My boss is a real jerk when I'm late by even a minute."

"Don't you work for yourself?" Clare asked.

"Yup. And I meant just what I said, the boss is a real jerk."

Everybody but Danielle laughed, and Chris loped off to his truck.

"You practically threw him out," I commented as soon as he was gone.

Danielle frowned. "I did not. I just didn't want him to be late for work."

"What do you care if he's late for work? If his business goes bust? You're not going to marry him, right?"

"He's so nice," Clare said quickly, before Danielle could reply. "He seems so genuine."

"Yeah," I agreed. "But personally, I'm more interested in his body. When you're done with Chris, pass him on to me, okay?"

"What about Rick?" Danielle shot back, clearly angry at me.

"What about him?" I replied, pretending nonchalance. "I'm not the one who wants to get married. I'm not the one with a system and a checklist."

"But—"

"But nothing. Don't put words in my mouth."

"Okay," she said, "the Rick question aside, let me just say that a guy who dates Danielle Leers is not going to be interested in dating Gincy Gannon."

"Is that an insult?"

"No, just a reality check. Gincy, we are, like, total opposites. We're barely the same species, let alone the same sex."

"You *are* insulting me!" I cried.

Danielle remained calm in the face of my growing rage. "No," she corrected, "I'm just pointing out the visible truth. Look at what you're wearing. Look at your hair. When was the last time you got it cut? Have you ever used a blow-dryer? What about gel? When was the last time you wore a skirt? Have you ever had a professional manicure?"

"Of course I've used a blow-dryer!" I spat back. "Where do you think I grew up, in a swamp?"

"Well," she drawled, "the way you talk about your hometown, I have wondered."

"Oh, Danielle," Clare said now, shooting me a look that said, please don't throw that punch. "You're making too big a deal about silly little differences. Things that mean absolutely nothing in the long run. You and Gincy are each hardworking, intelligent, kind women. That's all that matters. Any man worth his salt would be happy to be with either of you."

Danielle and I stared at each other until, finally, she shrugged and looked away.

Good ole Clare. Ever the peacemaker.

And I had my own way of conceding to peace. I ordered us another round, in spite of Clare's protests that one margarita was her limit.

"Eat more chips," I told her. "You'll be fine."

Halfway through our second margaritas, a couple was seated at the next table, close enough for observation but at an odd enough angle that they couldn't be sure if we were sneaking glances at them or the cute bartender just beyond.

She was straight out of the Young Female catalogue; he, straight out of the Young Male.

She had long blond hair, which she tossed with frequency, a flawless figure, and a pert and pretty face. She wore a mini-sundress and strappy high-heeled sandals.

He was muscled from regular workouts at the gym. His hair was not quite, but almost, cut in a buzz; on his left wrist was a heavy, round-faced, gold-tone Rolex. His crisp white cotton shirt was open to mid-hairy chest; his front-pleated black cotton pants flared just so.

Danielle, of course, helped refine my observations. I wouldn't have recognized a Rolex in a Rolex display case.

The woman's expression was alternately studiously bored and eyes-half-closed seductive.

The man's expression was alternately low-browed defensive and I'm-gonna-do-right-by-you-baby.

"Here's the difference between men and women, as I see it," Danielle suddenly announced.

"You really need to point out the differences?" I asked, incredulous. "The stereotypical male and female are on display right in front of us. You can extrapolate every detail just from the appearance and mannerisms of those two specimens! What more is there to say?"

"The difference is," she replied, "that with women there's always more to say. Men do; women talk. Guys go golfing and women get together for lunch."

"That's stupid," I said. "Eating lunch is doing something. You're biting, chewing, swallowing, digesting."

"Yes, but lunch is not really about the food, is it? It's about the conversation. It's about the juicy gossip and unwanted advice. It's about setting up your slightly overweight single girlfriend with your forty-five-year-old bachelor cousin."

"I think you're splitting hairs," Clare protested, "making a big distinction about talking and doing. You always—"

"Go on," Danielle urged, nonplussed. "I always what?"

Clare blushed. "I shouldn't have said 'always.' What I meant to say was that you try to categorize the world. A lot. Often."

Danielle shrugged. "So? A lot of things are just obvious. Categorizable. If that's even a word."

"But nothing is black-and-white," Clare argued. "Especially not people. Not behavior. Not—"

"Pardon me if I'm generalizing again," Danielle drawled. "But I've been thinking. See, my brother just asked his friend Jake, a guy he's known since kindergarten, to be his best man. David and Jake have had absolutely nothing in common since the age of, well, let's say five. I mean, Jake's a personal trainer. Nice, but dumb as a doornail. And David, well, he's a brilliant doctor. Still, they're like, best friends. And I've seen this kind of thing before."

"Your point?" I asked, bored enough to be fascinated by Young Male feeding Young Female fried calamari with his thick fingers.

"My point is that guys tend to find a few friends when they're like, toddlers, and keep them forever, even if they grow up to be totally different and have nothing in common but a penis."

"Well, I don't know," Clare said. Predictably. "Women keep some friends throughout their lives. My mother is still best friends with her best friend from high school. But it is true that women change so much. We move on, we shed friends and acquire new ones and . . ."

I pretended to shudder. "We sound like freakin' snakes with all the shedding. I don't like snakes."

"Of course," Danielle confirmed, ignoring my remark. "Women are about flowering and flux and flow."

"And so men are about stasis and stability and . . ." I hesitated. "I need another 's' word."

"You're still stereotyping," Clare said now to Danielle. "If that's all true, how do you explain the observable reality that women nest and men roam? Nesting is about stability. Roaming is about, well, chance. Instability. And if women are about change and flux, how do you explain the fact that they love boxes?"

I frowned. "They what now?"

"I've thought about this," Clare said earnestly. "Every little girl has a box for her secret treasures. Purses are just an extension of the treasure box. Think about it. What does it mean that a woman has a jewelry box for her watch and a pretty little dish for her change, while a guy throws his watch and change on the counter, all mixed up, right out there in the open?"

"Maybe it's about order versus chaos?" Danielle suggested.

"No, I don't think so," I said. "At least not in my case. I'm a slob and Rick is anally neat despite his clumsiness. I'm the one throwing quarters. Rick's the one collecting and rolling my spare change. Of course, he usually drops the roll on my foot, but . . ."

"Well then: Enclosure versus exposure?" Danielle asked.

"Safety versus risk?" Clare offered.

My turn. "It's about the fact that men are urged to spread their seed across the land and women are urged to hold themselves close."

"Good point," Danielle said. "And think about this: Women have a womb."

"Do I have to think about it?" I said. " 'Cause I'm not planning on using it for a while. Why does everything come back to the womb?"

But Danielle was warming to her train of thought. "A womb is a secret space for growing things. On the other hand, men have no secrets. They have a penis. And testicles. Just all hanging out there, shameless . . ."

"Ah, now we're onto something!" Clare cried.

She was more than a little tipsy. It was the first time I'd seen her that way.

She'd feel like crap in the morning, but right then, it was cute. I'd take happy drunk over belligerent drunk any time.

"Shame," Clare mused. "Women have always been taught to feel shame about their bodies, their feelings, their thoughts. Exposing any part of a woman's self is shameful. So women have learned to keep everything inside. Hidden. In a box. I am so smart."

"Yes, you are, honey," Danielle assured her. "And consider this: Women are urged not to go topless. I mean, in public. A woman without a shirt is a slut. Except on a nude beach. But it's okay for men to go shirtless. Tacky but not illegal."

"Yeah," I said, "and tell me who enjoys some stranger's nipples in their face. Or some stranger's big fat gut."

"I wouldn't mind seeing Ashton Kutcher's nipples," Danielle said.

"Ashton Kutcher isn't a stranger," Clare corrected. "He's a celebrity. There's a big difference between a stranger and a celebrity."

"While we're on this strange topic," I said, "let me just say that I don't particularly want to see any part of a stranger's naked body. Even his stomach. Or her stomach. Even if it's flat. I mean, I respect a person's right to put it out there, but why can't that person respect my right not to have to look at it put out there?"

"Secrecy versus frankness," Clare piped.

"Shame," Danielle said.

"Oh, no," I groaned. "The dreaded circular conversation."

"Polly Pocket! toys!" Danielle looked very pleased with herself. "Those teeny little dolls. Very easy to hide."

"Miniatures. Tiny little statues. And dollhouses. A little girl is given a dollhouse," Clare said. "An enclosure. A place that she can lock up tight. While a little boy is given a racetrack. How different is a dollhouse from a racetrack? Very different."

"Things are changing," I pointed out. "Things have changed. Look at all the little girls on soccer teams and, I don't know, doing amazing computer stuff. It's not like they're all skipping around in frilly dresses anymore."

"True," Clare admitted. "About the dresses, anyway. But have you seen the Barbie section at FAO Schwarz? Have you? And the baby-doll section? Pink still rules. There are still plenty of traditional girly things being pushed on kids."

"Well," Danielle said, "I, for one, don't see anything so wrong in that. I grew up with plenty of pink and I turned out just fine. And shut up, Gincy."

"Me! I didn't say anything!"

"You were going to."

"You really think you know me that well?"

"Yes, I do."

"There's a rock star named Pink," Clare said.

Danielle sniffed. "She's not the kind of pink I like."

"Russian stacking dolls," Clare said, suddenly. "A series of dolls within dolls."

"Who plays with them?" I asked. "I always thought they were, like, ornaments. Stuff you find in old lady houses. Old lady houses in Brighton Beach."

"Diaries that lock," Danielle said. "Electronic diaries that have, like, sirens if your little brother tries to open them without the password. I've seen them on TV."

"Do you remember your first suitcase?" Clare said suddenly, with the genius of someone gearing up for a major hangover.

I snorted.

"Suitcase? You mean, like, duffel bag? Backpack? We didn't really travel in my family. We piled in the rat-ass car and drove for an hour to AntLeg, New Hampshire. You don't need an actual suitcase to go to AntLeg, New Hampshire."

"Oh. Well, we used to go to Chicago. We have some relatives there. And the Upper Peninsula. I suppose you didn't need actual luggage for going to the lake house but . . ."

"Excuse me," I interrupted. "The lake house? You had a second house?"

Clare had the decency to blush. "It was no big deal," she protested. "Really. I mean, everyone we knew had a house on a lake. I mean . . ."

"Spare me."

"What color was it, anyway?" Danielle asked. "Your first suitcase."

"Blue. Kind of a dark baby blue. My parents had matching navy bags. I think it was an American Tourister set."

"I had a hatbox," Danielle said. "It was very impractical. Very chic but very impractical. Not that I cared about practicality."

"You still don't," I pointed out.

"My grandmother gave it to me. I loved it. It was pink patent leather. God, I wish I still had that hatbox. It would be perfect for storing some hair pieces."

"First makeup kits, first dress-up pocketbook . . ."

"So, what it's really about is stuff," I said with some distaste. "Girls have a lot of stuff. And they need places to put all their stuff."

Danielle considered. "Boys have a lot of stuff, too," she pointed out. "And men. Like tools and toolboxes and tool belts."

"I have a toolbox," Clare said brightly. "A shiny black one. The screwdriver's handle is fluorescent purple."

"I never thought I'd say this," I muttered, "but thank God for Win. He can use a screwdriver, right? Fix a broken toilet? Change a light bulb?"

"Briefcases," Clare went on, ignoring my rhetorical questions. "Both men and women have briefcases."

"And lunch boxes," Danielle said.

"Not my family. Tommy and I took our lunch to school in brown paper bags. They leaked. Especially, for some reason, when we had cream cheese and jelly. It didn't happen with peanut butter and jelly. Something about consistency, I suppose."

"Remember how exciting it was to open your lunch box even if you already knew what was inside?" Danielle sighed. "I miss being a kid. I just loved eating Twinkies."

"Twinkies?" I cried. "Gack. I preferred Suzy Qs. And, of course, Sno Balls."

"How could you?" Clare said with what sounded like genuine horror.

"What, like Suzy Qs are any worse than Twinkies? What did you eat for dessert?"

"Mostly, my mother baked. Sometimes she bought Little Debbies. It's a brand."

"What have you got against Hostess?"

"Nothing! I'm just telling you what we ate for dessert. We just ate what my mother told us to eat. I remember a little cake with caramel icing. Or maybe it was butterscotch. I remember the color distinctly. Whatever it was, I loved it."

"It's amazing what sticks with us, isn't it?" I remarked. "I mean, I can't remember major events, like grammar school graduation, but I can totally remember what the nerdiest kid in class wore every single day of school."

"Which was?" Danielle asked.

"A gray clip-on tie. Every single day, the same tie. Maybe he had an entire drawer full of them, I don't know. I can't remember my grandmother's face, and I loved my grandmother, but I can remember that tie. It was kind of shiny after a while. And it had a perfectly circular stain on the bottom left corner. Why do I remember that and not important stuff? What does that say about me?"

"What does it say about memory in general?" Clare wondered. "About history, about biography, about autobiography."

"What was the kid's name?" Danielle asked.

"I don't remember." I shrugged. "Tie Boy."

"I remember a boy who sat across from me in class, maybe in second or third grade," Clare said. "I don't remember his name or even what he looked like. But I remember there was always a huge plug of wax sticking out of his ear . . ."

"Oh, God," Danielle cried. "I'm going to be sick! Clare, how could you!"

"I know," she said, draining the last of her glass and smacking her lips. "It's a horrifying little detail to remember. I can still see, so clearly, the side of the boy's head and that dirty ear. Didn't his mother ever check him before he left for school in the morning? Didn't she ever make him bathe?"

"I wonder why the teacher didn't send a note home to his mother asking her to wash her kid!" I cried, remembering in a flash my own mother wielding a Q-tip with more determination than caution.

More lovely memories.

"Why is that awful memory still with me?" Clare went on. "What can it possibly mean to me now? I guess at the time it was kind of fascinating, in a gross sort of way. But why does my mind waste brain cells storing that bit of memory? Why can't I remember the French word for, say, shelf, but I can remember Ear Wax Boy?"

"It's only one of God's many sick jokes," I said.

"To remember things that horrify us and not edifying bits of information we learned in language class?"

Clare looked seriously distressed.

"Or pleasant memories," I continued. "Like a great afternoon of sleigh riding. Or the details of one of the books I loved as a kid. I remember certain titles and I know I loved the stories, but I can't remember exactly why I loved them. What kind of memory is that? It's like a black-and-white memory. Why can't we have memory in full color? Like the sunset? Look, isn't it amazing. And I guarantee that by tomorrow's sunset I won't remember the details of this one at all."

That melancholy observation put a temporary damper on our festivities. The damper was relieved when Young Male and Young Female got up to leave. Male put his massive arm around Female's teeny waist and unnecessarily guided her off the deck.

Danielle nodded in a manner she no doubt thought indicated wisdom. How many margaritas had she had?

"That guy? He's just like all the rest. All men are the same. And they're just completely the opposite of women. Venus and Mars. You just don't understand. Opposite ends of the pole. Men are idiots."

"There you go again," Clare scolded. "Generalizing. I don't think you should talk like that."

"Why not?" I challenged, as Danielle seemed inordinately interested in the bottom of her glass at the moment. "What Danielle's saying isn't hurting anyone. It's not like she's dictating behavior. She's just observing and commenting, that's all. That's her right as an American citizen."

"Things are never really opposites, you know," Clare went on, ever so patiently. "So-called opposites exist because of each other. Opposites define each other. Light is the opposite of dark because it's not dark . . ."

Danielle looked up from her glass, befuddled. "So everything is part of everything else? What?"

"God, we're boring!" I cried. Or seriously loaded. "How old are we anyway? Like, fifty?"

"Intelligence doesn't have anything to do with age," Clare said. "Necessarily."

"This conversation is about intelligence? What we're doing here while guzzling margaritas is being intelligent? Huh. I never would have known."

Danielle grinned. "You mean, you wouldn't recognize intelligence if it bit you in the ass."

"Of course not. Do I have eyes in back of my head? Now, if it bit me on the belly, I might have a chance. And I can't believe you said the word 'ass.' Ha! I'm rubbing off on you!"

"God forbid. Men don't like a woman with a foul mouth."

"That's absurd!"

Danielle preened. "Well, the kind of men I want to associate with don't like a woman with a foul mouth. Okay?"

I stuck out my tongue and ordered a final round. An hour later we stumbled back to the house and within minutes, though it was barely nine o'clock, the lights were off, Danielle was snoring, and Clare had disappeared into the second bedroom, mumbling something about Barbies and boobies.

It occurred to me later that night, as I lay on the couch, eyes wide, waiting for the room to stop spinning, that I'd never heard Rick use a four-letter word, much less a foul or rough or dirty word. I wondered if that was because of having a kid; maybe he'd just gotten out of the habit of cursing since Justin was born. Or maybe he never had been in the habit of using "bad" language.

Huh. Now that I thought about it, I'd never heard my father use a nasty word, either. That didn't mean he didn't curse with his buddies from work, but in the house, in front of the family, never.

Unlike my piggy brother, Tommy.

Unlike me.

Maybe you should work on the language thing, Gincy, I thought, just as the room stilled and I began to drift off to sleep. *Maybe guys like Rick don't marry gutter-mouths like you . . .*

I shot up and clutched my head.

Marry?

"Holy crap, Gincy," I whispered to the room. "You really have to watch those margaritas."

Clare

Mothers and the Daughters Who . . .

Mother called to announce that she was coming to Boston. Ordinarily, I enjoyed her visits. We'd shop and have lunch at fancy restaurants. Sometimes we'd just stay at the apartment, reading, sipping tea, and chatting about nothing in particular.

Our time together was always very pleasant.

But I knew this visit would be different. Now that I was about to become a married woman, Mother would be all business.

The lazy afternoons of fun were over. Now, there was work to be done.

As a precaution, I tucked my journal under the mattress where it would be safe from Mother's keen eyes. The only room Mother didn't enter, out of delicacy, she said, was our bedroom. I don't know what she expected to find going on in there.

And Win never did a bit of housework; he didn't need to tell me he thought it was woman's work. There was no chance he'd be changing the sheets any time soon.

After Mother had unpacked her bag and inspected the guest room for all amenities, she emerged with a look of determination I hadn't seen on her face since she chaired a big fund-raiser at Daddy's university.

"Clare," she said, "have you considered the vows?"

Her question startled me. Since the time I was a little girl first dreaming of her wedding day, I'd thought it would be nice to write my own vows. For my husband to write his.

But now, faced with the actual event, I wasn't so sure.

What, exactly, would I say about my feelings for Win? About why I was marrying him and no other?

My own words, spoken aloud to Win, in the hearing of friends and family. It seemed frighteningly intimate. Suddenly, I wasn't sure I wanted to do it. I wasn't sure I could.

"Uh—" I said.

"Well, I hope you'll be more eloquent than that," Mother replied, frowning.

Then she turned to Win. "Win, dear, what do you think about the vows?"

Win looked surprised. "Me? I don't care. Whatever Clare wants is fine by me."

And then he grinned his oh-so-charming grin. "But I have to warn you ladies. I didn't major in English."

"I think the standard vows of the Church are perfectly lovely," I said firmly, decision made. "We'll go with them."

Mother wasn't ready to let the subject rest. "Clare, honey, are you sure? Even as a little girl you used to talk about how romantic it would be to write your own wedding vows—"

"We'll go with the standard," I said hurriedly, scared I'd lose my nerve. "It'll be easier for Win."

Win chuckled. "Thanks, sweetie. I owe you one."

Mother gave me a searching look but moved on. "Clare, have you thought yet about music for the ceremony? You might want to work with the church's music director and meet with the choirmaster—"

"Win," I blurted. "Do you have a favorite hymn you want sung at the ceremony?"

Win looked up again from the computer screen and sighed good-naturedly.

"Look, sweetie, just tell me where to be and when to be there, okay? This shindig is yours. I'm just the guy in the black suit."

Mother seemed pleased by his answer and began to rattle off a list of musical pieces she considered suitable.

I nodded on cue but tuned out her words.

Danielle said it was wonderful, every bride's dream, for the groom to back off and let the bride have her way with the planning. I guess she had a point. I mean, I wouldn't want Win taking charge, which he tended to do with everything.

Still, his total lack of interest in the "project" made me feel alone. Like he thought the wedding was all for me when really, it hadn't even been my idea in the first place.

I watched Win squinting at the online news. I noted the perfect line of his hair against his neck. It struck me that I knew every inch of Win's body as well as I knew my own.

Of course Win thought I wanted a wedding.

Of course he thought I wanted to get married.

Because I hadn't told him otherwise.

Gincy
Who's Lying Now?

Danielle was decked out for the holiday. I mean, she was actually wearing a red, white, and blue outfit.

"You look like Shirley Temple in some World War Two propaganda film," I said as the ferry made its approach to the Vineyard.

It was a gorgeous day, boding well for a sun-filled weekend.

"Or whoever starred in those things. Don't you think you're being a little obvious?"

Danielle looked at me with disappointment. "That's the point, Virginia," she said. "And it's not like I'm wearing a cheesy T-shirt with a silkscreened flag across the back. I'm wearing a classic red, white, and navy ensemble. It's all Ralph Lauren, you know. Even the sandals. I think I look quite spiffy. Very nautical. Very appropriate for the ferry."

I shrugged. I didn't really care what Danielle wore. I just liked to pick on her. She was generally pretty unflappable.

"I can't believe Clare's staying in Boston this weekend," Danielle said suddenly. "It's, like, the official start of summer on the Vineyard! What is she thinking?"

Why did I feel the need to play devil's advocate?

I shrugged. "She's thinking she has a fiancé and they need to spend time together. It's perfectly normal."

"Well, she could have brought him out to the house. I wouldn't have minded."

"I'd have minded," I admitted. "It would have been weird having Win around. I think it would have put a cramp in my style."

Danielle lowered her aviator sunglasses and looked me up and down. From worn black T-shirt to torn jeans to ratty old Keds.

"I wasn't aware you had a style," she drawled. "Of any sort."

"Very funny. Come on. We're about to dock."

We gathered our bags and watched as the shore grew closer. And then, I spotted him. A guy on the dock, carrying an armload of wildflowers, and waving at us. Or . . .

"Danielle? Why is that guy waving at you? Wait. Is that Chris?"

"Oh, my God, it is!" she squealed, waving merrily back at him.

"Damn, he looks even hotter than the first time I saw him. I hope you appreciate what you have," I said to my preening companion.

"What?" Danielle was now studying her face in her compact mirror. "Oh, right. Yeah."

A few minutes later we stood with Chris by his truck.

"To what do I owe this pleasure?" Danielle cooed, clutching her bouquet.

Chris shrugged. "Well, I'm going to be tied up a lot this weekend but I wanted to see you, so . . . here I am."

I feigned a need for a pack of gum and left the two lovebirds alone. At the door of a tiny gift shop I turned and saw them embrace.

That's so not going to work, I thought. *Too bad.* They were both good people, just seriously mismatched.

Yeah, and I was a such a freakin' expert at love.

That evening before Danielle and I left for separate adventures, we spent some time hanging out in the tiny living room. She had put on a CD of some techno dance music stuff, which I loathed and despised but some counterimpulse made me keep my mouth shut about it.

I flipped through the latest issue of the *New Yorker* but not much more than the cartoons registered. I was thinking about the plans I'd made for the evening.

I'd arranged to meet a guy I'd spent some time with over the past visits to Oak Bluffs. He was a few years younger than me, African-American, and very good-looking. Better, he didn't seem to know about the good-looking part.

We'd have sex—of that I was sure—but we'd never make it as a couple. He was too sweet. Which was fine by me because I wasn't looking for a relationship.

I had a relationship back in Boston.

So, what the hell . . .

You might not want to overthink this, Gincy, I told myself, suddenly all uncomfortable.

Damn Rick! He was ruining my good time!

In a mood of defiance, I announced my plans for the night to Danielle.

"Hmmm," she said.

"Hmmm, what?"

"Nothing. Have a good time. Be careful."

"You're dying to say something else," I pressed.

Why? Did I really want to hear from Danielle what I'd already been telling myself?

Danielle sighed. "Fine. I think the only reason you're going out with Jason tonight is because you're afraid of commitment. You say that everything's good with Rick, so why are you bothering with a boy toy?"

And there it was.

"Me, afraid of commitment?" I cried. "What about you! Why are you going out with that Eurotrash guy tonight when you've got Chris, huh? He's gorgeous. He's sweet. What's not to like?"

"Mario is not Eurotrash," Danielle said. "He just dresses like Eurotrash. Besides, my situation with Chris is totally different from your situation with Rick."

"No it isn't! What's different about it?"

"For one, I haven't slept with Chris and you've slept with Rick."

"Well, jeez, what are you waiting for!"

"Excuse me if I don't just jump into bed with every guy I meet," Danielle said loftily.

"Are you implying that I do? Are you saying I'm a slut?"

"I'm not implying anything. Why would I imply? Besides, a guilty conscience needs no accuser."

"I don't have a guilty conscience!" I cried. "About anything. Rick and I never said we wouldn't date other people."

Danielle pinned me with her eyes. "I bet he isn't seeing anyone else. And not just because he has a child to care for."

Huh. I didn't think Rick was seeing anyone else.

I hoped he wasn't.

He had better not be!

"Well," I said weakly, "that's his problem."

"Besides," Danielle said, "Chris isn't a contender. He's not in the running."

"For what? Being chosen as one of your hapless male victims?"

Danielle looked daggers at me. She really was an incredible actress with her eyes.

Bravely, I persisted. "So you don't care if Chris is seeing someone else?"

"No."

"And you don't care if he knows you're seeing other people?"

Danielle's mouth opened and closed and opened. "I'm not talking to you anymore," she said finally.

"Fine, because I'm not talking to you, either. You know, I'm beginning to wish Clare were here, even if she had to drag Win along. She's like a buffer. You and I, we're just way too different to get along without that soft center. Our personalities are way too strong. And you can't bend."

"Why should I! Anyway, like you can bend?"

"I can bend. I just choose not to. About most things. And look! We're talking again!"

Danielle grinned. "Well, what can you expect from two big-mouths?"

She really was a good sport. Annoying, but a good sport.

"Well," she said then, "the truth is I really do wish Chris were around this weekend. Mario's insanely rich but he's just too oily to make it past this next date. Maybe one more after that."

"Bring the blotting paper."

"On another topic, I wonder when we're going to meet the elusive Win Carrington?"

"I don't know. And I don't care," I added truthfully.

"Doesn't it strike you as odd that Clare's never suggested we get together with them?"

"No. Anyway, he sounds like a drip."

"Why?" Danielle said. "Just because he's a corporate lawyer?"

"No. Do you think I'm an idiot? I'm not that addicted to stereotypes. It's just that Clare's marrying this guy, right? And she never lights up when she talks about him. Come to think of it, she never even smiles. And have you ever heard her go, 'Win's so great' or 'Win's so cute. Guess what Win did for me'? Have you?"

"Well, no," Danielle admitted. "But Clare's kind of shy."

"Uptight."

"Whatever. I don't think she's the type to gush. That doesn't mean Win's not worth gushing over."

"Speaking of gushing," I said, noting the dusty clock that hung over the stove, "it's almost seven o'clock. Shouldn't you be getting ready for your date with the oil slick?"

Gincy

Interruptus

Jason Davis was the kind of guy who probably had a good relationship with his mother.

The kind of guy who usually avoided sharp-mouthed types like me like the plague.

I'd met Jason a few weeks earlier at one of my favorite dives. His family owned a summer house in Oak Bluffs and a primary residence back in Newton. Jason worked in Boston as a financial analyst, so he didn't make it out to the Vineyard all that often. Apparently, crunching twenty-digit numbers requires far more than a forty-hour week.

Anyway, that night I joined him at a bar distinctly nicer than the dive at which we'd met, and after a few beers we headed for his family's house. He assured me that he was there alone that weekend. There'd be no awkward moments of our running into Mom and Dad in their bathrobes and slippers.

"Seriously nice house," I said, practically choking on my first-ever case of house envy.

"We've had it for years," Jason explained. "My dad's architecture firm did some major renovations recently. The back deck is new and the kitchen's been totally redone."

He showed me the kitchen. My mother, I thought, would pass

out if she saw this. A double oven. An indoor grill. A Sub-Zero refrigerator.

Oh, yeah. Mom would be on the floor. Drooling. And then condemning it all as wasteful. Sour grapes were my mother's favorite fruit.

There was no romance about the evening's tryst; just two consenting adults, two basically nice people out for some fun. We had another beer and Jason put on some CDs and before long, we were in his bed.

There were the usual preliminaries. And then the clothes all came off and I froze.

What the hell am I doing? I wondered, catching a glimpse of an unopened box of condoms on the massive antique dresser.

Damn. I just couldn't go through with it.

It was all Danielle's fault.

It was all Rick's fault.

It was all my fault that I was naked in Jason's bed.

"I can't do this," I muttered, extricating myself from his embrace. Jason was too deep into the moment to realize at first what was going on.

"Mmmm," he said.

"No, Jason," I said, speaking more loudly. "I mean it. I can't do this. I have to go."

Oh, my God, I thought, getting to my feet on the Oriental carpet. *I'm a tease! A classic cocktease!*

The fog had cleared from Jason's eyes. "I can't believe you're leaving!" he cried. "What's wrong?" He leapt from bed and I turned away from the sight of his erection.

"Nothing's wrong," I said, hurriedly yanking on my clothes. "I mean, nothing's wrong with you. It's me. It's just—"

"I thought we were getting along," he protested. "Did I say anything weird or something?"

Poor guy. He was the innocent victim in this. The innocent, seriously disappointed victim.

"No, no, no! Look," I said, grabbing my bag and retreating to the door of his room, "it's only ten o'clock. You can still go out and maybe meet someone—"

Jason's erection flopped as if it had been shot down. He reached for his boxers and slipped them on.

"What kind of person do you think I am?" he said, his voice thin. "I'm not some sort of slut, you know. I thought we were connecting. But I guess I was wrong."

Guilt swarmed over me like a horde of flies. I felt sick to my stomach. "I'm sorry. Really, I'm so sorry. I'll go now."

"That's a good idea," Jason said quietly. "Pull the front door tight when you leave. It tends to swell in the heat."

"Okay," I mumbled. And I got out of there fast.

Danielle
In Flagrante Delicto

I wondered if Gincy was having a good time with her hottie. *Everyone,* I thought ruefully, *is probably having a better time than me.*

Even though I'd just had a fabulous meal and excellent wine, all paid for by my handsome date, who had picked me up in his fabulous car.

Mario wasn't as horrid as Gincy assumed he was. I'd never have agreed to go out with him if he didn't have some good qualities.

If I can tolerate him for a few more dates, I thought, noting again the rather large diamond in Mario's gold pinkie ring, I just might get some jewelry out of my efforts.

Mario wasn't unattractive. And he was very clean. He smelled crisp.

I could have sex with him, I determined. It could be done.

Mario and I and one of his European friends, a short, balding man named Vinikourov, were standing outside the restaurant, chatting, Mario's arm around my waist, when it happened.

A black pickup truck rolled down the street, slowly, as if the driver was looking for an address.

Or as if the driver had seen someone he thought he knew?

Chris! I tried not to look directly at the truck as it passed us though I was suddenly desperate to know if he was behind the wheel.

Though the night was warm I pulled my wrap closer around my shoulders. Mario removed his arm from my waist and his friend lapsed into animated French.

I was left with my own thoughts, which weren't very pleasant. I felt horrible. I felt guilty.

Danielle, I scolded. *What's wrong with you? It's not as if you've been caught in a lie. You never promised anything to anyone!*

Oh, but I wanted to know!

Had it been Chris's truck? All trucks looked alike to me! And I hadn't bothered to learn Chris's license plate number. Why should I have?

Mario and his friend were deep in heated conversation now, about what I had no idea. Mario liked the sound of his own voice; I assumed we'd be standing on that sidewalk for some time.

Maybe, I thought, that truck will come around the block again. Maybe this time I'll see the driver. And maybe he'll really see me. Out on a Saturday night with another man.

And did I really, truly care?

I wondered.

Would I feel any more comfortable if my date were an average American guy and not a wealthy European visitor with his silk jacket and diamond pinkie ring and one hundred and fifty thousand dollar Ferrari?

And then I had a horrible realization.

I was actually ashamed of myself.

Not a lot, just a little bit, but even a little bit of shame was bad news.

I was ashamed of myself for going out with Chris.

I was ashamed of myself for hiding him from David.

For pushing him off when my friends wanted to chat that evening at Keith's.

I was ashamed of myself for choosing Mario.

For wanting to hide him from Chris.

I took a deep breath and tried to calm my thoughts. Get some perspective, Danielle, I urged. Forget this shame nonsense and let's look at things logically.

Fact: Chris and I had never talked about an exclusivity agreement.

Oh, but did that mean I could assume we had no responsibility toward one another?

Didn't the terms of decency dictate that I tell Chris I was dating other men?

Maybe Chris just assumed that I was seeing only him.

You know what they say about people who assume? They make an "ass" out of "u" and "me."

That was one of my father's standard lines. He said he got it from an episode of the old TV sitcom *The Odd Couple.*

While my wealthy date gesticulated and debated with his cohort, and couples strolled by enjoying the warm summer night, I thought about assumptions.

The act of making an ass of everyone around you.

Everybody assumed. Nobdy was immune from assuming.

Men assumed. They assumed that women dated only one man at a time.

And they assumed that men were free to date several women at a time.

At least until one of their buddies decided that it was time for everyone to settle down. Then each man weeded out the "women you had sex with" from "the women you married"—the assumed madonnas from the assumed whores—until finally, only one woman remained for each guy.

Assumed wife material.

The blare of a car horn roused me from my thoughts and I shot a look up and down the street. No black pickup truck.

Relief.

Because something told me that Chris wasn't a guy who dated several women at once. And the same something told me that he absolutely would not appreciate my seeing other men.

Especially men like Mario.

Of course, Danielle, I thought, *that's an assumption on your part.*

So there I was, making an ass out of us all, Chris, Mario, and myself.

But what did I really care about any of it? Mario was a passing fancy. And Chris was only a diversion.

He couldn't be anything but a diversion.

No matter how special he was.

"You want now to go to the club?" Mario asked, nuzzling my neck with his artfully stubbled face. I noticed that his chatty friend had gone.

"Sure," I answered distractedly. "Whatever."

Clare
Do As I Say

Mother left for Michigan after imparting several tidbits of unasked-for advice.

One concerned the July 4th holiday. I'd told her that I'd be spending it on the Vineyard with my new friends.

With a stern voice and a look to match, she argued that I should stay in Boston for the Fourth of July holiday and spend quality time with Win.

I thought of all the nice things I'd be missing—the beach, a parade, fireworks—and reluctantly agreed. Win worked hard for us. He deserved to spend the holiday with his future wife. Besides, there were plenty of events in the city we could enjoy.

So why did it feel as if I were making a huge sacrifice?

After dinner one evening, when Win had retired to his favorite armchair to enjoy a half hour of CNN before bed, I told him that I'd decided to stay with him in Boston for the holiday weekend.

I knelt by the chair and smiled up at my fiancé. I expected him to be thrilled. At least, grateful.

Did I expect to be rewarded, a dog at his knee?

"Oh, sweetie, that's so nice of you," he said, in that you-poor-thing, I-feel-so-sorry-for-you voice. "But I just assumed you were going off to the Vineyard. I've already made plans with some of the guys from the firm. We're going fly-fishing in upstate New York."

I was stunned. Win had never gone anywhere without me, except home to visit his family when his grandmother died and I was too sick with the flu to accompany him.

All I could say was, "Oh."

"I'm sorry, sweetie. But I really can't back out of these plans. We've already booked and I'd lose a good chunk of change. You understand, don't you?"

"Of course I understand," I told him. "You go and have a good time. I'll be fine."

"After all," he went on, his manner very earnest, "you do have the Oak Bluffs house and I haven't been able to get away at all since—"

"It's fine," I said, a bit sharply. "It's no problem. Really."

Win bent down and kissed my head. When he'd gone off to the bathroom, I wiped my hair where his lips had touched. And then was shocked at what I'd done.

I went directly to bed though I couldn't sleep for what seemed like an eternity. While I lay there next to Win, wide-eyed, it occurred that Win might be punishing me with this trip.

Or by telling me about it at the very last minute.

Or maybe Win was innocent of nasty intent and it was my own guilty conscience that made me feel as if I were being slapped for daring to carve out some personal space.

Win left the next morning at dawn. I pretended to be asleep so I wouldn't have to face the possibility of sex.

Or, maybe worse, of helping him pack, making him coffee, wishing him bon voyage with a sweet kiss.

Because every woman knows that a kiss is far more intimate than sex.

Clare

Declaration of Independence

As soon as Win was gone I got up and walked through the entire apartment as if it were a completely unfamiliar space.

Which in a way it was, without Win. Sure, he was gone every day for hours, but knowing that this time he'd be gone for days changed things.

It changed the way I saw everything.

In spite of spending so much time alone because of Win's devotion to work, I wasn't used to doing much on my own. Chores were one thing. But social activities—well, I usually opted to stay home rather than go to the movies or lunch by myself.

I don't know. Maybe spending time with Gincy and Danielle was changing me. Helping me to be more independent.

Because right there and then, alone in the vast apartment, I decided to spend the weekend in Boston instead of changing plans and joining my friends on the Vineyard.

And I would do fun things.

Like go to hear the Boston Pops's Fourth of July concert at the Hatch Shell on the Esplanade, even if going alone would be a bit scary.

The forecast told of heavy showers later in the afternoon so I loaded my backpack with an umbrella, a baseball cap, and a slicker.

I poured a bottle of white wine into a thermos and slid it down next to a turkey sandwich and an apple. Alcohol is illegal in the parks but this was a new Clare.

This was a Clare who took chances.

Besides, if I spotted a policeman I could discreetly pour the contents of the thermos into the grass.

The Pops were very popular. People staked out space early in the day for an early evening concert. People in need of lots of space, people with friends and family in tow.

Since I was going alone, I left the apartment around three and walked over to the Charles.

It was very hot and very humid and by the time I reached the Esplanade I was soaked through with sweat and very much in need of a cool glass of water.

Pushing my sunglasses up on my nose I looked around for a free inch of grass. There weren't many options. Finally, I thought I saw a small space near the middle of the field between a group of young married couples with babies and a group of middle-aged gay men.

Gingerly I made my way through the crowd, apologizing each time I stepped on an edge of blanket though no one seemed to care. When I reached the teeny square of grass, I spread out the old picnic sheet and got settled.

You're on an adventure, Clare, I thought, noting a black bank of thunderclouds over the water to my left. It might not be a long-lived adventure but at least you're on one.

"Hey."

I looked up and around. "Oh, hi," I said when I caught sight of a young guy standing almost directly over me to my left. He was smiling as if we were old friends.

"Crowded, huh?" he said.

I smiled back. "Yeah."

"Um, do you mind—I mean, do you think I could—"

The guy pointed to a beach towel folded under his other arm.

"Oh. Sure." I gathered up one side of my sheet to make room for him.

"Thanks," he said when he was settled. "I was beginning to think I'd have to stand all the way in the back."

"You like the Pops?" I asked politely.

He was younger than me. Unruly dark hair. Big dark eyes. Slim. His T-shirt read "Life is good"; he wore a pair of baggy cargo shorts.

The guy shrugged. "They're okay. Not really my kind of music. But I love the crowds, all mellowing, having a good time. And I love being outdoors. Nothing better."

"Me, too," I said. "Love the outdoors, I mean. I'm from Michigan. I kind of grew up outdoors."

The guy extended his hand. I noted he wore a silver ring with some scrolling I couldn't interpret. "My name is Finn, by the way."

I took his offered hand. "Clare."

"Hey, Clare. So what are you doing in the city. Visiting?"

"No. No I live here. I moved here with—"

I stopped cold. An adventure. I could have an adventure.

I could be a completely different person, even if only for an afternoon.

Clare the Wild and Uninhibited.

Wearing an engagement ring.

Had he noticed? Did it matter?

"I came here with my college roommate after graduation," I lied. "I guess I just stayed. I don't know."

Finn laughed. "Yeah, sometimes it feels like life just happens. I'm here for a reason, though. I'm at Berklee, studying jazz."

A musician! I'd never met a real musician before. I mean, except for the music director at York, Braddock and Roget.

"What do you play?" I asked.

Finn shrugged. "A little guitar, a little bass, and a lot of sax."

I jumped as a crack of thunder exploded and the crowd around us ooohed and shrieked with anticipation.

"Here she comes!" a woman near us cried.

"Look!" Finn said. "The hair on my arms always stands up in a storm. Cool, isn't it? It's like, every nerve goes live."

"Oh," I said eloquently. "Yeah. But shouldn't we, I don't know, leave? It might be dangerous, especially if there's lightning."

Finn grinned. "No way. We're safe enough here. Hey, I'll move onto your sheet and we'll use this towel as cover. We'll watch the show! Celebrate our independence from the tyranny of Mother Nature!"

And we did. Keith Lockhart and his orchestra played valiantly through the short-lived storm and the lingering drizzle afterward. The crows had thinned but only slightly. The mood was joyous.

Everyone is on an adventure today, I told myself, sitting close enough to Finn to brush arms when one of us lifted a cup of wine or shifted for comfort.

Finally came the 1812 Overture and fireworks display. It was moving in the way that spectacle always is. For some.

My father scoffed at spectacle and called it just another opiate of the people.

When the show was over I felt the inevitable letdown, the adrenaline hangover, that awful deflation of spirits that makes you wonder if the excitement was worth it all in the first place.

"So," I said, suddenly unwilling to let my adventure end.

Finn rocked on his heels. "So."

"Do you have to be anywhere?" I blurted, standing up to face him.

Back to the ordinary world tomorrow. Back to the daily sameness.

The calm after the storm.

"No," he said.

With my thumb I twisted my engagement ring so that the massive stones were hidden in my palm.

"Do you want to get a drink or something?" I asked.

Clare the Bold and Free.

Finn's eyes burned into mine. I hadn't seen that look since the very early days with Win.

It was the look of desire.

"A drink sounds good," he said. "But the 'or something' sounds better."

"Or something," I mumbled inanely.

Finn took my face in his hands and we kissed. He was the one who finally pulled away. I felt dizzy.

"Do you want to go back to my place?" he said, wiping stray raindrops from my cheek with his thumb.

He smelled so good, his hands were slim and beautiful, his stomach hard and flat.

"I'm alone for a few days. My roommate went home for the holiday."

I wondered if my nerve would hold out on the way to Finn's apartment.

There was only one way to find out.

"Okay," I said. "Yes."

Gincy

Last-Ditch Effort

Don't ask me why I answered a personal ad.

Okay. I'll tell you why.

I was a glutton for punishment. That was one of my father's favorite phrases.

The older I got the more I found myself ordering the world in terms of my father. Or ordering the world in my father's terms?

It was both amusing and slightly disturbing. Was I more of a Gannon than I'd realized?

Anyway, after the disaster that was the night with Jason I should simply have given up other men and concentrated on my relationship with Rick.

I should have done the right thing.

But no. That would have been too mature.

And I was so not ready to be mature.

I didn't tell Sally or Danielle or Clare what I had in mind, which was probably a clue that I shouldn't have been doing it in the first place.

I'd learned early on that, generally speaking, secrecy was not a healthy thing.

Another confession: I hadn't told Danielle the truth about the outcome of my rendezvous with Jason. I hadn't exactly lied about it either but I'd left the night open to interpretation.

Another not-so-mature decision on my part.

But back to me and the second disastrous date of the summer.

The basic idea wasn't all bad. I mean, I know lots of people have successfully hooked up through personals and dating services and sponsored singles events.

I just really should have known that I wasn't the type with that kind of luck. I really should have.

But in the words of my father, you live and learn.

Not that he seemed to have learned all that much in his fifty-eight years. Probably because he hadn't really lived all that much. I knew for a fact that he'd never traveled farther than two hundred miles from BadgerPellet, New Hampshire.

Unlike his utterly urban and urbane daughter.

The mature one. The one going on a blind date when she had a perfectly great guy already.

I'd suggested to Rob, the guy who'd placed the ad, that we meet at the bar at Joe's American. Witnesses and all.

Though on paper the guy sounded pretty harmless, you never could tell. He'd listed his occupation as assistant marketing director. Of what, he didn't say. He also claimed to be thirty-two and a graduate of Brown. Whatever.

Where a person went to college didn't impress me. It was what he'd done with his life since graduation that impressed or depressed me.

At five minutes after seven a tall, very thin, almost pretty guy came in and after a quick glance around the bar, made a beeline for me.

"Gincy?"

"Rob?"

You can't be Rob, I thought. *You're, like, twelve! Well,* I thought, *I'll give him the benefit of the doubt. Some people just don't show their age.*

"Yeah. Hi. Thanks for coming out."

What was I, his audience? But all I said was, "Yeah."

Rob settled on the barstool to my left and ordered a light beer. He seemed nervous. Was I that intimidating?

Okay, my nose was peeling from that sun-sun-sun–filled week-end on the beach, but what was a little flaking skin? It hadn't seemed to bother Jason.

My running out on him at the last minute had bothered him, but not my flaky skin.

"So," he said abruptly, "I have a confession to make."

Another one? Contrary to the information contained in his ad, I was now convinced this kid was no more than twenty-two.

"Yes?" I said sweetly.

"Well, you know how people can be, right?" he said earnestly. "Discriminating. Judgmental."

"Mmm."

Oh, I wasn't going to give this kid an inch.

"Well, okay, so in my ad I said I was an assistant marketing director, right? Well, I'm not. Actually."

"Oh?" I said, taking a swig of my own beer. "And what are you? Actually?"

Besides a pathetic fool.

"Actually," Rob explained, leaning in toward me and lowering his voice, "I'm a Cher impersonator. I know it's not a traditional career choice, but I love what I do and it pays pretty well. Mostly. Well, the tips can be good."

What about health insurance, I wondered. *What if you fall off your stilettos and break your neck?*

I declined to ask.

Instead, I said, "So, are you gay?"

The kid blushed. Blushed! I hadn't blushed since I was—

Well, maybe I'd never blushed.

"No way," he protested. "I mean, a lot of impersonators are, so I can see why you'd ask, but I like girls."

"Enough to make a career out of lampooning them."

The kid looked utterly confused.

Ah. A new word for his vocabulary.

"And I'm missing a rerun of *Friends* for you," I muttered.

"Why are you so hostile?" Rob shot back. "I thought someone who looks like you would be more open."

Now who was being judgmental?

"Well," I responded, "let's see if I can put this so that you'll understand. You. Lied. To. Me. And I don't like liars."

"Hey, it's just—"

"It's just nothing." I grabbed the check off the bar. "You can go now. After you pay for your drink. Six dollars, with tip."

Rob tossed a five and a one onto the bar and, looking highly offended—and on the verge of tears—ran from the bar.

If I could turn back time . . .

What would the real Cher have done to this kid, I wondered.

I finished my beer in one long draw and gestured for another.

The bartender, a plump chick with a mop of red hair, served me with a scowl. "You were a little harsh with him," she said. "He seemed very sensitive."

Yeah. As sensitive as my alcoholic uncle's pickled liver.

"Oh, so you're paid to eavesdrop?"

"I'm just saying—"

"And I'm just saying it's none of your business. Besides," I added in a sudden burst of lunacy, "I only go out with men to mock them. I'm a mocker. It's what I do. And by the way, I guess you won't be needing your tip."

Miss Nosy took her chubby, interfering self off to the other end of the bar with a huff and I finished my drink in relative peace.

Once outside, I was hit with a big and despairing sense of loneliness. I felt like I'd been sucker punched in the gut. In my heart's gut.

It made sense at the time.

Anyway, it was only eight-thirty. I didn't want to go home yet, all alone.

Poor me.

Rick, I thought. *I'll call Rick!*

But as soon as the thought occurred, another one pushed it aside.

Rick can't come out to play at any old time, Gincy. He's got Justin.

And that was the thing.

Rick wouldn't—couldn't—always be there when I called. No matter how much he might like me.

That sort of thing—someone you could call on at any time—had never mattered to me before.

What the hell was happening?

Commitment was not something I'd ever pursued and it wasn't something I was supposed to be pursuing this summer.

The summer before I turned thirty.

The summer before I stepped over the hill.

Clare

Sex, Lies, and Observations

Gincy called at about eight forty-five and asked if I could meet her for a drink.

Win wasn't home yet—he'd called to say he was staying late to deal with some work that had piled up while he was on his fishing trip—and I didn't have anything in particular to do, so I said yes.

Besides, since the night with Finn, I'd felt oddly uncomfortable in my own home. Almost as if I had no right to be there.

And maybe I didn't.

I got to Flash's a half hour later and met Danielle in the vestibule, also just arriving.

"Did she tell you why she wants to see us?" she asked, a woman on a mission.

I shrugged. "No idea."

Together we went inside and found Gincy slumped in one of the comfy chairs by the window facing onto Stuart Street.

"Hey," she said, almost sheepishly. "Thanks for coming."

"It's no problem," I said, thinking of how I'd dragged her to that perfectly lovely, perfectly awful baby shower.

If Gincy needed help, I owed her.

We sat and gave our drink orders to the waiter. When he'd gone, Danielle folded her hands in her lap, all business.

"Spill," she commanded.

So Gincy told us about Rob, her blind date, the Cher impersonator.

"I can't believe you went on a blind date!" Danielle hissed. "I can't believe you didn't tell us what you were up to! Do you know how dangerous that could have been? What if the guy was a rapist or something!"

"I can't believe I told you even after the fact," Gincy muttered. "What's happening to me?"

"What's happening," Danielle went on, "is that you're learning—slowly—to trust us. We're all becoming friends. Isn't it great?"

Gincy groaned but Danielle was undeterred.

"Well, I think it's great. And don't you feel better for confessing?"

"It wasn't a confession!" Gincy protested. "I didn't do anything wrong! If I'd committed a crime do you think I would have told you?"

Danielle shook her head. "I think maybe you would have. Say, if you cheated on a guy you were committed to. I think it would feel good to get such an awful burden off your chest. Get some perspective. You know."

"Uh," Gincy said, looking absolutely miserable, "speaking of awful burdens, there's something else. I didn't exactly tell the truth about what happened with that guy Jason."

Danielle gasped and quickly filled me in.

"So, what did happen that night?" Danielle then demanded.

"Nothing. I couldn't have sex with him. It felt too weird. I kept thinking about Rick and I felt all guilty. So I just left. You know, in the middle of things. I'm not such a horrible person after all, right? At least, in terms of Rick. I'm pretty sure Jason thinks I'm scum."

Danielle beamed. "I am so proud of you! Aren't you proud of Gincy, Clare? You kept your promise to Rick."

"We don't have a promise," Gincy protested, but weakly.

Danielle continued to chatter on about Gincy's moral courage. I feigned great interest in my colorful drink, hoping to hide the guilt I knew was all over my face.

Gincy might have been a heroine, but I'd done something terribly wrong. I'd cheated on the man I was bound to marry. A man who, as far as I knew, had never cheated on me.

Oh, how I wished that Win was having an affair! That he was staying late at the office three or four nights a week because he was cheating on me with his secretary or that sexy woman in the office down the hall from his. Macey something.

It would all be so easy then. I could break up with Win, call off the wedding, and feel justified in the process.

I'd be the injured woman, not the adulterous fiancée.

I wouldn't have to continue this excruciating examination of myself.

All by myself.

I knew friends were supposed to tell each other everything. I knew they weren't supposed to be afraid of being judged or ridiculed.

Still, I couldn't bring myself to tell Gincy or Danielle what had happened on July 4th. I was just too ashamed to reveal such moral weakness to people I'd known for so short a time.

Maybe if we'd been friends since childhood . . .

But I doubt even then I'd have had the courage to admit such frailty.

Wellmans weren't in the habit of revealing weakneses.

Better to live all alone with your wrongdoing, I told myself, than to confess it to anyone. Even to your journal. And especially to the one you hurt most.

Win.

Oh, I had cheated on him so casually!

What could Win ever do to me that would be as bad as what I had done to him?

God, a one-night stand. I deserved the awful burden of a secret infidelity.

Why, why had I gone home with Finn, a total stranger?

Temporary insanity.

Sexual frustration.

Boredom?

Whatever the reason, the reality was that what had happened between Finn and I was too wonderful to remember with blushing.

The abandon. The passion. My frenzied need for Finn's boyish body . . .

"Clare," Gincy said, and I startled. "You're just sitting there like a bump on a log. Are you okay?"

"Fine." I tried to smile. "I'm fine. Just a lot on my mind."

Danielle nodded wisely. "Of course. The wedding. Every bride-to-be gets totally distracted the closer she gets to the big day. By the night before, you won't even know who you are!"

My feeble smile died.

Great.

The last thing I needed was a more serious identity crisis than the one already plaguing me.

Gincy
If the Truth Were any Bigger

You had a summer house, you had guests.

It was an unwritten rule but a rule all the same.

Interestingly, Clare had yet to bring Win to the Vineyard. The fiance remained a mystery, which was fine with me.

Danielle had brought her brother and his ditzy fiancée, Roberta. She'd been good for a sick sort of laugh but by the end of the weekend, even Danielle had seemed glad to see her go.

Now it was my turn. Danielle and Clare were spending the weekend in Boston running wedding-related chores, which left the Vineyard house all to me.

Briefly, I'd considered asking Rick to come out with me but I shied away from the idea. An entire weekend alone together was big.

Plus, there was the issue of Justin. Would Rick insist he come along? And if so, would Rick be sleeping in the second bedroom with his son and not with me?

Besides, I hadn't even met the kid yet.

And that was a potentially major trauma.

See, I'd never met a kid I really liked. Or maybe it was that any kid I'd ever met hadn't liked me, so I'd responded in kind.

Finally, it seemed much simpler to avoid the Rick and Justin issue and invite Sally to the Vineyard.

It's not that I was dying to spend the weekend alone with Sally. It was that she left me little choice. She was the queen of unsubtle hints.

Still, she feigned enormous surprise when I finally offered the invitation.

"Yeah, you can close your mouth now," I said dryly. "Just be on time and bring your own towels. Danielle will kill me if she finds out anyone's used hers. She's very sensitive about her stuff."

"Since when do you care about other people's feelings?" Sally shot back.

I wasn't quite sure how to answer.

Early that Friday afternoon we settled on the ferry's open deck. The sun was hot but the humidity was low. My mood was good.

"Look, just so you know," I told Sally, face turned up to the sun, "I'm not going to cramp your style. If you meet someone and you want to bring her back to the house, fine by me. Just keep the noise to a minimum."

"No," Sally said quickly, "that's okay. I'm in a celibate phase right now. I'm centering and cleansing."

I looked at her closely. "What, are you into yoga now? Some bizarre Eastern feel-good practice? Are you going to be eating seaweed all weekend? Drinking some brown mess?"

"It's nothing so formal," she replied, suddenly intent upon the star tattoo on the back of her left hand. "It's just something I'm going through."

"Yeah. Whatever. But just so you know, I'm scattering and getting dirty."

Okay. It wasn't exactly the truth but I enjoyed teasing Sally. "So I might meet someone and—"

Sally's face took on a greenish cast.

"You're not going to hurl, are you?" I said, scooting away.

"No!" she protested.

Warily, I scooted back.

"Then, what? I thought you'd be thrilled to learn I'm not get-ting serious with Mr. Corporate Scum."

Another lie.

By the way, Sally was the only one in our office I'd told about my dates with Rick. No details, just that we were dating.

"Of course I am," Sally shot back. "He's so not right for you. What I meant was . . . It's just, don't you think you should—"

"What? Be careful? Of course I'm careful. I'm not a moron."

Sally clutched her pink hair in frustration. "I didn't say you were a moron! God, Gincy—"

"Look, chill, okay? 'Cause if you don't I'm gonna toss you overboard and you can swim back to Boston."

I waited for it.

Finally, Sally laughed. "You wouldn't dare."

"Try me." I patted her leg as if to belie my threat. "Go get us some sodas? I'll save the seats."

"You're paying, right?" Sally asked. "You make more money than I do."

With a phony grumble I handed her a five-dollar bill. "Keep the change," I called as she walked off. "You might want to get yet another piercing. Like, in your brain."

Clare
Kicking and Screaming

Danielle met me at the loft that rainy Saturday morning. "It's a perfect day for the mall," she pronounced as she strode through the door in a shiny red slicker and matching boots. "We won't feel like we're missing anything on the Vineyard."

"Do I really need to do this?" I asked, wondering if it was too late to feign a debilitating headache.

Danielle put her well-manicured hands to her head. "For the last time, yes, you do need to do this. What is your big problem with registering, anyway?"

The real problem is that I don't want to get married.

"Well," I said, "I guess I'm embarrassed about asking people to buy me things. I mean, particular things. It seems so selfish."

Danielle sighed magnificently. "Honey," she said, "let me explain to you the joys and convenience of a wedding registry. One: Everyone expects you to register and you can't let everyone down can you?"

"I—"

Danielle went on. "And everyone expects you to register at some high-end shops, like Tiffany, for all sorts of outrageously expensive gifts you can't possibly afford. That's the fun part. You get to go on a fantasy shopping spree and someone else has to pay the bill. Are you following?"

Not really.

"Yes," I said.

"Good. Now, everyone also expects you to register at places like Williams-Sonoma and Crate and Barrel for everyday items. Once you're in their systems, relatives and friends all across the country—with all sorts of budgets—can go into any store location, call up your registry, see what hasn't yet been bought, and make a purchase. Do you see the beauty of this?"

I nodded. Did it really matter what I saw or didn't see?

"Believe it, Clare," Danielle went on. "In the long run, you're doing your guests a favor by registering. You're saving them the trouble of having to think. Nobody likes to think when they don't have to. Am I right?"

"I guess," I mumbled.

Just then I heard the bedroom door open. A moment later, Win shuffled through the hall to the bathroom. Thank God he was wearing his robe.

Danielle peered after him, then turned back to me with a grin. "So, can I meet him?"

"Uh, now's not a good time," I said. "Win's not a morning person and he hasn't had his coffee yet and—"

"I get it, I get it. Some other time." Suddenly, Danielle grabbed my arm. "Wait a minute. Win's not getting involved with the registry, is he?"

"No," I admitted. "I asked him to but he said it was girl stuff. I told him I've seen lots of couples registering together but he wouldn't budge."

"Well, thank God! Trust me, he'd only be in the way. Now, do you have the bottles of Evian I told you to pack? Good. Registering is thirsty work. And wear comfortable shoes. We'll be doing a lot of walking. Oh—have you thought about stationery? I'd suggest Crane's. We'll make that our first stop."

So, we set out. The reluctant bride and her super-wanna-be-a-bride assistant.

Crate and Barrel. Williams-Sonoma. Victoria's Secret. That was so Danielle could make suggestions about my wedding-night attire.

"I don't feel comfortable in this sort of thing," I whispered, embarrassed by the lacy white ensemble she'd chosen as sure to drive Win wild.

A wild Win was a person I had never met.

"It's not about feeling comfortable," she said. "Anyway, it will be off before you know it so—"

"I'll think about it," I lied. "Can we leave now?"

Next stop was Tiffany.

"Why here?" I asked when we were just inside and past the security guard. "I mean, exactly?"

Danielle regarded me like a mother short on patience might regard her deliberately slow four-year-old. "Because," she said evenly, "you need to consider crystal. Follow me. It's in the back."

"Why?" I asked, trotting after her.

The store made me uncomfortable. Everything was so hushed. And there was that guard at the door. His presence made me feel guilty in general.

"I don't really like crystal."

Danielle came to an abrupt halt and turned to me. Now her look was one of extreme exasperation.

"You have to have crystal," she said. "You're getting married. Doesn't your mother have crystal?"

"Yes," I said. "If you mean vases. She has a few crystal vases. And bowls."

"Well?" Danielle said, as if her point was self-evident.

It wasn't to me. But what did I know about anything?

"Okay. I'll think about crystal. Um—what am I supposed to think about it for?"

Danielle put her hand to her temple.

"Do you have a headache?" I asked innocently.

"All I'm saying is thank God I'm a patient person."

After storming the gift department—crystal, silver, and china—Danielle suggested we take a break. I readily agreed. We got two iced coffees and sat on one of the many wooden benches that line the halls of the mall.

"I guess it's dumb of me to think you've considered any of the details," she said after gulping half of her drink.

I looked at her blankly. Crystal wasn't a detail?

Danielle sighed, opened her ever-present notebook, and began to scribble.

"Bubbles, how many dispensers to a box; giveaways for the wedding guests, think seed packets or mini-picture frames, Lenox or silver plate; disposable cameras on each table. Maybe. I'm not a huge fan. Too many chances for unflattering photos of the bride. And speaking of photos, I'm assuming you never had a formal engagement picture taken but it's not too late you know. I'll just go ahead and make an appointment . . ."

Danielle worked on.

I let my mind drift to memories of that one incredible night with Finn.

I'd vowed never to see him again and I would keep that vow. But I couldn't promise myself not to remember.

Gincy
Rug Rat

The weekend on the Vineyard with Sally was pretty fun. We hung around on the beach and ate nachos and drank beer and made fun of people who looked even worse than we did in shorts.

One night I flirted with a jerk in a bar and then, just when he was sure he was going to score, I told him sweetly that I was hooked up with the massive bouncer. He stalked off, furiously thwarted.

I thought it was pretty amusing, if a little infantile of me. Sally didn't get as much of a kick out of the game as I did, but, whatever. I encouraged her to flirt a little, too, but she reminded me of her period of centering and cleansing.

By the time we were back on the ferry Sunday evening, both of us a few pounds heavier and very relaxed, I was kind of sorry to be heading home.

"We should do this again sometime," I told Sally as we watched the Vineyard fade from view.

"You mean it?" she asked.

"Yeah. I had a good time. Why, didn't you?"

Sally shrugged. "Yeah, it was okay. Just give me some advance notice. You know. So I can plan."

"Right. Because your social schedule is so full," I joked.

Sally just smiled.

The next morning, as I was checking e-mail at my desk, Kell popped in.

"What's up?" I asked, eyes still focused on the computer screen.

"Rick's got his little boy in the office today. He's a cute kid. If you have some time, maybe you could entertain him a bit. We're all going to take turns so Rick can get some work done."

"Sure, sure," I mumbled, typing madly. Kell left and I let the panic overtake me.

Jesus, I thought, *I can't meet the kid! Where can I hide—*

"Gincy!" And there was Rick, standing at the door to my office with a kid.

His kid.

Who looked like Rick's Mini-Me. Some odd little being who had sprouted from Rick's forehead without the benefit of another set of DNA.

"Er," he said, "I want you to meet Justin. His sitter is sick so he'll be spending the day with me. Here. In the office."

I came around to the front of the desk, every step an effort.

The kid stared up at me with a look of such intense concentration on his face I assumed a pimple the size of Seattle had just appeared on my chin.

"What?" I said.

"You look like my teacher."

"I do?"

"Yeah. His name is Mr. Randall. He's old."

You know what W.C. Fields said about kids? A lot. None of it good.

Here's my favorite: "I like children—fried."

Rick opened his mouth but nothing came out.

"Uh," I said, "that's nice. I guess."

Justin nodded. "Yeah. He's pretty cool. He has a pet rat."

"White or gray?"

"White. You should have seen when it almost got eaten by a snake."

"Yeah, that's great, kid. Great. Uh, Justin. How about we—"

What, Gincy? Go Xerox our butts? What did you do with a five-year-old, anyway?

I shot a panicked look at Rick. He looked blankly back. Did he expect me to baby-sit the kid all day? I had a job to do . . .

Then Rick's brain kicked in. "Justin, why don't we go back to my office. Gincy's got a lot of work to do."

"Dad," Justin said solemnly, "your office is kind of boring."

"Well, that's because it's an office. It's supposed to be boring."

"Why?"

"I don't know. It just is, I guess."

Justin looked up at his father with a look that said, "Come on, Dad. You can do better than that."

At least that's what I read the look to mean.

But Rick just looked puzzled.

"Gincy's got a rubber-band ball on her desk," Justin pointed out.

Observant kid. It was almost hidden behind a tilting pile of loose papers and industry magazines.

Rick shrugged. "What's not boring about a rubber-band ball?"

Oh, come on! Had Rick never been a kid? His poor son was doomed.

"Are you kidding?" I said. "Do you know what you can do with a rubber-band ball? Come on, Justin. You can hang with me while Rick—your dad goes back to his boring office."

From the look on Rick's face you'd think I'd just done something highly noble.

"Are you sure it's all right? I mean—"

"Yeah, yeah, it's fine. Now go. We'll be fine. Right, Justin?"

"Yeah, Dad. You can go now."

Rick hesitated. I made a shooing gesture with my hand and he turned to leave. At the doorway he tripped. Justin gave me a little smile that revealed genuine fondness for his goofy dad.

"So," I said when the other adult was gone.

"So," Justin repeated.

"So, I'm going to get back to work here. You can, you know, hang with the rubber-band ball. I've got some markers, too. And some paper. You know."

Justin reached for the ball and settled himself on the floor. "You can go back to work now," he said calmly.

I did. And I got a lot done. Every so often I'd remember there was a five-year-old on my floor and shoot a glance his way.

Each time, I found Justin absorbed in some task that involved his poking at the rubber-band ball with his forefinger, a deep frown of concentration on his face.

As long as he wasn't tearing apart any important documents he could spend the entire day with the silly thing for all I cared.

And then at one point I sensed someone else in the room. I looked up from the computer to find Sally standing in the doorway.

She was scowling but Sally was often scowling.

"Hey," I called. "Come in and—"

Sally shot a look of pure loathing at Justin and walked away.

Okay. Clearly, Sally still had something against Rick and now, not only against Rick but also against his son.

Was it all about their being male? Who knew.

Male was a good thing in my book. With a few notable exceptions, starting with my brother.

Men. Sex.

Thoughts of me and Rick in bed began to flash through my head as I watched Justin futilely try to count the top layer of rubber bands on the ball. I tried to stop the lascivious images but the harder I tried the more they bombarded.

What kind of lowlife was I to be thinking about sex with a little kid in the room?

Here's what I was thinking about most: How Rick's clumsiness totally vanished in bed. He was sure and strong and gentle in all the right ways and places. Amazing. Rick's sexual prowess was a well-kept secret.

Suddenly, I was aware that Justin was staring at me.

"What?" I said guiltily.

"You have a funny look on your face. Are you sick?"

"Uh, no. I'm fine. You okay?"

"Yeah. I lost count though."

"I have an idea," I said. "Why don't you start your own rubber band ball? Look, I've got a whole box of rubber bands here. Different colors, too."

"I don't know how to start," he said, taking the box from me.

"I'll show you. It's easy. Just watch and listen."

"Okay. But sometimes I'm not a very good listener. I'm smart but I don't listen."

I looked at the kid with a frown. "Who says you don't listen good? Well? Who says you aren't a good listener?"

Justin shrugged. "Mr. Randall. And my dad. It's okay. It's no big deal. My dad says he was the same way when he was my age."

I could see little Rick in my head as clearly as if he were sitting cross-legged on my office carpet. The image made me smile.

"My dad's pretty clumsy, isn't he?" Justin said suddenly, looking right up at me.

Was the kid testing me?

Had he been reading my mind?

"Uh," I said brilliantly, "I guess."

"He broke my dump truck the other day, on accident. He stepped on it."

"Oh."

I began to sweat. Like, serious wetness under my arms.

Justin shrugged. "That's okay. I love him, anyway."

"That's good," I breathed. "That you love your dad."

Justin spilled open the box of rubber bands I'd given him. "Yeah," he mumbled, already busy at work.

You know, I thought, noting the boy's hair was the exact same color as Rick's, *if Justin could retain his beguiling honesty, he'll be one hell of a catch someday.*

Like his father?

Clare

She Wants To Be Alone

I threw out my journal.

First, I ripped out all the pages, even the still-blank ones, and tore them into tiny pieces. I put the pieces in a paper bag and the paper bag in a plastic bag and put the entire mess into the kitchen trash, on top of which I added the morning's coffee grounds and orange peels.

I couldn't bear to see my pain and confusion in writing. Bad enough my mind was plagued by doubts and worries and random flashes of anger at no one.

At everyone.

And what if Win had found the journal? What if he'd read all those damning, revelatory words?

Words I wanted to say to him but couldn't.

Words like: "I'm so sad. You don't understand me."

Seven words—with contractions—seven simple words that told a story eleven years in the making.

Seven nonargumentative words.

Just words that stated an unhappy fact.

I am so sad. You don't understand me.

I am so sad because you don't understand me.

I am so sad because I have finally come to see that you don't understand me.

I was so sad. Angry, yes, and hurt, but mostly, just sad.

You can get over anger, direct it somewhere out of yourself; it can even be cathartic.

Hurt, too, can be mended; the pain can be ameliorated and time almost always aids in the healing process.

But sadness is different. It doesn't seem to ever go away; it rests deep inside.

Sadness is profound disappointment. Once you've been made sad by someone, once you've been disappointed by someone—say, by the failure of someone who claims to love you to truly understand you—that's it, hope is quite suddenly dead and the world an entirely new and puzzling place.

Everywhere I went the words were a mantra in my head. I walked to their beat, breathed to their rhythm, let their import color every person I passed. Their power was in the car horns honking and their finality was in the litter fluttering across the sidewalk and into the gutter.

I was so sad.

A city is not a good place in which to be sad.

I went home one afternoon midweek and packed. Then I called Win at the office and left a message on his voice mail telling him I was going to the Vineyard.

Clare
Static

It was nice being at the house alone.

It was peaceful.

No one stealing my yogurts. No TV blaring. No one hogging the bathroom.

For a day and a half I came and went as I pleased.

I had a bedroom all to myself, a luxury I hadn't experienced since high school. In college I'd had a roommate and when I wasn't sharing a bedroom with her, I was sharing a bed with Win.

I took long walks on the beach, collected pretty shells, and tossed them back in the ocean before heading home.

I read a novelization of the life of Eleanor of Aquitaine and counted my good fortune in having been born in the twentieth century.

I gazed at the stars. I thought. I was quiet.

In that day and a half I spoke to no one, not even a store clerk. The solitude was restorative.

But it wasn't to last.

When the phone rang one morning at eight-thirty, the last person I expected to hear on the other end of the line was Win's mother.

The formidable Mrs. Matilda Carrington.

"Hello, Clare," she chirped. "Did I wake you?"

"Oh, no," I said.

I'd been up since six. Sleep hadn't come easily since the engagement.

"How are you, Mrs. Carrington?"

"Well, I'm just fine dear. But what about you? Win told me you're all alone out there and suggested I call to make sure you aren't too lonely."

If I was lonely, I thought, I'd—I'd what?

Go home to Win? That wouldn't exactly solve the problem.

"Oh, I'm fine," I said brightly. "It's very pleasant by the beach."

"Well, now that I have you on the phone, there are a few matters I'd like to discuss with you, concerning the wedding."

I thought of telling her it wasn't a good time, that I was meeting someone for breakfast, but I knew she'd ignore me.

Win hadn't fallen far from his mother's tree.

"All right, Mrs. Carrington," I said, settling heavily into a chair. "What would you like to talk about?"

"Clare, dear, you are taking my son's name, aren't you? I can't really see you as being part of the family if you're not a Carrington."

My grip on the receiver tightened. What in the world could I say to that?

I'd talked about the name issue with Gincy and Danielle.

"Of course I'm taking Win's name," I'd said.

Gincy had just rolled her eyes, as if I was a lost cause.

Danielle had suggested another option.

"Why don't you use both last names? Wellman-Carrington. It's a bit long but it's a good compromise."

"But I don't want a compromise," I'd insisted. "I'm fine with taking Win's name. Really. I know who I am. I don't need to keep Wellman to keep my identity as an individual."

Gincy had challenged me, of course. "Do you really know who you are, Clare? And by the way, Wellman is your father's name, after all. Do you really know who you are apart from the men in your life?"

"Does anyone?" Danielle had said, before I could open my

mouth to gape. "No person's an island, Gincy. We all exist in relation to everyone else we know, especially our families."

"Miss Philosophy 101 over here," Gincy snapped.

"Ms. Feminist Bullshit," Danielle snapped back. "Oooh, it's all the patriarchy's fault!"

Now, on the phone with my future mother-in-law, I suddenly knew I didn't want to be a Carrington or a Wellman.

I wanted to be me. Clare.

I wanted to be myself!

"Of course I'm taking Win's name," I said.

Mrs. Carrington sighed audibly. "Good. That's settled. Now, about your dress."

"Oh. What about it?" I asked.

Was she going to offer to pay for it? Of course, I'd graciously decline the offer.

"I would be honored if you would wear my dress at your wedding, Clare. As you know, I have no daughters and, well, now that you and Win are marrying, it's as if I do finally have a daughter. Someone I can advise. Someone I can . . ."

Mrs. Carrington rambled on but I no longer heard her words.

I'd seen photos of the dress—and Mrs. Carrington in it—at Win's house back in Ann Arbor. The dress was classically simple and probably would look beautiful on me.

But . . .

I was overcome with conflicting feelings of resentment and appreciation.

How dare Mrs. Carrington present me with such a loaded offer!

And yet, how nice it was of her to consider me her own flesh and blood.

Offering her dress is a gesture of love, Clare, one compelling voice pointed out. *Of family solidarity. One generation passing on its prized possessions to the next.*

And then, another compelling voice argued its case.

Be real, Clare, it said. *Trying to guilt you into wearing her wedding gown is only the first of many acts of an overbearing mother-in-law. She wants to advise you? On what? How to please her son?*

Danielle was right, I realized. I wasn't only marrying Win. I was marrying his mother, too.

But what about my own mother? How would she feel about my wearing Mrs. Carrington's wedding dress?

She'd feel bad. Left out. Not that her dress was an option. Mother was four inches shorter than me and very tiny. Still.

The second voice in my head won out.

I'd take Win's name. But I would not wear his mother's dress. I just wouldn't tell her that yet.

"Thank you, Mrs. Carrington," I said as firmly as I could. "I— I'll certainly consider your kind offer. See, I've been working with a small bridal shop on Newbury Street. They have some nice ideas. But I'll certainly think about . . ."

"Excellent, dear!" she interrupted. "I'll have copies made of the best of my wedding photos and send them along to refresh your memory, all right?"

We chatted about nothing for another moment or two and then ended the call.

I'd gone out to the Vineyard to be alone for a while, to think, to hide.

To rest.

But they had pursued me. They always pursued me.

Gincy
Good, Bad, Ugly

When Clare returned from her alone time at the Vineyard she called me at the office one afternoon and invited both me and Danielle to a cocktail party at the Ritz hotel on Tremont Street.

It was to be sponsored by Win's firm.

"I know Danielle's been wanting to meet Win," she explained, with an odd laugh. "Well, here's her big chance."

"Do I want to meet him?" I asked, surprising myself with the odd way I'd put the question.

Clare was silent a moment before answering. "Probably not," she said. "But you're invited."

Okay, I noted. This was a newer Clare. One who was speaking her mind right up front.

Maybe I'd been a good influence on my formerly uptight roommate.

It would definitely be the first time I'd been a good influence on anyone.

"Win's older brother Trey will be there," she went on. "He's visiting from San Francisco. He used to be a high school history teacher but he's changing careers. He works in the public defender's office during the day and goes to law school at night.

He's really bright. He just won some big award, I don't know, Win didn't really explain it to me. He's still getting over the shock of an illustrious Carrington wanting to become a public defender."

"So, are you trying to fix me up with this moral paragon?" I asked, half-jokingly.

"Oh, no! Trey's gay. I was just telling you about him because . . . Well, I think you'll like him."

"And you think I won't like Win."

Silence, for long seconds.

"Yes," she said, finally. "I think you won't like Win. But he probably won't like you, either, so what does it matter."

"Oh," I said. "Okay."

I wondered: Would this newer Clare become as annoyingly blunt as I was? Had I created a monster?

Either way, Danielle and I showed up in our finest. Which for Danielle meant a belted dress which, she told me, was an update of an old Diane von Furstenburg style. Whoever she was.

For me, it meant a French blue blouse—Danielle couldn't believe I actually knew the color—and black pants from the Gap. I'd gotten them on sale and sale pants were the best kind of pants.

And who cared if there was a Monsieur or Lady von Gap?

"I'm so glad we're finally getting to meet Win," Danielle said, popping a mini-quiche into her mouth and chewing with gusto.

"I think you're more excited about the free food," I commented.

"Free food is a good thing," she admitted, "especially when it's good quality. Have you tried the champagne? Veuve Clicquot. Very fine."

"I'm not a champagne person."

"Oh, please, Gincy. You're always trying to pretend you're so lowbrow when you've got as much sophistication as the next girl. Why you insist on hiding it is beyond me."

There was no point in arguing with Danielle. If she wanted to think I was Miss Emily Post, fine, let her think it.

Clare soon introduced us to Win. He looked like thousands of other guys. Medium height, brown hair neatly cut, brown eyes, navy suit, wingtip shoes.

There was nothing remarkable about him that I could see; even his affect was medium.

Maybe that's what had attracted Clare to Win.

Better her than me, I thought, thinking of Rick and his brutal honesty, rumpled clothes, and affinity for bluegrass music.

The four of us made very tiny talk for an interminable few minutes. And then a tall, handsome guy waved to Clare from across the room and she excused herself to join him.

"My brother," Win said. "He and Clare have always hit it off." Win hung his wrist in the age-old gesture.

Suddenly, the guy with no personality was obnoxiously loud and ragingly clear.

"What?" I said sharply. "What's that supposed to mean?"

"You know. Trey. He's queer. He's a homo. I don't know where he came from, boy. No one in our family has ever been a homo."

As far as you know, dickwad.

"Is that right?" I said, straining not to spit.

"Yeah. It's not something we're proud of. Trey being gay, I mean."

"I understand Trey was a teacher," Danielle said, her voice perfectly modulated.

I should have known she was an expert at polite conversation, even with jerks.

"And that he's getting his law degree," she went on. "And I believe Clare also mentioned that Trey recently won some prestigious award . . ."

"Oh, sure," Win said, as if the admission was a magnanimous act. "No Carrington is dumb."

Danielle pinched my arm in warning. I kept my mouth shut. For the moment.

Win continued to blab. "When Trey came out," he said, in a tone of confidentiality, "I had to seriously consider if I could maintain a relationship with him. Mother almost had a heart attack. She was rushed to the hospital . . . Mother can be a bit dramatic, but can you imagine the shock? Dad thought about cutting him out of the will. We had to wonder if it was worth including Trey in our lives. Well, you know how it is."

"Not really," I said with a big innocent smile. "See, I'm not— OW!"

Danielle had stomped on my foot with her stiletto.

"For Clare," she whispered through a fixed smile.

Win was so absorbed in his own idiotic pontifications and asinine ponderings he hadn't noticed our tussle.

"Frankly," he was saying now, holding aloft his martini, "I don't get this whole gay thing. I mean, suddenly there are all these people claiming to be gay. What's up with that? What's their point?"

"What's your point?" I said brightly, ignoring Danielle's frantic hand signals. "Being such a condescending—"

Before I could finish my tirade, Danielle grabbed my arm and with a false wave at nobody across the room, she dragged us both away from Mr. Winchester Carrington III.

We found the much-maligned Trey standing alone by the bar, sipping a glass of the fancy champagne.

"Your brother's an asshole," I said without preamble. "Shrimp?" I offered my heaped plate.

"Thanks." Trey popped an entire jumbo shrimp in his mouth. "I know," he mumbled.

"I'm Gincy by the way. Clare's friend. This is Danielle."

Trey introduced himself and took another shrimp from my plate.

"I don't know how Clare can stand talking to him," I went on, blood still seething, "let alone marrying him. Jesus Christ. He makes me want to spit."

Trey swallowed and grinned. "I'm glad Clare finally has a friend like you. She needs an advocate. She needs to learn to say, 'screw you.' She's not a bad person. She's just been pushed around a lot."

"Yeah, yeah," I said. "Clare's great and all. But what I want to know is how you can stand to be here. I mean, what are you, a saint? How can you stand to be in the same room with Win? He's despicable."

"He's an asshole and despicable and pathetic. But," Trey said, with a wry grin, "he's also my little brother. Family owes something to family. Even if it's just pretending to get along."

"You're a far better person than I am," I said.

"I doubt that."

"You don't know me very well."

"You don't have the look of a creep. Trust me, I've seen my fair share."

"Looks can be deceiving."

"Not to me. I have super-laser vision."

"Okay, you win," I said, laughing. "I don't suck. Totally."

"I can't imagine David ever turning his back on me," Danielle said, more to herself than to us. "And nothing he could ever do would make me turn my back on him."

"David's her big brother," I explained, and Trey nodded wisely.

I neglected to mention my own brother. I was sure Tommy would rat me out to the enemy for a quart of lighter fluid.

As for my loyalty to him, well, that was still up for debate.

Hours later, Danielle and I were hunched at the bar at Silvertone. Well, I was hunched; Danielle sat straight as she always did, except when lounging. More than once she'd reminded me of the importance of good posture.

"I don't think I can help Clare with the wedding any longer." Danielle looked genuinely pained. It cost her to abandon such a project. "How can I encourage such a sweet kid to marry such a horrible jerk?"

"You can't," I replied shortly.

"But I just can't walk out on the planning, can I? Clare's relying on me. There's so much still to do . . . And what excuse would I give? I can't tell her that I loathe her fiancé!"

We sat in silence for a few moments, until Danielle said, softly, "You know, I can't help but compare Win to Chris. Can you imagine Chris ever being such a jerk?"

"No," I said readily. "That's not what he's about. I mean, I hardly know him but I can just tell. Maybe I'm like Trey. I can spot a creep a mile away."

"And it's not what Rick's about, either," Danielle said. "If I can believe everything you've told me about him. And I don't see why you'd lie."

"You can believe me," I said. "Rick's one of the good ones. He's a man. Like the kind they used to grow. Like Gary Cooper or someone. He's always thinking of other people before himself. Not macho but manly. Women and children first but without all the condescending crap that goes with that."

"He sounds like my father," Danielle said. "He's a real caretaker. My father is very kind."

And so is mine, I thought, suddenly remembering how he'd go grocery shopping for the ancient Mrs. Kennedy down the street, and shovel the paths outside the church early every snowy Sunday morning, and bring my mother flowers just for the hell of it.

Not that she ever appreciated the flowers. Ellen Gannon had swallowed a bitterness pill some time in the early seventies— about the time I was born—and it had taken rapid and permanent effect.

But back to my father. I hadn't thought about any of those nice things for years. The memories hit hard.

"My dad's pretty okay, too," I said, feeling a bothersome tickle in my throat. "I guess we're both lucky daughters."

Clare

Girls on Film

When I first met Gincy I noticed she never looked fully at ease on the beach unless she was flinging rocks back into the ocean, as if she had some point to prove to the never-ceasing waves.

But for some reason, as the summer wore on, she spent more and more time sprawled with me and Danielle on our towels, chatting, reading, and sipping cold drinks.

And she'd even bought a bathing suit. It was a one-piece black racing suit. Gincy actually had a nice figure. It looked as if she might have gained a little bit of weight in the past weeks. It was attractive.

I wondered if her slow and partial transformation had anything to do with Rick. Was Gincy actually happy?

"I'm sorry I didn't get to talk to you after the cocktail party," I said, laying aside my novel. "We had a dinner reservation at eight."

"That's okay," Gincy said. "We understand. I'm sorry we didn't have more time to hang with Trey, though."

I smiled. "Trey is wonderful. He just started seeing someone new. A professor of urban studies, I think. Or urban design. Anyway, Trey seems to think this could be it."

"Is he cute?" Danielle asked. "This professor?"

"Why is that important?" Gincy demanded.

Danielle threw her hands in the air. "I'm not getting into this with you again. Go ahead and marry the Creature from the Black Lagoon if you want. No one's stopping you. Maybe the Elephant Man is free this evening. Here, you can use my cell phone."

"So, what did you think of Win?" I asked, interrupting the familiar wrangle.

A trick question? I don't know what I was hoping to hear.

"Well, he's very nice looking," Danielle said promptly. "Very neat. And his suit was impeccable. Do you help him pick out his clothes?"

"No. Win's mother visits once a year and they go shopping together."

Danielle opened her mouth but had nothing to say to that. Nervously, she cleared her throat and took a drink of iced tea.

"Gincy?" I said. "What about you?"

She scratched her head and frowned, as if debating her answer. "I insulted him right to his face," she said finally, "and he didn't seem to pick up on it. I'm not saying he's an idiot or anything . . ."

"Win's not stupid," I explained. "He just hears what he wants to hear. He scans for criticism or ridicule and converts it to compliments or neutralizes it somehow. It's rather amazing."

"It must be hard to have a real argument with him," Danielle noted. "I mean, a productive one."

"It's impossible," I said flatly. "The only time he listens is when I start a sentence with, 'I'm sorry, I know it's my fault, but.' "

Gincy frowned. "I just have to ask this question, Clare. It's a tough one."

"Go ahead."

"Do you know how Win talks about his brother? I mean, I won't speak for Danielle—"

"You can," she interrupted.

"Okay then, Danielle and I were really—"

"Shocked."

"Disgusted by his behavior. It was so offensive. And he just assumed we'd be right on board his gay-bashing train. I swear, Clare, I almost hit him."

"She did," Danielle said, nodding. "I stopped her."

"Yeah, by stomping on my foot!"

I was silent for a moment. I could feel Gincy and Danielle tensing, worried they'd upset me.

I looked out at the water sparkling with sunlight. It was so pretty. It posed no awkward dilemmas.

Yes, I knew how Win spoke about his brother. About all homosexuals. I'd tried to argue him into tolerance and understanding. I'd tried to cajole him into generosity of spirit, into kindness.

But Win was Win. His ideas were set in stone and had been from childhood.

His ideas were his father's.

Not mine. Never mine.

Finally, I had gotten Win to agree not to share his opinions on homosexuality with me. But I knew he held those opinions.

Was I in collusion by living with Win, by marrying him? Was I by proxy a narrow-minded, spiritless person?

How could I ever explain myself and my choices? Especially when more and more they seemed no longer my choices.

"Yes," I said, finally. "I know how he thinks. And talks. I hate it. But it's not me."

"We never thought it was," Danielle said, reaching for and squeezing my hand.

Mercifully, Gincy let the awkward subject drop.

And then another subject bounced into sight. I watched them strutting in our direction, three young women in teeny bikinis, swinging bright beach bags and giggling.

"I think I might just be a rocket scientist," Danielle murmured.

"Compared to the Bouncie sisters," Gincy grumbled, "you are. And I'm a physics professor. With a second degree in genetic engineering."

Well, the girls weren't acting like intellectuals, but why should they be, I thought. They're at the beach, a place of fun and relaxation. Okay, there was an awful lot of hair tossing going on but . . .

"Is there a hidden camera somewhere?" Gincy said. "Are we on the set of yet another Baywatch spin-off? Baywatch Vineyard?"

"Why do they have to sit so close to us?" Danielle complained when the three girls had tossed their towels not ten yards from us. "We're invisible next to them! What if Chris comes by?"

"That's the point," Gincy said. "They know what they're doing. Girls who look like that are never as dumb as they appear."

"As dumb as a bucket of hair," Danielle said.

"A big sack of stupid."

"Nice cupboards, no dishes."

"A few sandwiches short of a picnic."

"Oh, come on, you two," I scolded. "They're just having fun. Goofing around. We don't exactly sound brilliant all the time. Maybe never."

"You're a softie, Clare," Danielle snapped. "These girls are a serious threat to women like us. And it's only going to get worse the older we get. Because every year a new crop of Bouncies comes up, ready to replace wives and give middle-aged men heart attacks."

Gincy snorted. "If my husband left me for a Bouncie, he'd better freakin' have a heart attack. A big one. One that kills him. Dead. Like the roach that he is."

"Oh, crap, one's coming over here!" Danielle lifted her magazine so that it almost entirely covered her face.

"What are you hiding from?" I asked.

"I'm not hiding," she snapped. "I'm afraid I might spit and I don't want to start a girly-fight. My nails are long but look at their abs!"

The girl was now upon us—the blond one. She leaned forward and I was suddenly embarrassed being confronted with all that cleavage.

Was all that really necessary?

"Could you, like, take our picture?" she asked.

"I could," Gincy said blandly. "The question is, will I?"

The girl's smile faltered. Her pale blue eyes went blank.

"I'll do it," I said, suddenly taking pity on the girl.

Just because she was gorgeous and dumb didn't mean she was a bad person.

"How does the camera work?"

"Oh, it's totally simple," the girl replied, big, toothy smile back in place. "Just look through there and push this button. That's it!"

I climbed to my feet and followed the blond girl back to her friends. There was more giggling and then some squealing as they arranged themselves in a pose they thought was cute.

Arms around each other, butts and breasts sticking out everywhere.

Maybe they're contortionists, I thought stupidly.

"Smile," I mumbled, but lips were already open and teeth already flashing.

The blond girl snatched back the camera and thanked me with yet another giggle.

Glumly, feeling I'd somehow been abused or mocked, I made my way back to my own friends.

The sand was hot on the soles of my feet. I had to use the bathroom. My bathing suit was riding up.

"Oh, my, God, Clare," Gincy said when I'd flopped back down on my towel. "You've just shot your first *Playboy* centerfold! How does it feel to be a genuine member of the porn industry? Maybe you should join a union or something. I hear they provide good health insurance, job security . . ."

"Oh, be quiet," Danielle snapped. "Maybe we should just move."

"No way! We were here first."

While Gincy and Danielle bickered, I thought about Win.

I wondered if he was attracted to women like the three cavorting on the sand before us.

While I was out here on the Vineyard, was he spending his evenings reading *Playboy* and watching pornographic videos? Did he go to strip bars with so-called clients?

It was hard to imagine because Win had never been overly interested in sex.

Maybe, I thought uncomfortably, as the brunette squirted tanning lotion on her already brown and very flat stomach, maybe that was my fault.

Maybe Win held back because he sensed that I wasn't all that interested in sex. With him.

Maybe Win just didn't find me all that attractive.

I was the kind of girl a man married, not the kind a man fooled around with. I'd known that since adolescence.

My encounter with Finn? An aberration.

Was that part of the problem with me and Win, the lack of intense sexual attraction?

But how important was that in a marriage, how important over the long haul?

All the experts said that animal lust faded over time and was replaced by a deeper relationship built around comfort and friendship and mutual respect.

But what if the animal lust had never been there in the first place?

Maybe, I thought, *I should ask Gincy what she thinks. Maybe I should ask her how things are between her and Rick. Sexually.*

Maybe I should ask Danielle about Chris.

Maybe . . .

One of the bikini girls shrieked and her two friends took up the cry. They were in the water now, having a splash fight.

"I hope they drown," I muttered. "I hope they get shredded by a shark."

Gincy burst out laughing. "I knew you'd come around! Nobody's that generous."

Danielle patted my arm. "Welcome to the real world, honey. It ain't pretty."

August

Gincy
Blood Is Thicker

Rick and I had just finished eating a simple dinner of pasta with garlic and oil, salad, and bread—he'd cooked, of course—and I'd just dumped the dirty dishes in the sink when my doorbell rang.

And then rang again.

And again.

"Who the hell can that be?" I said, heading for the door.

I peered through the dirty peephole and saw my worst nightmare.

Holy crap. It was my brother.

Maybe I just wouldn't open the door.

Could I do that?

I mean, he had to have heard my voice. I wasn't exactly a low-talker.

What would he tell my parents? That his own sister, his own flesh and blood, had left him standing alone in the hallway like a dog.

"Shit."

"Gincy? Who is it?" Rick had come out of the mini-kitchen, a dish towel in one hand, a frown on his face.

"It's my brother," I mouthed.

"Well, let him in."

"I—"

"Yo, Gince. Open up!"

I cringed.

"Are you embarrassed of me?" Rick teased.

"Jesus, no. But just remember. You asked for it."

And I opened the door, halfway.

Tommy. In all his dirtbag glory. Wife beater T-shirt. Jeans riding below a beer paunch that had no business being on his skinny frame. Thin hair cut in a mullett.

"What are you doing here?" I snapped. "In Boston, I mean. You can't stay here tonight, you know."

"Whoa, Gince," he said, putting his hands up in the universal sign for surrender. "Slow down. Dude. Me and Jay came in for some fun, that's all."

"Jay?" I tore open the door and looked up and down the hallway. "That delinquent piece of crap is not coming anywhere near me, I hope you know that, Tommy."

"Uh, yeah? That's why he's downstairs. Dude, he's like scared of you."

I glared at my idiot brother. "He should be."

Behind me, Rick cleared his throat enquiringly. Oh, he'd hear the whole story later, all right.

"So, why are you here?" I repeated. "In my apartment." Though technically he was still in the doorway.

"Can't a guy say hey to his sister?"

"Hello. Now time to go. Don't let the door hit you on the back of the head on the way out."

Tommy shook his head. "Man, what is your damage? Me and Jay, we were like thinking you could tell us where to go have some fuuuunn. Like, get some beers and par-tay."

"No. I can't. You'll just have to find some fuuuunn on your own. Now—" I pointed into the dark hall behind him.

Suddenly, Tommy peered over my shoulder and scowled. Damn. He'd finally noticed Rick. "Who's this, your landlord?" he said in that mocking way all dumbasses have.

"No." I swallowed hard. Here we go. "He's my boyfriend."

It took almost a full minute for that bit of juicy news to sink into my brother's beer-soaked brain. Finally, a slow grin spread across his greasy face.

"Whoa, what's Mom gonna say when she finds out you're seeing some old dude?"

Rick could barely control his laughter. I shot him a warning glance and he backed into the living room, mumbling, "Hey, I'm only thirty-five."

"Mom's gonna say nothing," I snapped. "Because she's not going to find out. You keep your mouth shut, Tommy!"

"Make me!"

"You stink," I spat.

Tommy sneered. His cheesy, three-haired mustache twitched. "Yeah, well, you stink on ice."

Ah, there we were, my brother and I, the proud progeny of the Gannon-Bauer line.

I vowed right then and there never ever to reproduce. And I wondered how I could get Tommy's lines cut so he could avoid sending more stooopidity out into the already sadly stooopid world.

After another round of pointless wrangling, I told Tommy to go to Dick's Last Resort on Huntington and take the night from there. With a final smirk, he oozed off into the dark. I thoroughly enjoyed slamming the door after him.

"What?" I demanded, whirling to Rick. "Go ahead and say it."

If he broke up with me over this . . .

Rick's lips twitched. "So, ah, that was your brother. Interesting. I mean, he seems—"

"Go ahead. Say it. He seems like scum. That's because he is scum."

Rick came close and kissed me on the forehead. "What I was going to say was that he seems very different from you."

I beamed. "Really? Thanks. I mean, I know that but sometimes I'm afraid some weird genetic trait is latent in me and suddenly I'll sprout a mullet and start drinking beer for breakfast."

Finally, Rick burst out laughing. "I'm sorry, Gincy. But the idea of you with a mullet is ludicrous. It's so never going to happen."

"Yeah," I admitted, "I know."

"You want to tell me what happened with this Jay character?"

"No," I said emphatically. "Someday. You wanna fool around?"

Rick did, so we did.

Later, after Rick had gone home, I thought of Trey Carrington and how he tolerated, even loved, his younger brother. Was Trey a masochist or simply very mature?

What, exactly, do we owe to family, those people foisted upon us at birth, those people from whom we descend, those people who share our DNA, our stumbling youth, our pudgy middle age, our incontinent old age?

I wondered if I would ever know the answer to that bothersome question.

Gincy

Misfit Air

I took the Blue Line out to Logan and met Danielle at the Delta shuttle.

Because we were staying at her parents' house I'd invested in a new travel bag. Something clean and not plastic. Appearances mattered to Danielle and I assumed they mattered to her parents.

I might not have been all warm and cuddly, but I did respect other people's parents.

Danielle saw me coming. "Gincy!" she cried. "Your bag! Is it new?"

An armed airport security guy glared from Danielle to me.

"And I packed it myself!" I told him brightly as I passed.

Clearly, I still wasn't past the age of occasional idiotic behavior in the presence of law enforcement.

Danielle grabbed my arm and smiled winningly at the scowling security guy. As if to say, "Please don't arrest my moronic friend."

And then she glared at me.

"What? Oh, okay. I'm sorry. I'll behave."

"Good. Now, about the bag. It's got to be new?"

I grinned, self-satisfied. "Why, yes it is. And it was a bargain, too. I got it at Marshall's."

"Well, I am just so proud of you. And new capris? You know, you clean up pretty good."

"Look, thanks again for all this," I said.

Danielle waved her well-manicured hand, a now-familiar gesture. "Don't mention it, Gincy. A girl only turns thirty once. Thank God."

"I mean it, Danielle. I can't believe your parents are paying for me and Clare to fly home with you. I mean, number one: It's totally generous. And number two: Why us, anyway? Don't you know other people in Boston better than you know us?"

I asked the question in all innocence. Really. With no ulterior motive to embarrass or provoke.

"Truth?" she said, with a funny look on her face. "No. I'm not really close to anyone in Boston. Except you and Clare. I mean, sure, there are some girls at work I have drinks with sometimes but . . ." With one delicate fingertip Danielle blotted away a tear from the corner of her left eye.

"But what?" I said, suddenly feeling very itchy. I'd never been good with tears. Mine or anyone else's.

Danielle laughed one of those sad, aren't-I-silly laughs. "But, I don't know, I've never been very good at making friends. I guess I've never really, really tried. I don't know why."

I shrugged. "That's okay. I suck at friendships, too. Maybe that's why you and I get along even though we're so different."

"Maybe we get along because we're so different. It's like I don't know what to expect from you. Ever. And that's interesting."

"There's a theory. It's more flattering than mine. Hey, here comes Clare."

"Why isn't Win coming, anyway?" I blurted, when she'd joined us, all perky and shiny in a lime green brushed cotton sundress.

Danielle identified the brushed cotton part for me.

"Well . . ." Clare bit back a smile. "I told him it was just us girls. I didn't really want him to come along. You know."

There was an awkward silence.

Why, I wondered, do people always say, "you know," expecting to hear, "of course," when the reality is that no one knows diddly-squat about anyone else's situation?

Were we supposed to understand Clare's pleasure in lying to her fiancé?

"Look," I said, determined to avoid unpleasantness, "we're all going to have a blast, right?"

"Right," Danielle said, but she didn't sound so sure. "Even without the guys. Especially without the guys."

Maybe. Clare hadn't invited Win. I didn't really care why but I was glad. I might have been forced to punch him.

Chris hadn't been invited, either. And though Danielle hadn't admitted her reasons for leaving him out of the festivities, I knew immediately and without a doubt her motives.

Chris was a pleasant diversion and nothing more. To invite him home would be to cause a whole lot of unnecessary complication.

In the end, she thought she was doing them both a favor.

Rick, however, had been invited. And he'd accepted.

And then, he'd cancelled.

I was pissed at him for backing out. But I understood, too. And I respected his decision.

Jeez, his kid was sick. The kid who'd lost his mother to cancer. Of course Rick had to stay home. Of course he wasn't going to dump Justin on a sitter for an entire weekend when the kid couldn't stop throwing up.

It's just that I missed Rick's company.

I wanted him with me.

I missed his intelligence, his wit, his gorgeous dark hair, his crashing into walls, his crashing into me.

It's the territory, Gincy, I told myself as we boarded the small plane for LaGuardia Airport behind a family of four, their two strollers, two car seats, and one giant stuffed teddy bear in tow.

Get used to it. You date a dad, you get the kid.

Accept that up front and you'll be just fine.

Clare
Friendly Skies

All buckled in and ready for takeoff.

It was the first time in a long time I'd been on a plane to anywhere but Ann Arbor, via Detroit. Win and I hadn't been away together on a romantic vacation for at least two years. He'd been so busy at the firm, moving fast on the partner track.

Which wasn't all bad. Lately, it was simply more peaceful to be without Win than to be with him. Not that my worries and questions disappeared the moment he was out of sight. But they definitely receded.

Life seemed broader, more breathable and airy when I was alone. Even if I wasn't entirely alone. Even if I was with my friends.

My friends. Now that was new.

I still couldn't bring myself to admit to them what had happened with Finn. But there were related issues I felt comfortable discussing. "Do you ever feel lonely?" I asked.

Danielle brushed the notion away with her hand. "Never. Not much. Sometimes. Why?"

"Gincy?"

"Uh, yeah, sometimes. More as I get older. It's no big deal," she added quickly.

"Are you ever lonely, Clare?" Danielle asked.

"I'm lonely all the time," I stated boldly. "It's worse when Win and I are alone together at home. It shouldn't be that way, should it?"

No one's going to tell you what to do, Clare, I reminded myself. *No one wants the responsibility of advising you to break your engagement.*

Danielle cleared her throat nervously. "Maybe it's pre-wedding jitters. You know, classic cold feet. Or something."

"Maybe."

"I'm not a big fan of therapy," Gincy said, "but maybe you should talk to someone. About the loneliness and all. That sort of thing can wear you down. So I've heard."

I laughed and mimicked Danielle's famous dismissive wave.

"Oh, I'll be all right," I said. "Danielle's probably right. It's probably just classic cold feet."

But I knew it wasn't.

Danielle

You Can Take the Girl

My parents met us at the door to our four-thousand-square-foot, split-level contemporary house. With a two-car garage. A patio out back. And a Jacuzzi.

Mom covered my face with kisses and squeezed first Clare, then Gincy.

Mom had often been described as effusive. She was born to be a grandmother. To her credit, she was remarkably restrained when it came to pressing David and me for grandchildren.

My father politely shook my friends' hands and offered each a big, genuine smile.

"The lawn looks great, Dad," I said, noting with some dismay that his face was thinner than it had been the last time I'd seen him only months earlier. "Still doing it all on your own?"

"Of course," he boomed. "I'm not an old man yet. In spite of this birthday of yours."

Dad soon went off to the garage to check his 1972 custom maroon Cadillac for fingerprints. It was only one of the many daily checks he made of the property, though as far as I knew we'd never suffered a robbery or an act of vandalism.

Mom led us girls inside. After she had shown Gincy and Clare to the guest bedroom, which, I noted, had been redone since my last visit, she went off to the kitchen.

I took them to see my room, the room where I'd spent almost every night of the first eighteen years of my life.

The room where I'd be sleeping that night.

A little haven. Or not.

"Danielle?" Gincy said, standing very still in the room's center. "Has anything changed since you last lived here?"

I surveyed the room. Plush pink carpet.

An array of dolls on the pink bedspread.

An embroidered wall hanging of a pink and purple butterfly, my one sad attempt at needlework.

A rocking chair I hadn't been able to fit into since about the age of five.

"No. Not really," I said. "It's pretty much as it was when I left for college at the age of eighteen. Oh, except for the poster of Paris at night. I bought that the summer after sophomore year, I think."

"Doesn't your father want to turn the room into, I don't know, a media room?" Gincy asked.

"No. He did that already with David's room. We can watch a DVD there later if you want. Surround sound and everything."

"This sounds so much like my family," Clare said. "My brothers' rooms are now a guest room and an office for my mother. She does do a lot of charity work, on the organizational, fund-raising side. All my brothers' trophies and awards are on display in the library and Daddy's home office. And I guess their other belongings are in the attic. But my room is exactly as I left it all those years ago. Sometimes . . ."

"Sometimes what?" I prodded. I had my own theory about why my room was a museum.

Clare shrugged. "Sometimes I think my parents expect me to fail spectacularly and come crying home to live out my lonely miserable life with them. The spinster daughter in her fading pink bedroom."

"That's probably your own insecurity talking," Gincy said.

"And where do you think I got that insecurity?" Clare shot back.

I peered into the hall to be sure we were alone.

"Well," I whispered, "sometimes I think my parents would just love me to come home and live with them. Not forever. Just until they found me a nice husband. Until he and I bought a house across the street. I think my parents keep my room this way because they want me to feel welcome. You know. If I ever lose my mind and decide to leave Boston."

"I think it's sweet," Clare said. "I think your parents really love you."

Gincy ran her finger along a shelf laden with miniature wicker furniture. "Look at this! No dust. Your mother even keeps the room clean!"

"What about your room?" I asked.

"Yeah, Gincy. Tell us. Do your parents preserve the memory?"

Gincy snorted. But behind the gross gesture I thought I sensed a genuine sore spot.

"Yeah, right," she said. "The minute I was out the door my mother put all my stuff in boxes and stuffed them in the basement. Where everything proceeded to mold. She made my room a sewing room. Or so she calls it. Last time I was home the sewing machine was covered in about three inches of dust. The bottom line is it's her room now. For her stuff. I swear I think she sleeps in there most nights. I don't think she likes my father much. I'm not sure she ever did."

"Oh, Gincy," Clare said feelingly, "that's horrible. Where do you sleep when you go home to visit?"

"In the basement. On a cot next to my moldy possessions. Which is only one of the reasons I don't go home all that often."

What could I say to that horror story?

"Girls!"

My mother to the rescue.

"In here, Mom!" I called.

A moment later my mother appeared at the door to my bedroom.

"I've just made some delicious cookies," she said, beaming. "A nice variety. Nice and hot from the oven. Why don't you come into the kitchen for a nice snack."

And then my mother reached out and poked Gincy's arm. "You're too skinny, young lady," she scolded. "Come and eat."

And there was the reason I lived in Boston . . .

"Mom! Don't insult her!"

Gincy shrugged. "I'm not insulted. I am too thin. I'm going to look grotesquely old by the time I'm forty if I don't fatten up a bit. Look at the lines around my eyes already. So, let's go have some of those cookies."

"Thanks, Mrs. Leers," Clare said as we trailed down the wall-papered hallways after my mother. "I love home-baked cookies. My fiancé doesn't have a sweet tooth so I don't bother to make them for myself . . ."

I smiled as I followed them all to the kitchen.

Danielle, I thought, *I don't know how it happened, but you've got two pretty fabulous friends.*

Danielle
Cry If You Want To

My thirtieth birthday party was held at Captain Al's, a combination event hall and restaurant overlooking The Sound.

My parents had booked the Sea Shell Room for four hours, at no small expense. We'd all remembered the room from my cousin Mena's wedding a few years earlier. I, especially, had been impressed by the dusky rose-colored wallpaper.

The Johnny Orchestra Band, the darlings of my parents' set, had been hired for the evening to play classics like "Satin Doll" and party favorites like the ever-popular "Celebration."

"It's like a mini-wedding!" Gincy hissed when we'd first arrived. "Jeez. I'm glad I didn't bring a gag gift."

Clare and Gincy wandered off as I greeted each guest in turn. Sarah, Michelle, and Rachel were all there, husbands in tow. Aside from those six, the three of us from Boston, and David and Roberta, every other guest—with one notable exception I was soon to meet—was over fifty.

Some might have said it was more of a party for my parents than for me. But I was pleased. I liked when various generations socialized together. It seemed real and valuable. Who was anyone without context?

Take the Rothsteins. They had been good friends of my parents' for years. For the past ten of those years they'd lived directly across the street.

Wednesday nights the two couples met for bridge or various board games.

Every other Saturday they went to dinner at the club's restaurant.

Every Sunday the men played a round of golf.

Every so often the women took the train into Manhattan and caught a show or did some serious shopping.

The Rothsteins were more like family than friends. Like my aunt and uncle. If there really was a difference at that point.

I greeted the Rothsteins at their table. Among the long-familiar faces was one new face.

Mrs. Rothstein introduced him as Barry Lieberman.

Clearly, he'd been asked to attend the party for a specific reason. Mrs. Rothstein was making a match. And really, she was doing a good job of it.

A commendable job.

Her candidate was straight and Jewish.

He was somewhere between thirty-five and forty, nicely within age range.

His haircut was good and his suit well-tailored.

He was a professional.

And as a friend of the Rothsteins, he came recommended and could be held accountable. That was nothing to sneeze at.

Barry was perfectly eligible and perfectly pleasant.

But I felt not even the tiniest spark of interest in him.

When Mrs. Rothstein moved off to greet an old friend at another table, Barry and I chatted for a bit. Then he gave me his card on which were no less than three phone numbers, one of which was for a cell phone, an e-mail address, a fax number, a post-office-box number, and a street address.

"I'll be in Boston some time in the next few weeks," he said. "I'd love to take you to dinner."

"Call me," I said pleasantly, and excused myself to greet other guests.

I would go to dinner with Barry. Maybe a spark would ignite if we went to one of my favorite restaurants. Good food and a lively atmosphere were known to do wonders for romance.

I stopped by the bandstand and watched my guests talking, laughing, eating, and drinking with relish.

How could I have asked Chris to come to this event? He would have been a fish out of water.

Right?

It would have been setting him up to fail, dropping him in a room full of professional types in Hugo Boss ties, Armani suits, and Kaspar dresses.

Right?

The truth was, I'd never seen Chris in a large, sort of formal social situation. For all I knew he was totally at ease in a suit, sipping champagne, nibbling Popsicle-sized lamb chops.

But I hadn't given Chris a chance to prove himself away from home.

Why?

Maybe—and this was a scary possibility—maybe I was more concerned with how I would handle introducing Chris to my family. Concerned with what my parents—and David?—would say about my choice of date for such a major family event.

Face it, Danielle, I told myself, as my sixty-year-old, red-haired aunt Myra shimmied by laughing up a storm. Every event is major in your family. The Leers could make opera out of your getting a new haircut.

Maybe I would be better off out of context. At least on occasion.

I slipped out onto the terrace and using my cell phone, I called Chris. He answered on the first ring.

"Hey, Danielle," he said brightly. "I knew it was you. I've got your number loaded into my cell. So, how's it going? Is it good to see your parents?"

God, how I missed him at that moment. "Oh, yeah, it's great," I said. "You know. Look, Chris, I was thinking. Um. Well, I was wondering how you would feel about coming into Boston some time when I get back. To celebrate my birthday."

"Instead of out here on the Vineyard?" he asked, sounding a bit puzzled.

Or was that my imagination?

"Um, yeah. Would that be okay?"

"Danielle, I'd love to," he replied, and all I heard was true enthusiasm. "I hardly ever get to Boston. Summer is tight for me with work but I'll arrange something. Just pick a day, okay?"

Just then the door to the terrace opened and a loud shout of laughter burst through.

"Where are you?" Chris asked, with a smile in his voice.

"Oh, just at home," I lied. "My family's kind of loud. They like to have a good time."

"Sounds good to me. Danielle, thanks for calling. It means a lot. I'm sorry but I've got to go. Johnny and I are just about to load—"

"That's okay," I interrupted. "I . . . I miss you, Chris."

"I miss you, too, Danielle. I'll see you soon?"

"Yes," I whispered, too close to tears.

We ended the call and I stood looking out over the water until I could regain my composure. When I went back into the event room, I caught sight of David standing alone by the bar.

David's presence had always made me feel better. He was predictable, reliable, solid.

"Hey," I said, joining him, "where's Roberta?"

"Frankly, I don't care where she is right now. She's becoming a royal pain in my ass."

"David!" I shot a glance over my shoulder.

Thank God no one but the bartender was in earshot, and like any good bartender, this one hadn't blinked an eye at his client's private conversation.

"That's your fiancée you're talking about," I whispered fiercely. "The future mother of your children. What's wrong with you?"

"I'm sorry, Danielle. It's just . . ." David sighed hugely. A habit we both got from my grandfather.

"It's just what? You can tell me."

First, David ordered another gin and tonic. When he was served we moved off a bit to allow others access to the bar.

"It's just that we're looking for a house, right?" he said, when we'd come to stand by the big window overlooking the water. "And this one she's fixated on looks like Scarlett O'Hara's mansion—"

"Tara."

"Whatever. Well, we just can't afford it right now. I can't afford it. I mean, maybe in five years, if I plan right and the practice grows. I'm hopeful. But not now."

Where was the problem? I wondered.

"Okay," I said. "So, tell her that."

"Ah, therein lies the difficulty, little sister. I have told her. I've told her five, ten times. But the reality doesn't seem to sink in. It's like she doesn't even hear me. Do you know she's told her mother we've put in an offer on the place? And when I confronted her about it, you know what she said? She said, 'Oh, David, you'll make it work.' Do you believe it?"

I wasn't quite sure what David wanted to hear from me. Roberta's response sounded positive. Though her lying to her mother about the offer was not good news.

"Well," I said, weakly, "at least she has faith in you."

David finished off his drink in one long swallow. "I don't see faith," he said shortly. "I see pressure. I see that she's spoiled rotten and instead of helping me she's setting me up for failure. The relationship isn't about us, a team, a family. It's just all about her."

The force behind David's words stunned me.

"Is this new?" I dared to ask. "I mean, has Roberta changed since you met her? Since you got engaged?"

David shook his head. "No. To be fair, no. I'm the one who's changed. Who's changing. Whatever. But listen to me. I'm ruining my baby sister's big birthday party by moaning about my woes. I'm sorry, Danielle."

I threw my arms around him and held him tight. "I'm worried about you, David. I want you to be happy."

"Don't worry," he said, kissing the top of my head. "I can take care of myself. Really. I promise. And I will be happy. Okay? So you just enjoy the celebration."

David walked off in the direction of our parents. I watched him go.

How could I enjoy the party after that exchange?

Was nobody happy?

Clare was marrying a horribly narrow-minded, self-centered snob.

David had finally realized what I'd caught a glimpse of earlier that summer, that his fiancée was spoiled rotten and totally self-absorbed.

And Chris . . .

Nothing was wrong with Chris other than the fact that he was who he was. And I was who I was.

And that even though I had agreed to go fishing on his boat and he had agreed to come to Boston to celebrate my birthday, the fact was that we were horribly mismatched.

Even though he made me so happy.

The band came back from break and struck up a lively tune. Couples swarmed the dance floor.

Couples in their seventies. Couples who'd been together for forty years.

Couples in their thirties and forties, many second or third spouses.

People just keep trying, I thought. *They just keep trying to be happy.*

Maybe things will work out between Gincy and Rick, I thought, turning away from the dancing couples, trying hard for hopefulness. Though Gincy was still adamant about not getting serious with a guy who came with a child.

As if summoned by my thoughts, Gincy and Clare joined me. Clare looked lovely in a pale lime green sleeveless dress with cream-colored princess heels and matching bag.

Gincy had disappeared into the bathroom that morning with one of my hair-care products and somehow had managed to produce a pixielike look that was very flattering.

I considered her efforts and good results partly my own doing. I was a good influence on the girl, no doubt.

"We want to give you our presents," Clare said brightly.

"You guys! You didn't have to get me anything!"

"Yeah. Right."

Gincy handed me a heavy box wrapped in pink glossy paper. "Anyway, if you hate it I have the gift receipt so you can return it."

"I so won't hate it," I swore, tearing open the package to find a book about Kevin Aucoin, the famously talented makeup artist who had died tragically a year or two earlier.

"Oh my God, it's . . . God, I'm going to cry, here it comes! Gincy, thank you, really . . ."

Gincy patted my shoulder awkwardly. "I asked a salesperson in Barnes & Noble what someone like you might want. You know, someone heavily into all the girl stuff. It was down to that book or the big Elizabeth Taylor one—"

"*My Love Affair with Jewelry*? I bought a copy the first day it came out."

"I figured as much," she said, laughing.

Clare held out a thick white envelope. "My turn."

It was a gift certificate for Belle Sante, a lovely spa on Newbury Street.

"Oh! Oh!" I cried. "This is enough for a massage and a facial! Oh, Clare, you shouldn't have!"

"Enjoy it in good health," she said.

Gincy poked my arm. "You know," she said, "maybe we should all have a glass of champagne. What was that stuff we had at Win's party?"

"I thought you didn't like champagne!" I teased.

"Well, you know, it's good to keep an open mind."

So the three of us raised a glass.

"To the birthday girl."

"To you guys, for coming all the way to Long Island."

"To us," Clare said.

And we clinked glasses.

Okay. Maybe I'd been wrong not to trust in Chris.

But I'd been right in trusting Gincy and Clare to come home with me.

My two friends.

Clare
When You Least Expect It

Win was reading the *Wall Street Journal* and sipping a bourbon when I walked through the living room.

He looked up, surprised. "You're going out?"

"Yes," I said simply.

I do have a life without you. Even though it's a mess right now.

"Can I ask where you're going?"

"Of course. I'm going to a reading at the library at Copley Square. One of my favorite authors is in town."

"Oh?" Win said, looking almost puzzled. "Who?"

"You wouldn't know her," I said.

"Have you mentioned her to me?"

"Yes. It's Barbara Michaels. She also writes under Elizabeth Peters."

And I own all of her books. They're right there on the shelves behind you.

Win considered. "No, you're right. I don't recognize the name."

I opened the hall closet and pulled out a mini-umbrella.

"The library smells," Win said suddenly. "It's a dump for the homeless. I don't know how you can bear it. Why don't you just go to a B&N superstore? At least they're clean. And you can get a decent cup of coffee."

I tried to smile. I did. "Because," I said, "Barbara Michaels isn't reading at B&N. She's reading at the library."

Win's eyes were glancing back to the paper. He was done with the conversation. "Well," he said, folding the paper to a new page, "don't let anyone pick you up."

I thought I would faint. My stomach clenched, my mouth watered, sweat broke out on my neck.

Oh, God, what did Win know? Maybe one of his colleagues had seen me with Finn back on the Fourth of July!

But Win's creeping smile belied any knowledge of my betrayal.

I shoved away my nagging conscience.

Win, I realized, thought he was being funny. He thought that at a silly reading and book signing there'd be no eligible men to make a pass at me, only sad homeless losers and pathetic homosexuals.

Those would be his terms.

Maybe he thought that even if there were eligible men at the event, none of them would notice me, let alone make a pass at me.

Why? Because I wasn't the type men made passes at. I wasn't sexy, outstanding, irresistible.

I was Clare.

Sweetie.

A nobody.

"I'll be fine," I mumbled. I grabbed my bag and left the room. As the door shut I heard Win calling, "What time will—," but I didn't stop to answer.

The reading and signing was attended by about fifty people, which to me seemed a great success. Afterward, clutching my autographed copy of the latest in the Amelia Peabody series, I examined the display of photographs of late-nineteenth–early-twentieth-century archaeological digs, digs that took place around the time Ms. Michaels's famous heroine was busy in Egypt.

And then I was aware of someone close on my right, also studying the display.

A man. Maybe five or seven years older than me.

I'd noticed him earlier. It hadn't been difficult given that he was the only man in the room aside from two members of the library staff.

I shot a quick glance at him. Tall. Reddish brown hair, cut close. An artfully scruffy beard. A good profile, strong nose and chin. He looked Viking-like.

I looked away, afraid he'd catch me staring.

Too late.

"Hi," he said, and I turned back to him.

"Hi."

He gestured to the book I held in my arms. "You were at the reading."

I smiled. "Yeah. I love her work."

The guy's neat, clean attire precluded his being homeless. And if he was gay, well, it wasn't going to matter to me in the end, anyway. Being engaged to Win.

And there would be no more slips. No more betrayals. Ever.

I gestured at his own book, under his arm. "You, too."

The guy nodded. "I admit, I'm a fan. My sister has Ms. Michaels's books all over her apartment and one day I picked one up, just to browse. A chapter later, I was hooked."

Well, there was no harm in talking about books, was there? I asked myself.

"Her characters are always strong and intelligent," I said. "But not perfect. You feel like you know them. You feel like you are them. At least, I do. I feel like I could be a heroine. Except . . . Except . . ."

"Go on," he urged. "Except that real life is more complicated than fiction? Because instead of just one author making decisions there are countless 'authors' contributing random, conflicting ideas and no editor to pull everything together into a meaningful whole?"

"Well, that wasn't exactly what I meant," I admitted, smiling. "But it's a very interesting observation. What I mean is that even if they're afraid or sad, the heroines in Ms. Michaels's books seek out their fate. They have adventures because they have convictions and interests and they pursue ideas and justice and rest for weary souls . . ."

I stopped, embarrassed. "I'm sorry," I said, blushing. "Am I making any sense?"

"Perfect sense. And why don't you think you're like a Michaels/Peters heroine?"

"Because I'm not."

The guy gave me an odd look. "You sound so sure of that."

"I am."

"Well, maybe you're working up to being a heroine. The heroine of your own life."

An interesting idea.

"That would be nice," I said. "Maybe I should make that my goal. Thanks."

He glanced at his watch and then looked back to me. "Hey," he said, "it's only eight o'clock. I was wondering, would you like to get some coffee, maybe continue our conversation?"

For the second time that night I felt as if I would faint. I wondered if I'd heard him correctly. But the open, anticipatory look on his face affirmed that I had.

"Oh, I'm—I'm so sorry," I said. "I'd love to have coffee with you but, you see, I'm engaged."

Stupidly, I wiggled my left hand. And only then realized that I wasn't wearing my engagement ring.

"Oh. No, I'm the one who's sorry." He laughed awkwardly. "I didn't see a ring."

I looked down at my empty hand.

At my hand the way it should be?

"It's being resized," I said. As if he cared. "Of course you wouldn't know . . ."

"Yeah . . . Well, I guess I'm going to take off. Have a good night."

"Thanks," I said, forcing a smile. "You, too."

There followed a moment of supreme mutual discomfort.

And then, with a quick smile, he left me standing alone by the photographic display.

I stood there for a moment, staring blindly at the other attendees around me.

I hadn't even asked for his name.

The stranger. An admirer.

The misunderstanding had been all my fault.

I was guilty of false advertising. I wasn't wearing my engagement ring. I'd lost so much weight the ring kept threatening to fall off my finger so Win had taken it to a jeweler to be resized.

Without the ring, I appeared to be a free agent.

I wondered. Should I have hidden in the apartment until the ring was back on my finger, good and tight?

Of course not.

But why had the stranger spoken to me?

I must have been giving off a vibe that said I was available. Right?

Danielle would know the answer. She knew everything about male dating behavior and she had a notebook to prove it.

But I would never know.

And now the stranger probably thought I was just a tease, a heartless flirt.

As if it mattered what the stranger thought. I'd never see him again. I couldn't!

What a mess, Clare, I scolded. *Everything you touch dissolves into disaster.*

Win. Finn.

My heart heavy, I left the library and hailed a cab on Bolyston Street.

Alone in the dark on the hard backseat, I tried for peace of mind.

Nothing happened, Clare, I told myself, watching the streets go by, *just forget it.*

It wasn't like the July 4th incident.

Nothing happened.

But something had.

Danielle
Meet the Parents

It wasn't the first time I'd been invited to a guy's parents' house for dinner.

Except that it was. Meaning that back in high school Seth Levenkron, my senior prom date, was living with his parents, whereas Chris had his own small place behind his parents' house.

A few days before the big night Chris had asked me if I had any food allergies or intense dislikes.

"I love food," I said. "Have you ever seen me be fussy?"

"No. It's one of the things I really like about you. You're sensual. Sensuous. You embrace life."

Yes, I do, I agreed silently.

Take that Lara Flynn Boyle! Kim Cattrall! Michelle Pfeiffer!

Saturday evening Chris and I arrived at the Childs' family property in rural Chilmark.

The Childs' property covered about twenty acres. Everything was so green and lush. The air was so fresh I felt almost light-headed.

The three-story, nineteenth-century house was white with black shutters. Colorful petunias spilled from window boxes on the first-floor windows. There was a wild garden off to the side and behind the house, just outside the kitchen door, an herb and vegetable garden.

The first floor consisted of a parlor-like front room, now used as a bedroom, complete with fireplace; a kitchen; a dining room; a half-bath; and something Chris called a mudroom. On the second floor there were three bedrooms of varying size, each with a fireplace, one used as a home office; and a full bath.

I asked where the washing machine and dryer were located. Chris gave me a funny look and told me his mother did all the laundry down by the creek.

It took me a moment to realize he was joking. Mrs. Childs had a very nice laundry and ironing room set up in the basement.

Chris introduced me to his parents as his girlfriend. It gave me a start but no one could tell my surprise thanks to my excellent social training.

Mr. Childs, a plump, red-cheeked man, was in a wheelchair. Chris had implied that his father wasn't well but he'd never offered any details. I hadn't asked, partly out of delicacy and partly because, well, I'd never expected to meet Mr. Childs or to become involved in the Childs family.

But there I was, in their home for dinner.

Mrs. Childs was tall and fair; Chris got his height and coloring from her.

Dinner was served almost immediately. Though I was used to a relaxing cocktail hour first, what could I say?

The dining table was simply, though expertly, set with everyday white china. Sunflowers graced the table, their stems cut short so as to create a lush, low centerpiece. The napkins were deep blue to match the enameled vase that held the sunflowers.

And the food! We started with homemade New England clam chowder. The entree was a juicy roast beef. Chris had put together a salad of bright, sweet tomatoes and fresh, locally grown greens.

And for dessert, we feasted on Mrs. Childs's homemade peach-and-blueberry cobbler, served with vanilla ice cream.

After what seemed like hours—and very pleasant ones at

that!—I patted my mouth with a napkin and sat back in my chair with a sigh of contentment.

"I like to see a girl with a healthy appetite," Mr. Childs said with a twinkle in his eye.

Mrs. Childs swiped his shoulder with her napkin but I wasn't in the least offended.

"That's me." I laughed. "I don't understand skinny. It doesn't speak to me. I think it's genetic."

"Speaking of family," Mrs. Childs said cleverly, "we heard you had a birthday recently."

I thanked her for remembering and told them I'd gone home to see my parents. I omitted the fact that Gincy and Clare had gone with me, as Chris thought I'd gone to Long Island alone.

"But we'll be celebrating on our own soon," Chris said, taking my hand. "In Boston."

I didn't miss Mrs. Childs's quirked eyebrow as she looked at her son and then, briefly, to our joined hands.

Gently, I slipped out of Chris's grasp. I was pretty certain Mrs. Childs liked me. Most people did. But I was also pretty sure she didn't understand my relationship with her son.

That made two of us.

Deftly, I turned the conversation to a more general, less personal topic.

About an hour later, Chris and I took our leave and went to his own home, which he said he was eager to show me. I wondered if he was going to suggest we have sex and I had my answer all prepared.

It was a gentle no.

The house was a smaller version of his parents', built in the 1970s for a bachelor uncle. Chris had inherited it at the age of eighteen, the uncle long since having passed away.

The rooms were spare but not spartan, the style simple but not cold bachelor pad. While looking at a framed photograph of the Gay Head lighthouse during a storm, I wondered who had decorated Chris's house. His mother? A former girlfriend? Or Chris himself?

There was so much I didn't know about Chris Childs. He wasn't the sort to talk much about himself and I had neglected to ask. Neglected or chosen not to ask?

Did he have a brother or sister? Had he ever been married or engaged? How old was he, anyway?

Oh, my God, had he even gone to college?

It struck me then, absolutely for the first time, that if Chris were eligible husband material, I would have acquired the answers to those questions and many more before the end of the first date.

I shuddered, mentally. I so didn't want any bothersome thoughts to spoil an otherwise pleasant evening.

"Your mother is wonderful, Chris," I said, thinking also that she was shrewd and protective of her baby. "You're so lucky. And your father is a sweetheart! He's so cute!"

Chris grinned. "I'll tell him you said so."

I playfully swatted his arm. "Oh, don't do that! I'd be so embarrassed! But really, your parents are so nice. The perfect hosts. And my God, can your mother cook! I'd be as big as a house if I lived near her. And I'm not sure I'd mind!"

Chris got a funny look on his face. He crossed the room to a side table, opened a drawer, removed something from it, then returned to me.

"I have something for you, Danielle," he said, and I swear his voice was unsteady. "I don't know if you'll like it. It's okay if you don't. I mean—"

My heart began to race. "Chris. Stop worrying. I love presents!"

He handed me a flat, square, white box; two tiny pieces of clear tape held it closed.

Jewelry, I thought. My heart continued to speed. *It's jewelry.*

Okay, wrapping paper would have been nice, or at least a big shiny bow, but it was what was inside that mattered.

A bracelet. If the size and shape of the box was any indication, it had to be a bracelet.

Fingers quivering, I sliced the tape with my nail and lifted the lid of the box.

And there it was.

It was a bracelet, all right. And it was made of thin panels of pale shell, sort of opaline, glued to a metal circle. Not even silver, just some low-grade jewelers' metal.

"I've never had a shell bracelet before," I said truthfully. Brightly.

Though I almost felt like crying. I don't know what I'd been expecting. I don't know what I'd been dreading.

"I figured as much," Chris said earnestly. "I mean, I've never seen you in anything like it but when I saw it, I don't know, I just thought of how beautiful it would look against your skin."

He really was so sweet. I smiled and reached up to kiss him softly on the lips. Chris took me in his arms and wouldn't let me go.

"Danielle," he said, his voice husky, "there's something I want to ask you."

His closeness lulled me. For a moment.

And then I was struck by a dreadful thought.

A shell bracelet just could not be an engagement offering, could it?

It had better not be! Because then I would have to turn Chris down for more than one reason.

"Hmm?" I murmured, pretending I was still under the spell of his embrace.

"We've been seeing each other for a while now—"

"Ten weeks," I said, unaware until that moment that I'd been keeping track. "Twenty times. Ten actual dates. Not including the two times we bumped into each other."

"Oh," Chris said. "Okay. Well, I was thinking, there's no one else I want to be dating. I was wondering if you felt the same. Because if you do, well, I thought we could see each other exclusively. Just us two."

The wonderful meal I'd just eaten threatened to come back up in a torrent of panic.

Oh, God, I thought, *why is this happening?*

Stupid girl, accepting an invitation to his parents' house for dinner!

"Silly," I said, trying for a softly teasing tone, one fairly seductive and reassuring, "of course I love being with you."

"But will—"

"I mean, we have such a nice time. Don't we? Everything's just so nice."

Chris looked down at me and though I tried, I couldn't read his face.

In so, so many ways Chris was an unknown.

Had my words fooled him into thinking I'd agreed not to see anyone else? Or had he read the real meaning behind them?

Chris wasn't stupid. If he had understood me, then he was saving his dignity by pretending not to have.

I tried to salvage what I could of that evening's romance. I drew back from him just a bit and held up the arm with the bracelet.

"Look," I said, "if you turn it this way it flashes the palest pink. I love pink."

Chris smiled briefly. "I know," he whispered.

Then he drew me back to him and said nothing more.

How can I not love this man, I asked myself as we embraced.

Because you're not allowed.

Gincy

Playing House

I took the plunge.
Made the leap.
Bit the bullet.
How else would my father describe my brave action?

I screwed my courage to the sticking point and invited Rick and Justin to spend a day in Oak Bluffs with me.

It was a nerve-wracking prospect, but something happened during the week that completely took my mind off the impending weekend visit.

I received a letter from The Doctor.

Let me set this up.

After years of ignoring the reality of my health—i.e., self-diagnosing and skipping yearly physicals—I'd finally succumbed to Sally's pressure and made an appointment with a doctor. Really, it was more to shut her up than because I really cared about my vital signs.

The visit went okay. There was some minor poking and prodding, nothing annoyingly invasive.

And then The Doctor, a superfit-looking woman about thirty-five years old, wanted to draw some blood.

"What for?" I asked. Somewhat belligerently.

"I want to check your cholesterol levels," she said, scribbling in my chart. "And I want to test for a thyroid problem."

"Thyroid?"

"Your eyes look a little bulgy," The Doctor said matter-of-factly.

Doctors, it seems, can insult your looks and get away with it. That has to be a perk of the profession.

"Can I say no?"

I fully intended to say no.

"You can," The Doctor replied, looking steadily at me.

Suddenly, I felt ashamed. Had I really been acting like a pissy child?

"It's your life," she went on. "But if I'm going to treat you properly, you need to work with me, not against me."

"Okay," I murmured.

So my blood was drawn by a large Jamaican woman full of attitude. She made the procedure bearable; I imagined her sitting on a struggling patient and enjoying it. When she was done she told me I'd get the results in a few days, via snail mail.

I forgot about the test about five minutes after leaving the doctor's office and making my way back into town from Chestnut Hill on the Green Line D extension.

About a week later, as I was leaving for work, I found an envelope on the floor of my building's lobby, addressed to me. It must have been put in someone else's box, someone who kindly tossed it on the floor for me.

It was an envelope from The Doctor.

My heart started beating madly and I stuffed the envelope in my bag. As soon as I got to the office I dialed Sally's extension and told her to hightail it to my office.

"Look!" I hissed, waving the envelope in her face. "This is all your fault."

"What?" Sally said, snatching the envelope. "Oh. It's probably the results of your blood test. What's the big deal?"

I snatched back the envelope.

"The big deal is . . . The big deal . . ."

"Gincy, just open it. If there's bad news at least you'll know so you can do something about it. Fix the problem, find a solution, solve—"

"Shut. Up."

I tore open the now-mangled envelope and read the contents. Then I read the contents again.

"Well?" Sally prompted. "Don't keep me hanging."

I cleared my throat. "It says, and I quote, 'Your levels are essentially normal.' "

Essentially normal?

What did that mean, essentially?

No, what did that mean, exactly?

Another question: What the hell was a level? Levels of what?

"That's how doctors talk," Sally explained. "Don't worry about it."

"Don't worry about it?" I shrieked. "It's my blood, I'll worry about it if I want to. You know, before you made me go to the freakin' doctor, I never even thought about my blood. About my—what is this? My freakin' expialadocious? What does this mean? How do they expect you not to worry when they don't explain these stupid medical codes—this could be ancient Egyptian for all I know!—and they tell you your blood is essentially normal?"

"Calm down, Gincy," Sally said. "You can ask the doctor when you go back."

"Go back? Why would I go back?"

"For a follow-up. Didn't she tell you to make another appointment?"

"No. And I'm not going to. I'm going to try really, really hard to forget this whole thing ever happened. Essentially normal. Jesus Christ. What next? Slightly insane? A little bit pregnant?"

Sally shook her head and walked off. In retrospect, I couldn't blame her.

The whole thing was still bugging me when Rick and Justin stepped off the ferry that morning in August, but I vowed not to mention The Doctor until Rick and I were alone.

First I brought the guys to the house to meet Danielle and

Clare. We stayed only about five minutes but it was long enough for Rick and Justin to make a good impression on my roomies.

On the way back out, I turned to catch any nasty faces. Instead, Clare smiled broadly at me and Danielle shook her right hand and mouthed, "Hot!"

From the house we went straight to the Flying Horse Carousel on Circuit Avenue, Oak Bluff's main street. Rick hoisted Justin on a prancing purple horse while I got us ice cream cones. Then we plopped down on a bench from where we could keep an eye on the rotating kid.

While Justin went round and round on his purple horse, I told Rick about my visit to The Doctor and about the blood test results.

"That sounds good," he said, finishing off his ice cream cone.

"Don't you think the language is a little vague?" I pressed. "Essentially normal?"

"That's how doctors talk," he said, wiping his mouth and balling the napkin. "They learn early on to avoid definitive statements. Other than, "He's dead," of course. It's a way of protecting themselves against malpractice suits. And probably also a way of admitting that they're not gods. That they might have missed something lurking in the shadows."

Well, that was disturbing.

"So, you're saying precision isn't a big thing for physicians?"

Rick shrugged. "In their language if not in their actions, no, it's not."

"That's criminal," I said angrily. "Why do people bother going to doctors anyway if all they're going to hear are diagnoses like, well, you look like you have a thyroid problem but the tests say you don't so let's just wait and see if you curl up and die before tomorrow?"

Rick laughed. "Would it make you feel better if I told you my own favorite doctor diagnosis?"

"No. Yes."

I wondered how he could be so matter-of-fact, so Zen about medical stuff, when his wife's freakin' doctors couldn't prevent her from dying of cancer at the age of twenty-nine.

Oh, my God, I realized. *That's my age. I'm twenty-nine. And I could die . . .*

"Gincy?"

"What?" I blurted.

"Are you okay? You just went pale."

Yeah, pale like a corpse. Like the corpse I soon could be!

"I'm fine," I lied. "Just tell me the story. And it had better be funny."

Rick took a deep breath. "Okay," he began, "well, it was about six years ago, I guess, and Annie had just been diagnosed. She was feeling very depressed and tired so I decided I'd try to do more around the house. You know, take some of the pressure off so she could concentrate on getting well."

Like that worked, I thought grimly.

"Anyway, one day I pulled out the vacuum and the dust mop and the Ajax and put on the TV for some background noise and got to work. At one point, I was bending over dusting a baseboard—"

"You dust baseboards?"

This was an interesting fact.

"Not anymore," he assured me. "So, I was dusting a baseboard when something on the TV caught my interest and I straightened up to check it out and crashed my head into the edge of a heavy wood shelf."

"Ow."

Rick touched the very top of his head with one finger, as if it still hurt. "Yeah, ow. I blanked out for a minute and the pain was bad but I didn't want to cause more trouble for Annie, so when she got up from her nap for dinner I didn't mention it. But four days later I still had a headache and my eyesight was a bit blurry so I went for a CT scan."

I felt my stomach drop to my knees. My knees throbbed with the weight.

"Was it scary? They put you in a tube, right?"

Rick shrugged. "No, it's no big deal, you just lie there. I kind of fell asleep. Anyway, when it was over, I asked the technician if he saw anything. And he told me that he'd leave the official readings to my doctor but that he saw no gross abnormalities."

Rick laughed. I mean, he guffawed. "It still cracks me up. No gross abnormalities. Implying, of course, there were only millions of tiny abnormalities."

I didn't get the humor. "Rick, how can you laugh about that?" I cried. "First of all, the technician guy should never have just blurted out that information. Was he trying to be funny? He probably wasn't even qualified to give an opinion!"

I grabbed Rick's arm and shook it, as if that would make him understand my point.

My fear.

"And, God, you could be a freakin' walking time bomb! What if all those little abnormalities get together and decide to make one big-ass—i.e., gross!—abnormality, and POW! you're dead."

Rick slipped out of my grasp and gave me a one-armed, cheer-up kind of hug. "Gincy, the doctor read the scan and concluded I didn't have a concussion, so there was nothing to worry about. There is nothing to worry about."

I wasn't appeased. "Essentially normal, my ass," I muttered.

"Look," Rick said, "here comes Justin. Guess he's finally tired of the merry-go-round."

"Okay. I get it. We'll drop the subject. For now."

The rest of the afternoon was spent having fun. Which I managed to do after some serious effort at putting the gross abnormalities story out of my mind.

Rick and I had fried clams for lunch; Justin went for a hot dog. Rick bought a second ice cream cone, which he managed to drop two seconds after the purchase.

"Dad," Justin said, matter-of-factly, "you might want to try a cup next time."

After lunch, Justin and I had a contest to see who could toss small rocks farthest into the ocean. I won, fair and square. Justin was a good loser so it all worked out.

Using a one-time-use camera I'd bought in CVS we took goofy pictures of each other splashing in the surf. A passing couple in their late sixties or so offered to take a picture of "the entire family." Without missing a beat, Justin grabbed my hand and Rick's, and suddenly we were a unit.

Rick winked at me over Justin's head. It was a weird moment but also really wonderful. I felt tears prick my eyes and was glad I was wearing sunglasses.

Later, I watched as the ferry pulled away from the dock, taking Rick and Justin back to Boston. The sun was almost down. My guys appeared on deck, almost shadows now, and we waved to each other until we were all lost to sight.

I was sad to see them go.

I hoped that made me essentially normal.

Gincy

It's All in the Presentation

On a wild and crazy whim, Clare and I had stayed home that night instead of wasting money at a bar. We poured our own beer and ordered a pizza.

Clare was reading some mystery set in late-nineteenth-century Egypt and I was enjoying a biography of Benjamin Franklin when Danielle came home around eleven o'clock, dragging her date behind her.

Clare, wearing only a thin cotton nightgown, grabbed a throw pillow to her chest and remained curled up in her chair. Dressed in a T-shirt and jean shorts, I got up to shake hands with this newest in a long line.

It was like shaking a few strands of limp pasta. The guy's wrist was the circumference of a matchstick.

Danielle introduced him as Stuart and announced he'd only be staying a moment.

Stuart blushed furiously and looked to Danielle. She pointed toward the bathroom. While he was gone, Clare and I shot each other questioning looks. Danielle hummed and emptied her purse on the kitchen counter.

After a moment or two Stuart scurried back and Danielle walked him to the door. There was no kiss, not even a peck on the cheek.

His head bobbed as if he were an overly humble Japanese man begging pardon for some social misstep.

"So," I drawled when Danielle returned alone. "How was your date?"

She shrugged and didn't meet my eye. "Fine. He asked me out again and I said yes. He's a lawyer, you know."

"He's a lawyer?" I said. "Jeez, I hope he's more alive in the courtroom. The guy's got no affect. He's without affect. He's affectless."

Danielle pouted. "That's not true. Okay, maybe it's a little true."

"I could hardly hear him when he said hello," Clare said, joining us now in the kitchen. "He seems far too gentle for court."

I laughed. "He's too skinny for court."

"What!" my roomies cried in unison.

"Just what I said. He's too skinny for court. He makes no impression. One breath and I could knock him over. He's the weenie guy at the beach the macho dudes kick sand at."

"That's so mean!"

I shrugged. "I'm not saying he's not super-intelligent. Maybe. Or nice. Or rich. Family money or something. But I can't imagine he's successful, at least not if he has to argue cases in court in front of a jury. If the guy sits behind a desk all day making whizbang deals, okay, I can see that. Maybe. Maybe he uses his meek appearance to throw off the opposition."

"Do you really think appearance has that much to do with professional success?" Clare said, doubtfully.

"In this case," I said, "yes. Tall men are more noticed than short men. Well-built men are considered more powerful than fat or skinny men. Juries are going to be persuaded by the hero guy, the handsome guy, the guy women want to date and men want to be. Or hang out with."

"I think I'll break our next date," Danielle said suddenly. "Gincy's got a very good point. Plus, I don't know, his name does nothing for me. Stuart. Stuart-shmoouart. Blah."

I grinned. "Stuart Little. See? A mouse, not a man."

"You're breaking up with a guy because of his name!" Clare

cried. "I don't believe you. How would you feel if a guy broke up with you because he didn't like your name?"

Danielle shrugged. "His loss. Besides, how could any normal man not like 'Danielle.' Please. Although one guy called me Dani-elle on our first date and, let me tell you, that was the end of that relationship."

"Why are you dating other guys, anyway?" Clare asked then. "I mean, you've been to Chris's house and met his parents. Isn't that kind of big?"

Danielle actually flushed and turned to open the refrigerator. "Is there any diet soda left?"

"She doesn't want to discuss it," I explained. "Chris isn't in the running. She doesn't take him seriously. She's intending to break his heart."

Danielle slammed the fridge door and whirled around. "Oh, please! Chris isn't in love with me!"

"Of course he is," I answered calmly. "You're just in denial."

Clare walked over to Danielle and put a hand on her shoulder. I'd never seen her touch anyone before. The girl was just full of surprises.

"Danielle, I think Gincy's right. It is pretty obvious. He looks at you like—like he's glad to be alive just so he can gaze at you."

"He—" Ah, Danielle couldn't deny it.

"And you're in love with him, too," I said.

"I am not!"

"Okay, then. You have strong feelings for him."

"No, I don't!"

I shot a look at Clare. It said, "Watch this."

"Oh, yeah?" I pointed to Danielle's right wrist. "Then what's that thing you're wearing?"

Danielle nervously—guiltily?—touched the wide bracelet on her arm. "What thing? Oh, this? It's nothing. It's just a shell bangle. Nothing."

"And who gave it to you?"

"All right," she cried, "Chris gave it to me. At his parents' house. But it doesn't mean anything. It's not like—like a promise ring."

"Then why are you wearing it? It's not gold. It's not diamonds. It's so not—"

"Okay, okay. Just—just stop. It does mean something to me. God."

"Why is it so hard to admit that you really like Chris?" Clare asked, far more gently than I would have. "He seems awfully nice."

Danielle clutched her head. The shell bangle slid farther down toward her elbow.

I think I'd like one of those, I thought.

"Because it's just not going to work out, okay?" Danielle answered, clearly near tears. "It's just not."

Clare didn't push for an explanation. I'm sure she knew as well as I did what Danielle's answer would be.

"Then why don't you cut him loose now?" I asked, "if your mind is made up? Don't drag him along, letting him think you guys are building something special when you have no intention of seeing him after the summer."

Clare shook her head at me, ever so slightly.

"Can we please change the subject?" Danielle cried, eyes glistening. "Or I'm out of here. I mean it. I don't want to talk about Chris anymore."

"Of course," Clare said before I could further antagonize anyone. "I think there's some diet soda on the porch. I'll go get some. It's warm but we have ice."

"Thanks," Danielle whispered.

Gincy
Personal Responsibility

After the grilling I had given her the night before, I wasn't sure Danielle was ever going to talk to me again.

But Danielle was remarkably buoyant. Maybe inside she was all coiled up about Chris, but when she appeared for breakfast I couldn't detect a trace of sadness or anger.

As I'd noted before, she was generally a good sport. That, and a damn good actress.

By ten o'clock we were installed at our favorite area of the Oak Bluffs town beach. The Bouncies were nowhere in sight. The day boded well.

I was half asleep, my hat over my face, when Danielle asked, apropos of nothing, "Does Rick have a nickname for you?"

I lifted the hat and squinted at her. "What? No. Sometimes he calls me Gince. That's just when he's being lazy."

"No," she said, "I mean a pet name, something only he calls you."

I scowled and sat up on my towel. "I'm not big on pet names. I find the whole concept sickening. My own name is good enough."

Danielle grinned. "You mean you don't call him Rickie-wickie or Loverboy?"

I reached for Clare's sunblock and squirted some on my pasty legs.

"He'd spit in my eye if I did," I assured Danielle. "And I'd deserve it. Well, he wouldn't actually spit. I'm the hot-tempered idiot in the relationship. Rick is annoyingly mature."

"Back when we were first together," Clare said then, "Win used to call me Clare-bear. His little Clare-bear."

"Ugh."

"Oh, I think it's kind of cute," Danielle said. "So what does he call you now?"

Clare made a face. "It's kind of embarrassing."

"Why?" I asked, returning her sunblock. "Too icky?"

"No," she said with a sigh. "Actually, it's embarrassing because all his friends at the office and from law school call their wives the same thing."

"Which is? Don't keep us hanging here!"

"Sweetie."

"Okay," Danielle said with a roll of her eyes, "that's pretty condescending."

"Sweetie?" I repeated. "As in, 'Sweetie, will you get me another beer?' and 'Sweetie, call my mother for me, would you? You really should call her more often, you know. Good little wives call their mothers-in-law at least once a week.'"

"And, 'Sweetie, have you done my laundry yet?'" Danielle added.

"Something like that," Clare admitted. "But I don't think Win means it to be condescending. I think he just calls me sweetie because all the other guys use the term."

"Ah, that's what bothers you, isn't it?" I said, putting my hat on my head where it belonged. The sun was super-strong. "The fact that you're no longer a special individual to him. You're just one of the gals. One of the stable of fiancées and wives."

"Yes," she said fiercely. "That's it exactly."

I guess I'd hit a sore truth. Danielle shot me a warning glance and I just shrugged.

"And it also bothers me that Win is so one of the guys."

Clare sat up now, too, and wrapped her arms around her knees.

"He's so one of the crowd. Everything he does seems so, I don't know, by the book, exactly what a successful corporate lawyer is supposed to do. Buy a 7-Series BMW. Upgrade his cell phone every three months. Play golf on Saturday mornings. Buy his shirts at Brooks Brothers. Marry the college girlfriend. Move to the suburbs."

"He wants to move to the suburbs?" Danielle asked. "Where, Lincoln?"

"Or Lexington. Maybe Concord. As soon as I get pregnant with our first child."

"So don't get pregnant," I muttered.

"Oh, I wouldn't mind living in a nice suburb," Clare said, neatly ignoring the pregnancy issue. "I miss living in a real house. I just—It would be nice if I had a say in our life decisions, that's all."

"Tweetie," I said. "He might as well call you his wittle yewoh Tweetie Bird. And keep you in a cage."

"Was Win always this way?" Danielle asked. "Was he always part of the pack? Was he ever really an individual? Or was that just your perception of him?"

Clare didn't answer right away.

"Or maybe you once liked that he was solid and ordinary," I said, remembering my first impression of Win at his firm's cocktail party.

Before he'd opened his big mouth.

"Maybe Win hasn't changed so much. Maybe it's you who's changed."

Clare still had no answer.

"Put your foot down now, Clare," Danielle urged, twisting open a bottle of diet iced tea, "before it's too late."

"I hate to bring everyone down even lower than we already are," I said, "but it's already way too late. Win's not going to change. Why should he? The system works fine for him."

Danielle frowned at me. "So, what are you suggesting Clare do?"

"I'm not necessarily suggesting anything," I said carefully, speaking only to Danielle. "I'm just offering my opinion. I think the only way Clare's going to have her own life—or, at least, a say in a shared life—is by dumping Win and finding another guy. A very different sort of guy."

I turned back to Clare then. "Start all over with a new guy, Clare," I said, "fresh and clean. Set new precedents. Make new rules."

Clare frowned down at the massive diamond ring that tightly encircled the fourth finger of her left hand.

Oh, crap, I thought. *I've done it again.*

Channeled Ralph Kramden. Gone one step too far.

Me and my big mouth.

Finally, Clare looked up, first at me, than Danielle. "I appreciate your thoughts," she said, voice tight. "I do. But it's my life. And I'm the one who's going to have to live it. That way I won't have anyone to blame but myself if I screw it all up."

Well, what could we say to that?

I laid back down on my towel and took a vow of temporary silence.

Danielle
What You Asked For

I made the reservation at Grille 23.

Not that Chris couldn't have handled such a simple task. Of course he could have. It's just that I was so used to dealing with personnel at high-end restaurants it seemed silly not to make the call. And to choose the place and time.

Frankly, I would have chosen Locke-Ober for dinner but I thought the prices might be too unfairly high for Chris.

I was thinking of him all along. Even though it was my birthday celebration and, technically speaking, the birthday girl should be the center of attention and shouldn't have to do any of the work.

Chris came to my door at five that afternoon. He looked very presentable. The double-breasted suit was a few years out of style, but for Boston it was just fine.

Au courant, most Boston men were not.

His hair was a bit plastered down at first but during the course of the evening it fluffed up nicely.

And, of course, he carried a small overnight bag.

One issue was left outstanding and that was the issue of where Chris was going to spend the night. In my apartment, of course, but on the couch or in my bed? With me. Having sex.

I can't really say why we hadn't slept together before then except that I had never let it happen. I'd never set up a situation in which Chris felt comfortable suggesting we spend the night together.

I wasn't entirely sure why. I wasn't entirely sure of anything where Chris was concerned.

We took a cab to the restaurant. Chris had wanted to walk but I didn't want to arrive all sweaty, even though taking a cab meant another expense for my date.

The woman never pays for transportation.

We were seated at a corner table, per my request. I didn't want Chris to be stuck right in the middle of the hustle and bustle. I wanted him to be comfortable.

I ordered the prime rib. Chris had the filet mignon.

We hardly spoke during the meal but when we did the conversation was fine. Light and fine.

Everything was going swimmingly.

Until the waiter had cleared the meal and brought dessert menus.

"Danielle," Chris said, the moment the waiter had moved off, "there's something I have to say."

I can dash off to the ladies' room, I thought wildly. I could delay whatever was coming.

But could I stop it all together?

"Yes?" I said innocently.

Chris's bright blue eyes held mine. I couldn't look away. "Danielle, I want us to be together. I want you not to see anyone else. I want us to be exclusive."

Where, where, where to begin?

How, how, how to extricate myself from this . . . trap.

I smiled feebly. Social training only goes so far.

"But Chris," I began. I prayed for inspiration. And then . . . "We haven't even, you know."

Chris gave me nothing. He continued to gaze at me with those brilliant eyes. I was a butterfly under his pin.

I swallowed hard, leaned forward, and dropped my voice to a whisper. "We haven't even been intimate yet. How can we, you know . . ."

"Commit to each other?"

I nodded.

Chris's voice was tight. "Do you need to know how I am in bed before you'll agree not to see other guys?"

"No, no, it's not that!" I assured him.

It wasn't that, entirely.

Where to go from there!

"Of course," I went on, hoping desperately that the waiter would reappear that second, "sexual compatibility is important in a relationship. But I'm not worried about that with us, really. It's just . . ."

"Just what, Danielle?"

I felt panic rise in me.

How, how, how could I tell him that I didn't want a commitment in the first place?

Well, I did want a commitment, just not with Chris.

But you do want a commitment with him!

That bothersome little voice in my head again.

You're in love with him. How can you turn your back on love! Love doesn't come around all that often, you know.

When was the last time you were in love, Danielle?

A better question: *Have you ever been in love?*

Chris spoke again before I could answer his last question. "I'm going to be away for a while, maybe as long as a week," he said. "I don't know for sure. I hate to leave right now with one of the guys sick, but I have no choice. Johnny will cover for me as much as he can."

"Where are you going?" I asked, surprised by the sudden change in topic.

"Portland, Maine. A guy named Tristan Connor contacted us, Childs' Seafoods. He's some big restaurant guy, an entrepreneur. He was on the Vineyard recently and was impressed by our reputation. I never really thought too much about it but everybody on the island knows Childs' Seafoods. Anyway, he thinks there's money to be made by opening a Childs' Seafoods restaurant."

Chris shrugged. He seemed almost embarrassed by the prospect.

"I don't know. If things work out it could mean big business for Childs' Seafoods. That's what Connor thinks, anyway. I've hired a lawyer in Portland to help me figure it all out."

"Chris, that's wonderful!" I said, raising my wineglass as if to toast him. "You'll finally be a success!"

The second the words left my mouth it hit me how insensitive and insulting I'd sounded.

The evening was so not going according to plan.

"Oh, Chris," I cried, setting the glass down heavily and spilling red wine on the snowy table linen, "not that you aren't already a success. I didn't mean . . . I just meant that . . ."

Chris's face was inscrutable. "I know what you meant," he said evenly.

I wondered if he really did.

"Anyway," he went on, "it's a big 'if' but it's a chance I think is worth taking. And when I come back, I'm going to ask you the same question I asked tonight. I'm going to ask you to make a commitment to me."

I sat straight in my chair and tried to remain composed.

I thought back to the night Chris had given me the shell bracelet. He'd asked me then to promise to date only him.

I'd sidestepped the question, not very neatly. Chris hadn't been satisfied, but he'd let the matter go.

For the moment.

Now he was asking again, and again I was avoiding.

This time, Chris wasn't about to let the matter go.

There was something fierce about Chris Childs. Suddenly, I found his persistence attractive; he was the wild hero of old, pursuing his feisty heroine with a vengeance.

Suddenly, I found his persistence repellant.

We hardly knew each other, though maybe that was largely my fault. Still, in terms of time, in terms of days and weeks and months, we were so new.

Why was he pushing, why was he trying to lock me up as his?

I looked across the table at Chris Childs and I saw a stranger. A dangerous stranger.

"Are you giving me an ultimatum?" I said, my voice quivering with a sudden fury.

And then, in an instant, the dark pursuer was gone, replaced by a sweet man in love.

"God, no, Danielle," he said, all earnest. "I don't mean it that way. I just want us to be together. I don't want to lose you."

I took his hand across the snowy white tablecloth. "You're not going to lose me," I promised.

Liar. It's over as soon as you hand the keys to the house back to the rental agency.

Chris squeezed my hand in return. "Will you think about it while I'm away? Please?"

"Of course I will. Of course. Now, how about dessert?"

Chris stayed in my bed that night. We made love. It was our first time and it was intense and erotic and desperate.

The next morning, as I watched Chris from the living room window, on his way back home to the Vineyard, suit stuffed in his overnight bag, I wondered if it had also been our last.

Gincy

Duty

They say it's bound to happen at least once in the life of every American citizen. For almost thirty years I'd dodged the bullet. But finally I got my day in court.

I was called for jury duty.

I showed the no-nonsense notice to Danielle and Clare over drinks on the terrace of Keith's, by now our favorite bar overlooking the water.

"Jury duty?" Danielle wrinkled her nose. "Ugh. You have to get out of it."

"I don't think I can," I said, worriedly. "My boss has no problem with my doing it. Kell knows I'll still get my work done."

"Fine. Then show up and if you get called to a courtroom and asked questions by the judge or lawyers, lie. Make them believe you're unfit to be on a jury."

"I can't lie," I whispered, hoping no law-enforcement types were in earshot. "It's the government, Danielle. You can't lie to the government. Especially not in court. I think it's called perjury. Or something."

"You wouldn't exactly be in court at that point, would you?" Clare asked, also in a whisper.

I shrugged. "Court is court. The way I see it, if I'm in the building, I'm in court."

Danielle gestured for our waitress and we ordered drinks and a plate of fried calamari. When the waitress had gone to place our order, Danielle sat back and sighed.

"Well, I'd lie," she proclaimed. "There's no way I'm serving on a jury. No. Way. I'd say anything to get myself sent home."

"Oh, please. You'd claim to be a racist or certifiably insane?" I asked.

"Exactly. I don't care what a bunch of strangers think of me. Look, those—people—are not my peers. I don't want any of them judging me. I don't even want to be in the same room as them."

"Those people?" Clare asked. "Who, exactly, do you mean?"

"You know, the average person. The man and woman in the street."

"On the street."

Danielle rolled her eyes. "Whatever. I mean, have you seen how the average person dresses to go to work? Sweatpants. Polyester suits. Reeboks with pantyhose. I wouldn't wear that garbage to—to take out my garbage."

"You don't take out your garbage," Clare pointed out. "You pay someone else to do it."

"Well, see?"

"Look," I said, "I'm not saying I don't agree with Danielle, sort of. I mean, most people are morons. I know that. I am fully aware of that. But . . ."

Danielle put her red-nailed hand on my arm. "But what? Go ahead, say it. You know I'm right. You don't want to spend an entire day in an airless room with a random bunch of morons any more than I do. The average person is not like you and me, Gincy. It's okay to admit that."

"But it's wrong," I argued, "to act on it. If I lie to avoid being on a jury panel, aren't I, I don't know, rejecting the social structure of democracy or something? Like, all men are created equal. All women, too. At least, we're supposed to be."

"So, you're saying it's okay to be prejudiced against morons, and it's okay to call people morons in the first place—"

"Behind their backs," I amended.

Danielle shrugged. "Whatever. But it's not okay to say, 'Hey, I'm not going into that room because it's full of morons and I don't want to spend time with them'?"

"Yeah. I guess. It sounds stupid, I know . . ."

"You can't judge a book by its cover," Clare said suddenly. "No, I mean it. You can't. Just because someone looks, I don't know—"

"Stupid?" Danielle snapped. "Uneducated? Cheesy?"

"Any of those. Just because someone looks odd doesn't mean he is odd. Or stupid or whatever. Every person has value. Every person deserves respect."

"Not necessarily from me," Danielle retorted, looking around for our slow-moving waitress. "That's all I'm saying. Where is that girl?"

"I'm with Danielle on this one," I admitted. "I'll respect anyone who respects me back. But if someone treats me with disrespect, well, I can choose to ignore her. There's no law that says I have to like everybody."

"But," Clare argued, "there are laws that say you have to respect everybody's property and privacy and lives."

"Okay," I conceded. "If I come face-to-face with a person. But I can choose to stay far, far out of the way of morons and their property whenever possible."

"Gincy's right," Danielle said. "And there are morons being called to serve jury duty every day. I simply choose not to spend my time with them."

The waitress finally appeared and apologized for the delay. I wondered how much of our conversation she had overheard and hoped she'd heard none of it. I gave her a big smile, as if to prove that I was a nice person and not an elitist snob. She didn't seem to notice.

When the waitress had gone, Clare, who looked on the edge of having a stroke, picked up the subject.

"You would refuse to serve even if your being on a jury might save an innocent person's life? Even if you might be the only really smart person on the jury, the only chance an innocent person has to get a fair trial?"

Danielle took a sip of her fruity martini before answering. "Oh, please. The court system doesn't need little ole me."

"You're horribly elitist, Danielle," Clare said angrily. "And Gincy, you're not much better."

"Have you ever done jury duty?" I asked her, faking bravado but suddenly very self-conscious. Jeez, I'd just called myself an elitist.

"No," she admitted. "I've never been called. But you can be sure that if I am called, I'll show up and I'll tell the truth and I'll perform my civic duty."

"Well, bully for you."

Danielle swatted away an invisible bug. "That's the beauty of democracy, you know. To each her own."

I spent the rest of the evening drinking in silence.

Gincy
The Dirty Truth

I don't know why I'd bothered to wear a suit. Most of the people gathered in the main jury-pool room were dressed for street cleaning.

Men sat slumped, legs spread, arms folded across their chests. Women clacked gum and filed their nails. Some people settled in for a nap; others sat staring into space, no book or newspaper in sight. Ten people in direct sight slurped cold coffee drinks and chomped donuts.

Was I the only one who was taking this seriously? I wondered. Suddenly, I wanted to yell out, "Hey! Wake up! Sit up straight! Spit out the gum!"

Danielle was right. The average person was a slob. The average person didn't care.

God, I prayed, *I know it's been a really long time since I talked to you. Sorry about that, really. But this is important. Please, please, please don't ever let me be arrested. Because I know I'll be innocent and I just can't face a jury of so-called peers who look like these people do! Because you just know they're not big into critical thinking. And you can just bet they have a tenuous relationship with the English language, regardless of where they were born.*

After almost two hours of being lectured by a judge on the im-

portance of jury duty, and watching a film outlining the basics of
the judicial system for those who hadn't made it past fifth grade,
my number was called and, along with a small mob, I was sent to
a courtroom in which were gathered a judge, a defendant, various armed guards, a court recorder, and two teams of lawyers,
defense and prosecution.

My stomach knotted and I began to sweat. *Crap,* I thought, *I'm
going to faint! Some trigger-happy guard will think it's a trick and he'll
shoot me before I hit the floor.*

I didn't faint. And after an hour of "selection process" I was
thanked and sent back to the main jury-pool room. Thanked
and rejected. Maybe it was how I'd answered a particular question that eliminated me from consideration.

"Juror Number Fifty-Seven. Would you have any difficulty remaining fair and impartial toward this defendant who is being
charged with molesting a three-year-old girl?"

Or something to that effect.

"Yes," I replied. "Yes, I would have difficulty. I would have difficulty not spitting in his general direction whenever he walked
into the courtroom."

Yeah, in retrospect it was probably my answer that got me
thrown out.

Anyway, the only good thing about jury duty in Boston was the
"one day or one trial" policy. I'd done my duty to the city, even
though I'd been rejected for a jury, and now I was free to go.

I left the Post Office Square courthouse in a big hurry.

The city felt ugly, dirty, hot, and sticky.

I was deeply glad I hadn't been chosen for the jury. I don't
know how I would have survived such an emotional ordeal without breaking down or killing the defendant, a large, sweaty fellow with heavy black plastic glasses, whom I'd convicted at first
glance.

No one who looked like that slack-jawed slob in the defendant's chair was ever innocent.

Right?

Hence my answer to the attorney.

I wondered: Why were some people so perverted? How did it

happen? Where they just born defective or did life twist them into an ugly shape? Was it a combination of both predisposition and circumstance?

And how did psychologists not go crazy dealing with the morally decrepit and criminally insane?

There was a reason I hadn't gone into the mental sciences. The presence of lunatics could not be conducive to one's own peace of mind.

All I knew was that if anybody ever touched my kid in an inappropriate manner I'd—

I came to a dead halt on the corner of Franklin Street.

My kid? As in, a kid who was mine?

My son. My daughter.

Holy crap. What was I thinking?

Was this Justin's fault?

Because I'd never said I wanted kids. Ever.

I'd never fantasized about names and tricycles and trips to Disneyworld. I'd never dreamed of how my son would grow up to be the first truly honest president and how my daughter would be the head of a global corporation devoted to preserving the environment by developing Earth-friendly products.

And now I was ready to beat the shit out of some hypothetical pervert who was eyeing my hypothetical kid in a hypothetically inappropriate manner?

Coffee. I decided to get a cup of coffee, something to calm a sudden onset of nerves. Maybe something to eat, too. I spotted a bagel store up the block and headed for it.

As I walked, I tried to rationalize. Maybe I was just reacting in a normally protective manner. Didn't everyone automatically try to protect her property, even if something wasn't technically property, like a human being or a pet?

My boyfriend. My apartment. My car. My cat. My dog.

Even if you didn't actually have something in your possession, wasn't it normal to assume that if you did have that something in your possession you'd do anything you could to protect it—and to punish anyone who tried to hurt it?

Sure. The protective instinct was perfectly normal.

But wasn't it also part of the maternal instinct?

Whoa.

For the first time in my life I'd actually imagined myself as a mother. Even if it was in a roundabout sort of way.

I flung open the door to the bagel shop.

The situation called for extra cream cheese.

Danielle

Off Its Axis

Sometimes, one phone call can change your life.

One phone call from someone you love whose personal decision has ramifications he never even dreamed of.

David called one evening as I was reading the latest issue of *InStyle.*

"Hey," I said. "It's almost ten. I thought you doctors went to bed early. You know, early to bed, early to rise . . ."

"I've got some news, Danielle," he said. His voice sounded funny. Serious and more full of energy than it had sounded in a long time.

"You and Roberta decided to go to Hawaii on your honeymoon after all?" I guessed, somehow knowing that wasn't the news David had called to tell me.

"Uh, no," he said with a small laugh. "There's not going to be a honeymoon, Danielle. Roberta and I aren't getting married."

The news took a moment to sink in.

And then I shouted, "That bitch!"

I heard David take a deep breath. "Danielle," he said, "I broke the engagement. And no more yelling. I've already got one woman furious with me."

Suddenly, I felt sick to my stomach. Literally sick.

I stumbled to the kitchen and poured a glass of cold water.

"David, how could you?" I gasped, water dribbling down my chin unheeded. "Everything was all planned. The ring, the synagogue, the dress! My God, the reception! Bacon-wrapped shrimp and Beluga caviar! Why are you doing this?"

"I'm sorry you're so upset, Danielle. I mean, I thought you didn't even like Roberta."

"I never said I didn't like her!" I cried.

"You didn't have to say anything," he replied. "I know you were trying to be nice, but I could tell what you really felt that last morning on the Vineyard."

I didn't bother to deny it.

"Danielle," David went on, "I hope you can understand. I just can't marry her. I can't marry a woman I'm not in love with. I can't marry a woman I don't respect."

I loved my brother. Of course I wanted him to be happy.

Of course.

I held the cold glass of water against my flushed cheek.

But David was ruining the plan. He was bucking the system. He was destroying the family!

"David?" I croaked, remembering the anger and disappointment he'd revealed at my birthday party. "Why did you ask Roberta to marry you in the first place?"

"I don't know," he admitted. "Well, I sort of know. It just took me some time to figure out the whole thing was a big mistake. What can I say? Better now than two years into the marriage, right?"

Right.

But maybe if they'd just go ahead and get married things would change. David would fall in love with his new wife and she would grow an inner self and . . .

"Have you told Mom and Dad yet?" I said. "They must be so upset."

"They'll get over it. They want me to be happy, Danielle. What do you think, they'd force me into a situation that would make me miserable?"

Wouldn't they? I wondered.

"No," I said. "Of course not."

But maybe if they just encouraged David to give this marriage a try everything would be all right. It happened with arranged marriages, didn't it? Sometimes? If total strangers could make a marriage work . . .

"Let's change the subject," David said. "Let's talk about something positive. Hey, what about you and that guy Chris? The one I never got to meet because he was on vacation or something. The one who couldn't make it to your party. What's going on with him?"

Chris.

I rubbed my temple with my free hand and remembered our one night of extraordinary passion. I remembered also how the next morning I'd watched from my living room window as he'd loped down the block on his way home to the Vineyard, sleeves rolled to the elbow.

"Nothing's going on," I said dully. "Nothing at all."

Gincy

Unforeseen Contingency

Sally wanted to meet at Brasserie Jo on Huntington Avenue so she could watch a review of that day's stage of the Tour de France on the big flat-screen TV set up over the bar.

"I didn't know you were into cycling," I said when I'd hopped up onto a stool.

"I'm not, really. But Sido is. She's French."

"Hey," I said to the painfully skinny, sallow woman sitting to Sally's left. Sido gave a brisk nod of the head and took a long drag of her Gauloise.

I noticed that Sally's hair was streaked with acid green. So was Sido's.

"Did you guys meet at the beauty parlor?" I asked with a raised eyebrow.

Sido either ignored my question or simply was not interested in conversation.

"I don't go to a beauty parlor," Sally said with a frown. "I do my own hair. So does Sido. We met at a club."

"You have no sense of humor, you know that?"

Sally shrugged.

I leaned in and lowered my voice. "So, are you two, you know, involved?"

Sally shot a glance at Sido's sharp profile and then turned back to me. "No! We're just friends." Now it was Sally's turn to whisper. "Sido's got a girlfriend named Barbara. She's much older and has lots of money. She keeps Sido on a very tight leash. Sido's only out alone tonight because Barbara had to go out of town unexpectedly. Some business thing. I'm paying for her drinks so Barbara doesn't notice any charges on Sido's credit card."

"That sounds like an abusive relationship to me," I said, feeling my blood rise. Sido looked tough as nails, but looks, as we all knew, were massively deceiving.

Sally shook her head and I dropped the subject. She ordered a pastis, I ordered a gin and tonic, and Sido ordered a Belgian beer. Actually, she gestured for the beer. Sido, it seemed, wasn't a woman of many words.

Had she been bullied into silence?

"How can you drink that crap?" I asked when Sally's drink arrived. "It looks like phlegm."

But drink it she did. By the third disgusting glass, Sally was becoming feisty.

"Why the hell can't women be in the Tour anyway, is what I want to knew. Know."

"You got me, kiddo," I said. "I know nothing about pro sports. I'm sure there are all sorts of rules and boards and panels and traditions—"

"It stinks is what I say!"

I looked at my friend carefully. Her eyes were droopy and bloodshot. Her mouth looked strained. "And what I say is that maybe you should lay off those nauseating drinks."

"I know when I've had enough," she snapped.

I shrugged. I'd done my job. Now she was the bartender's problem. Or Sido's.

She certainly hadn't come with me.

"I gotta go pee," Sally mumbled. She slid off her barstool and stumbled off to the ladies' room. *Great,* I thought, stuffing a few French fries in my mouth. *I'm alone with Sido the Silent.*

"She like you."

I jumped. She speaks!

"What?" I asked, turning to face Sido, who, by the way, hadn't eaten a thing all night.

"She want to be your girlfriend," she said throatily, taking another puff of her Gauloise. "Sally."

Probably for the first time in my life, I was speechless. For a moment. "What! No way."

"You see how she look at you. You cannot lie."

Well, I could lie, but maybe I wouldn't. If I were perfectly honest with myself, I had to acknowledge that maybe, just maybe I'd had some inkling of Sally's feelings.

I mean, why else would a single gay woman spend so much time with a heterosexual woman, forgoing nights out in bars where she could maybe meet the love of her life, unless maybe the love of her life was right there under her nose?

The heterosexual woman. Her best bud from work.

A little full of yourself, aren't you, I chided. *Who said Sally thinks I'm the love of her life? Maybe she just wants a little below-the-belt action.*

The idea freaked me out.

"I have to run," I said to Sido. I tossed a crumpled twenty-dollar bill on the bar and grabbed my bag, hoping to get out of there before Sally returned from the ladies' room.

Sido shrugged and lit another cigarette. I ducked out of the bar through the revolving door.

Clare

Help from Above

"Marriage is about compromise."

I'd heard that all my adult life.

What I hadn't fully understood was that the compromise starts far before the nuptials. And that it also involves parents and in-laws.

For Mrs. Carrington's sake I would take Win's name.

For my mother's sake, I agreed to have the bridal shower back home in Michigan so that aunts and cousins and neighbors could attend. People I hadn't seen in years. People I didn't really want to see then.

But a bridal shower is as much for the mother as it is for the bride.

Which is maybe why the closer the date came, the more panicked I began to feel about the command performance.

Briefly, I considered claiming illness as an excuse not to make the trip to Michigan. Not to appear at my own bridal shower. But I rejected the idea as far too hard to pull off.

In Boston, I'd have to fake it with Win. And if I decided to get to Ann Arbor before falling ill, I'd have to fake it with Mother.

I was already horribly mired in deception. I doubted I had the dubious skill to fool anyone with a mysterious stomachache. And lying took such enormous energy.

Lying alone probably accounted for my post-engagement weight loss.

Grimly, with the unsuspecting help of my friends, I soldiered on.

I met Gincy and Danielle one evening in Boston for drinks at a place called Out of the Blue. Somehow Gincy had gotten her hands on a discount drinks ticket, good between five and seven o'clock.

Truly, she had a knack for finding bargains. I suppose growing up in near-poverty had its advantages later in life.

When we were seated at the bar—Gincy's choice; she often preferred the bar to a table—and had ordered, Danielle pulled a newspaper from her bag and asked us to bear with her while she finished reading an article.

Danielle claimed not to read, but she almost always had a magazine or newspaper in hand. Her sometimes ditzy personality belied a curious and informed mind.

Well, informed on certain topics.

"What's up with this contemplative lifestyle?" Danielle said with a frown, finally tossing the paper on the bar. "Have you read the review of that tiny French movie about some old monastery? I don't understand the whole nun and monk thing. They just sit around all day praying? Like that will make an exciting movie! Why don't they do something useful for society?"

"They do," Gincy replied calmly. "Praying is useful. They pray for your soul because you don't have the time to. You're too busy going to the mall."

"What if I don't want them praying for my soul?"

"Too bad. They're praying. That's what they do."

"A little prayer never hurt anyone," I said, then felt like an idiot for using a cliché.

I'd noticed that in the past year my diction had gotten lazy. I'd gotten lazy.

And laziness was about not caring.

"Anyway, what do you care?" Gincy was saying. "It's a free

country. You have to let them do their thing. You don't see any nuns trying to stop you from going to the nail salon, do you?"

"Of course I have to let them do their thing." Danielle rolled her eyes. I noticed there was a line of pink shimmer just under her brow. "But I don't have to like it."

"You mean," I said suddenly, pretending nonchalance, "contemplative people pray for the souls of people who aren't even Catholic?"

"Well, yeah, I guess," Gincy said. "Sure. They're holy. They pray for everybody. They're equal-opportunity pray-ers."

I guess that's what makes them holy, I thought.

"So, say I wanted them to pray for something, for example, a cause, something special, you know . . ."

"No, I don't," Gincy said. "But go on."

"How would I go about asking a contemplative to pray for me? It. The cause."

"Yeah," Danielle said. "How would you even go about finding a contemplative nun in the first place? Aren't they secluded?"

"Sequestered. Or maybe the word is cloistered." Gincy frowned. "I don't know, exactly. I suppose you could go online . . ."

"Contemplatives have Web sites?" Danielle shrieked.

"Oh," Gincy said, as if really struck by the oddness of the idea. "Maybe not. But hey, these days? Marketing is everything. The nuns have to live, too, you know. Like, say an order feeds itself on donations from people they pray for especially well. Okay, but first they've got to advertise so people know they even exist. Right? Then they have to remind people they're still there. That's marketing."

"May I see the paper?" I asked, trying again for nonchalance.

Danielle handed it to me and while she and Gincy talked, I sought the review of that tiny French movie.

Clare

Sisterhood

Later that night, after Win was asleep and snoring fitfully, I sat down in the kitchen with my laptop and went online.

I didn't turn on any lights; the glow from the screen was enough for me to see by and I didn't want to wake Win only to have him find me typing keywords such as "prayer" and "monastery."

Unbidden, I heard his fond yet derisive laugh in my head.

Win indulges your little whims, a voice inside me whispered. *How sweet of him.*

It didn't take long before I found a rather simple Web site operated by a group of nuns called the Sisters of the White Rose of Mary. Their cloistered convent was located in a neighborhood of Chicago I knew as quite gritty; the home page indicated that the convent had been there since the early twentieth century.

Nervously, I typed my petition.

That's what they called it. A petition for prayer.

"Hello," I typed, then deleted the word. Too casual.

Maybe this is a stupid idea, I thought. But just then, I didn't have any others.

I took a deep breath, thought quietly for a moment, and then the words came.

"Dear Sisters: Thank you for considering my petition. You should know that I am not a Catholic. However, my friend Virginia, who was raised in your church, assures me that you do not turn away anyone in need of your help."

And then I explained my situation. Truthfully. Almost. Instead of admitting to having cheated on Win, I spoke of having thoughts about other men.

These women might be more worldly than nuns of the previous century, but I didn't want to shock them unnecessarily. Also, I didn't want them to consider me a lost cause.

"Please," I typed, "pray for me. I want to make the right decision. Thank you. Very sincerely yours, Clare J. Wellman."

Gincy

Mommyzilla

Three times she'd come to the office. Three times in one week!

At least to me, her reasons were patently bogus.

Mommyzilla.

The monster after my boyfriend.

Rick told me the monster—Laura DeCosta—had a daughter who went to Justin's summer day-care program. Rick had met her a week or two earlier at a parents' meeting.

Mommyzilla was a single parent. Divorced.

How convenient.

And I just knew that she knew Rick and I were involved.

Maybe Rick had told her. Maybe she'd just sensed our bond on that first visit to the office. Either way, she was out to eliminate me.

I just knew it.

Let me tell you about the first attack.

Mommyzilla invaded on a Monday morning about ten o'clock.

It seems she'd promised to give Rick a recipe for the oatmeal raisin cookies Justin had liked so much, and instead of e-mailing it or jotting it on a card and sending it the old-fashioned way, she'd chosen to make a surprise appearance at his office.

At my office.

A special visit in from Charlestown just to hand-deliver a freakin' cookie recipe?

My ass.

Rick introduced us. Laura DeCosta barely acknowledged my greeting, and turned back to Rick. They headed for his office— why?—and until I saw her pass back through the hall on her way to the elevators, I couldn't concentrate.

Mommyzilla was up to something. My father didn't raise a stupid daughter. I knew trouble when I saw it pad down the hall in flip-flops and a ponytail.

The second attack came on Wednesday at about three.

I sensed someone watching me, looked up from my computer screen, and there she was. A foot or two into my office. Just standing there in her bright yellow T-shirt and flip-flops.

Again with the flip-flops. Today they were bright yellow to match her T-shirt.

Too freakin' cute.

"So, do you have children?" she asked, without preliminary niceties.

No, I thought. *But I do have manners. If I didn't, I'd kick your sorry ass out of my office right now.*

"No," I said, as evenly as possible.

I wanted to convey absolutely nothing. No feelings.

No regret, no desire, nothing.

"Oh," she said, with an odd little smirk. "Well."

And then the bitch just walked out of my office.

I'd been totally dismissed. No one had ever done that to me before.

Well, I could have kids, given the chance! I wanted to scream after her. *I have the same equipment as you! And mine's younger!*

But I sat there at my desk, paralyzed by disbelief.

According to Rick, Mommyzilla had popped in just to say hi. And to deliver a book she'd come across while browsing in Barnes & Noble. A book she just knew Justin would loooove. And it had been a bargain, too, only $4.99.

Rick didn't seem impressed with the gift.

He didn't seem nervous and secretive, either, as if he were hiding a sordid truth from me. His girlfriend.

He seemed perfectly normal, if a bit annoyed at having been interrupted, first by Mommyzilla and then by me, who'd charged into his office immediately after the monster had gotten back on the elevator.

"You want the book?" he said, tossing it aside and beginning to type. "Justin already has it."

The title was *One Hundred Best-Loved Fairy Tales.*

"Okay," I said, though I was loathe to touch it after Mommyzilla had sweated all over it.

But beggars can't be choosers. The book was a freebie. I'd send it to my pregnant teenage cousin as a wedding/baby gift, though I wasn't quite sure she could read.

I went back to my own office and kept the earlier encounter with the monster to myself.

Thursday was blissfully monster-free. And then Friday morning, another invasion.

That time, I had some advance warning. I'd stopped at the receptionist's desk for messages on my way back from the ladies' room. Ken, phone at his ear, shook his head as I approached.

"Rick," he said as I passed. "While you were on the phone you got a call from a Laura. She didn't want your voice mail. She said she'd be here sometime before noon. What? I don't know, she didn't say."

Desperate times called for desperate measures.

Once safely back in my office, I summoned my friends.

Okay. That's what Danielle and Clare had become.

My friends. Through no fault of mine.

They stepped off the elevator within a half an hour. On our way back to my office, I introduced Danielle and Clare to Sally.

Sally greeted them with her usual gruff indifference and then claimed an urgent need to use the copy machine.

"She's interesting," Danielle commented with a raised eyebrow.

"She's all right," I defended. "She is what she is. Anyway, she's not the problem." Okay, a tiny lie. "Mommyzilla is the problem.

And here she comes!" I hissed. "Right on schedule. Now, just watch and tell me what you think."

I shoved my friends into my office where they would pretend not to be spying on me.

I hovered in the doorway. Mommyzilla approached.

"Hello!" I said brightly, noting yet another pair of flip-flops. These were decorated with ladybugs.

Mommyzilla slowed. She tilted her head and looked at me quizzically.

"Oh," she said, stopping momentarily. "I didn't recognize you."

I prayed for calm.

"Gincy," I said, ever more brightly. "We've met twice this week."

Mommyzilla smiled for about a tenth of a second. And then she walked on!

Shaking, I watched her go.

Then I dashed back into my office.

"She's stopped by the office three times this week," I hissed to my friends. "Doesn't she have anything better to do, like go grocery shopping or get her lip waxed? I'm telling you, she's after Rick."

"What's her name?" Clare asked matter-of-factly.

"Laura DeCosta. She's divorced. She's got a four-year-old kid. Kristen or Kirsten or Kris Kringle or something. I don't know."

Danielle folded her arms across her chest and frowned at me. "I cannot," she said, "believe you find that woman a threat."

"Well, I do find her a threat."

"But why?" Clare said. "She didn't seem at all special."

I balled my hands into fists. "I'll tell you why she's a threat," I said fiercely. "Because she's proven she can do it. Go the distance. You know, get married, have the kid. She's an adult."

"That's debatable," Danielle murmured. "Ladybugs?"

I raged on. "What have I done with my life so far? Nothing. Nada. Face it: It would be way less of an adjustment for Rick if he got together with her. Laura knows how to be married. She knows how to be a mother. I bet she can make a sandwich and clean a toilet at the same time. While doing the laundry. And cleaning up after the dog."

"Gincy." Danielle grabbed my arm, careful, I noticed, not to lacerate me. "Gincy, listen to me. Clare and I saw what just happened out there. The woman treated you with disdain. Rick can't possibly like that kind of person. Not the Rick you've described."

Yeah. But had I been describing the real Rick?

"I've never been treated with disdain before," I said, carefully removing Danielle's hand. "Was that disdain? I thought it was disrespect."

Clare shook her head. "No, it was disdain. Also known as contempt or scorn. Trust me. I know. And don't ask why. I just know."

Danielle glanced into the hallway to be sure we were still alone. "I still don't understand what, exactly, you find intimidating about this Laura person. I mean, she wasn't even wearing any makeup. No offense, honey. But, seriously, it can't be her looks."

"There's more to life than looks, you know," I shot back.

Like pregnancy and childbirth and motherhood.

And mortgages and hospital bills and divorce lawyers.

Danielle sighed. "Oh, you poor, innocent thing. Honey, it's always all about looks. At least at first. And trust me, this woman doesn't have them."

And I did? *There's a flaw in your argument, Danielle,* I thought.

"But she does have a kid," I countered. "And she's got Rick's attention."

Clare smiled kindly. "Gincy, I think you're in love."

I flopped into my desk chair and Clare closed the door to my office.

"God. I know. It sucks, doesn't it? Especially since I'm going to lose Rick to a woman with a good forty pounds on me."

"You're not going to lose him," Clare said firmly.

"At least not to that cow!" Danielle exclaimed. "No wonder her husband dumped her. You can be sure she didn't dump him, because when you look that bad you'd be crazy to dump your man unless he was a brutal wife-beater."

I had to laugh. "Thanks, Danielle. You're so reassuring. And so awfully kind. I like that about you."

"I'm just telling you the truth," she said, unperturbed. "You're cute and smart, and even though you're full of piss and vinegar, as my grandma used to say, you're a good person. Now, come on, we're taking you to lunch."

"I usually work through lunch hour," I protested.

"Skipping meals isn't healthy," Clare pointed out.

"And men don't like skinny women."

"Or cows?" I said, feeling the laughter rise again.

Gincy
The Bull by the Horns

That night, after Justin had gone to bed, exhausted after a day spent on a field trip to the Franklin Park Zoo, I confronted Rick.

"I need to know something," I said. God, I was nervous. "I need you to tell me the truth."

Rick sat on the couch, sorely in need of replacing, and motioned for me to join him. "Okay. Shoot."

I looked him straight in the eye.

His eyelashes were longer than mine.

"Are you interested in Laura DeCosta?" I asked. "Don't lie, Rick."

He actually flinched. "Kirsten's mother? Or is it Kristen? Whatever happened to names like Kathleen? Anyway, you mean interested as in, am I attracted to her?"

Don't laugh, Rick, I prayed. *Whatever your answer, don't laugh at me.*

He didn't laugh. In fact, he suddenly looked kind of grossed out. "Jesus, Gincy, no, I'm not attracted to her at all. Did I do something to make you think I was? I'm so sorry. Tell me what it was and I'll make sure I never do it again."

Whoa. Seriously right answer.

I felt relief flood every inch of me. It was very very sweet.

"No," I said, "you didn't do anything. I guess . . . It's all me. I just . . ."

"You never have to be jealous," Rick said, saving me having to speak the word. "It's you and me. Right?"

"Yeah. I guess."

Rick took my hands and said, "Don't guess. It's a fact."

"So, you're sure I'm your type and Laura's not?"

Rick grinned. "Well, don't think I'm a creep for saying this, but, aside from all the other reasons I'm not attracted to the DeCosta person, like the fact that she's the most boring person I've ever met, and why is she showing up in the office every other day on some bogus errand?, she's not exactly good-looking."

"Danielle called her a cow," I told him.

"Well, I wouldn't call her a cow, exactly. Maybe a heifer . . ."

I slapped Rick's arm playfully.

Rick grasped my hands in his. "Here's the deal, Gincy," he said. "I love you."

Oh, boy. There it was.

The moment I'd been dreading.

The moment I'd been craving.

Could I say it back?

Rick sat quietly, patiently, my hands resting in his.

"I love you, too," I said. My voice was a bit wiggly but God, I'd said it!

We hugged for a long time.

Take that, Mommyzilla.

Clare
Pleasantville

The wedding shower.

My wedding shower.

Though Danielle had hinted that she would be happy to come with me to Michigan in case I needed any assistance—whatever that meant; probably, I thought, something to do with crystal—I didn't ask either Danielle or Gincy to join me.

Honestly, I don't think Danielle was particularly offended.

Gincy, I know for a fact, was downright relieved.

"That freakin' baby shower was enough lady-party for me for years," she told me. "But have a good time and all."

Win and I took a cab to Logan. We made our way through security with the usual minor annoyances. I was asked to remove my shoes. Win's laptop rasied suspicions.

Just before takeoff, Win took my hand in his. "I'm so happy, Clare," he said. "I really believe this is the best thing for the both of us. Don't you?"

His eyes were sincere behind his gold-rimmed round glasses. He always wore his glasses and not his contacts when flying. He suffered from dry eyes.

I didn't hate Win.

Sometimes I didn't much like him, either.

And as for love? I knew I was no longer in love with him. I hadn't been for years.

But I did love Win in the way you love someone you know so well it's almost like loving yourself.

Or, at least, being used to yourself. Win was just there like I was just there.

My love for Win was a habit.

Now the question was: A good habit or a bad one?

"Clare?" Win said, squeezing my hand. "I asked you a question."

I shook my head and smiled. "Sorry, Win. There's just so much on my mind . . . Of course I think it's the right thing. Of course."

Mother and Daddy were waiting for us when we emerged from the Detroit airport with our luggage.

"My girl," Daddy said, kissing my forehead. "I'm so proud of you."

"Why, Daddy?" I asked, feigning innocence.

I'd been at the same job for several years. Had I accomplished something extraordinary without being aware of my feat?

"You're finally getting married," he replied.

Ah. The apex of my career as a woman. Until I had children, of course.

"I was beginning to think I'd never be a grandfather."

And there it was.

"You have James, Junior," I pointed out.

Daddy shook his head. "It's not the same," he declared, and I declined to pursue the topic.

"Everyone is just so excited to see you," Mother gushed, linking her arm with mine as we walked toward the car.

Behind us I heard Win and Daddy chuckling, no doubt sharing golf stories and fishing tales, bonding as men like Winchester Carrington III, Esquire and Doctor Walter Wellman would.

"Aunt Isabelle's coming, and all your cousins," Mother was saying. "And guess who's also coming to the shower? Marianne Brightman, all the way from Chicago! I know you haven't seen her since high school so I thought it would be a nice surprise to invite her. Do you know she has four children!"

"Wow," I said. "Four. That's . . . that's a lot."

I thought about the bustling airport terminal behind us. I thought of all the families heading for and returning from vacations, of all the old and infirm in wheelchairs, of all the young and obese in motorized carts driven by bored airport personnel, of all the happiness and sorrow each person carried with him or her.

I thought: *I could tell Mother I need to use the ladies' room. And once inside, I could just slip away into the crowds.*

I thought: *I could just never come back.*

I kept on walking.

"And Clare, you really must decide on your maid of honor!" Mother was urging now. "People need to make travel plans and all. And you really must choose a dress and a color scheme right away or the maid of honor will be stuck with some dreadful gown off the rack. And the bridesmaids—"

"No bridesmaids," I said. "Just a maid of honor."

"Oh, but—"

"The wedding is going to be small."

Mother looked wounded.

"I mean intimate," I amended. "It's a trend. Intimate."

"Well, all right, I'm sure you know best . . ."

Like hell I do.

"I'll ask Jessica to be my maid of honor," I said, deciding on the spot.

What did it matter that I hadn't seen or talked to my cousin in years? We'd been close as children. And I had to pick someone.

Mother brightened immediately. "Oh, Jessica will be so pleased!" she cried.

I wasn't at all sure she would be, but I smiled and nodded.

"The people at the Gandy Dancer have been just marvelous about arrangements," Mother went on.

I thought about taking a nap in my old room. And then I remembered that Win would want to come with me.

Clare
The Show That Never Ends

My cousin Jessica was indeed thrilled to be chosen maid of honor. Even after the registry had been handled and the shower planned and much of the footwork already completed in Boston.

Maybe that was why she was thrilled. There wasn't much left for her to do but show up a few days before The Big Day with her dress. And I'd made that easy for her, too, by suggesting she choose something she really could wear again as long as it wasn't black.

"Ohhh, I'm so jealous!" she squeaked as we arrived at the Gandy Dancer, once a train station and still retaining much of that historical charm. "Marrying a handsome, successful guy like Win Carrington. I hope I'm lucky enough to find someone like Win before I turn thirty. Does he have a brother? Maybe you can introduce me to some of his friends when I get to Boston!"

Mrs. Carrington was there, of course.

"Well, dear," she said, pulling me aside just before I was to open the gifts. "Have you thought about my dress?"

Her pale blue eyes sparkled with hope.

Around me women laughed and chatted. Everyone was all dressed up. Everyone was so excited to be part of a wedding.

They were excited all because of me.

"Yes," I said to my future mother-in-law. "I would love to wear your dress."

Mother will understand, I thought as Mrs. Carrington wiped tears from her eyes. *I'll make sure I make her happy, too.*

I got lots of crystal, all from Tiffany. I forget the name of the style. Danielle had chosen it for me. She would be very happy, I thought. Maybe I'd give her one of the pieces.

Jessica urged me to make a toast. I did and I thanked everyone. Finally, I said, "This is for the most important person in my life. My mother. Without her I would be nothing."

Mother cried and hugged me. Mrs. Carrington bawled. Everyone clapped.

Then it was time for the cake to be served—a mini-wedding-style cake, complete with plastic bride and groom. I tried to refuse a slice, but a worried look from my mother made me accept the plate from Aunt Isabelle.

By that time the event had taken on the feel of a dream. Or of a circus. Noise. Color. Frenzy.

"Every woman's dream . . ."

"You just don't know true happiness until . . ."

"The day every woman's dreamed of since she was a little girl . . ."

"You're going to be one of us now!"

I smiled, as I was expected to do.

Clearly, marriage was only partly about your husband. It was mostly about other wives. It was about being one of the group, a member of an exclusive club, with spin-offs for those wives who were divorced and had been replaced by younger women, for those second wives with their stepchildren and new babies, and for those wives left widowed.

Marriage was about belonging.

Well, I thought, *it would be nice to belong.*

Wouldn't it?

I didn't have time to answer my own question because just then a high-pitched, multi-voiced shout of glee went up as Win and my father and Mr. Carrington and Win's cousin Alan, his best man, appeared in the doorway of our private party room.

It was as if a band of conquering heroes had returned from years at war. The women were suddenly ultra-animated and giggly. The children, many of them my cousins, shouted with joy and rushed to greet Win and his cohorts.

I sat still on my throne, the queen with the crown of ribbons and lace, and watched.

Win beamed with pride and pleasure and magnanimity, as if he alone had created the scene before him. The king.

In fact, all four men glowed with responsibility. Even Alan, who looked as if his glow was largely due to the many gin and tonics I guessed the men had been downing at Mr. Carrington's club.

Alan's gaze swept the room and alighted on Jessica. He favored her with a wink.

"Oh, he's cute," Jessica whispered, pulling on my arm. "Who is he? Is he single? He must be, he winked at me!"

The men made their way into the room. Win came straight to me and everybody applauded as he bent to kiss my cheek.

"You look like a queen," he said, and I saw tears in his eyes. "I'm so happy you're going to be my wife."

And then he knelt at my feet, my vassal, my knight.

I leaned forward and we clasped hands. "I'm happy, too," I said. "Really."

And at that moment, I thought that maybe I was.

Gincy
In Vino Veritas

"Gincy! It's me, Sally. Let me in!"

Freakin' midnight. And I'd been in such a sound sleep.

Bang, bang, bang!

What, was she using her fists or a battering ram?

"I'm coming!" I grabbed a robe and shoved my way into it.

Bang, bang, bang!

"Jesus Christ," I muttered, making my way to the door, "hold on already."

No one had to go to the bathroom that bad . . .

I unlocked and opened the door. Sally practically fell into the room. She looked a mess, all bleary-eyed and rumpled.

And she stank of booze.

"You're drunk," I said unnecessarily.

"I know."

"You should go home."

Man, I so didn't want her to stay in my apartment.

"I don't think I can."

I sighed. "Look, if you're too loaded you can sleep—" Where? I didn't have a couch, per se. Just an old beanbag thing. "On the floor. I've got an extra blanket."

"Why not in the bed, with you?"

"Because you're drunk, that's why. I don't want you snoring in my ear and puking on my sheets. Correction: On my one and only sheet."

"Is that the only reason? Maybe you don't want me in your bed 'cause you're afraid of what might happen, huh?"

Weren't snoring and puking enough to be scared of?

"What are you talking about?" I asked, though I had a sneaking suspicion I knew exactly what she was talking about.

Sally stumbled forward. I noted her mascara had started to slide down her cheeks. "I love you, Gincy. I'm in love with you. You have to know that, right? I mean, God!" Here Sally broke into wild laugher. "I've been so obvious!"

And I'd been so stupid.

Sido, Sally's skinny French friend, was right. How could I not have seen this episode coming?

I took a step back to avoid her drunken embrace. "Sally, come on, you know I'm seeing Rick."

"What can he give you that I can't?" she demanded.

If you weren't shit-faced, I thought, *you would never have asked such a moronic question.*

Be kind, Gincy. Firm but kind.

I took a deep breath and looked her right in the eye. "I'm in love with Rick, Sally. It's not about you. Look, I'm not gay. I don't know what else I can tell you. I'm sorry."

She stood there, eyes averted, mouth opening then closing as if she were trying to say something.

"Sally?" I said. "Do you understand?"

Still, Sally had no words.

She tried to leave, but friends don't let friends stumble through the streets drunk. Finally, she gave up trying to grab the doorknob and collapsed on the floor. I covered her with my spare blanket and unfolded a plastic garbage bag in case she got sick in the night.

Or decided to suffocate herself.

Sally was snoring within seconds. No such luck for me. I lay awake most of the night feeling like a fool.

Around six o'clock I finally fell asleep.

When the alarm clock woke me, swollen-eyed, at seven-thirty, Sally was gone.

September

Danielle
Act of God

I enjoyed the ritual of preparing for bed.

Lotions and potions, creams and emollients. The simple, sooth-
ing rituals demanded almost no concentration and allowed my
mind to wander.

That evening in early September as I prepared for bed, my
mind wandered to Clare.

Since the wedding shower, Clare seemed rededicated to Win.

Or dedicated for the first time, at least for the first time since
I'd known her.

I wondered what had happened out there in the wilds of
Michigan.

Maybe, I thought, *she'd just decided to shut up and play the hand
she was dealt.* I could understand that. Clare had chosen to fulfill
her obligations. She had chosen to perform her duty to family
and tradition and . . .

Herself?

I squeezed toothpaste onto my electric toothbrush and began
to brush.

Or maybe, I thought, *just maybe, Clare had fallen in love with Win
again. Maybe she'd remembered why she'd fallen in love with him in the
first place.*

I didn't know and Clare wasn't telling.

And she wasn't the only one with a big secret.

I frowned at my reflection in the mirror over the sink. Was that another line? I reached for the little jar of eye cream.

Secrets could take their toll on your appearance.

See, I hadn't told Gincy or Clare about my one night of passion with Chris. They didn't even know he'd come to Boston to have dinner with me. Every time in the past days they'd asked about us, I'd neatly avoided answering.

Once, Gincy had pressed for a real answer, eyes narrowed for the kill, but I shut her down with a look I usually reserve only for potential perverts on the T.

Chris.

He was still in Portland but we'd spoken twice. The meetings and negotiations with Tristan Connor, the investor and idea man, were going well, and we talked mostly about the potentials for his business. He never once mentioned the Unanswered Question, and I was grateful, though the Unanswered Question was there, looming.

The third time Chris called I didn't answer the phone.

I couldn't.

I'd made absolutely no progress in terms of understanding our relationship and I wasn't sure I could handle another conversation in which we studiously avoided the topic we both cared most about.

Yes, I thought, looking carefully at my reflection. *Another line.* And my pores were stretching by the second.

The entire situation was wreaking havoc on my skin. I knew that if I didn't come to a conclusion soon about Chris and what it was we had together, I was going to need an appointment with a very, very good dermatologist.

I flipped off the bathroom light and went into the bedroom.

What was driving me most crazy was that I'd always been so decisive about practically everything.

I knew immediately whether I liked or disliked a dress or pair of shoes. I knew immediately whether a certain fabric would work on a certain piece of furniture. I knew immediately when a man was history.

Until Chris.

Did I love Chris? I wondered, undressing. I still wasn't sure.

People married the person they loved. That was huge. How could I love Chris if I wasn't even able to commit to dating him exclusively?

I wondered: Was there a difference between loving someone and being in love with that someone?

Yes. Wasn't there?

So maybe I was in love with Chris.

Yes, I thought, *I probably am in love with him.*

Probably.

Though how much of those feelings could really be called lust?

And did it even matter?

What I had going was a classic summer romance. Every single woman hoped to find a special summer romance, something wonderful to remember for the rest of her life.

Love, lust, who cared?

I did. I cared. And so did Chris.

Chris wanted more.

And I kind of wanted more, too.

Kind of.

I thought again of my parents and wondered why, why, why I was even considering making a commitment to Chris. He was so totally not acceptable as a husband. Why didn't I just let him go?

A better question: Why couldn't I just let him go?

With a noisy sigh I crawled into bed and stretched out flat. The air-conditioning was on high and before long I was chilly, but I left the covers at the end of the bed and stared up at the ceiling.

Suddenly, I remembered the conversation my friends and I had had about those Catholic nuns and monks who spent their lives praying for people.

I'd never been much for the whole religion thing. At least, the prayer part and all, the kind of stuff you did alone, like yoga and meditation.

But I needed help, bad. Chris would be back on the Vineyard in a few days. I had no time to hunt down some professional pray-er and explain the whole situation.

I was on my own.

"God," I said to the ceiling, "this is Danielle Leers. And I'm in trouble. I've got this big decision to make and I don't know what to do. I won't bother you with the details because you're supposed to know everything, right? So could you maybe send me a sign or something, so I can know what to do about Chris? Maybe you could perform one of those things, what do you call them, an Act of God? So I won't have to do this all on my own. Thanks."

Well, that was weird, I thought as I pulled up the covers and turned out the bedside lamp. *Weird but okay.*

Gincy

Every Woman Is an Island

Sally wouldn't talk to me at work the day after her drunken declaration.

Instead, she made a point of avoiding me entirely. The one time we accidentally met by the elevator she shot me a look full of death rays and took the stairs.

I was sorry for hurting her but I was glad that things were out in the open.

You'll miss her company, Gincy, I told myself. But it had been like the company of a mascot. And that just wasn't right, for either of us.

I sat at my desk and tried to focus on work, but my conscience was not through giving me a hard time.

I thought back to the invasion of Mommyzilla and how that third time she'd come to the office she'd treated me with disdain. Contempt. Scorn.

Even my friends had said so.

Wasn't there something of disdain in the way I'd treated Sally all along?

I put my head in my hands, hiding from myself in shame.

I'd made a joke of her to some extent, hadn't I? It was a disgusting admission but it was true. I could be a disgusting person.

I'd underestimated Sally's person. I'd underestimated her capacity for joy and pain.

I was beginning to think I didn't understand anything about love and kindness and friendship. That maybe I never really had.

I was beginning to think I didn't understand anyone, least of all myself.

And then Kell, his face grim, called a meeting of our department.

It was horrible news.

A woman named Gail Black from the graphics department had committed suicide the evening before.

She'd left no note; at least, none had yet been found.

Friends—of which she had few—reported no odd behavior in the months, weeks, days just before Gail's suicide.

Family claimed Gail had always been a good daughter, responsible, caring.

Coworkers, like me, realized we knew virtually nothing about the quiet, pleasant woman three cubicles down the hall.

Everybody was puzzled. Everybody was shocked.

We all straggled out of Kell's office, subdued, stunned.

And all day long I couldn't help but think about—dwell on—those last few minutes of Gail's life.

What had she been feeling?

Had she felt sad or lonely? Or had she been beyond feeling bad, beyond any concern with life?

Had she forgotten for a split-second that she was about to die—the habit of life being so strong—and wondered what she'd have for dinner that night?

And as she walked up that last dark staircase to the roof, had she been trembling? Had she been excited, eager to cast off this troublesome life and enter a new and better place?

Had she believed in an afterlife? Or had she simply craved oblivion?

And at the crucial moment, had she taken a bold step into the still air, or had she simply allowed herself to fall, angling her upper body far enough so that gravity grabbed hold and she tumbled, headfirst . . .

And had she then panicked and tried to stop herself, arms windmilling, mind screaming . . .

Had she been dead before she hit the filthy pavement?

What a horrible, public way to die, I thought.

What could possibly make someone choose such an openly humiliating death?

In my mind I saw Gail's paisley-print skirt bunched up over her panties, her legs splayed shamelessly, her face a mess of gore. How could she have wanted anyone to see her like that?

Maybe she'd been beyond caring about appearances. Maybe she'd so hated herself that she craved the postmortem violation. Maybe she'd been so far gone into gloom she never even thought of—after.

But how could she not have, an angry voice in my head countered. Suicide—especially one so public—was in some ways an act of aggression, wasn't it?

At least, it seemed so to me.

An unmistakable "fuck you" to the world.

"Okay, here I am, splattered across your public sidewalk. Now, clean up the mess! You didn't notice me while I was alive, you didn't hear my cries for help, well you're damn sure gonna have to deal with me now that I'm dead."

I could toss around idea after idea, I realized, but I'd never know what made forty-one-year-old Gail Black climb those gray concrete stairs to the roof of her apartment building, knowing she wouldn't be coming down in quite the same way.

Suicide was also the ultimate act of secrecy.

I shut the door to my office and slid down to the floor, my back against the door.

And I cried.

Clare

Chance Encounter

I was browsing through the fiction stacks when I saw him again. The stranger. The admirer. The Viking-like guy from the reading.

My first instinct was to scurry around the rack and into the next aisle.

I was getting married. I was dedicated to Win. The trip to Ann Arbor had changed things.

It had. I hadn't complained once to my friends since coming back East.

"Hi," I said.

He startled and looked up.

The stranger. The admirer.

Had I noticed just how beautiful he was?

Butterflies fluttered madly through my body.

And then he smiled. "Hi. Wow. This is a coincidence. Well, maybe not really. I mean, we met at the library and now here we are, at the library again . . ."

I smiled back. "It's nice to see you. You look well."

"Thanks. Oh, by the way, my name is Eason."

"Clare," I told him.

Around us, homeless men sat at blond wood tables reading

the daily papers, teens typed madly at computerized card catalogues, and book-group ladies searched for new ideas.

All oblivious to the man and woman making awkward conversation among the stacks.

Star-crossed lovers?

Eason bounced on the balls of his feet, clearly uncomfortable.
"So," he said, "how are the wedding plans going?"

I'm not getting married. Would you like to go out with me?

"Fine. Okay." Oh, at that moment I felt so very conscious of
my engagement ring.

It felt like an anchor on my hand, weighing me to the ground,
when all I wanted to do was float free. At least for a while . . .

Remember Ann Arbor, Clare. Remember how everyone was
so happy. Remember how you felt everything would be okay in
the end.

"By the way," I said quickly, hoping to keep Eason there for
just a bit longer. Hoping to memorize his face. "I never asked
what you do. That night, at the reading."

"I teach high school," he said. "Public school system. I know. It
sounds insane—so much work and so little pay—but I really like
teaching."

"It doesn't sound insane at all!" I blurted. "I'm a teacher, too.
I teach fifth grade at York, Braddock and Roget."

"Oh. Great. It's a wonderful school."

"Yes," I said. "It is."

Silence followed, then Eason pointed to the plastic-covered
hardback he held in his left hand. "Well, I should get going. I
found what I was looking for . . . I mean, the book."

I smiled, nodded, shrugged.

"Okay," he said, backing away a step or two, "well, it was good
to see you again. And really, I'm sorry I asked you out that time.
I didn't mean to—"

"No," I blurted. "I mean, that's okay."

I'm the one who's sorry. So sorry.

Eason hesitated a moment. Our eyes locked.

And then, he was gone.

Danielle
All the Right Moves

Barry Lieberman called to say he was coming to Boston on business.

I agreed to have dinner with him, partly as a courtesy to Mrs. Rothstein and partly in an attempt to get my mind off Chris.

And to be honest, partly because Barry fit perfectly the profile of a potential husband and, well, I certainly wasn't getting any younger.

For better or worse, even during the worst moments of the whole Chris affair, I never quite lost my practical perspective.

Barry picked me up at my apartment right on time. He was very sweet and just amusing enough to be entertaining but not obnoxious.

He also was nice-looking, in a slightly hairy way. Like that actor, Peter Gallagher.

I mean, Barry's haircut and eyebrows were a lot neater, thank God. There was some hair on the backs of his hands, which made me suspect there might be some hair on his back, too.

But he was so clean and neat overall the thought didn't really bother me.

Besides, I thought, *there's a very good chance I'll never see him naked, so what does it matter if his chest is as hairy as Austin Powers's?*

We had dinner at the Oak Room in the Copley Fairmont. Then we went for drinks to the Top of the Hub. Barry admitted he was a sucker for tourist traps.

That was another positive. He was unaffected, and not in a studied way. I mean, he was real.

Still, I felt no great spark.

But Barry felt otherwise.

While gazing out over the city of Boston he told me he had tickets to an opening-night performance at the Metropolitan Opera and asked if I'd be interested in coming to New York for that late-September weekend.

A night at the opera! Not that I was such a huge fan, but that meant an opportunity to dress up, to see and be seen.

And an autumn weekend in New York! I could shop. And I could check out some new restaurants. I could . . .

Remember, Danielle, I told myself, *Barry will be there with you. You'd be going to New York primarily to be with Barry.*

I told Barry I'd check my schedule and call him within the week.

Barry brought me home, and at the door to my apartment he kissed me good-night. It was very appropriately done, just enough to remember him by. And his face was smooth. He was a good shaver.

When Barry had gone I changed into a nightgown and flipped on the TV. For a while I watched a mystery show on Lifetime, but I wasn't really paying attention.

My mind was awhirl with thoughts of the men in my life.

Dad.

David.

And . . .

Sitting there on my couch, watching some red-haired actress solving a crime of domestic abuse, I decided that if I weren't so preoccupied with Chris, I could really like Barry.

In spite of his being perfect husband material.

Gincy
Hope and Glory

When Justin had gone to bed and I'd finished loading the dishwasher, I joined Rick in the living room.

"The Gail situation is really bothering me," I admitted, flopping down next to him on the couch. It groaned loudly and I wondered just how much longer the old thing was going to last.

Rick aimed the remote at the TV and shut off the nature show he was watching on Discovery.

"Gail's suicide is going to stay with everyone for a while," he said softly.

"I suppose. But I didn't even know her! I mean, I knew who she was, but honestly, I don't think we ever spoke. And yet every time I think about what happened I feel sick. Almost physically sick."

"You could see a grief counselor."

"No, no, no," I protested, "I'm sure I'll be fine. Maybe I'll get a book or something. Yeah, that's an idea. I'll go to Barnes & Noble at lunch tomorrow. I just need to understand a bit more."

A strange look crossed Rick's face. He opened his mouth as if to speak but shut it again.

"What? No, tell me," I begged. "You were going to say something."

Rick sighed. "It's not that I'm trying to keep secrets from you, Gincy," he said. "I just don't want to burden you."

"Well," I said, fighting a horrible feeling of doom, "you've already freaked me out with this setup so you'd better just spill it."

And he did. "At one point," Rick told me, "Annie thought about suicide. She was miserable and her latest prognosis wasn't good. She was just so tired of everything."

Now there was a bombshell. And I'd begged for it.

"I'm so sorry," I said, and I was. Would he go on?

Yeah.

"You know, the last months of her pregnancy were colored by cancer," Rick said. "I can't imagine what she went through, even though I was with her the entire time. And then Justin was born and she couldn't even be there for him, not really. Anyway, that's how she felt. Like she'd failed our child, even though he was perfectly healthy. And he was happy, too, which surprised both of us. We were so worried he was going to drink in all the sadness and be a miserable little guy."

"Justin is pretty amazing," I said. "He's the only kid who's ever liked me. I think he's got some natural anti-negativity shield or something."

Rick sort of smiled, but it was Annie he was thinking about again, not me and Justin.

"I didn't even know what to say to her," Rick admitted angrily. "How could I ask her to hang on when every doctor was telling us there was no hope? Hang on for what? So I could see her emaciated face for a little while longer? How selfish could I be? Or so Justin might, just might, bond with a mother he'd never consciously remember?"

I wanted to know if Annie had asked Rick to help her die. And I didn't want to know.

"It must have been horrible," I said inanely.

"It was a bad time, Gincy. The worst."

Could I ask? Was I supposed to ask?

"What happened, Rick?" I said.

Rick sighed deeply. "I don't really know what happened, but Annie decided to live on. Something clicked over and she seemed more peaceful from that point on. Until the end, which wasn't far off. Too soon and too far."

Rick grabbed my hands and leaned close. "Gincy, I didn't want her to die," he said passionately, "but I didn't want her to live, either. Not the way she was living. Do you understand that?"

"Yes," I said softly. "I think I do."

Gincy
An Offer She . . .

I stayed over that night and we slept wrapped in each other's arms, something that wasn't our usual habit.

The next morning I woke before Rick and started the coffee. Then I roused Justin and got him ready for day camp. When the bus came by at seven-thirty, I helped him up the steps and went back up to the apartment.

Rick was just out of the shower and drinking coffee. He looked refreshed, better than I felt. I'd dreamed all night of bad things, murder and mayhem, losing my job, my parents dying, Rick's leaving me.

After my own shower, I joined him in the living room with my third cup of coffee.

"I was thinking," he said suddenly.

Oh, God, I thought. Thinking is rarely a good sign. Telling someone you've been thinking is just about the worst sign there is.

I knew because in the previous ten years I'd told lots of men that I'd been thinking.

"Oh?" I said squeakily.

"Yes. About us. About our moving in together, seeing how it goes."

You know that old expression, you could have knocked me over with a feather? Another one of my father's all-time favorites.

Well, let me tell you. If Rick had had a feather, I'd have been on the floor.

"You mean," I said carefully, "I'd move into your place?"

"Yeah. There's plenty of room and you hardly have any stuff, so moving will be easy. We can rent a van and do the entire move in a few hours."

I got to my feet and narrowly avoided spilling the dregs of my coffee. I put the messy cup on a shelf half-stacked with books and turned back to Rick. "Jesus, Rick, it's not that. Your apartment is a palace compared to mine! It's just—whoa. Wow. I don't know what to say. Wait, here's something: Where did this come from?"

Rick grinned up at me. "It came from the fact that I love you. Maybe I should have started this conversation by restating that bit of information."

I threw my arms in the air and let them smack back against my sides. "Well, I love you, too. We know we love each other."

He looked at me keenly. "You sound angry about it."

"No!" I cried, flopping back down next to him. "Well, it's just that I didn't expect to fall in love. Now, this year, this summer. But I did and it's great," I said, grabbing his hand and squeezing. "Unless you cheat on me and then you're in seriously big trouble. I will so kick your ass."

"If I were thinking about cheating on you, would I be suggesting we move in together?"

"No," I admitted. "I guess not. But Rick, this is huge. We've only known each other for a few months. Not even."

"Yeah, but why wait? Life is short, Gincy. When something good happens, you embrace it."

This man would love my father, I thought. *At least, the clichéd wisdom part.*

"I've never been in a long-term relationship, you know."

Rick nodded thoughtfully. "I'm aware. You've told me at least a dozen times. But you're doing okay so far, aren't you?"

"What do you think of my relationship performance?" I asked, half-teasingly.

"It doesn't matter what I think. You're the only one who knows if you're doing okay. If you feel right."

"I feel fine," I admitted. "I guess. I don't think I've screwed up. Too badly. Yet."

"Maybe you're a natural."

"Hmmm." I felt my mind drift and suddenly found my knees very fascinating.

"Is there someone else?" Rick asked abruptly, and I realized that of course he would wonder.

I looked back to Rick.

His expression was heartbreaking. And suddenly I thought of the photo on Justin's nightstand, the photo of Rick taken when he was about three years old. Little overalls. A little baseball cap. Little sneakers.

I realized then that you knew you were in love when no matter how angry you were at a guy, a photo of him as a little boy reminded you of what you liked about him, of what he really meant to you. You felt flooded by tenderness, and even if the guy had farted at the dinner table or smeared bike grease on your best towels, you forgave him.

And Rick had done nothing wrong but throw an enormous monkey wrench into our works.

"No," I answered truthfully. "There's no one else." And then I took a deep breath. "Honestly? For a while, at the beginning, I kind of hoped there would be. But with you in my life, there just wasn't room for anyone else. There isn't room. That's a good thing, but at first it scared me. You know."

Rick sighed and his relief was obvious. "I do know. I feel the same way. Love is always scary, even for people like me who've been married. Maybe especially for people like me, who've lost love so brutally. I don't know. I shouldn't assume my situation is any harder than anyone else's."

There was something I needed to know. "Annie was really devoted to you though, right?" I asked carefully. "It was horrible that she died so young and that Justin never got to know her. But she never cheated on you, did she? She never betrayed you?"

"No," Rick said emphatically. "We were good. Maybe that's part of why I can love again. I had a good experience. It gave me hope."

No "once burned twice shy" here.

But was I as resilient and brave as Rick?

"What if . . ." Jeez, how to say it? "Rick, I can't help but think you're going to compare me to Annie. Compare what we have to what you guys had together. And I can't be—"

"Try not to think that way, Gincy. I don't want the past. I want the present. And the future. With you. Please believe me."

I wanted to believe him.

And then I leapt from the couch again. "Oh, my, God, what about Justin! How's he going to react to all this?"

Rick sighed and messed up the hair on his head. By now, it was a familiar gesture. "Justin likes you, Gincy," he said. "A lot. I know we'd all have to adjust and grow into a family, but I really believe we can do it."

Holy crap. A family. Did that mean . . .

"Wait a minute," I said. "I think I've been a little slow on the uptake here. Are you thinking that if I move in it'll be like a trial run? Or something."

If Danielle tried to make me wear white . . .

Rick nodded. "Yeah. For the long haul. For marriage. I wouldn't ask you otherwise. It wouldn't be fair to you or to Justin. Or to me."

No, I thought, *it wouldn't be fair.*

"Rick," I said, "I've got to think about this. Okay? This is huge." I checked the clock on the VCR. "Look, we both have to leave for work now. Maybe I should just go home tonight, by myself. Try to—try to figure things out."

Rick opened his mouth but closed it without saying anything. Like, "Don't run off, okay? Let's figure this out together."

And then he got up off the couch. It wailed in relief. "Of course," he said. "And whatever I can do to help, let me know. Promise?"

I took his hand. "Yeah," I said. "Promise."

Gincy

Sharper Than a Serpent's Tooth

The phone rang at nine o'clock that night.

It was my father.

"Who's dead?" I blurted.

"What?"

"Someone must be dead. You never call me. Who is it? Oh, my God, is Mom okay?"

Okay, I didn't really like my mother but I didn't want her dead. Yet.

My father sighed. "Virginia, you get that morbid habit of thinking from your mother's Aunt Bessie. All that woman could talk about was death and dying and—"

Poverty and disease and sin . . .

"Dad! Why are you calling me?"

Dad cleared his throat. "Well," he said, "this is a bit awkward, Virginia. You know I've never interfered with your, uh, with your personal life . . ."

Ah. "Tommy told you about Rick?" I asked, sparing the poor man.

"Now, Virginia, I know your brother doesn't always show it, but he does care for you—"

"Dad," I interrupted, "what did Tommy tell you?"

In short, that I was seeing some "creepy old guy."

"You've always had good sense, Virginia," Dad went on, cutting off my shriek of horror. "And you've been on your own for some time now. Maybe you don't think you need your father's advice, but here it is. I want you to be careful. Men, well, most men aren't what they seem. This person might seem on the up-and-up but you have to be very careful. He's not taking money from you, is he?"

Poor Dad.

Poor me.

Such deep miscommunication.

As gently and as firmly as I could I told Dad the truth about Rick.

That he was only thirty-five. That he was a well-respected professional and a good father. Dad wasn't glad to learn that Rick was a widower, but he was glad to learn he wasn't divorced.

And that he wasn't taking money from me.

As if I had any to give.

I did not tell my father that Rick had just asked me to move in with him. One step at a time.

I think I reassured Dad that I hadn't allowed myself to fall into the clutches of a dastardly villain. By the time we said good-bye, his voice wasn't quite so grim. And he actually asked me to call him if I needed anything. Like advice.

It was probably the best conversation I'd ever had with my father. And it had taken almost thirty years to happen.

Later that night, while lying sleepless in bed, I was overwhelmed by a sense of my own frailty. Every hurtful, selfish thing I'd ever done was suddenly right before me in a glaringly bright light.

I'd been a rotten friend. I should have taken Sally more seriously as a person. Maybe I'd led her on without even realizing it. Even if I hadn't, I should have been sensitive enough to pick up on her feelings and maybe spend less time with her.

But sensitivity had never been my strong suit.

And maybe I hadn't been a very good daughter, either. I hadn't given my father much credit for anything, least of all for caring so much.

There was a slight breeze coming through the window. I pulled the sheet up around my neck and suddenly felt like a little kid, sent to bed without supper for some stupid infraction.

Gincy, I told myself sadly, *you have an awful lot to learn.*

How could I possibly move in with Rick and Justin and take on all that responsibility when I was such a screw-up?

Clare

Charity Begins

It was a letter from the convent of the Sisters of the White Rose of Mary.

I was glad that Win hadn't seen it before I could retrieve the bulky envelope from the mailbox.

Once inside the apartment I tore open the Sisters' response to my plea. I'd made my decision to go through with the wedding, but still, I was curious to hear the Sisters' words of wisdom.

I put aside the card on which was printed a poorly painted bleeding heart, and with it the card on which an insipid Jesus looked up at me with watery blue eyes.

Horrible. I'd never understand the appeal of such things.

There was a handwritten letter from someone named Sr. Richard Marie, blue ink on white paper. The penmanship was perfectly regular, a lost art. Certainly none of my students wrote half as legibly. Neither did I, come to think of it.

I read. "You must turn your mind to your duty," Sr. Richard Marie advised, "and to the promise you made to your fiancé as well as to God."

But I don't know God, I thought. *I was never really introduced. Not properly.*

I read on, spirits falling. "Think always of Our Blessed Virgin

Mary, both wife and mother, and of the sacrifices she made in the name of love. Follow her example always and you will walk in the Grace of God."

Her example. I didn't know much about the Virgin Mary— aside from the obvious—but I knew enough to guess that she didn't snap at Joseph the way I'd been snapping at Win in the past months.

Poor Win. He tried, he really did.

He wasn't a bad man. He had his flaws and his faults, but so did I. So did everyone.

No one is perfect, Clare, I reminded myself.

And then I heard my mother's voice in my head. She was angry, and something else. Manic.

Are you thinking there's someone out there so much better than Win? Are you? she demanded shrilly. *So utterly made for you that it's worth throwing away what you have in hand, what you've worked at for over ten years?*

Mother fell silent and I thought about her questions.

I'd been with Win for over ten years.

What was there to show for it? What had I earned? What had I received?

What had I given?

And then I wondered: Was longevity alone an accomplishment? Were forty bland, possibly soulless, years of marriage better than forty years of shorter-term alliances?

Especially if those alliances brought intense emotion and unexpected flashes of supreme passion and knowledge of the sort you just couldn't find in a long-term, exclusive partnership.

Of course longevity is an accomplishment, Mother shrieked. *If it isn't, then what have I . . .*

I looked back at the handwritten letter.

"Remember," Sister Richard Marie wrote, "Jesus Christ gave up His life. He suffered and died for our sins."

The poor man, I thought, folding the letter. *Why had he bothered?*

Gincy

Domestic Trappings

We dropped Justin off at a neighbor's house for a play date and walked to the Congress Street loft district.

I'd never been to the furniture store called Machine Age. Rick promised I'd enjoy it.

I didn't.

"What do you think of this couch?" Rick nodded at some long thing covered in a nubbly pea green material.

"It's not exactly the style I'd considered but . . ."

Rick sat down on the monstrosity. Was he color blind?

"I don't know," I said. "It's okay."

The place made me nervous. Everything was so expensive and severe. And ugly.

"Pretty comfortable," Rick went on, running his hands over the seat. "Tough fabric. That's important, considering Justin's been begging for a dog. Maybe I should just get a secondhand couch. Or go to one of those outlets on Route 1. Jordan's or something. With a kid and a dog, and let's face it, the way I spill stuff, the thing's going to be destroyed before long . . ."

"Rick!" My own voice startled me. A salesperson glared. A customer hurried off to another section of the store.

Rick frowned. "What's wrong?" he said, rising from the couch. "Do you feel sick?"

I took a step back from him. "No. I mean yes, in a way. Rick, I just don't understand how you can be making this life choice."

"Buying a couch is a life choice?"

He wasn't joking.

"No, no," I said, clutching my head. "Marriage. I'm talking about your getting married again. To me! After all the pain of losing Annie and . . . Rick, what if I die? What if I screw us up? What about Justin?"

Rick didn't try to reach for me. He'd been good from the start at reading my antipathy to being touched at certain peaks of emotion. "Life can't be about expectation, Gincy," he said quietly, "or it's all a waste. Nothing's ever as you expect it to be. Life has to be about risk. If you want to be happy there's no other way."

Fine words but . . .

"But what if you take the risk and you aren't happy?" I pressed.

Rick shoved his hands into the front pocket of his faded black jeans. "Look," he said, "when I married Annie we'd already known each other for five years. Getting married, then Annie's getting pregnant, it was like my life was all set, everything in place, the road all paved to the distant end. I was sure of Annie. But what I didn't realize was that I couldn't be sure of life. When she got sick, I was totally shocked. I'd never even considered one of us could die before being grumpy old grandparents."

"What's your point?" I said, though I knew what he was trying to say.

"My point is that if I had to do it over again, knowing I'd lose Annie, I would. I'd take what I could get and be grateful for it."

I didn't answer.

"Sometimes," he went on, "life kicks you in the teeth. And there's nothing you can do about it but go on. Maybe your grin's a little lopsided for a while, but what's the alternative? Give up?"

I shrugged and thought of Gail. Had she given up? Was that what suicide was all about?

Maybe. Maybe not.

"Well, I couldn't give up," Rick went on, his tone urgent. "I had Justin. He was only a few months old. Annie would have been seriously disappointed in me if I'd fallen apart. In a way, Justin saved my life."

And then, I snapped. I swear I went insane.

Annie, Annie, always Annie. Justin was Annie's child, not mine. He'd never be mine.

"Annie was prettier than me," I blurted, choking back tears. "How can you ever love me like you loved her?"

Rick looked absolutely stunned. He reached for me then, but I turned and ran out of the store, startling the owner who probably thought I was an escaping thief.

Once on the sidewalk I turned right and kept going. Behind me, I heard Rick's running feet.

"Gincy!" he called, and he sounded panicked. "Come back!"

Tears streamed down my face. I kept running. Behind me, Rick's voice grew tinier and tinier until finally I could no longer hear him.

Maybe he'd stopped calling for me. Maybe I was just too far out of range for anything to reach me.

Eventually, I slowed to a stumbling walk. My chest heaved from the physical exertion as well as from the overflowing of my heart.

I thought of Gail again, dead so suddenly, though maybe her death had been long in coming.

Had anyone loved her?

Was love ever enough to save a person from despair?

I thought of Sally, bestowing her love on someone who just couldn't give love back. Our friendship was ruined, and I blamed myself.

And I blamed love. Love got people into trouble.

On Summer Street I stopped and leaned against a building. A middle-aged man passing by, briefcase in tow, scowled at me as if I was a druggie and maybe just then I looked like one, all hollow-eyed and sad.

Why couldn't anything be guaranteed? Why couldn't you

know with confidence that a marriage would last, that a child would grow up to be healthy and wise, that you would die peacefully at a ripe old age, surrounded by loved ones?

I pushed off the building and stepped blindly off the curb.

A horn blasted and I stopped dead. An SUV rounded the corner and missed me by inches.

"You are one stupid bitch!" the woman in the passenger seat screamed at me.

I didn't even want to yell back.

Maybe she was right. Maybe I was one stupid bitch. A stupid bitch full of piss and vinegar.

I walked on in search of a T station.

This is what you wanted when you moved to the big city, Gincy, I told myself.

Experience. Challenge.

Life.

Can you deal with it, after all?

Danielle

Nothing Good Ever Came Easily

"So, what are you going to tell him?" I asked.

Gincy and Clare sat on my couch and I presided from a leather armchair I'd gotten on sale at Adesso.

I'd never imagined Gincy to be such a drama queen. Actually running from a store, tearing down the street, ignoring the pleading cries of her lover?

"I think I already told him my answer," she snapped. "You don't run away from someone who's shouting for you to stop without sending a pretty clear message."

"I'm sure he hasn't cut you off," Clare said gently. "I'm sure he understands."

"Understands what?" Gincy cried. "That I'm stringing him along until I work up the nerve to say no? Which ends our relationship. It has to. And it makes me sick to think about losing him."

"So you're definitely going to say no?"

"Yeah," Gincy said, rubbing her temples. "I have to. I'm just not ready."

"No one's ever ready," Clare murmured.

"It . . . It feels like there's so much death," Gincy went on, more to herself than to us. "Annie is dead but she's not, you know? But the fact that she died and they didn't just divorce . . . Sometimes it creeps me out. I can't explain it."

This girl had to get it together.

"So," I said, "you'd rather Rick have a bitchy, money-grubbing ex-wife prowling outside his apartment door? You'd rather him be a divorced dad instead of a widower? Believe me, you're better off with Annie dead than with her living on his paycheck and slamming your character to Rick's former so-called friends."

Clare's eyes widened to ridiculous proportions.

"You're despicable," Gincy said, her voice shaking with fury. "Do you even have a heart? That is one of the coldest things I've ever heard."

"I'm just trying to be realistic," I replied, perfectly in control. Not cold. Never cold.

"Look," she went on, "I'm not you. We're not even close to being members of the same species. So don't start spouting your screwed-up philosophy of men and women to me, okay? Like you know what you're doing? Like you know anything about commitment?"

I gripped the arms of the chair and felt something inside just break in two.

All right, I thought. If Gincy could reveal herself to be a drama queen, I could reveal myself to be one, too.

That or a doomed heroine. Because I was the victim in the whole affair, wasn't I?

"I'll have you know," I said calmly, "that Chris asked me to make a formal commitment to him. And that he's waiting for my answer."

Clare gasped. "The bracelet . . ."

"After that," I said. "When he came to Boston to take me to dinner for my birthday."

Gincy shook her head. "You never told us . . ."

"I don't tell you everything," I snapped. "I can handle my own life."

"I don't understand," Clare said gently. "Did he ask you to marry him?"

"No," I admitted. "But the idea is the same. He wants us to be exclusive."

"Which means he wants to get married at some point," Gincy said, undeterred by my anger at her. "Step one, go steady. Become his main squeeze. His one and only."

Married at some point . . .

The moment of truth had arrived. Suddenly, I knew I'd made my decision.

"Yes," I said, "except that I won't be marrying Chris Childs. Or making a commitment to him. Ever."

The words, now out of my mouth, horrified me. But I would not take them back.

"Are you in love with him, Danielle?" Clare dared to ask.

I sat staring at my knees for a long moment.

"Dan—"

"Yes, no, I don't know!" I cried. "It doesn't matter because I'm not allowed to marry Chris!"

"Who says so?" Gincy shot back. "Have you ever actually talked to your parents about marrying someone not Jewish? Have you? Because it's about Chris's being Christian, isn't it?"

No, I hadn't ever talked to my parents about marrying a non-Jew. But I knew what was expected of me.

"You don't understand," I cried. "To the Leers, a fishing business is not a glamorous thing. It's the old country, it's drudgery and poverty and dying before you're fifty without a tooth in your head."

Clare cleared her throat. "Danielle," she said, "I met your parents. They don't strike me—"

"Once! You met my parents once! I know them, you don't." I got up from the chair and began to pace the living room. "Believe me, my mother won't care that the Childses have hundreds of acres or whatever, or that they live in a beautifully restored nineteenth-century house overlooking a pretty pond. Esther Leers will care that Chris's father didn't finish high school. She'll care that Chris didn't finish college. My God, she'll be horrified to learn that his mother wears an apron to walk to the mailbox at the end of the drive."

"Do you really care that much about what your mother thinks?" Gincy asked, and I thought I saw a look of sympathy cross her face.

I didn't want her sympathy.

"I care enough," I said, "to want my parents and aunts and uncles and cousins to come to my house for the holidays. I don't want to isolate them. I don't want to make them feel I'm betraying all they've worked so hard to give me. I'll do what I have to do to keep my family."

"Even if it means giving up Chris?" Clare's voice was hushed.

For a moment I couldn't reply. "Yes," I said finally, my voice choked. "Even if it means that. I want tradition more. I can't—I won't!—be an outsider to my own family. They have expectations. I have to live up to them."

"What are those expectations?" Gincy asked. "Exactly. I mean, have your parents ever sat down with you and handed you a checklist? Or are you just assuming—"

I cut her off. "Giving up Chris is a sacrifice? So big deal. Like other people in my family didn't make sacrifices? Please. Giving up Chris is a minor sacrifice compared to what my Great-aunt Ruth gave up in the war. To what my grandparents lost. The prejudices they faced. My sacrifice is nothing compared to theirs. And it's one I'm totally willing to make."

There was a horrible, heavy silence. Finally, Gincy stood and walked to the door of the apartment.

"I don't think this is about sacrifice," she said quietly, her hand on the knob. "I don't think it's about your family at all. I think it's all about you and your own cowardice. I think you're chickening out of your own life. And I'm sorry for you."

Clare covered her face with her hands.

I was sorry for me, too.

Gincy
Braveheart

I'd called Danielle a coward. I was not unaware of the irony. I decided to break up with Rick face-to-face, though the coward's way out was so tempting. A phone call, an e-mail, an old-fashioned Dear John letter.

I called and asked if it would be okay to come over. Rick told me that Justin was at a friend's house and that it would be fine. His voice was flat.

I let myself in; Rick often forgot to lock the door. He wasn't in sight; I imagined he was in the bedroom.

I took a moment to look around, to remember. And something odd happened.

For the first time, the framed photos of Annie, alone and with Rick and Justin, didn't seem threatening. In fact, I realized, the photos seemed perfect right where they were.

Annie was Annie. Gincy was Gincy.

Rick and I were who we were.

We were the couple in the photo taken on the beach, the photo taken by Justin with my one-time-use camera. The couple with their arms slung over each other's shoulders, smiling into the sun.

Past, present, future. We were going to hold it all in our hands.

I went into the bedroom. Rick was standing at the window, looking out at the darkening sky. I knew he'd heard me come in, but it was a moment before he turned.

His eyes were tentatively hopeful. Not assuming. Not defeated.

And in that moment I realized that I loved him for allowing me this freedom.

This is the face I will cherish forever, I thought.

Wow.

Rick took a tentative step toward me. "Gincy?"

"You know," I said, feeling a big old smile dawn on my face, "I think we should go to Jordans for the couch. I'm not any less destructive than a five-year-old or a dog. Or you. I mean, all of us together? Maybe we should just buy disposable cardboard furniture or something."

And then we were in each other's arms, crying, laughing, kissing.

The necessary leap of faith. Someone had to take it.

So Rick did. And I followed.

Danielle
The Cruelest Month

I'd been avoiding Chris since he'd come home from Portland. He had to know the reason for my missing his calls. For my staying in Boston one weekend due to a sudden and severe summer cold.

He had to know the reason, but I had to speak it to his face. I owed him that much. Finally, I called Chris and we made plans to meet on the Vineyard.

Once there, the conversation was brief and awkward.

"I don't understand why we just can't go on the way we are," I said. "Why do we have to change things? Everything's so nice the way it is."

"For who?" he asked.

I had no answer. Things weren't really nice for either of us.

"Look," Chris said, pointing to his heart. "I've got to take care of this. I don't think I can do that with you. Not without further commitment, Danielle. I'm sorry."

"How do you even know I'm not already committed to you?" I cried stupidly.

Chris had the decency to look embarrassed. For me? "I saw you with another guy one night. I know you've been seeing other people on the island."

"Have you been following me?" I demanded, though I knew the notion was absurd.

"No, no. But the Vineyard's a small place. My friends talk. It's okay. I mean, we never had an agreement."

No. We hadn't had an agreement.

Chris went on. "And I don't know about back in Boston. If you're seeing someone else there, too. I guess I just don't know much at all about your life, Danielle."

"That can change," I said, though I knew I was lying. Words just kept coming, making no sense. I was clinging to Chris at the same time I was pushing him away.

And he had had just about enough. "Danielle," he said, angrily, "you're making this too hard. For both of us. Face it. You don't want what I want."

"I do! I do. Just—"

"What?" he shot back. "Just not with me? That's nice. And I thought we had something special."

"We did," I said lamely.

Chris grunted. He was furious. "Not special enough for you to say yes without having to qualify your answer. I'll be with you—but. I'll be with you—except. I'll be with you—until. Until what? Until a more eligible guy comes along? Come on, Danielle, I'd have to be stupid to accept a relationship on your terms."

I shook my head. "So I should accept a relationship on your terms?"

"No. We should build one on our terms. But there is no 'we.'"

I couldn't argue any longer.

"Look," he said, after a moment, his voice gentler. "I've got to go. I've got to get out of here. I hope things work out for you, Danielle. I hope you get what you want."

I watched as he drove away.

I, too, hoped I got what I wanted.

Whatever the hell that was.

Gincy

Leaving the Nest

Moving was hell.

Packing sucked. And I just bet unpacking would suck, too.

I wondered if I'd miss my little Allston apartment. I mean, it was pretty much of a dump but it was my dump.

And the contents of the apartment. The lopsided wooden table I'd bought in college and had been lugging around with me ever since. The warped plastic colander I'd found at a flea market. The green folding chair that doubled as a laundry drop.

None of those things would come with me.

Miss the place?

Not so much, I realized. Because it was time to go, time to move on. It felt okay, the decision I'd made so surprisingly, on the spur of the moment.

And Justin was okay with it, too. Sure, we'd all stumble through a period of adjustment, but the fact that Justin had already asked me to share his room boded well for our future.

There was only one major chore left to tackle.

I still had to tell my parents that I was moving in with Rick.

The guy with the kid and the dead wife.

Or did I have to tell them?

Maybe, I thought, *maybe I just won't say anything.*

I'll cancel my phone service and just use my cell phone and . . .

But what about the mail?

And what if Tommy shows up again, unannounced? He'll frighten the new tenant to death . . . The Mullett Monster.

I stared at the stupid phone.

It bothered me to realize that I was actually afraid of my parents' reactions. Well, not so much of their anger as of their disappointment.

What did they want me to do with my life?

Would my being with Rick fit into their hopes?

Did they have any hopes for me? Had they ever?

I wondered: Are we ever not children, hoping to please, needing to rebel, craving attention in some form or another?

What a chore to be a parent!

If things went okay with me and Rick, if I became Justin's official stepmother, would I fall apart under the pressure?

And what would happen if we had a kid together? Would I scar him for life before his first birthday, assuring years of therapy and drugs for all sorts of problems from uncontrollable quivering to pyromaniacal tendencies to severe panic attacks in the presence of vegetables?

That way lies madness, Gincy, I warned myself. *In more ways than one.*

One foot in front of the other. Like Dad always said.

Dad.

I picked up the phone, hoping my father would answer.

Luck was with me.

"Hi, Dad?" I said, voice quivering. "It's me. I have some good news."

Danielle
Singleton

I decided to go alone to Clare's wedding.

David would have been my escort. But he'd taken a few days off and was visiting his best friend from medical school in Colorado. Regrouping, he said.

I wished him well, as did our parents. To my total surprise, they were thrilled with David's decision to break his engagement to Roberta.

It seems they'd seen her for what little she was right from the start. But they hadn't issued a word of warning. They hadn't interfered in David's life.

They'd let their thirty-six-year-old son make his own discoveries and decisions.

My parents' actions had made me start to reconsider some of the notions I held about them.

About the four of us as a family.

About their expectations and my own.

About bravery and independence.

About the fact that I wasn't David and never had been.

In short, I was a wreck. Nothing was stable, nothing was right. Everything I'd been so sure of now seemed dubious and questionable. Everything was a shade of gray.

Deception. Indecision. Uncertainty.

I'd ruined things with Chris by not being honest. I mean, maybe we hadn't been meant for each other but if only I'd been honest with him up front, I could have saved us both a lot of heartache.

I wasn't going to go through the same nonsense with Barry. So I called him and gently explained that I'd been involved with someone for several weeks and that our relationship had come to a sudden and unexpected end. I told him I felt all discombobulated and that it wouldn't be fair to Barry to spend more time with him when I was in no position to start another relationship.

Barry was very polite and understanding. At least, he acted like he was, and for that I was grateful. He didn't let me off the hook entirely, though.

"Danielle," he said, "if you were involved with someone, and I'm guessing it was a pretty important relationship if you're so upset that it's over, can I ask why you agreed to see me in Boston?"

"I'm not quite sure," I admitted. "But I'm glad I did see you. I know that sounds selfish and it is, but I like you. I had a really good time with you."

Barry chuckled ruefully. "Well," he said, "I'm sorry. For both of us. I hope you feel better soon about—about the breakup. As for me, well, I'm not going to lie and say I'm not disappointed. I like you, too, Danielle."

"I'm sorry, Barry," I said, tears threatening. "Really."

"Look, maybe in a few months, if neither of us is—"

"Maybe," I agreed. "In a few months."

Listlessly I went about choosing an outfit and hairstyle for Clare's big day.

I still had deep reservations about Win, but Clare was my friend and I was determined to support her choice.

Besides, I thought, *what do you know about true love, Danielle? What did you ever know?*

Clare

Fortitudo

The night before my wedding.

My last night as a single woman.

Though maybe the night before I'd met Win all those years ago had marked that occasion.

Either way, come the next evening I would be Mrs. Winston Carrington III. Clare Jean Wellman Carrington.

A lot of names to carry around.

A lot of roles to play.

We had the bridal suite at the old Ritz. It was ten o'clock and in everybody's opinion I was supposed to be in bed. But I just couldn't sleep.

I knew Win and some people in town for the wedding were still at the bar downstairs. I slipped into the dress I'd worn for dinner and took the elevator to the ground floor.

I halted just outside the door to the almost-empty bar.

Win's voice rose and fell like a tide. And I heard the rest of my life laid out. No surprises. Nothing new. All according to plan. Win's plan.

It wasn't a bad life. But was it really mine?

And if not, whose fault was that?

"Clare will probably want to get pregnant right away," Win was saying. "I want her to quit working as soon as she does, of course. It's not like we can't live comfortably on my salary. More than comfortably."

I heard the low rumble of male chuckling.

Oh, yes, Win. We all know you make lots and lots of money.

"I figure for the next few years we'll vacation back home, at the lake. That way the grandparents will each get their fair share of the kids. I know Clare wants to go to Paris, but that can wait. Maybe I'll take her for our tenth anniversary."

Ten more years . . .

It won't be a bad life, Clare, I told myself as I rode the elevator back to the bridal suite.

There will be consolations.

Clare
Impromptu

I stood at the altar.
Win stood next to me.

Behind us, our friends and family were gathered.

The reverend was reading from a sheet of paper.

And I was thinking.

Sometimes, I thought, *we women forget that men have feelings and emotions.*

Sometimes we forget that men were once little boys in need of cuddles and kisses. That in some ways men are always little boys, much as we women are always little girls.

Sometimes, I thought, *we women forget that men are as much in need of love as we are.*

And we really, really should never forget that.

I couldn't marry Win, as much for his sake as for mine.

The initial blessing had just been read.

The reverend looked smilingly at us.

Enough.

"I can't marry you," I blurted. "I can't do this."

The reverend frowned and stepped closer to Win and me. "My dear," he whispered. "Do you feel all right?"

Win was frowning, truly puzzled.

"I feel fine," I said firmly.

I didn't know if our friends and family could hear me. I didn't care.

"I feel fine," I repeated, "because I've told my last lie. I'm through with lies. My soul can't take the strain of one more falsehood."

Win's face darkened. The truth was dawning. "What are you saying?" he hissed.

He took a step toward me and reached for my elbow. His fingers dug into my flesh and I yanked my arm away. The reverend gasped and a murmur arose from those in the pews.

And then I began to run.

Gincy

She's Come Undone

I'd heard about a bride or groom abandoning the other at the altar but I'd never, ever thought I'd witness such a truly dramatic event.

It seemed unreal, like a movie, Clare fleeing back down the aisle, the reverend hurriedly ushering Win and his best man behind the altar, some old lady screaming, kids running after Clare, probably thinking it was all a big game.

A full minute later and Danielle's mouth was still hanging open. Gently, I pushed on her chin and shut it.

"Wow," Rick said. "Wow."

"I can't believe she did it," Danielle said. "I just—I'm stunned."

"I'm proud," I declared. "Win was a jerk. Clare can do much better."

Danielle began to fan herself with one of the programs we'd been given on the way in. "Yeah, but on the altar! She couldn't have dumped him backstage or whatever?"

"I'm with Danielle on this one," Rick said, and I glared. "Okay, maybe she just couldn't work up the nerve until the big moment. But you have to admit that even if the guy's a jerk, this has to be harsh on his family."

"I guess I'll have to return this gift," I said, poking at the perfectly wrapped box on the pew next to me. "I even used her registry."

"And she looked so lovely in that dress," Danielle murmured. "What a waste."

The exodus was continuing.

Mr. and Mrs. Carrington passed us first. Mrs. Carrington looked as pale as rice. Mr. Carrington's face was a dangerous purplish red.

Trey, looking dapper in his tuxedo, followed and winked at us.

And then came the Wellmans, carbon copies of their not-to-be in-laws. White and red. Shock and fury.

The church emptied rapidly after that, but we three still sat, stunned.

Finally, Rick stood. "Well," he said, pretending to haul us both up off the pew. "I know it's been a shock and all but I, for one, could use a drink."

Danielle smiled feebly. "Look at us. We're all dressed up. We just have to go someplace. Plus," she added, "I'm really kind of down right now. I could use some company."

I don't know what possessed me. I don't. But when we all had shuffled out into the center aisle, I gave Danielle a great big hug.

"Thanks," she said, her eyes tearing.

"Don't mention it," I answered, my own eyes welling up. "I mean it. Don't ever mention it again."

Clare
Postmortem

My father, furious, went back to Michigan on the very next plane to Detroit. My brothers and their wives dutifully joined him.

My mother, oddly calm, offered to stay with me for a few days. I hesitated before thanking her and accepting her offer.

That first night I holed up alone in one of the rooms of the hotel suite my father had abandoned.

The second night I slept in the king-sized bed with my mother. I cried for hours. My mother cried at intervals. Neither of us got much sleep.

At one point, very late, I thought I heard my mother whisper these words: "I'm sorry, Clare. I'm so sorry."

The next morning the words seemed like a dream and I didn't ask my mother to verify their reality. It was good enough that I had heard them, no matter the source.

I moved out of the loft immediately and rented a small apartment in the Fenway area. Mother flew home.

Finally, I called Gincy and Danielle. Each had left messages on my cell phone but I just hadn't been ready to talk. We met a week to the date after the wedding that wasn't. Gincy had another drink coupon for the Good News Bar and Cafe.

"I don't feel at all bad for Mr. Jerry McJilted," Gincy declared. "He was an idiot and he still got a vacation out of it. Win and his best man on the shores of Tahiti. I wonder if . . . Ugh. I forgot Win and Alan are cousins. Anyway, Clare, I think you should have kept the ring and then sold it and used the money for a fabulous vacation for yourself and your girlfriends."

"I had to give the ring back," I said. "It cost Win a fortune. It wouldn't have been right to keep it. Besides, I didn't even like it."

Danielle's eyes bugged. I noted she looked a bit haggard but I said nothing.

"What!" she cried. "It was a three-carat cushion-cut central diamond with two carats' worth of diamonds in the band! A platinum band!"

Gincy grinned. "I thought you only liked yellow gold?"

"I'd have made an exception. My God, the thing was gorgeous!"

"It was too much for me," I admitted. "Too big and flashy."

Danielle leaned against the back of her stool. "Water. I need water! I mean it, someone call the bartender!"

I smiled, glad to be with my friends again.

"Anyway," I said, "I'm sorry I broke the engagement the way I did. I think I'll always be sorry. But I just couldn't do it until that critical moment. It was now or never, do or die. And I just couldn't die."

Gincy raised her beer bottle. "You're a brave woman, Clare," she said. "I really admire you."

I smiled ruefully. "I hope I feel brave when I'm all alone at night in my new little apartment. I'm completely without all the amenities Win had installed in the condo. I mean, I hardly ever used the dishwasher but at least I had a choice. Now, I'm lucky to have a microwave."

"Can't your parents help you out?" Danielle asked, in all innocence.

So I finally told them about the monthly allowance my parents had been sending me. And about how as punishment for running out on my wedding, my father had sworn he'd never give me another cent.

"My mother's furious with him," I said. "She can't believe he wants to cut me off entirely. I don't know why she's surprised. I half suspected it would happen. But I am grateful for her support. Staying with me after the—well, after the almost-wedding. Helping me to find an apartment and move out of the loft."

I shrugged. "Who knows? Maybe this will be a turning point for her, too. Daddy's been pretty condescending to Mother for the past forty years. Maybe now it's finally time for her to fight back. Stand up for herself. You know, before my mother married she was accepted to several very good graduate programs in art history. Maybe now she'll go back to school . . ."

I trailed off, not wanting to put too much energy into vague possibilities.

"One person is brave enough to change and others follow," Gincy said, and I knew she was thinking of Rick and herself. "You are brave, Clare. And maybe you've helped your mom to be brave, too."

Maybe. But my only intention had been to save my own life.

"I wish I could have been brave years ago," I admitted, "before things got so—so settled with Win. Before I hurt so many people."

"We all wish we could have done things differently," Danielle said softly.

"I'm sorry about you and Chris," I said.

She shrugged. "It's okay. You never know what will happen."

Gincy eyed her shrewdly. "What's going on in that fluffy brain of yours?"

"Nothing. So, how's everything with you and Rick?"

"Ah, conveniently changing the subject. Things are fine. We've already had one fight over our stuff. You know, he thinks his stuff is more important than mine, which it's not, and I think my stuff is more important than his, which it is."

I laughed. "Sounds like you're doing just fine," I said.

I hoped she was. I hoped Danielle would be okay.

And I so hoped that I would be, too.

Danielle
Who's Sorry Now

My friends had inspired me.

Both had taken such enormous risks. Both had been so brave.

Gincy's bravery seemed to have snuck up on her. She'd gone to Rick's apartment to end their relationship. Both Clare and I had been ready for a phone call of distress. We'd been ready to rush to her apartment and sit up with her all night as she stamped out her grief.

Instead, we'd each gotten a brief call made from Rick's apartment telling us to go to bed. Telling us that she was fine. Promising that she'd tell us more in the morning.

"Be happy for me," she'd said. "I'm so freakin' happy I could plotz!"

Clare's declaration of independence had been a touch more deliberate. She'd been unhappy and discontent for months. In passive-aggressive ways she'd tried to show Win her anger and her disappointment. And, as usual with such methods, she'd failed.

Finally, at the very moment of truth, she'd found the courage to speak honestly.

My friends were strong women. Not perfect—who was?—but they were really trying.

I wanted to be worthy of them. So I thought I'd give it one more try.

I missed him in Menemsha, where the Childs' Seafoods major boats were docked. Johnny told me he'd gone in to Oak Bluffs.

I found Chris just coming out of the Rattlesnake, one of his favorite hangouts.

I wasn't at all sure he was glad to see me. His face was a rapid play of emotions. Surprise. Pleasure. And annoyance.

And certainly his greeting was less than encouraging. "Danielle," he said flatly. "What are you doing here?"

"I had to see you," I said. "I want us to . . ."

The air was wet and chilly, more than hinting at fall. I shivered, and Chris unenthusiastically suggested we go inside.

He indicated the barstool on which I should perch. He remained standing.

"Let me go first," he said. "One of the reasons I was first attracted to you was because you were so different from any woman I'd ever known. You were so exciting. Every moment with you was a surprise. A good surprise."

"Thank you," I whispered. "I felt the same. I feel the same. I—"

"Let me finish, Danielle." Chris pushed his hair off his forehead with both hands and sighed.

Was I such a burden?

"I think I was wrong to get together with you," he said, looking me square in the eye. "I don't think two people from such different lives can make it work. Not for the long run. Not for a lifetime. I should never have asked you to make a commitment to me, Danielle. It was unfair. I'm sorry."

"No," I pleaded, reaching for his arm. "It wasn't unfair, what you asked. I—"

Chris recoiled as if I were somehow contaminated. "I'm sorry, Danielle. I just can't do this. And . . . I think you've got to move on. You're bad news for me. You're going to be bad news for any guy until you figure out what it is you want."

To say his words stung me, to say they were a slap in the face, to say they wounded my pride—all would be a terrible under-statement.

No one—no one!—had ever said such a horrible thing to me.

And the worse part about it all was that Chris was right.

I was bad news even to myself.

"I hate that you're so smart," I said finally, my voice thick with emotion. "I can't even tell you to shut up because I know you're right."

Chris gave me a sad sort of smile. "I'm not any smarter than you are, Danielle. I just got here ahead of you, that's all. And I'm still alone, so what does it really matter?"

"I don't want to end up alone," I said, inanely.

"That's up to you, Danielle," he said, not unkindly. "Your life is totally up to you."

Gincy
Best-Laid Plans

Danielle lay facedown across her bed.

I wanted to shake her silly for having gone back out to the Vineyard in search of Chris. Sure, maybe it was partly my fault that she'd gone, all that stuff I'd said about her chickening out and all.

What had I been thinking? I'd never even been totally convinced Chris was the right guy for her!

Me and my big mouth.

"The only reason I took the house this summer was to meet Mr. Right," she sobbed. "I didn't do it to have fun or to get girlfriends."

"But you did have fun," I reminded her. "And you did get girlfriends. You got me."

"And me," Clare added, handing Danielle another tissue.

"It's what we all got. Friends. I'd say it was a pretty good deal all around."

"You got Rick," Danielle mumbled, wiping at her wet cheeks.

Okay. Good point.

"For now," I admitted. "Maybe it will last. I hope it does. But let's face it. Romance is a huge crap shoot. Finding someone who'll last over the long haul . . ."

"And sometimes the long haul itself brings out the inherent problems," Clare added. Not helpfully.

Danielle wailed magnificently. "I just . . . I just regret so much! I regret ever going out with Chris in the first place. What was I thinking!"

"You were thinking, 'what a cute guy! and he's so nice, too,' " Clare said. "Why shouldn't you have gone out with him?"

But our words of comfort were falling on deaf ears.

"I regret not inviting Chris to my birthday party. I regret not making a commitment to him. As if I had it in me to make a commitment to anyone!"

"Maybe," Clare said tentatively, shooting me a look of help-lessness, "maybe deep down you really didn't want to get all tied up with Chris. That's okay, too."

Danielle sobbed. "If deep down I didn't want to be tied to Chris, then I regret that, too!"

Poor kid, I thought. This was going to take some time.

I patted her shoulder. "You know what Katharine Hepburn said about regrets?" I asked.

Danielle shook her head and snorted into a tissue.

"She said that if you don't have any, you must be stupid."

Danielle sobbed even more loudly. "Easy for her to say! She was rich and gorgeous! And she had Spencer Tracy forever. Almost."

"I suspect their relationship wasn't all it was made out to be by the romantics," Clare assured her quietly. "Try not to focus on what other people have or don't have. Just think about how Danielle can be happy again."

Danielle flipped over to her back and sat up on the rumpled bed. She looked like hell. It was the first time I'd ever seen her looking less than perfect and I was pretty sure it would be the last.

"Maybe," she said, "we could make a promise to each other. Maybe we could promise we'll try to stay friends for as long as we live. No matter where we each wind up in life. Maybe we should promise that we'll meet once a year, even when we're old and creaky and incontinent and in wheelchairs and no one loves us and—"

"Jesus, Danielle," I cried, "can you be more depressing? Look, you're the only one who's thirty. Give us the chance to grow old after you and then we'll talk about the future. Sheesh."

Clare smiled. "I think Danielle has a very good idea. I can see us all forty years from now, crazy old ladies sharing our life stories . . ."

Danielle frowned anew. "I am saying this now. I am so not ever wearing a purple dress with a red hat or a caftan or a housedress or corrective shoes. I don't care how senile I get. Shoot me if I even think about it."

I rolled my eyes.

"Okay, we promise," Clare said.

And finally, finally, Danielle smiled. It was a good thing to see.

Epilogue

Gincy
All's Well That . . .

We didn't see much of each other after our lease on the Oak Bluffs house ended. We did keep up via e-mail, but without the excuse of a common destination—Martha's Vineyard—we each retreated to our separate lives.

I suppose it was normal. I suppose it was to be expected.

I mean, there was daily life to get through, jobs and responsibilities, and everyone's annual cold or flu.

Life.

Like turning thirty. Like celebrating the holidays for the first time with Rick and Justin. Like getting a promotion.

But by the time February grumped in I was ready to think again about my friends. And about the summer. I told Rick I had something kind of crazy in mind and he just shrugged.

"What else is new?" he said.

We met at George, just us three.

"So, what do you say? We rent a house?"

Danielle groaned. "Just not the same dump, please!"

"Oh, I think it would be nice to rent the same place," Clare said. "It's got memories now."

I laughed. "Oddly, I'm with Danielle on this one. Maybe it's living with Rick or maybe it's age but my taste is improving. I say we start the search now and get something decent."

Clare shrugged. "What about girls-only weekends?" she suggested.

We each thought that a good idea.

"Does Justin qualify as a guy?" Clare asked then. "I mean, he's only a child. Are you really a guy at the age of five?"

"Does he pee standing up?" Danielle asked.

"Uh, yeah," I said. "Of course."

"Then he's a guy. But okay, he can be the exception on girls-only weekend."

"He'd better be! I mean, he could be my own kid someday."

"Gincy!" Clare cried. "Are you and Rick talking about getting married?"

"Holy crap, not yet! But, you know, we are living together. You don't live with a guy with a kid without the topic of marriage coming up every once in a while."

"What's once in a while?" Danielle demanded.

I squirmed. "I don't know. Like, every week. Or so. Once every week or so. Twice a week, tops."

"I can help you plan the wedding!" Danielle said brightly.

Clare shot me a look that said, "Don't go there. Ever."

"You want to hear something funny?" I said. "Well, not funny, exactly. Get this. My father, a man who'd only been to Boston once when he was about nineteen, has visited me twice since I moved in with Rick. I know the first time was to make sure I wasn't living with some drug addict in a hovel."

Danielle nodded approvingly. "He only did what any good father would do."

"How does he get along with Rick?" Clare asked.

"Fine," I told them. "You know, Dad's not exactly a great conversationalist, but so far no punches have been thrown. And Dad and Justin have totally hit it off. I mean, we have to tear Justin away from Dad when it's time for bed. He calls him Pop. Isn't that cute? It's like they're buddies. Like, Rick's a menace with any kind of tool and Dad's a whiz, so suddenly, Dad's become this Construction Man hero-type. He even gave Justin his own set of tools. And believe me, they've put them to use on all the stuff Rick never got around to fixing. Like the bedroom door, which was hanging by one hinge. Thank God for screwdrivers and the macho guys who know how to use them."

"I never thought I'd hear you so psyched about family," Clare noted.

"Me, neither," I admitted. "But if there's one thing I've learned since we all met last May it's 'expect the unexpected.' I mean, my father had been telling me that since I was a kid but I never listened. You know, there's something to clichés. People use them for a reason."

"So what about your brother?" Danielle asked. "Tommy, right? Have you guys gotten any closer?"

Sure, I thought. *Let's talk about the one area in which I've made no progress.*

"You know," I said, "I only have so much energy. It's huge I'm with Rick and Justin. It's huge I'm actually getting to know my father and he's getting to know me. I just can't handle Tommy right now. Maybe some day. Or not."

"Okay, so what about your mom?"

I glared at Danielle. "You never let up, do you? Jeez. I don't know. Sometimes I think I'll never have a decent relationship with my mother. Who knows? She's never made an effort, but then again, neither have I. Right now, I'll take what I can get. End of this conversation."

"What ever happened to your friend Sally, from work?" Clare asked in all innocence. "How's she doing?"

I hesitated. I'd told Rick about what had happened that night in my apartment. But I hadn't told Danielle or Clare, less to protect Sally's privacy than to hide my own culpability.

But now, I revealed all.

"Ouch," Danielle remarked.

"Yeah, ouch. But I hope she's happy. She left Boston for a job out in California," I told them. "I don't expect I'll ever hear from her again."

"That's okay, honey," Danielle said, patting my hand as if she were my grandmother. "You have me and Clare. And we're all the girlfriends you need."

Oh, yeah.

Clare

The Start of Something

I was glad when Gincy called and suggested we get together. Life had been super-full since the aborted wedding, but still, I missed my girlfriends.

"My father still isn't speaking to me," I admitted. "It broke my heart at first. He just couldn't understand. Or he wouldn't. He says I embarrassed the family and that's an unforgivable act."

Gincy scowled and held her tongue. I knew it cost her.

"Either way," I went on, "I'm still not happy about the situation. But I am rethinking just about everything in my life. And I'm realizing Daddy wasn't such a great father to me. In a way I don't care if he won't speak to me because I have nothing to say to him. Yet."

Danielle sat back as if stunned. I knew family meant all to her.

"Do you ever hear from Win?" Gincy asked, tossing back the last of her beer.

I laughed uncomfortably. "Oh, no. I think that as far as Win's concerned I'm just too big of an embarrassing memory."

"I bet he's getting dates with his sob story of being left at the altar by his bitch of a fiancée," Gincy said.

"Maybe. His mother called me once, back around Christmas. It was horribly awkward. I'd sent a note of apology in October when I returned her dress, but . . . Well, let's just say all is not for-given."

"You poor thing," Danielle murmured.

Yeah, poor me. The victim. Or the victimizer?
I wondered.

What was the point in telling my friends now, all these months later?

What was the point in not telling them?

"I cheated on Win once," I blurted. "Last summer."

"What!" Danielle cried, leaping from her stool and grabbing my shoulders. "And you didn't tell us?"

"Ow," I said, removing her hands. "I'm telling you now."

And I did.

And then I filled them in on Eason. My new guy. The library guy.

"Sooo," Danielle drawled, "are we hearing wedding bells in the foreseeable future?"

"God, no!" I cried. "I had way too close a call back in September. There's no way I'm talking about marriage again for a long, long time. If ever."

"This guy Eason doesn't push?" Gincy asked.

"No, not at all. He respects my need to go slow. With the com-mitment part."

Danielle's eyes gleamed. "So you are having sex?"

"Of course!"

"And . . ."

"What? I'm not talking about that. It's personal."

"Personal?" Gincy repeated. "You just told us you cheated on your fiancé! Look, just tell us this. Compared to Win, how would you rate Eason?"

I hesitated. "Well, if Win was, say, I don't know—this is embar-rassing!"

"Oh, come on," Danielle coaxed. "After all we've gone through with you? Dealing with your furious father and your swooning mother after you'd run screaming from the church?"

"I wasn't screaming. And I didn't run. Exactly. But, okay. You're right. I owe you something. Okay. If Win was a—five—"

"Poor thing!" Danielle cried. "No wonder you left him at the altar."

"—then Eason is a . . ."

"A what?" Gincy was grinning. "A nine? A ten?"

"No." Could I say it? "A twenty."

"Whoo-hoo! Girlfriend hit the jackpot!"

"How did you two hook up finally, anyway?" Danielle asked.

"I know it sounds impossible, but we met again in the library in early November. It was the third time."

Gincy nodded wisely. "Ah, the charm."

"You do go other places, right?" Danielle asked. "I mean, like restaurants and movies?"

"Oh, sure. And when spring comes we're going to do some camping. Win wasn't a big fan so we never went. I've really missed the outdoors, and Eason's got all his own equipment. It should be fun. We'll do some hiking, too."

"Do you think you'd consider leaving Boston someday?" Gincy asked suddenly. "For some small town with like, a general store and a local swimming hole? God, I couldn't wait to get out of that kind of environment!"

"Well, you know how I feel about the L.L. Bean lifestyle," I joked. "Anyway, I'm not making any plans for the future yet, with or without Eason. He knows how I feel. He seems okay with it. We'll just have to see how it goes."

"You sound awfully Zen-like."

I laughed. "Either that or I'm still just so horribly tired from having faked my life for so long. I guess on some level I just don't care what happens with Eason in the end. I just want to be honest this time, with myself and with him."

Gincy eyed me carefully. "It's almost as if you're a completely different person from the girl I met last May. You were so hesitant. But there was also a sense that you were about to explode."

"And I did, didn't I?"

Danielle rolled her eyes. "Honey, it was spectacular."

Danielle
Back to the Beginning

I knew the subject was going to come up.

"Did you ever tell your family about Chris?" Clare asked me. "About what happened in the end?"

"No."

Gincy looked doubtful. "Not even David? He'd understand. And you two are so close."

I sighed. "No," I repeated. "Why should I bother talking about it? It's all over now, anyway."

My friends looked at each other and then back to me.

"But you were in love," Clare said gently. "Weren't you?"

How could I help my friends understand? "I don't think I was," I said. "Not really. I mean, Chris meant something to me. But in the end . . ."

I took a deep breath. Those two were always causing me grief. Testing me. Someday they'd give me a heart attack. "Okay, look," I said, "I kept that silly bracelet Chris gave me. The shell one. It's in a box and I'll never wear it again but I just couldn't bear to throw it out. I'm still not sure if Chris is a good memory or a bad one. Maybe I'll never figure it out."

"But the bracelet will remind you of an important lesson, right?" Gincy looked at me in expectation.

I looked back at her challengingly.

"Danielle," Clare said quickly.

Good girl. Once again defusing a potential fight.

"Last summer I was so preoccupied with my own situation with Win I didn't spend much time thinking about yours. But later, when I took the time to consider, well, I thought it seemed kind of odd that Chris was pressing for a commitment so early in your relationship."

Gincy nodded. "Yeah. I thought so, too. Okay, Rick wanted a commitment from me early on, too, but he didn't demand. He asked. Danielle, I'm thinking maybe it's way better you backed off."

"I think I might have idealized Chris, just a bit," I admitted finally. "I think I might have focused so much energy on him because the idea of finding Mr. Right and getting married really terrified me. Even though I thought that what I wanted was to hurry up and get married."

Gincy grinned. "Serious insight! Have you been seeing a therapist?"

"No, of course not. I'm not as empty-headed as you think I am."

"I never said you were empty-headed!" Gincy protested.

I just rolled my eyes at her.

"So," Clare asked, "are you seeing anyone special?"

"Yes," I told them. "I most certainly am. It started slowly, but we're picking up speed as we go."

"Well, who is he?" Gincy demanded.

I'd forgotten how fun it was to annoy her. She was so easily aggravated. Really, she was the one who should have been in therapy, learning patience.

"It's Barry, the guy I met at my birthday party last August. The Rothsteins' friend. And before you make any judgments, let me say that I really like him. Really. We're very suited for each other."

"But didn't you dump him?" Gincy demanded.

She really was impossible.

"I didn't dump him. I—Oh, never mind! Anyway, I called him again just before I was flying home for Christmas. And yes, my parents have a tree, why not. Anyway, luckily Barry was available. Since then we've been seeing each other about twice a month. He comes here and I go there. And we try not to spend the entire time with my parents."

"And in between?" Clare asked.

I knew someone would ask.

"Are you seeing other guys?"

"No. And that's fine. I'm working on falling in love."

"What about your system?" Gincy asked. "Still keeping that notebook? How does Barry rate on, oh, I don't know, hairstyle?"

"I abandoned the system. No more checklists. And his hair is great, by the way."

Both Gincy and Clare spontaneously clapped.

"Good for you!" Clare said.

We ordered another round of drinks and some appetizers.

"So," Gincy asked when the waiter had gone, "you never heard from Chris after that last time? Just after Clare's, uh, non-wedding?"

I cringed. But I'd admitted everything else . . .

"I sent him an e-mail in early November. And before you yell, yes, I know it was stupid."

"What did you say to him?" Gincy asked.

I sighed. "God this is embarrassing. I told him I could come out and see him if he liked. And other stuff. You really don't want to know."

"Oh, Danielle."

Clare patted my hand.

I tried to smile but I'm afraid it came out a grimace. "Anyway, he e-mailed back. His spelling was abysmal. He told me he'd moved on. He'd met some girl who'd moved back to the Vineyard after like fifteen years away. Some girl he'd known when he was a kid. God, I wouldn't be surprised if he was married by now! And he asked me not to contact him again. Can you imagine? I felt like a stalker."

Gincy's face turned red and I knew her well enough by then to know she was just aching to punch Chris in the face.

I loved her the more for it.

"That's horrible, Danielle," Clare said, consolingly. "But it's also probably for the best. At least he didn't play around with your heart. At least he was honest about his situation—"

"Right," I cut in. "Just like I was with him. Don't remind me."

Our drinks arrived and I took an appreciative sip of my martini.

"Jumping way ahead," Gincy said, "what happens if you and Barry decide to get married? Is he going to leave New York for you? Move to Boston?"

About some things the girl would never learn.

"Gincy, don't be silly. Men never change cities for women. Of course I'll move back to New York. Anyway, it's not like it will be a sacrifice. I love New York. It's my home."

"Yeah, but what about your job?" she pressed. "Your career?"

I smiled at her fondly. "That is a joke, right? You can't think I really care about my job. Gincy, I've been waiting all my adult life to quit work. I've always considered work just something to do until I decide to get married."

"And if you don't decide to get married?" Clare asked.

Good question.

"Well," I said, "if I don't get married . . . Ugh, then I'll just have to keep working. Can we please change the subject?"

"You, Danielle Sarah Leers, are priceless."

"I know!" I said.

And I finally believed it.

**Please turn the page
for a very special Q&A with
Holly Chamberlin.**

Q: You wrote *The Summer of Us* back in 2003. Had you read it since its publication in 2004?

A: No, I hadn't. I make it a policy never to reread my work once it's published. I'm not exactly sure why. So when my editor asked me to write a Reading Group Guide for the republication of *The Summer of Us* I was pretty nervous. What if I hated it? I would never have revisited this book unless specifically asked to do so.

Q: How does this book compare with your more recent novels?

A: Well, in *The Summer of Us* I was writing about three women on the cusp of thirty. For the past few years I've been writing about women in their mid to late forties. There are huge differences between tales about women in these two age groups. I have to say it was somewhat refreshing to go back to a narrative with concerns other than midlife crises, rebellious children, widowhood, and sagging necks! Which is not to say that Gincy, Clare, and Danielle don't have serious or annoying issues of their own to handle.

Q: Are there any other differences that struck you?

A: Yes. A few years ago I switched from using a first-person-point-of-view narrative to a third-person-omniscient one. There were several reasons for this change and I'm still content with it. But rereading *The Summer of Us* made me want to give the first-person point of view another try. There's something really fun about it. We'll see.

Q: You wrote this book, so you knew before rereading it what was going to happen. Was there any sense of suspense for you?

A: As a matter of fact, yes! I was almost thoroughly surprised by the characters and what happens to them. To realize that I had entirely forgotten characters I had created was a very odd experience. Fortunately, I was pleasantly surprised rather than disappointed. And I felt strangely protective of the three main characters, almost like a mother might feel watching a child go through a period of major decision making, wanting to help, hoping everything will turn out well.

Q: As in many if not all of your books, the subject of family looms large. What is the specific focus in *The Summer of Us?*
A: The three main characters are young enough to still be figuring out some basic rules of adult life and to be establishing parameters of their own. They're still trying to separate from their parents, to decide what lessons to keep and what to throw out. Maybe that process never entirely ends, but when you're writing about characters who are closing in on fifty rather than thirty, the "issues" they might have with their parents are less about separation and more about preparing to become a caretaker and, eventually, about preparing to say good-bye. And, chances are a character in her forties has children of her own, which brings another dynamic into play.

Q: In *The Summer of Us,* the characters talk about the nature of friendships among women. An argument is made that because women tend to change so much during the course of their lives, their friendships, too, are always in flux and sometimes temporary. This is a subject you also explore in your most recent book, *Summer Friends.*
A: Yes. In *Summer Friends,* two women who were virtually inseparable from the age of eight or nine until twenty-one or so come together again when in their late forties. The Maggie character seeks out this reunion while the Delphine character very reluctantly allows it. Through these two characters I explore how and why a close friendship can sicken and die, and how sometimes it can revive. Friendship is a very interesting and very difficult subject about which to write.

Q: If you were to write a sequel to *The Summer of Us,* with the three main characters now in their late forties, what kind of life might you create for them?

A: Well, I would want Gincy, Clare, and Danielle to be happy and healthy and successful. They are, in a way, my babies! But in order to write a book that would hold a reader's attention, I'm afraid I'd have to create some degree of unhappiness or dissatisfaction for each of the women. It would be nice if Gincy learned to tolerate if not love her brother and her mother, but I don't think that would happen. I would like to see Clare reconciled with her father—but I don't see that happening, either. And I would like Danielle to have successfully explored her somewhat undeveloped thoughts and feelings about men and marriage. I do see a marriage to the Barry Lieberman character as a real possibility. And Gincy would be married to Rick and taking care of her aging father. Clare and Eason would be married with children. I guess I'd have to think hard about creating more tension in their lives!

THE SUMMER OF US

Holly Chamberlin

ABOUT THIS GUIDE

The suggested questions are included to enhance
your group's reading of Holly Chamberlin's
The Summer of Us.

DISCUSSION QUESTIONS

1. In the beginning of the book, Gincy presents herself as "the go-to girl." Clare says that she's "pleasant and easy to please." Danielle claims to have good self-esteem. In what way is each character right or wrong in her self-assessment? By the end of the book, how might each character's self-description have changed?

2. Gincy despises her brother Tommy for being a drunken, unmotivated "dirtbag." Danielle loves and to some extent idolizes her older brother, David, a successful doctor. Clare's brothers, James and Philip, have little if anything to do with her, though she wishes they were close. How might the brother-sister relationship have influenced each character's chosen lifestyle or romantic decisions?

3. Gincy dutifully loves her father, though until certain events in this story, she hasn't truly appreciated his capacity for caring. Clare respects her father though he only values her through the achievements of her fiancé. Danielle genuinely loves her father, and he adores her as his "little girl." How might the father-daughter relationship have influenced each character's chosen lifestyle or romantic decisions?

4. Gincy has little love and no respect for her mother. Clare loves her mother, in spite of the fact that Mrs. Wellman's dashed hopes for independence might have negatively influenced Clare's ability to achieve the same. Danielle loves her mother but is wary of being smothered by her concern. How might the mother-daughter relationship have influenced each character's chosen lifestyle or romantic decisions?

5. Talk about the notion of parental pressure and how each character to some extent misinterprets her parents' expectations of her. For example, Gincy feels that her par-

ents have no expectations for her and don't even want
her in their house. Clare assumes that her parents expect
her to fail. Danielle thinks that her parents are eagerly
awaiting her move back home. How might each character
be right or wrong?

6. All three of the young women claim to have trouble forming friendships. Gincy has an unhealthy "mascot" sort of
relationship with Sally, her office mate. Clare longs for
the easy intimacy of childhood friendships. Danielle feels
alienated from the girls with whom she grew up. Gincy,
Clare, and Danielle's coming together is partly a matter
of timing; each character is ready, whether she knows it or
not, to reach out to another person. What other factors
might have contributed to the formation of this seem-
ingly unlikely bond?

7. Gincy feels great remorse for her behavior after Sally
drunkenly declares her love. She feels that she has not
taken Sally seriously as a person, that she has "underestimated (Sally's) capacity for joy and pain." Do you
think Gincy is right to feel remorse, or do you think she is
being too hard on herself? How do her feelings about her
behavior toward Sally relate to her grief over the suicide
death of her colleague, and to the anxieties about her potential life as Rick's partner?

8. Discuss the notion of privacy in a committed relationship.
Consider Clare and her concerns about keeping a secret
journal.

9. Explore how each character views marriage. In what ways
are their views naïve or mature? For example, Gincy, per-
haps with her parents' unspectacular marriage in mind,
has strenuously avoided the notion of commitment, and
yet, when Rick asks her to move in with him, the issue that
holds her back is her own perceived unworthiness. Clare,
on the brink of a wedding she doesn't quite want, sees
marriage as an inevitable duty, almost a trap. She also sees

it as a state of "belonging" with other women. There isn't much joy in Danielle's view of marriage. She sees it as a necessary goal, a sign of maturity, "an end to something."

10. Discuss the characters' ideas about men. In what ways are their ideas simplistic, realistic, or idealized? Which character do you think most understands and appreciates men as full human beings? Which character do you think least understands and appreciates them?

11. Discuss the notion of a "leap of faith"—what is required when we've told ourselves we want one thing and quite another thing suddenly presents itself as a viable option. How does each character take—or not take—that leap?

12. At one point Rick says, "Life is short, Gincy. When something good happens, you embrace it." But it's not always easy to determine what is good for us at any given moment. Sometimes we aren't prepared to make a big decision about our happiness. Discuss this in relation to Gincy, Clare, and Danielle.

13. Discuss the notion of honesty and fidelity, lying versus not telling the entire truth, in the case of each character. Consider Claire's one-night stand with Finn in Boston; Gincy's aborted one-night stand with Jason in Oak Bluffs; and Danielle's continuing to date other men even while dating Chris. How is each situation different? Is any situation understandable, if not exactly excusable?

14. Clare tells us that she is no longer in love with Win, but that she does still love him "in the way you love someone you know so well it's almost like loving yourself. Or, at least, being used to yourself. Win was just there like I was just there." Discuss the validity of love as habit, or its lack thereof.

15. Win's brother Trey says, "Family owes something to family. Even if it's just pretending to get along." Do you agree? Discuss in relation to Gincy, Clare, and Danielle.

16. Clare worries that by marrying Win, who holds opinions she finds offensive, she might be "by proxy a narrow-minded, spiritless person." Discuss the notion of collusion in a relationship. Is it possible to be with a person whose values and morals differ seriously from your own and not be somehow affected by them?

17. At one point Clare says, "You can get over anger . . . Hurt, too, can be mended . . . But sadness is different. It doesn't seem to ever go away; it rests deep inside. Sadness is profound disappointment." Discuss this.

18. Clare wonders if longevity in a marriage is a worthwhile accomplishment if the years together are "bland, possibly soulless." Is Clare's question naïve or mature? She also assumes that in a long-term exclusive relationship it is impossible to experience "flashes of supreme passion and knowledge." Do you agree with her?

19. Rick believes that "Life can't be about expectation. . . . Nothing's ever as you expect it to be. Life has to be about risk. If you want to be happy, there's no other way." Discuss this in relation to Gincy, Clare, and Danielle.

20. After Clare leaves Win at the altar, Gincy says, "One person is brave enough to change and others follow." Discuss how this is true—or not true—for each of the characters.

In this compelling novel set against the beautiful backdrop of Ogunquit, Maine, the bestselling author of Tuscan Holiday *and* One Week in December *portrays an unexpected friendship, and its consequences, for two very different women as time inevitably sweeps them into adulthood. . . .*

Over the course of one eventful summer, nine-year-old native Mainer Delphine Crandall and Maggie Weldon, a privileged girl "from away," become best friends. Despite the social gulf between them, their bond is strengthened during vacations spent rambling around Ogunquit's beaches and quiet country lanes, and lasts throughout their college years in Boston. It seems nothing can separate them, yet after graduation, Delphine and Maggie slowly drift in different directions. . . .

With her MBA, Maggie acquires a lucrative career, and eventually marries. Delphine is drawn back home, her life steeped in family and the Maine community she loves. Twenty years pass, until one summer, Maggie announces she's returning to Ogunquit to pay an extended visit. And for the first time, the friends are drawn to reflect on their choices and compromises, the girls they were, and the women they've become, the promises kept and broken—and the deep, lasting ties that even time can never quite wash away. . . .

Please turn the page for an exciting sneak peek of

Holly Chamberlin's

SUMMER FRIENDS

coming soon!

Prologue

1971

It was late August, the end of summer, at least, the end of summer for nine-year-old Delphine Crandall and almost-nine-year-old Maggie Weldon. Both would be starting school in about a week, the fourth grade, Delphine at the local public grammar school five miles from her home in Ogunquit, Maine, and Maggie at Blair Academy, a private grammar school in Concord, Massachusetts, where her family lived. It was the end of the summer but it also felt like the end of the world. It was bad enough having to go back to school, but it was far worse to be parting from each other for what would be a whole ten months. In other words, forever.

The girls were hanging out in the backyard of the Lilac House, the expensive and recently renovated home Maggie's parents had rented for the summer. There was a giant swing set, metal monkey bars, and a slide. Two banana-seated girls' bikes lay on the grass; each had a plastic basket in front and streamers from the ends of the looped handlebars. The new pink bike was Maggie's. The old red bike had once belonged to Delphine's ten-year-old sister, Jackie, but it belonged to her now.

Delphine, who was swinging ever higher, legs pumping furiously, wore a faded red T-shirt that, like her bike, had once belonged to Jackie. Across the front were the words—also now faded—RED SOX RULE. Her jean shorts had been cut down from full-length jeans that had badly frayed at the knees. Her sneakers, caked in mud from a morning's romp around the edges of the pond in the woods behind her house, had once been white, back when her mother had bought them at a resale shop in Wells. Her hair, which was thick and the brown of glossy chestnuts, hung in a messy braid down her back, fastened near the end by a rubber band that had once held together a bunch of scallions. Her eyes were as dark and luminous as her hair. Her skin was deeply tanned. Since school had let out she had grown an amazing three inches and was now as tall as Jackie, which meant no more hand-me-down pants. Secretly, Delphine hoped she would grow to be really tall someday. But given the fact that both of her parents were well under six feet, she doubted that she would.

Maggie was on the swing next to Delphine. She was too hot to move and was sitting as still as possible. The neck of her pale pink T-shirt was embroidered in darker pink thread. Her white shorts, which she hated but which her mother made her wear, came almost to the knee and, worse, had a crisp pleat right down the middle of each leg. Her sneakers were white, coated only that morning with that liquid paint-like stuff that came in a bottle with a picture of a nurse on the front. The coating was her mother's idea, too. Her hair, which was the color of jonquils, was neatly drawn into a ponytail and held in place by a woolly purple ribbon. Her skin, almost white during the winter, was now a pale gold. Her large, almost navy blue eyes were currently distorted by the thick lenses of a pair of tortoiseshell-frame glasses she had gotten right after school had let out for the summer. She was still embarrassed by them, though her parents and even Mr. and Mrs. Crandall had assured her that she still looked pretty.

Maggie was tall for her age, taller than Delphine, who, even though she had sprouted, was never going to be a towering Weldon. Her mother bragged about being "model tall" at five feet ten inches, and her dad was six feet two inches. Peter, her thirteen-year-old brother, was already the tallest kid in his class, though he was terrible at basketball, something Maggie found very funny. She was bad at basketball, too, but it didn't matter for girls to be bad at sports. Not at Maggie's school, at least.

Around her left wrist, each girl wore a macramé bracelet. Earlier in the summer, Dephine's sister had taught them how to make them and if the bracelets weren't as perfect as the ones Jackie turned out, Maggie and Delphine thought they were beautiful. Delphine's was already dirty and a bit frayed. Maggie's looked as fresh as the day Delphine had given it to her. Still, when it got dirty, which it would, she would not let her mother coat it with that white paint stuff she used on her sneakers. That would be so embarrassing.

"Are you sure these glasses don't make me look like a dork?" Maggie asked for what Delphine thought was the bazillionth time.

Delphine began to slow her swinging. "I'm sure," she said. "Why would I want to be friends with a dork?"

"Ha, ha, very funny. I just hope the kids at school won't laugh at me."

"If anyone laughs at you—which they won't—tell them your best friend in the world will come down from Maine and beat them up." Her feet dragged in the sand below the swing and she came to a stop.

"No!" Maggie looked genuinely shocked. "You wouldn't really beat someone up, would you?"

Delphine grinned. "Try me. I beat up Joey, once."

"Liar. Your brother's, like, huge compared to you."

"Well, I bet I could beat him up. He makes me mad enough."

"Because he's a boy, and boys stink," Maggie said emphatically. "And they're stupid."

"Mostly," Delphine said with a shrug. "My dad's okay, though. And your dad is pretty nice."

"Yeah, but my brother is gross."

"Maybe boys get nicer as they get older. Like, really old, like our dads. Well, anyway, remember you're leaving in, like, an hour. We have to do our swear about being best friends. We have to do a pinky swear."

"What's that?" Maggie asked.

Delphine laughed. "Come on! Everyone knows what a pinky swear is."

"Well, I don't. We don't do pinky swears in my school."

Delphine rolled her eyes dramatically. It made her feel slightly dizzy. Maybe it was all that swinging. And it was really hot. "Oh, all right," she said. "Stick out your pinky. Now I link my pinky with yours and we swear whatever we're swearing and then we pull our pinkies apart."

The girls linked pinkies and Maggie said, "Me first. I swear I will be your best friend forever and ever."

"Me too," Delphine said.

"No, you have to say all the words."

"Okay. I swear I will be your best friend forever and ever."

"Pinky swear."

The girls pulled their pinkies apart, and Maggie said, "Ow."

Delphine leapt off her swing and stood with her hands on her hips. "So, write to me the minute you get home later, okay?"

"Okay. And you write to me the minute I leave, okay?"

"Okay." Delphine considered. "But I won't have much to say. Maybe I should wait till just before I go to bed tonight. Maybe Joey will do something stupid at dinner. The other night he laughed so hard at something Jackie said, milk came out of his nose and all over the table. It was gross. Also kind of funny, though."

"I guess it's okay if you wait."

Delphine suddenly looked doubtful. "You're sure your parents promised you could come back to Ogunquit next year?"

"Yeah. Mom said Dad already gave the guy who owns the house some money. So it's all set."

"Cool. I'm thirsty. Does your mom still have stuff in the fidgerator?"

"Refrigerator," Maggie corrected her. "I think so."

Maggie got up from her swing, and with their arms around each other's waist, the girls trooped into the Lilac House for lemonade.

1

Maggie Weldon Wilkes steered her Lexus IS C 10 convertible around a slow-moving station wagon decorated with three bikes and a canoe. The Lexus had been a present to herself for a very successful bonus season. Retractable hardtop, cruise control, even a backup camera—this particular car was more of an indulgence than a necessity.

She reached for her iPhone on the seat beside her. She knew it was dangerous to text while driving—everybody knew that, especially after Oprah had made a deservedly big deal out of it—but she did it, anyway, occasionally. It gave her a bit of a thrill to do something possibly illegal and definitely reckless, though she could barely admit that to herself. Besides, it wasn't like she reached for her phone on a busy New York City street. Like right now, there were only a few cars within sight, and what was the harm in typing out a brief, abbreviated note to her husband? Nothing. Not much. Except that in spite of wearing bifocal contact lenses, she couldn't quite see what she was doing.

"In ME," she managed, the intelligence of habit overcoming the limitations of vision. "How r u?" She put her phone back on the passenger seat and realized that she hadn't actually heard Gregory's voice in days. They had tweeted and texted and e-mailed but not actually spoken, not even on voice mail. This, however, was par for the course with the Wilkes and not to be taken as a sign of marital distress or discord. Maggie reassured herself on this point with some frequency. She and Gregory were a highly successful career couple whose jobs took them out of each other's sight, not out of each other's minds. Maybe they weren't as close as they once had been, but . . . it was what it was.

So, she was on her way to spend a few weeks in Ogunquit, that "beautiful place by the sea." She had been so happy there, mostly, of course, because of Delphine Crandall, but also because of the sheer beauty of the area. She still remembered the slightly punky smell of the wildflowers that grew in profusion along the road to the Lilac House, the place her parents had rented for all those years. She could hear in her mind the absurdly loud chirping of the teeny peepers in the pond in the woods behind the Crandalls' house. She remembered the softness of the summer evening air. She remembered how she and Delphine and sometimes their siblings would go down to the beach at a super high tide, when the water would come all the way up to the parking lot. She remembered being both frightened and excited by the cold Atlantic rushing around her feet. She remembered the swing set behind the Lilac House and the new kittens at Delphine's family's farm. She remembered the joy.

Now, after almost three hours on the road, Maggie was finally getting close to her destination. So much had changed since she had last driven this far north. Traffic was definitely worse than it once had been, especially now along Route 1 in Wells. There were just way too many people, period. She didn't recognize half of the restaurants along the road, though she was pleased to see that the rickety old clam shack that Delphine's family had taken them to once a summer was still open. There was a whole new crop of summer cottage developments sprawled on either side of the road. Some of the cottages were unbelievably tiny; it was hard to imagine even a family of three being comfortable in them. Then again, kids could be comfortable anywhere, especially with the beach within sight. Still, Maggie could not imagine herself tolerating such tight quarters, not now, not as a forty-eight-year-old. She had become used to a degree of luxury. A high degree of luxury, in all honesty. Her hair color was professionally maintained at an award-winning salon on Newbury Street. She had a manicure and pedicure once every two weeks. Around her left wrist she wore a Rolex, another gift to herself after a particularly good year at the office. Around her neck, on a white-gold chain, she wore a two-carat diamond set in platinum. That was from Gregory, an anniversary gift, she thought, or maybe a birthday gift. She couldn't really remember. He had given her so many expensive presents. He was very good about that sort of thing. For their wedding, though he could barely afford them at the time, he had given her diamond stud earrings.

Thinking about those earrings, Maggie realized that the last time she'd seen Delphine had been at the wedding, and that was more than twenty years ago. She had invited her with a guest, but she had come alone, and had only accepted the invitation after ascertaining that Robert Evans, her former fiancé, wouldn't be there. He had been invited, also with a guest, but would be on an assignment in Thailand. It would have been ridiculous to turn down a major journalistic gig for the sake of a friend's wedding. Besides, Robert and Maggie had really only been friends because of Delphine. Once Delphine had gone back home to Ogunquit after breaking up with Robert, Maggie's friendship with him had steadily waned. She hadn't heard from him in more than fifteen years, though she could see his face, hear his name, and read his words all over the media. You'd have to be living in a cave not to be aware of Robert Evans.

Maggie adjusted the air-conditioning a bit and thought of the pale blue velvet box carefully tucked between layers of clothing in her suitcase. Inside the box was an aquamarine pendant on a gold chain. Aquamarine was Delphine's birthstone; her birthday was March twenty-third. The necklace should have been hers. And it would have been if Maggie had asked Delphine to be her maid of honor. But she hadn't. The necklace had been in that pale blue velvet box, in the back of Maggie's lingerie drawer, for more than twenty years.

She was crossing into Ogunquit now, and traffic was still at a crawl. Every other minute it came to a complete stop for pedestrians crossing the road, many of whom ignored the official crosswalks and dashed out at random. Maggie frowned. She did not care for traffic jams or for pedestrians who didn't follow the rules. Well, she supposed nobody did. As she waited for a family, which included a baby in a stroller and three small children, to organize themselves across the road, she let her mind wander.

Delphine Crandall. There had been long periods of her life in which she hadn't thought about Delphine at all. Like when business school had overwhelmed her, and when she was starting her career, and then, when the children had come along. There had been other long periods when she thought of her occasionally, randomly, and without much emotion. Like when her daughters did or said something that reminded her of her own childhood self, or when Robert Evans's face popped up on the TV screen. Once in a very great while Delphine would make an appearance in a dream, and mostly those dreams were somehow disturbing, though Maggie could never remember them clearly when she woke. Some details lingered—something about being forced to leave boxes of books behind, an eviction, someone crying, dirty floors. None of it made any sense.

But in the past two years or so, Maggie had found herself thinking more and more often of her old friend. Specific memories were coming back to her with a vividness that was startling. The time when they were about ten when they had stumbled on a teenage couple kissing behind a shack in Perkins Cove and had run away giggling and shrieking. The time when they were about sixteen and had snuck out one night to go to the only dance club in town, even though their parents had forbidden them. The time in college when Delphine had woken in the middle of the night with a raging fever and Maggie had bundled her into a cab and then to the emergency room. The time when Maggie had thought she was pregnant. She had been too frightened and ashamed to buy an at-home pregnancy kit, so Delphine had bought it for her, and had sat holding her hand while they waited for the result.

And the feelings, too, they were coming back, rather, memories of how it had felt to be so comfortable with someone, so loved and appreciated. She had begun to think of Delphine Crandall with a longing that seemed more than mere nostalgia. It was a longing that finally became too real to ignore.

So back in April, Maggie had made a decision to find her. She had no idea if Delphine was online or if she had married and changed her name, so she sent an old-fashioned, handwritten letter to Delphine in care of her parents. In it she mentioned her job, Gregory's job, her daughters being in college. She suggested that she come to Ogunquit to visit. August would be a good time for her. She had several weeks of vacation saved up. She would stay in a hotel so as not to burden anyone. She needed a low-key, quiet break from her busy life. She said nothing about the memories or the dreams.

She had waited a month, hoping for a reply, and when no reply came, she took the more direct measure of making a telephone call. There was a Delphine Crandall listed in Ogunquit. It was her Delphine Crandall.

She called one night, about eight o'clock, and was surprised to hear a voice groggy with sleep. She asked Delphine if she had gotten her letter. Yes, Delphine had. But she had been terribly busy and hadn't had time to reply. She said she was sorry. Maggie hadn't entirely believed her.

"So," Maggie had said, suddenly nervous, "what do you think about my coming to visit this summer?"

There had been a long beat of silence, one Maggie couldn't attribute to anything other than Delphine's reluctance. Just when Maggie, feeling both embarrassed and annoyed, was about to retract the suggestion of a visit, Delphine had blurted something like, "Yeah. Okay." The moment of retreat had been lost. A reunion was going to happen.